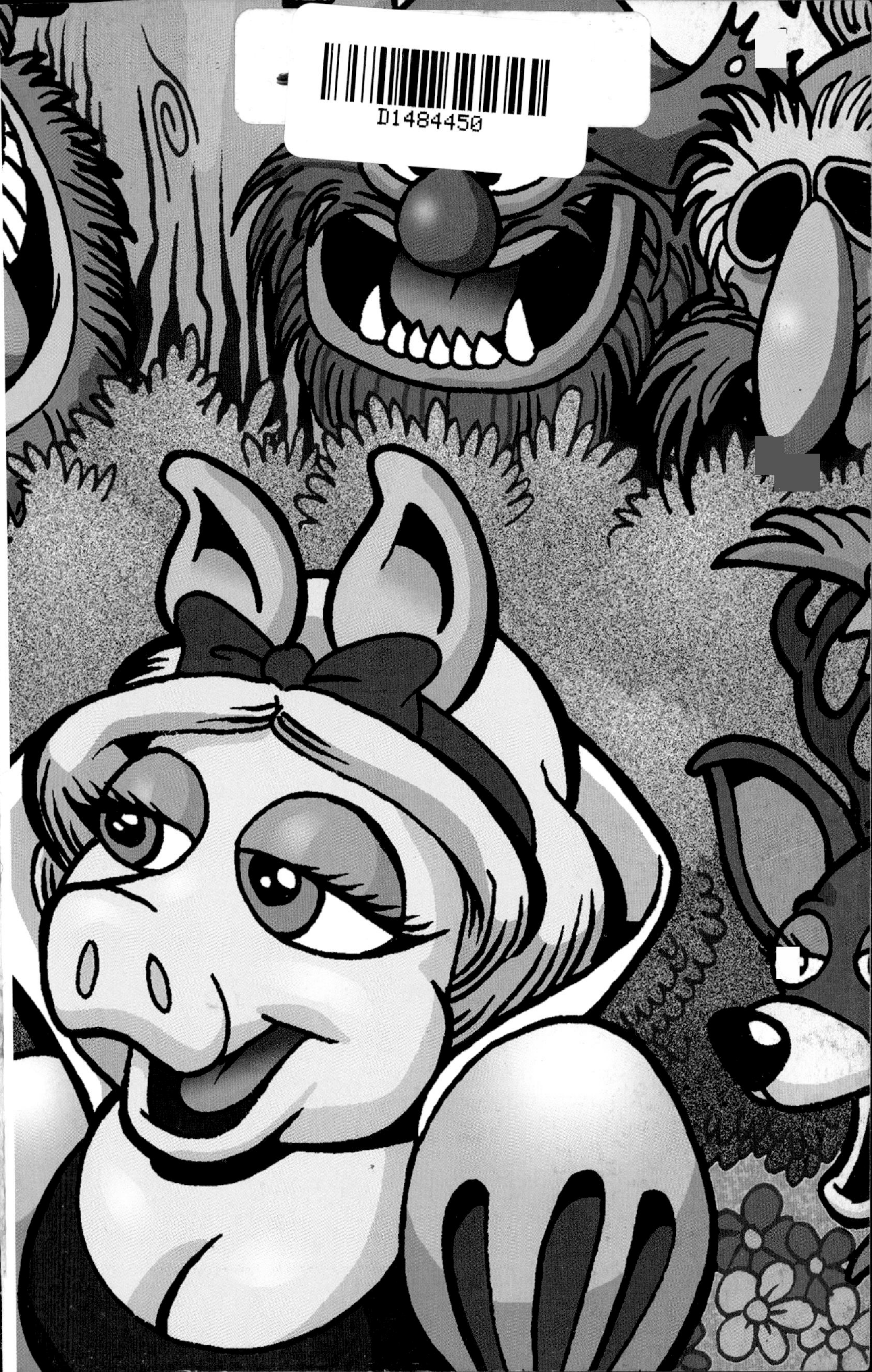

**ROSS RICHIE**
chief executive officer

**MARK WAID**
chief creative officer

**MATT GAGNON**
editor-in-chief

**ADAM FORTIER**
vice president,
new business

**WES HARRIS**
vice president,
publishing

**LANCE KREITER**
vice president,
licensing & merchandising

**CHIP MOSHER**
marketing director

FIRST EDITION: SEPTEMBER 2010

10 9 8 7 6 5 4 3 2 1

FOR INFORMATION REGARDING THE CPSIA ON THIS PRINTED MATERIAL
CALL: 203-595-3636 AND PROVIDE REFERENCE # EAST – 67573.

# MUPPET SNOW WHITE

**Writers:**
Jesse Blaze Snider with
Patrick Storck

**Letterer:**
Deron Bennett

**Artist:**
Shelli Paroline

**Assistant Editor:**
Jason Long

**Colors:**
Braden Lamb

**Editor:**
Aaron Sparrow

**Designer:**
Erika Terriquez

**Cover:**
David Petersen

**Special Thanks:**
Jesse Post and Lauren Kressel of
Disney Publishing and our friends
at The Muppets Studio

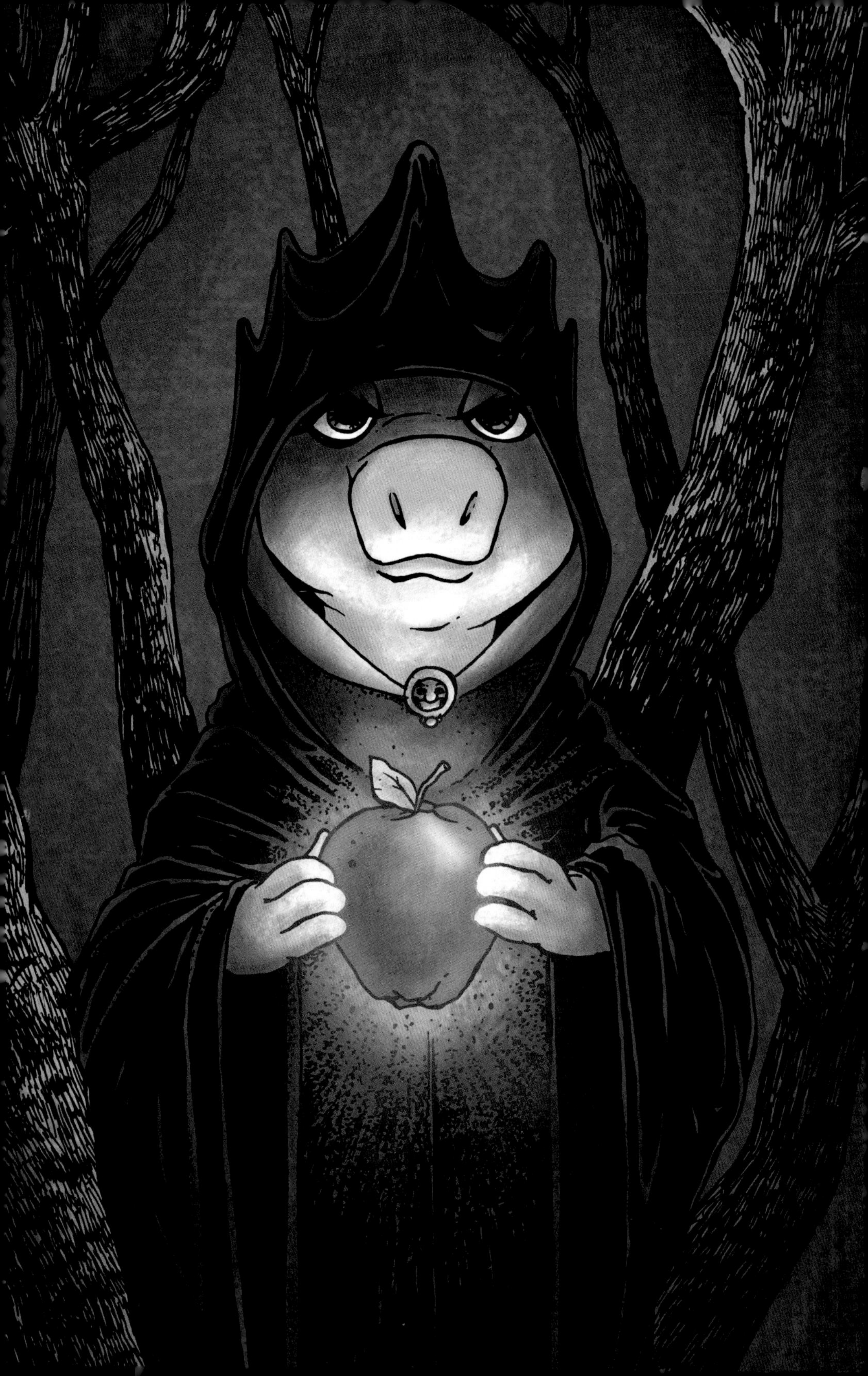

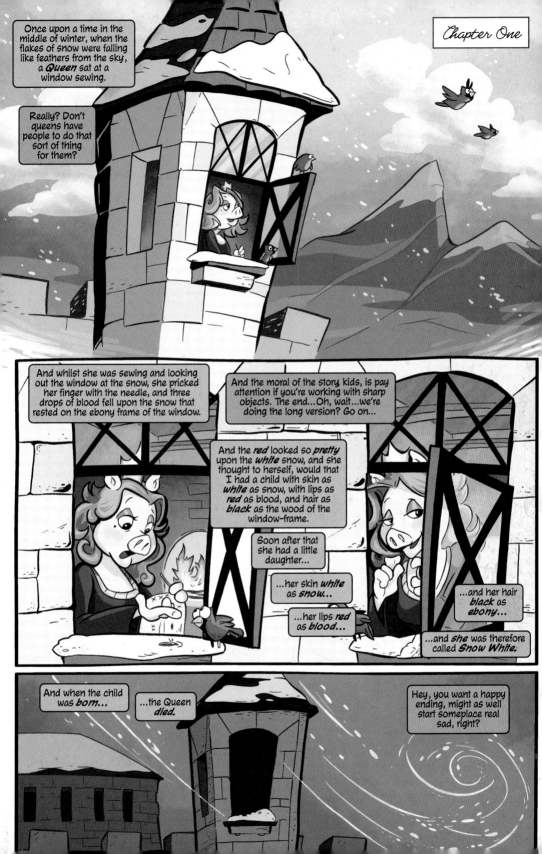

Once upon a time in the middle of winter, when the flakes of snow were falling like feathers from the sky, a *Queen* sat at a window sewing.

Really? Don't queens have people to do that sort of thing for them?

And whilst she was sewing and looking out the window at the snow, she pricked her finger with the needle, and three drops of blood fell upon the snow that rested on the ebony frame of the window.

And the moral of the story kids, is pay attention if you're working with sharp objects. The end...Oh, wait...we're doing the long version? Go on...

And the *red* looked so *pretty* upon the *white* snow, and she thought to herself, would that I had a child with skin as *white* as snow, with lips as *red* as blood, and hair as *black* as the wood of the window-frame.

Soon after that she had a little daughter...

...her skin *white* as *snow*...

...her lips *red* as *blood*...

...and her hair *black* as *ebony*...

...and *she* was therefore called *Snow White.*

And when the child was *born*...

...the Queen *died.*

Hey, you want a happy ending, might as well start someplace real sad, right?

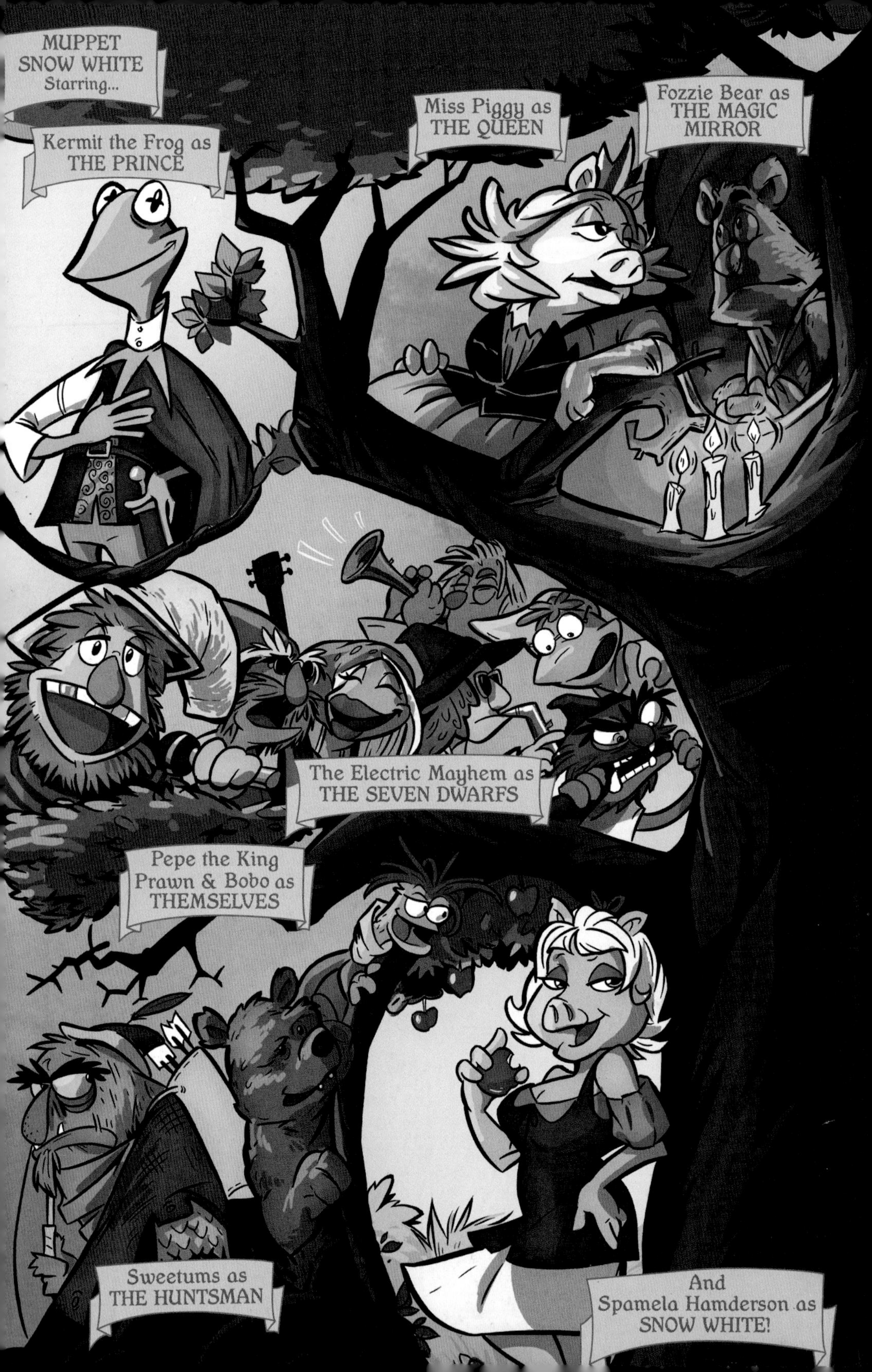
MUPPET SNOW WHITE Starring...
Kermit the Frog as THE PRINCE
Miss Piggy as THE QUEEN
Fozzie Bear as THE MAGIC MIRROR
The Electric Mayhem as THE SEVEN DWARFS
Pepe the King Prawn & Bobo as THEMSELVES
Sweetums as THE HUNTSMAN
And Spamela Hamderson as SNOW WHITE!

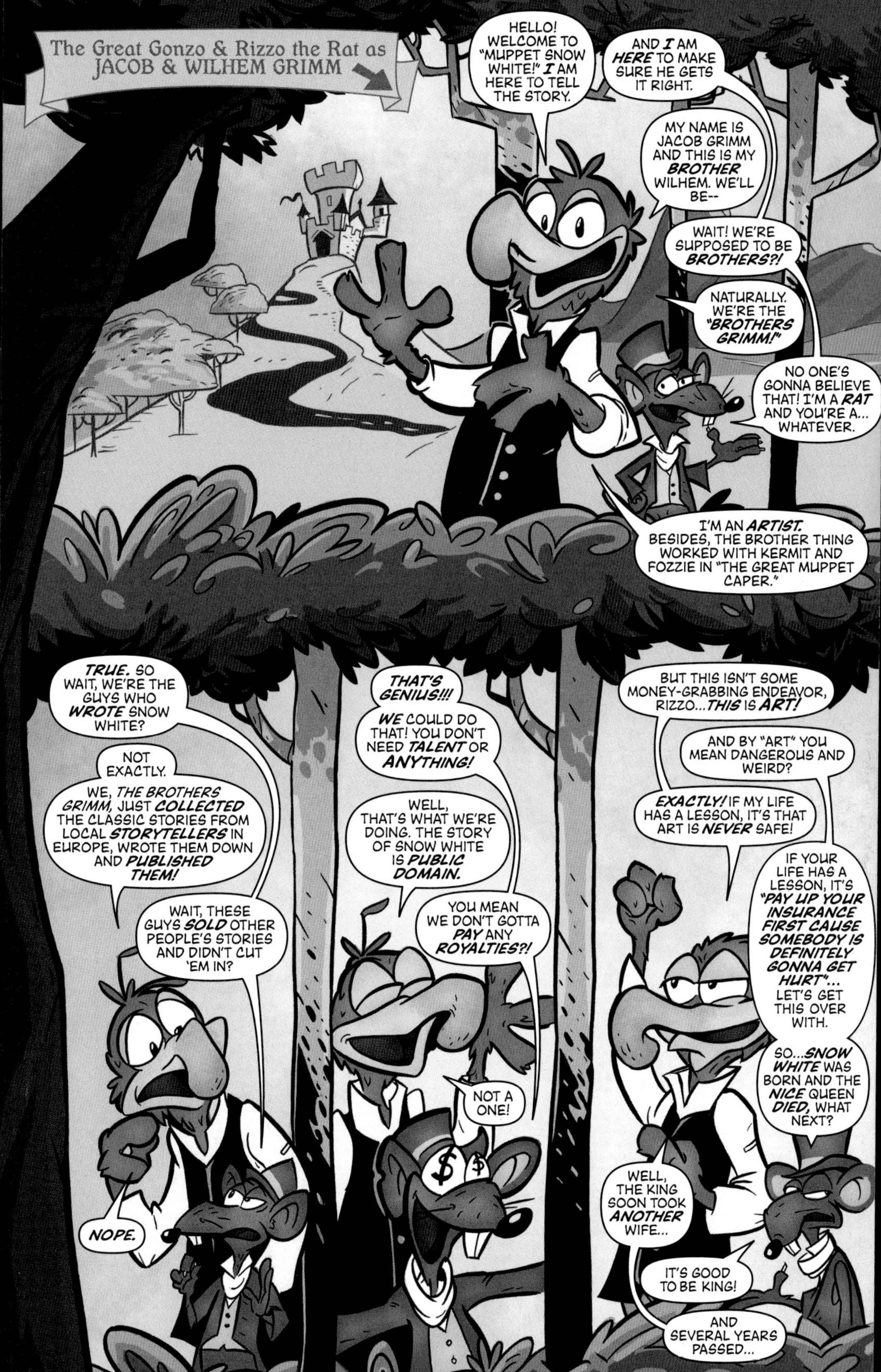

The Great Gonzo & Rizzo the Rat as JACOB & WILHEM GRIMM
HELLO! WELCOME TO "MUPPET SNOW WHITE!" I AM HERE TO TELL THE STORY.
AND I AM HERE TO MAKE SURE HE GETS IT RIGHT.
MY NAME IS JACOB GRIMM AND THIS IS MY BROTHER WILHEM. WE'LL BE--
WAIT! WE'RE SUPPOSED TO BE BROTHERS?!
NATURALLY. WE'RE THE "BROTHERS GRIMM!"
NO ONE'S GONNA BELIEVE THAT! I'M A RAT AND YOU'RE A... WHATEVER.
I'M AN ARTIST. BESIDES, THE BROTHER THING WORKED WITH KERMIT AND FOZZIE IN "THE GREAT MUPPET CAPER."
TRUE. SO WAIT, WE'RE THE GUYS WHO WROTE SNOW WHITE?
NOT EXACTLY.
WE, THE BROTHERS GRIMM, JUST COLLECTED THE CLASSIC STORIES FROM LOCAL STORYTELLERS IN EUROPE, WROTE THEM DOWN AND PUBLISHED THEM!
WAIT, THESE GUYS SOLD OTHER PEOPLE'S STORIES AND DIDN'T CUT 'EM IN?
NOPE.
THAT'S GENIUS!!!
WE COULD DO THAT! YOU DON'T NEED TALENT OR ANYTHING!
WELL, THAT'S WHAT WE'RE DOING. THE STORY OF SNOW WHITE IS PUBLIC DOMAIN.
YOU MEAN WE DON'T GOTTA PAY ANY ROYALTIES?!
NOT A ONE!
BUT THIS ISN'T SOME MONEY-GRABBING ENDEAVOR, RIZZO...THIS IS ART!
AND BY "ART" YOU MEAN DANGEROUS AND WEIRD?
EXACTLY! IF MY LIFE HAS A LESSON, IT'S THAT ART IS NEVER SAFE!
IF YOUR LIFE HAS A LESSON, IT'S "PAY UP YOUR INSURANCE FIRST CAUSE SOMEBODY IS DEFINITELY GONNA GET HURT"... LET'S GET THIS OVER WITH.
SO...SNOW WHITE WAS BORN AND THE NICE QUEEN DIED, WHAT NEXT?
WELL, THE KING SOON TOOK ANOTHER WIFE...
IT'S GOOD TO BE KING!
AND SEVERAL YEARS PASSED...

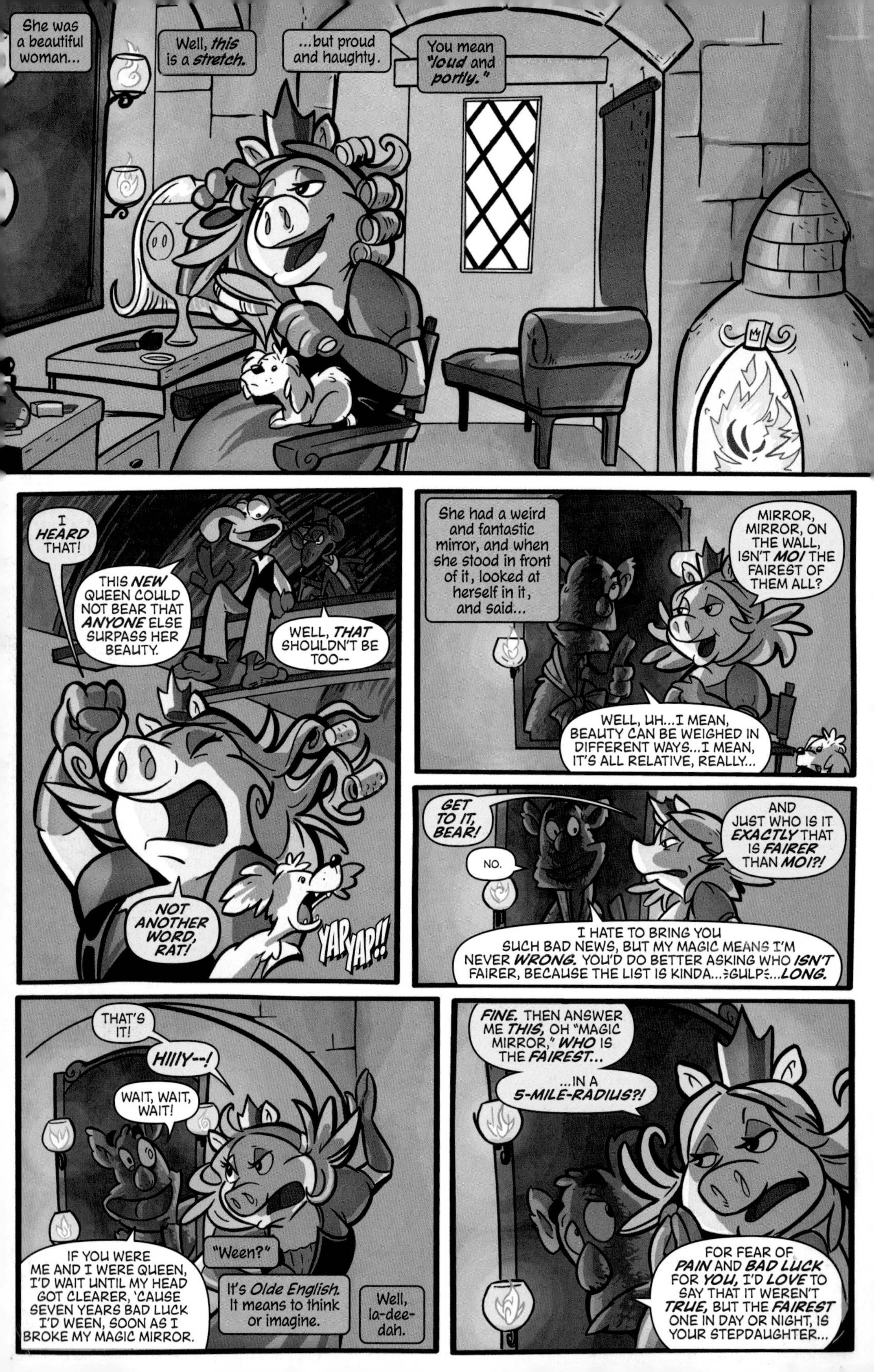
She was a beautiful woman...
Well, *this* is a *stretch.*
...but proud and haughty.
You mean "*loud* and *portly.*"
I *HEARD* THAT!
THIS *NEW* QUEEN COULD NOT BEAR THAT *ANYONE* ELSE SURPASS HER BEAUTY.
WELL, *THAT* SHOULDN'T BE TOO--
NOT ANOTHER WORD, RAT!
YAP YAP!!
She had a weird and fantastic mirror, and when she stood in front of it, looked at herself in it, and said...
MIRROR, MIRROR, ON THE WALL, ISN'T *MOI* THE FAIREST OF THEM ALL?
WELL, UH...I MEAN, BEAUTY CAN BE WEIGHED IN DIFFERENT WAYS...I MEAN, IT'S ALL RELATIVE, REALLY...
GET TO IT, BEAR!
NO.
AND JUST WHO IS IT *EXACTLY* THAT IS *FAIRER* THAN *MOI?!*
I HATE TO BRING YOU SUCH BAD NEWS, BUT MY MAGIC MEANS I'M NEVER *WRONG.* YOU'D DO BETTER ASKING WHO *ISN'T* FAIRER, BECAUSE THE LIST IS KINDA...GULP...*LONG.*
THAT'S IT!
HIIIY--!
WAIT, WAIT, WAIT!
IF YOU WERE ME AND I WERE QUEEN, I'D WAIT UNTIL MY HEAD GOT CLEARER, 'CAUSE SEVEN YEARS BAD LUCK I'D WEEN, SOON AS I BROKE MY MAGIC MIRROR.
"Ween?"
It's *Olde English.* It means to think or imagine.
Well, la-dee-dah.
*FINE.* THEN ANSWER ME *THIS,* OH "MAGIC MIRROR," *WHO* IS THE *FAIREST*...
...IN A 5-MILE-RADIUS?!
FOR FEAR OF *PAIN* AND *BAD LUCK* FOR *YOU,* I'D *LOVE* TO SAY THAT IT WEREN'T *TRUE,* BUT THE *FAIREST* ONE IN DAY OR NIGHT, IS YOUR STEPDAUGHTER...

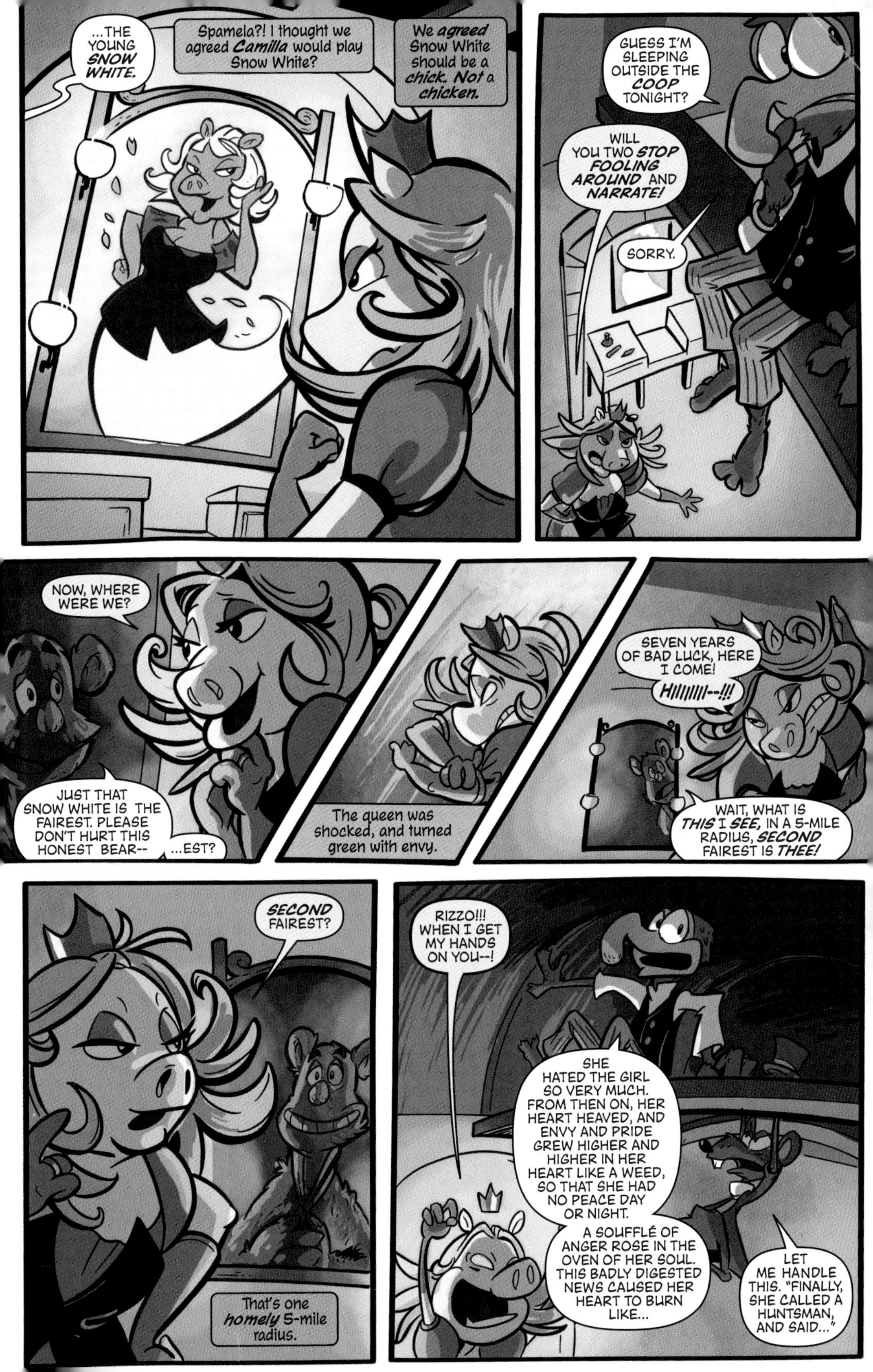
...THE YOUNG SNOW WHITE.
Spamela?! I thought we agreed Camilla would play Snow White?
We agreed Snow White should be a chick. Not a chicken.
GUESS I'M SLEEPING OUTSIDE THE COOP TONIGHT?
WILL YOU TWO STOP FOOLING AROUND AND NARRATE!
SORRY.
NOW, WHERE WERE WE?
JUST THAT SNOW WHITE IS THE FAIREST. PLEASE DON'T HURT THIS HONEST BEAR--
...EST?
The queen was shocked, and turned green with envy.
SEVEN YEARS OF BAD LUCK, HERE I COME!
HI!!!!!!!--!!!
WAIT, WHAT IS THIS I SEE, IN A 5-MILE RADIUS, SECOND FAIREST IS THEE!
SECOND FAIREST?
That's one homely 5-mile radius.
RIZZO!!! WHEN I GET MY HANDS ON YOU--!
SHE HATED THE GIRL SO VERY MUCH. FROM THEN ON, HER HEART HEAVED, AND ENVY AND PRIDE GREW HIGHER AND HIGHER IN HER HEART LIKE A WEED, SO THAT SHE HAD NO PEACE DAY OR NIGHT.
A SOUFFLÉ OF ANGER ROSE IN THE OVEN OF HER SOUL. THIS BADLY DIGESTED NEWS CAUSED HER HEART TO BURN LIKE...
LET ME HANDLE THIS. "FINALLY, SHE CALLED A HUNTSMAN, AND SAID..."

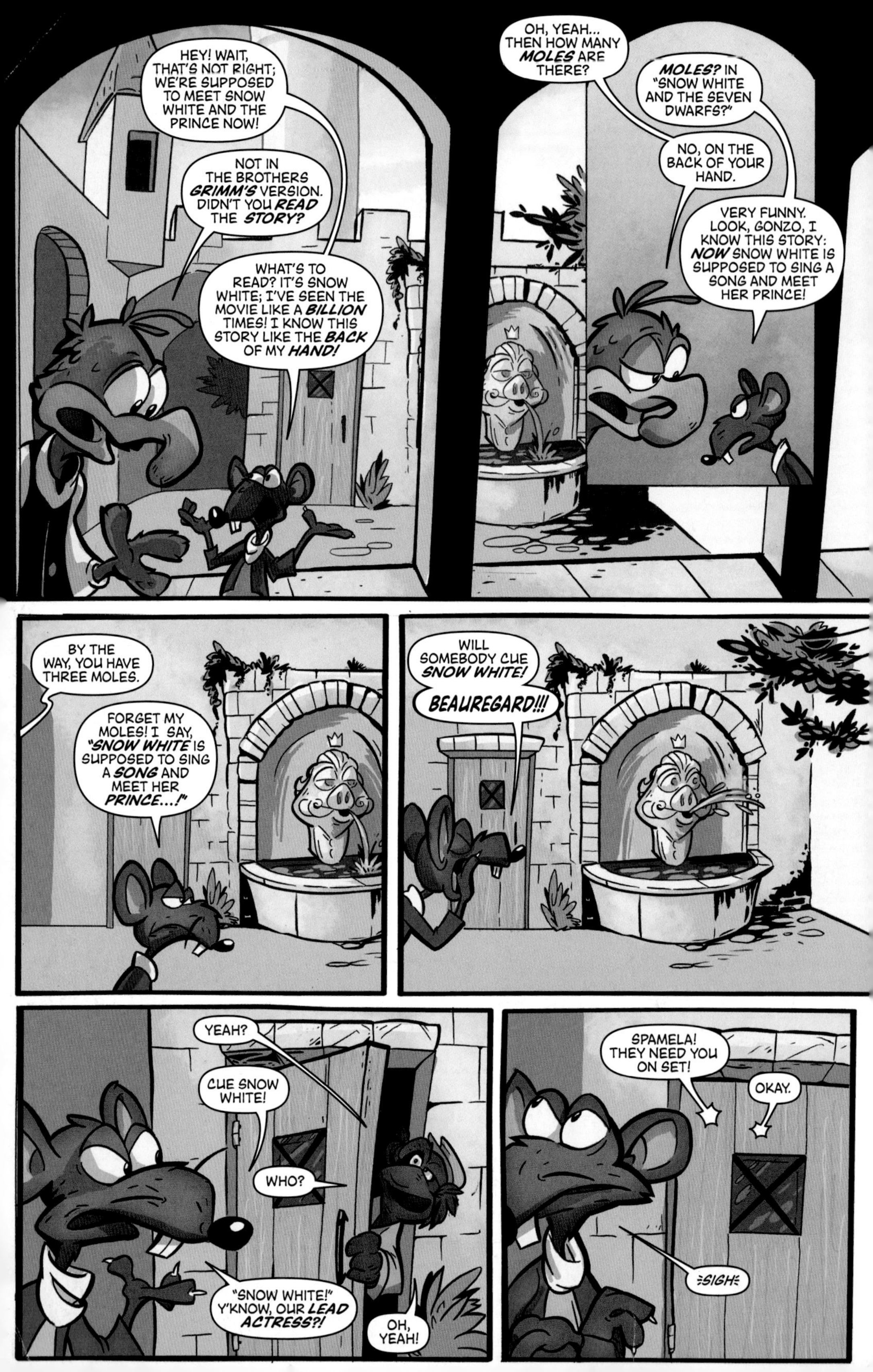
HEY! WAIT, THAT'S NOT RIGHT; WE'RE SUPPOSED TO MEET SNOW WHITE AND THE PRINCE NOW!
NOT IN THE BROTHERS GRIMM'S VERSION. DIDN'T YOU READ THE STORY?
WHAT'S TO READ? IT'S SNOW WHITE; I'VE SEEN THE MOVIE LIKE A BILLION TIMES! I KNOW THIS STORY LIKE THE BACK OF MY HAND!
OH, YEAH... THEN HOW MANY MOLES ARE THERE?
MOLES? IN "SNOW WHITE AND THE SEVEN DWARFS?"
NO, ON THE BACK OF YOUR HAND.
VERY FUNNY. LOOK, GONZO, I KNOW THIS STORY: NOW SNOW WHITE IS SUPPOSED TO SING A SONG AND MEET HER PRINCE!
BY THE WAY, YOU HAVE THREE MOLES.
FORGET MY MOLES! I SAY, "SNOW WHITE IS SUPPOSED TO SING A SONG AND MEET HER PRINCE...!"
WILL SOMEBODY CUE SNOW WHITE!
BEAUREGARD!!!
YEAH?
CUE SNOW WHITE!
WHO?
"SNOW WHITE!" Y'KNOW, OUR LEAD ACTRESS?!
OH, YEAH!
SPAMELA! THEY NEED YOU ON SET!
OKAY.
SIGH

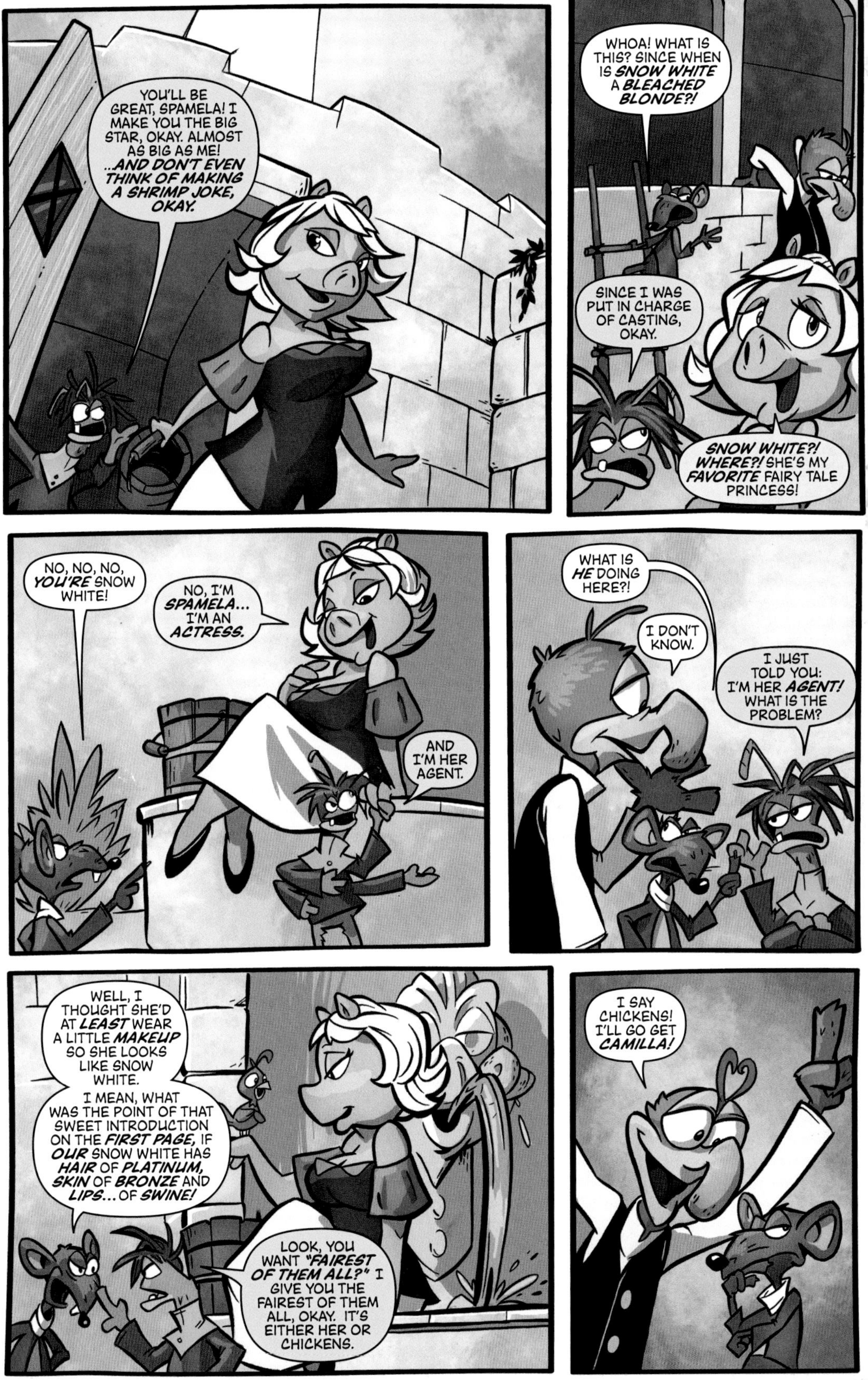
YOU'LL BE GREAT, SPAMELA! I MAKE YOU THE BIG STAR, OKAY. ALMOST AS BIG AS ME! ...AND DON'T EVEN THINK OF MAKING A SHRIMP JOKE, OKAY.
WHOA! WHAT IS THIS? SINCE WHEN IS SNOW WHITE A BLEACHED BLONDE?!
SINCE I WAS PUT IN CHARGE OF CASTING, OKAY.
SNOW WHITE?! WHERE?! SHE'S MY FAVORITE FAIRY TALE PRINCESS!
NO, NO, NO, YOU'RE SNOW WHITE!
NO, I'M SPAMELA... I'M AN ACTRESS.
AND I'M HER AGENT.
WHAT IS HE DOING HERE?!
I DON'T KNOW.
I JUST TOLD YOU: I'M HER AGENT! WHAT IS THE PROBLEM?
WELL, I THOUGHT SHE'D AT LEAST WEAR A LITTLE MAKEUP SO SHE LOOKS LIKE SNOW WHITE.
I MEAN, WHAT WAS THE POINT OF THAT SWEET INTRODUCTION ON THE FIRST PAGE, IF OUR SNOW WHITE HAS HAIR OF PLATINUM, SKIN OF BRONZE AND LIPS... OF SWINE!
LOOK, YOU WANT "FAIREST OF THEM ALL?" I GIVE YOU THE FAIREST OF THEM ALL, OKAY. IT'S EITHER HER OR CHICKENS.
I SAY CHICKENS! I'LL GO GET CAMILLA!

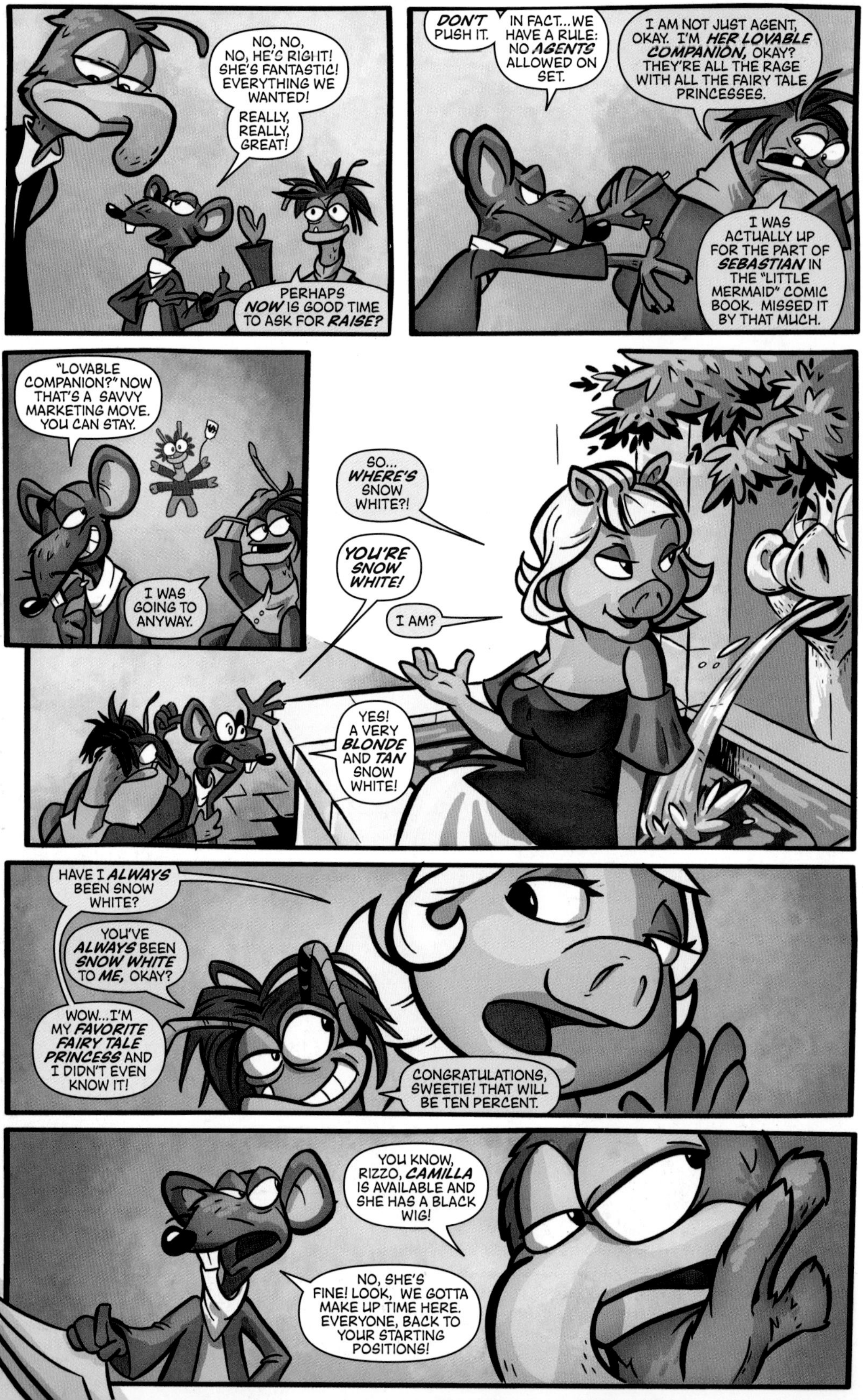
NO, NO, NO, HE'S RIGHT! SHE'S FANTASTIC! EVERYTHING WE WANTED!
REALLY, REALLY, GREAT!
PERHAPS NOW IS GOOD TIME TO ASK FOR RAISE?
DON'T PUSH IT.
IN FACT...WE HAVE A RULE: NO AGENTS ALLOWED ON SET.
I AM NOT JUST AGENT, OKAY. I'M HER LOVABLE COMPANION, OKAY? THEY'RE ALL THE RAGE WITH ALL THE FAIRY TALE PRINCESSES.
I WAS ACTUALLY UP FOR THE PART OF SEBASTIAN IN THE "LITTLE MERMAID" COMIC BOOK. MISSED IT BY THAT MUCH.
"LOVABLE COMPANION?" NOW THAT'S A SAVVY MARKETING MOVE. YOU CAN STAY.
I WAS GOING TO ANYWAY.
SO... WHERE'S SNOW WHITE?!
YOU'RE SNOW WHITE!
I AM?
YES! A VERY BLONDE AND TAN SNOW WHITE!
HAVE I ALWAYS BEEN SNOW WHITE?
YOU'VE ALWAYS BEEN SNOW WHITE TO ME, OKAY?
WOW...I'M MY FAVORITE FAIRY TALE PRINCESS AND I DIDN'T EVEN KNOW IT!
CONGRATULATIONS, SWEETIE! THAT WILL BE TEN PERCENT.
YOU KNOW, RIZZO, CAMILLA IS AVAILABLE AND SHE HAS A BLACK WIG!
NO, SHE'S FINE! LOOK, WE GOTTA MAKE UP TIME HERE. EVERYONE, BACK TO YOUR STARTING POSITIONS!

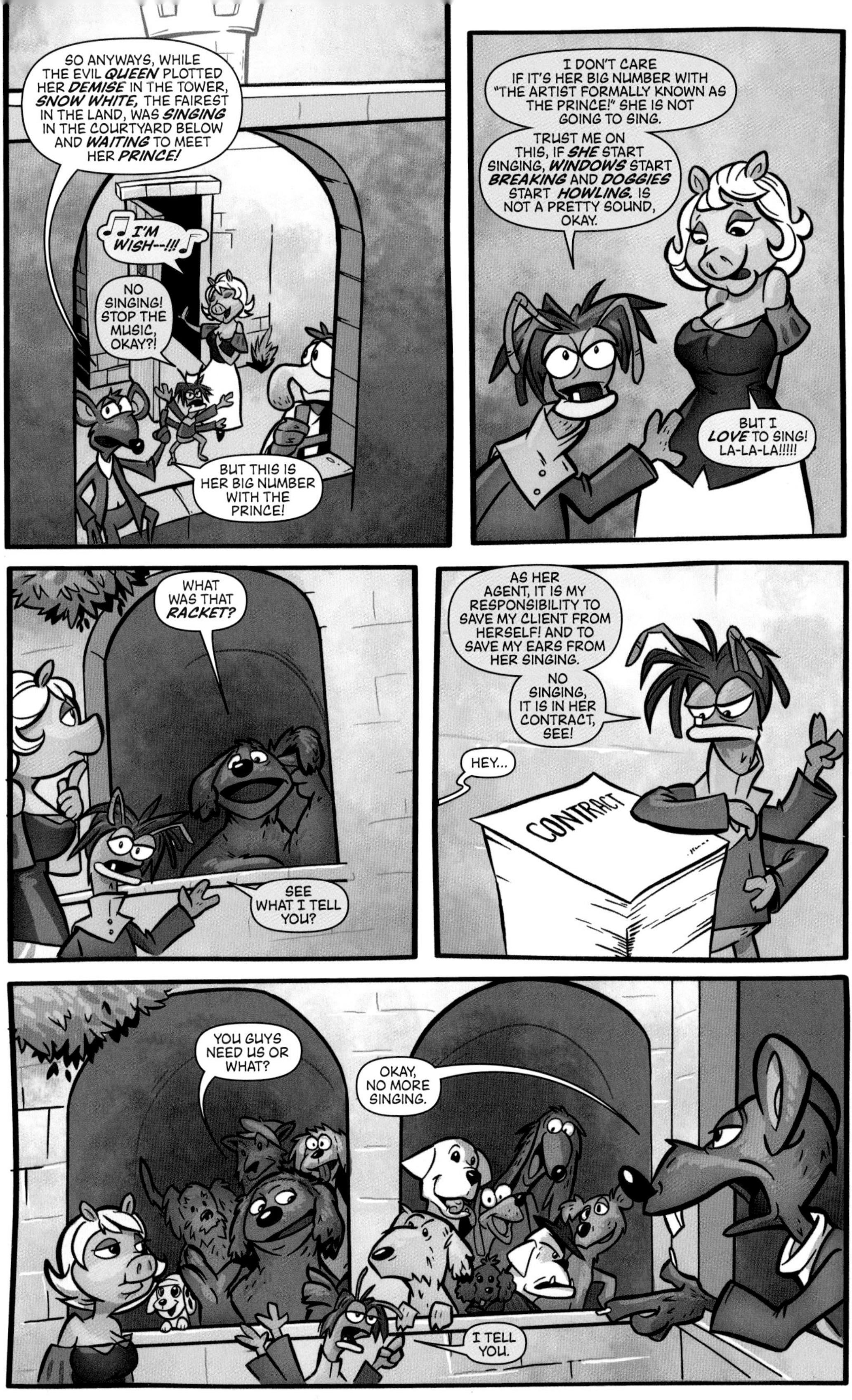

SO ANYWAYS, WHILE THE EVIL *QUEEN* PLOTTED HER *DEMISE* IN THE TOWER, *SNOW WHITE,* THE FAIREST IN THE LAND, WAS *SINGING* IN THE COURTYARD BELOW AND *WAITING* TO MEET HER *PRINCE!*
I'M WISH--!!!
NO SINGING! STOP THE MUSIC, OKAY?!
BUT THIS IS HER BIG NUMBER WITH THE PRINCE!
I DON'T CARE IF IT'S HER BIG NUMBER WITH "THE ARTIST FORMALLY KNOWN AS THE PRINCE!" SHE IS NOT GOING TO SING.
TRUST ME ON THIS, IF *SHE* START SINGING, *WINDOWS* START *BREAKING* AND *DOGGIES* START *HOWLING.* IS NOT A PRETTY SOUND, OKAY.
BUT I *LOVE* TO SING! LA-LA-LA!!!!!
WHAT WAS THAT *RACKET?*
SEE WHAT I TELL YOU?
AS HER AGENT, IT IS MY RESPONSIBILITY TO SAVE MY CLIENT FROM HERSELF! AND TO SAVE MY EARS FROM HER SINGING.
NO SINGING, IT IS IN HER CONTRACT, SEE!
HEY...
CONTRACT
YOU GUYS NEED US OR WHAT?
OKAY, NO MORE SINGING.
I TELL YOU.

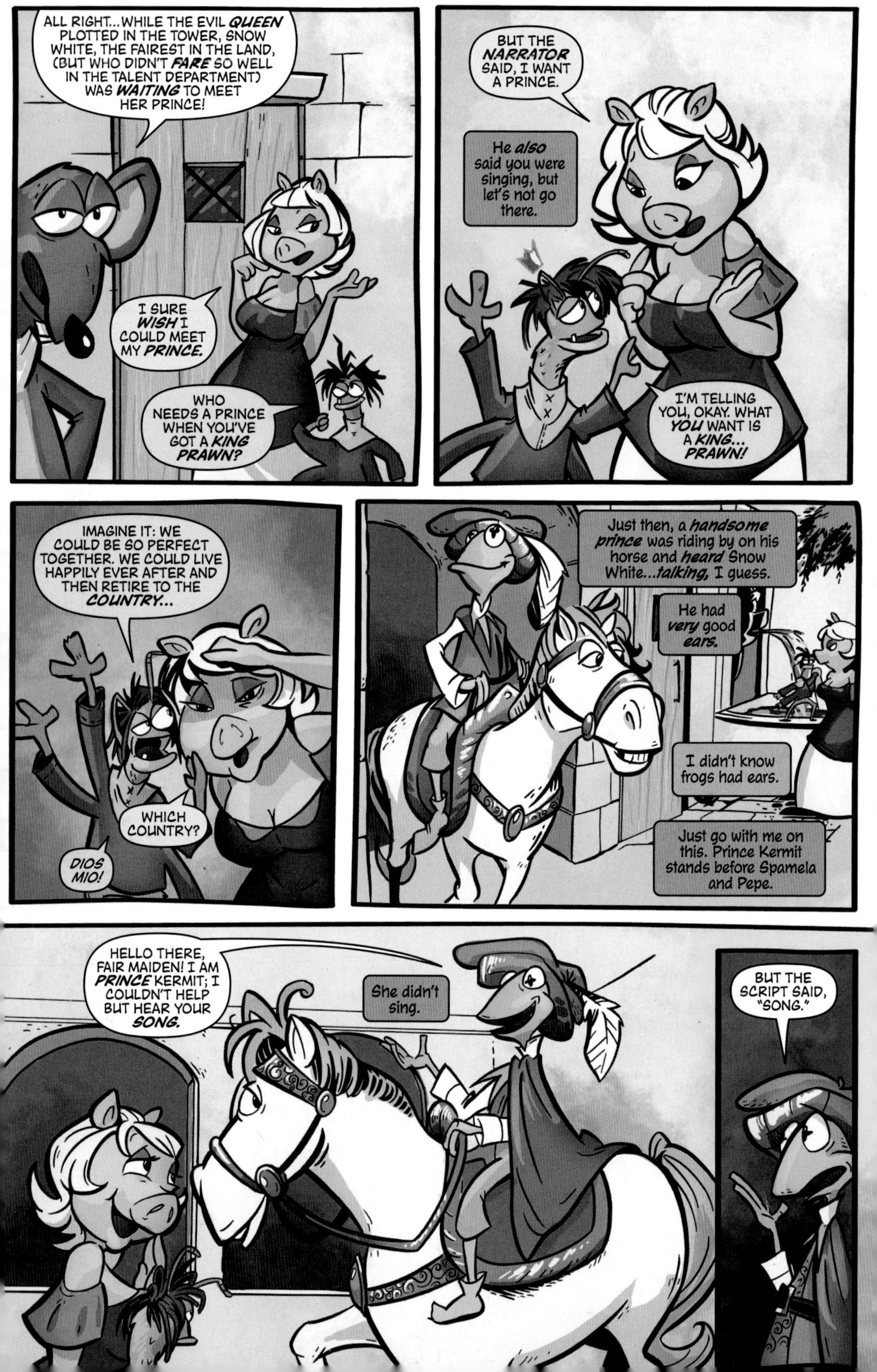

ALL RIGHT...WHILE THE EVIL QUEEN PLOTTED IN THE TOWER, SNOW WHITE, THE FAIREST IN THE LAND, (BUT WHO DIDN'T FARE SO WELL IN THE TALENT DEPARTMENT) WAS WAITING TO MEET HER PRINCE!
I SURE WISH I COULD MEET MY PRINCE.
WHO NEEDS A PRINCE WHEN YOU'VE GOT A KING PRAWN?
BUT THE NARRATOR SAID, I WANT A PRINCE.
He also said you were singing, but let's not go there.
I'M TELLING YOU, OKAY. WHAT YOU WANT IS A KING... PRAWN!
IMAGINE IT: WE COULD BE SO PERFECT TOGETHER. WE COULD LIVE HAPPILY EVER AFTER AND THEN RETIRE TO THE COUNTRY...
WHICH COUNTRY?
DIOS MIO!
Just then, a handsome prince was riding by on his horse and heard Snow White...talking, I guess.
He had very good ears.
I didn't know frogs had ears.
Just go with me on this. Prince Kermit stands before Spamela and Pepe.
HELLO THERE, FAIR MAIDEN! I AM PRINCE KERMIT; I COULDN'T HELP BUT HEAR YOUR SONG.
She didn't sing.
BUT THE SCRIPT SAID, "SONG."

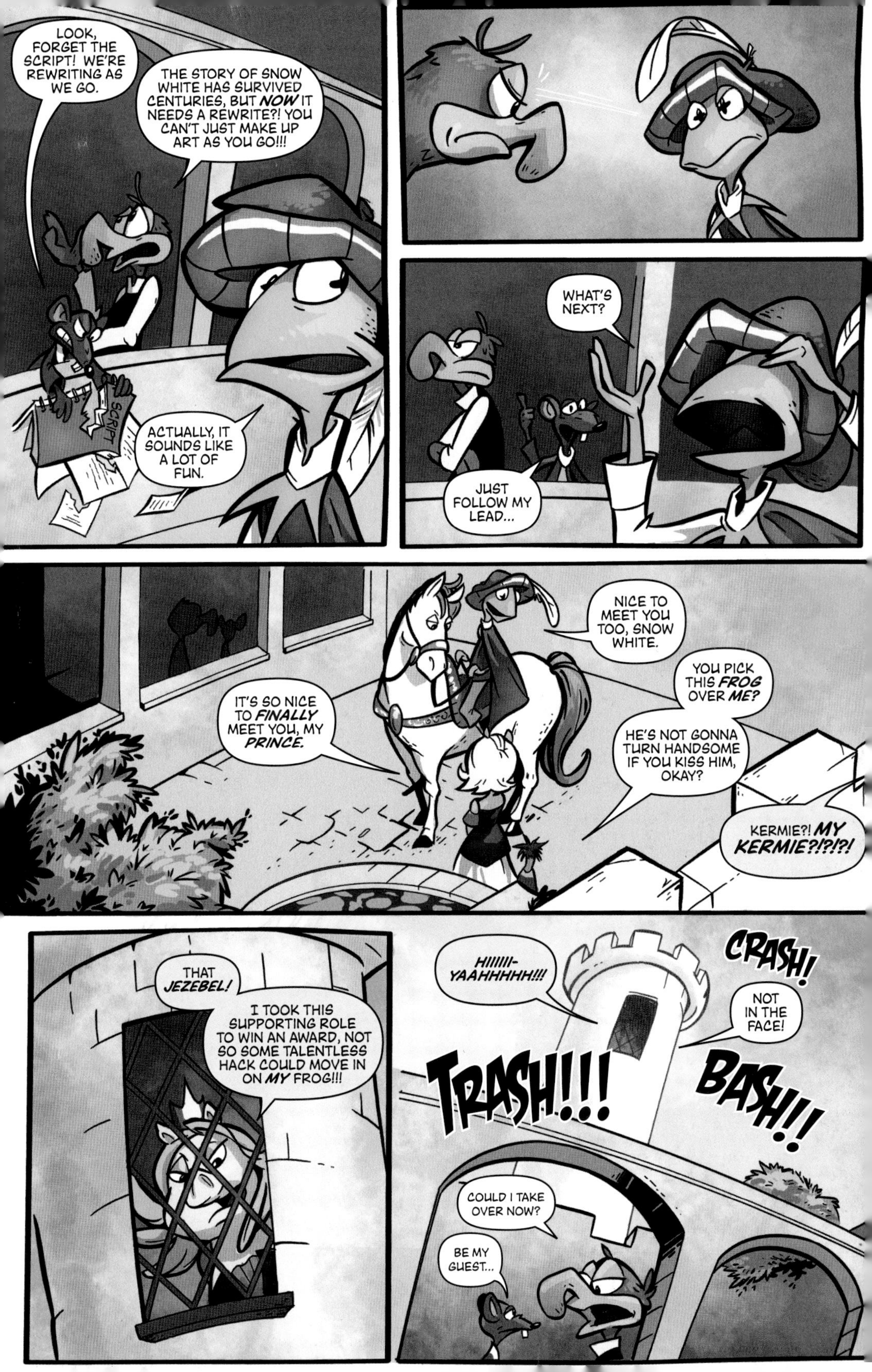

LOOK, FORGET THE SCRIPT! WE'RE REWRITING AS WE GO.
THE STORY OF SNOW WHITE HAS SURVIVED CENTURIES, BUT NOW IT NEEDS A REWRITE?! YOU CAN'T JUST MAKE UP ART AS YOU GO!!!
SCRIPT
ACTUALLY, IT SOUNDS LIKE A LOT OF FUN.
WHAT'S NEXT?
JUST FOLLOW MY LEAD...
IT'S SO NICE TO FINALLY MEET YOU, MY PRINCE.
NICE TO MEET YOU TOO, SNOW WHITE.
YOU PICK THIS FROG OVER ME?
HE'S NOT GONNA TURN HANDSOME IF YOU KISS HIM, OKAY?
KERMIE?! MY KERMIE?!?!?!
THAT JEZEBEL!
I TOOK THIS SUPPORTING ROLE TO WIN AN AWARD, NOT SO SOME TALENTLESS HACK COULD MOVE IN ON MY FROG!!!
HIIIIII-YAAHHHHHH!!!
CRASH!
NOT IN THE FACE!
TRASH!!!
BASH!!
COULD I TAKE OVER NOW?
BE MY GUEST...

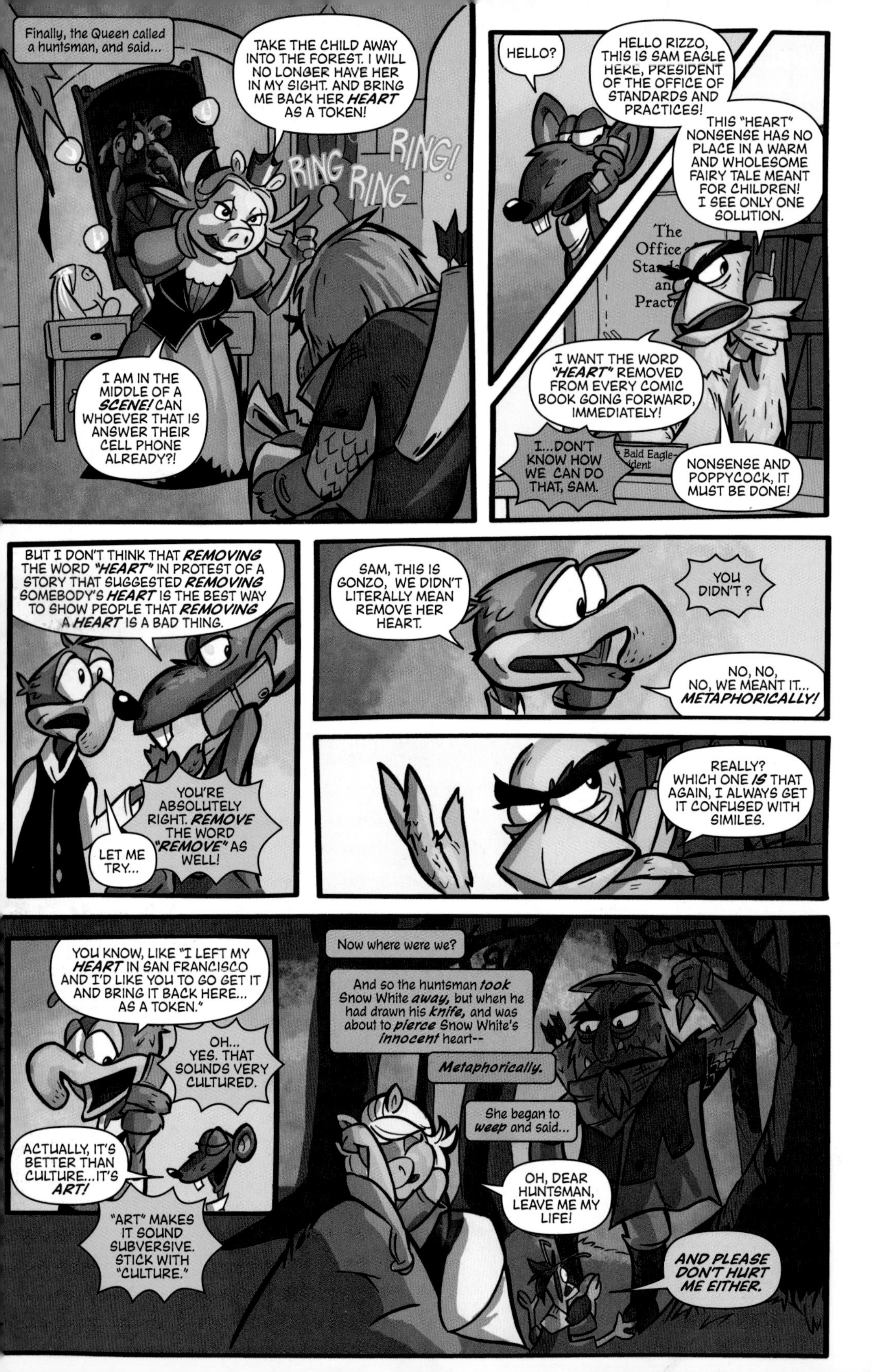

Finally, the Queen called a huntsman, and said...
TAKE THE CHILD AWAY INTO THE FOREST. I WILL NO LONGER HAVE HER IN MY SIGHT. AND BRING ME BACK HER HEART AS A TOKEN!
RING RING RING!
I AM IN THE MIDDLE OF A SCENE! CAN WHOEVER THAT IS ANSWER THEIR CELL PHONE ALREADY?!
HELLO?
HELLO RIZZO, THIS IS SAM EAGLE HERE, PRESIDENT OF THE OFFICE OF STANDARDS AND PRACTICES!
THIS "HEART" NONSENSE HAS NO PLACE IN A WARM AND WHOLESOME FAIRY TALE MEANT FOR CHILDREN! I SEE ONLY ONE SOLUTION.
I WANT THE WORD "HEART" REMOVED FROM EVERY COMIC BOOK GOING FORWARD, IMMEDIATELY!
I...DON'T KNOW HOW WE CAN DO THAT, SAM.
NONSENSE AND POPPYCOCK, IT MUST BE DONE!
BUT I DON'T THINK THAT REMOVING THE WORD "HEART" IN PROTEST OF A STORY THAT SUGGESTED REMOVING SOMEBODY'S HEART IS THE BEST WAY TO SHOW PEOPLE THAT REMOVING A HEART IS A BAD THING.
YOU'RE ABSOLUTELY RIGHT. REMOVE THE WORD "REMOVE" AS WELL!
LET ME TRY...
SAM, THIS IS GONZO, WE DIDN'T LITERALLY MEAN REMOVE HER HEART.
YOU DIDN'T ?
NO, NO, NO, WE MEANT IT... METAPHORICALLY!
REALLY? WHICH ONE IS THAT AGAIN, I ALWAYS GET IT CONFUSED WITH SIMILES.
YOU KNOW, LIKE "I LEFT MY HEART IN SAN FRANCISCO AND I'D LIKE YOU TO GO GET IT AND BRING IT BACK HERE... AS A TOKEN."
OH... YES. THAT SOUNDS VERY CULTURED.
ACTUALLY, IT'S BETTER THAN CULTURE...IT'S ART!
"ART" MAKES IT SOUND SUBVERSIVE. STICK WITH "CULTURE."
Now where were we?
And so the huntsman took Snow White away, but when he had drawn his knife, and was about to pierce Snow White's innocent heart--
Metaphorically.
She began to weep and said...
OH, DEAR HUNTSMAN, LEAVE ME MY LIFE!
AND PLEASE DON'T HURT ME EITHER.

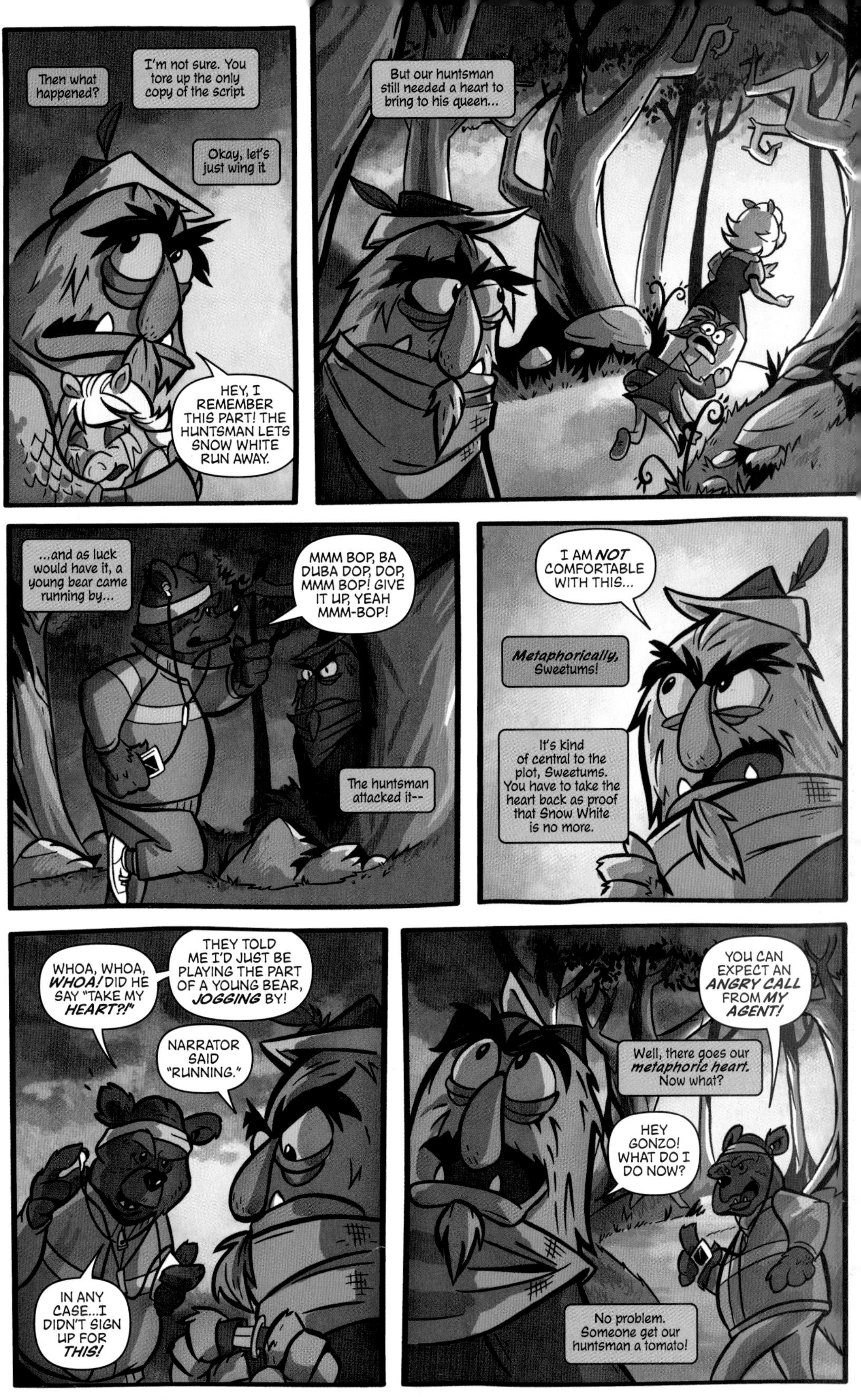
Then what happened?
I'm not sure. You tore up the only copy of the script
Okay, let's just wing it
HEY, I REMEMBER THIS PART! THE HUNTSMAN LETS SNOW WHITE RUN AWAY.
But our huntsman still needed a heart to bring to his queen...
...and as luck would have it, a young bear came running by...
MMM BOP, BA DUBA DOP, DOP, MMM BOP! GIVE IT UP, YEAH MMM-BOP!
The huntsman attacked it--
I AM NOT COMFORTABLE WITH THIS...
Metaphorically, Sweetums!
It's kind of central to the plot, Sweetums. You have to take the heart back as proof that Snow White is no more.
WHOA, WHOA, WHOA! DID HE SAY "TAKE MY HEART?!"
THEY TOLD ME I'D JUST BE PLAYING THE PART OF A YOUNG BEAR, JOGGING BY!
NARRATOR SAID "RUNNING."
IN ANY CASE...I DIDN'T SIGN UP FOR THIS!
YOU CAN EXPECT AN ANGRY CALL FROM MY AGENT!
Well, there goes our metaphoric heart. Now what?
HEY GONZO! WHAT DO I DO NOW?
No problem. Someone get our huntsman a tomato!

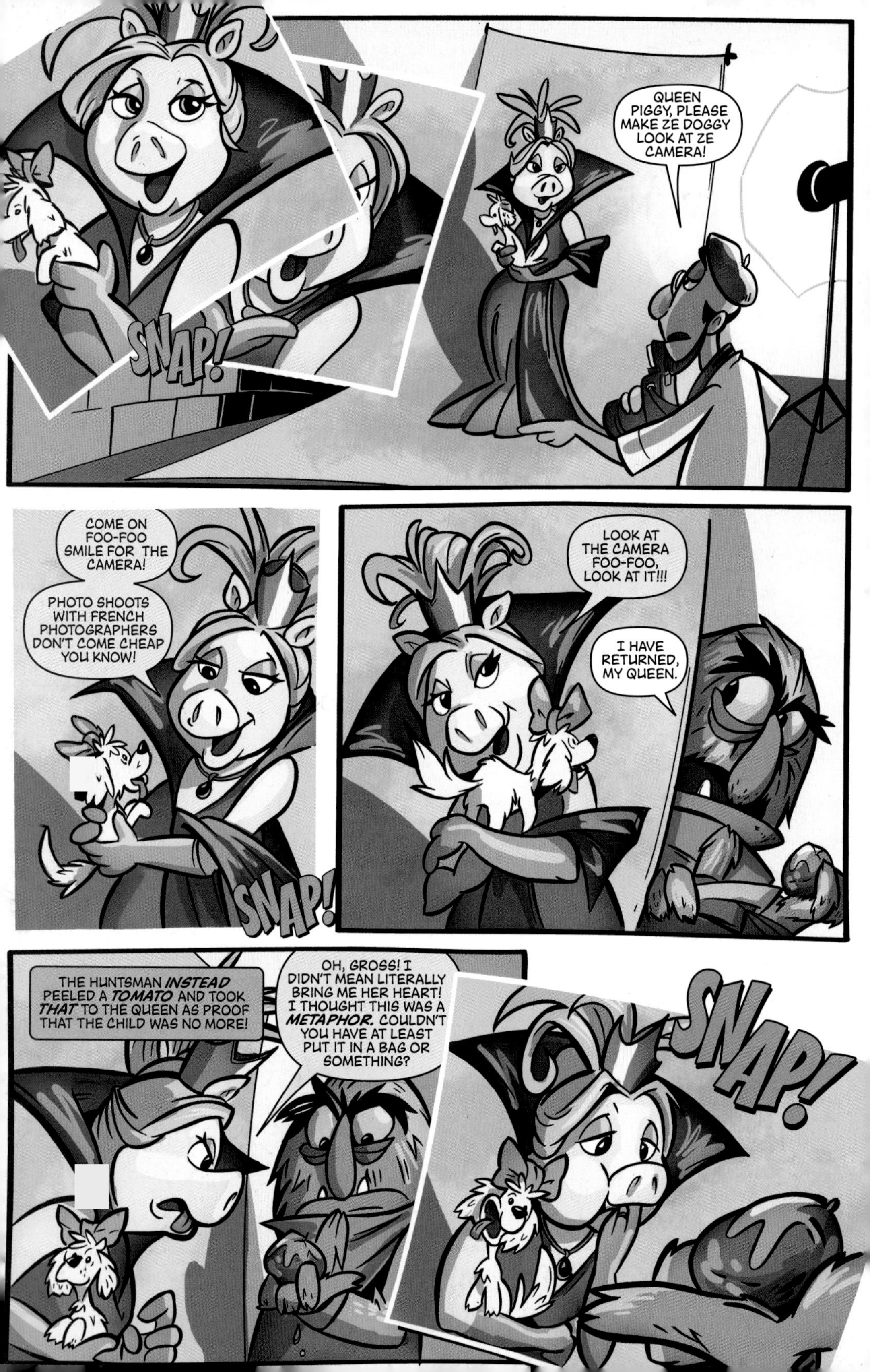
SNAP!
QUEEN PIGGY, PLEASE MAKE ZE DOGGY LOOK AT ZE CAMERA!
COME ON FOO-FOO SMILE FOR THE CAMERA!
PHOTO SHOOTS WITH FRENCH PHOTOGRAPHERS DON'T COME CHEAP YOU KNOW!
SNAP!
LOOK AT THE CAMERA FOO-FOO, LOOK AT IT!!!
I HAVE RETURNED, MY QUEEN.
THE HUNTSMAN *INSTEAD* PEELED A *TOMATO* AND TOOK *THAT* TO THE QUEEN AS PROOF THAT THE CHILD WAS NO MORE!
OH, GROSS! I DIDN'T MEAN LITERALLY BRING ME HER HEART! I THOUGHT THIS WAS A *METAPHOR.* COULDN'T YOU HAVE AT LEAST PUT IT IN A BAG OR SOMETHING?
SNAP!

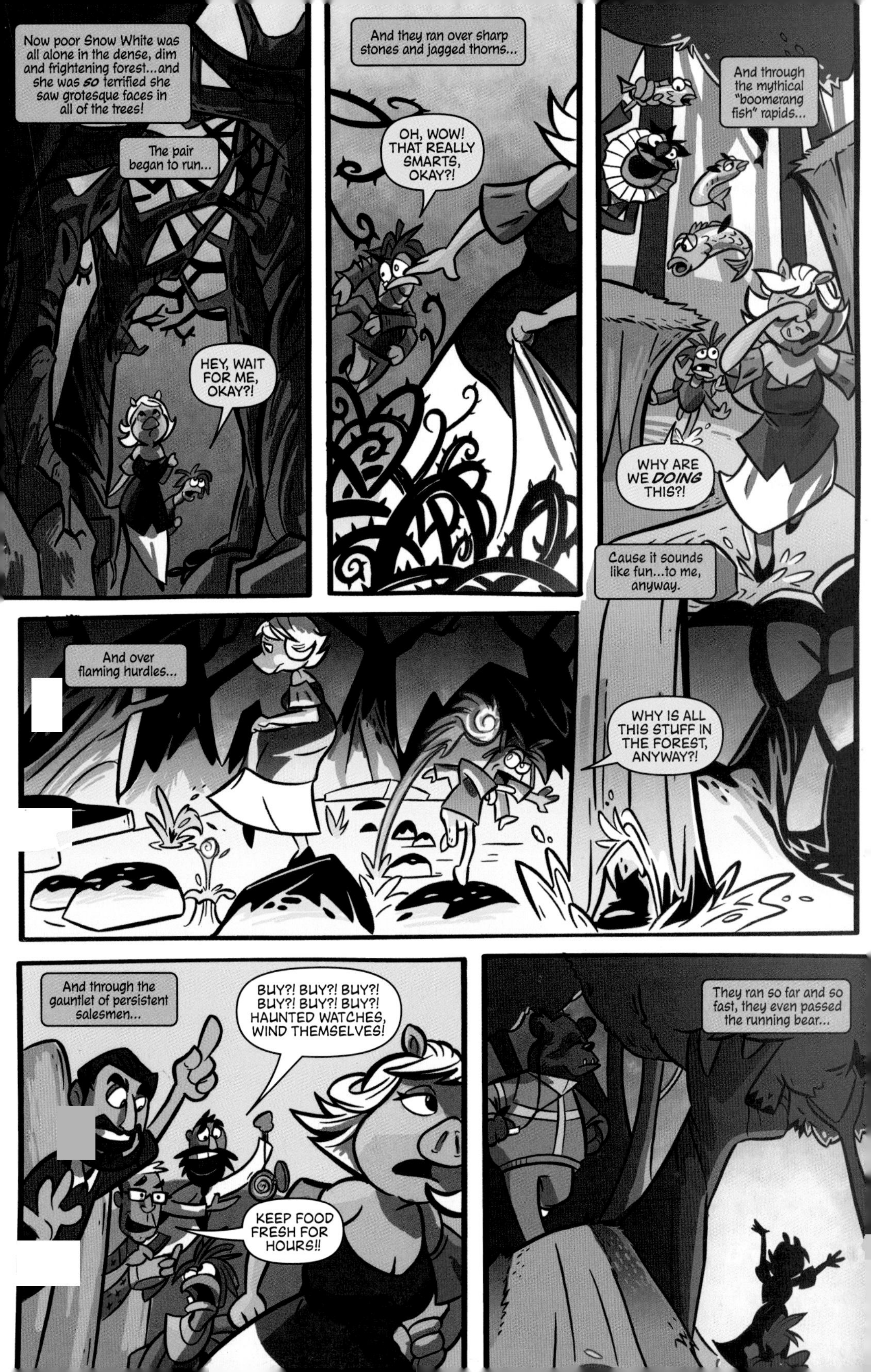
Now poor Snow White was all alone in the dense, dim and frightening forest...and she was so terrified she saw grotesque faces in all of the trees!
The pair began to run...
HEY, WAIT FOR ME, OKAY?!
And they ran over sharp stones and jagged thorns...
OH, WOW! THAT REALLY SMARTS, OKAY?!
And through the mythical "boomerang fish" rapids...
WHY ARE WE DOING THIS?!
Cause it sounds like fun...to me, anyway.
And over flaming hurdles...
WHY IS ALL THIS STUFF IN THE FOREST, ANYWAY?!
And through the gauntlet of persistent salesmen...
BUY?! BUY?! BUY?! BUY?! BUY?! BUY?! HAUNTED WATCHES, WIND THEMSELVES!
KEEP FOOD FRESH FOR HOURS!!
They ran so far and so fast, they even passed the running bear...

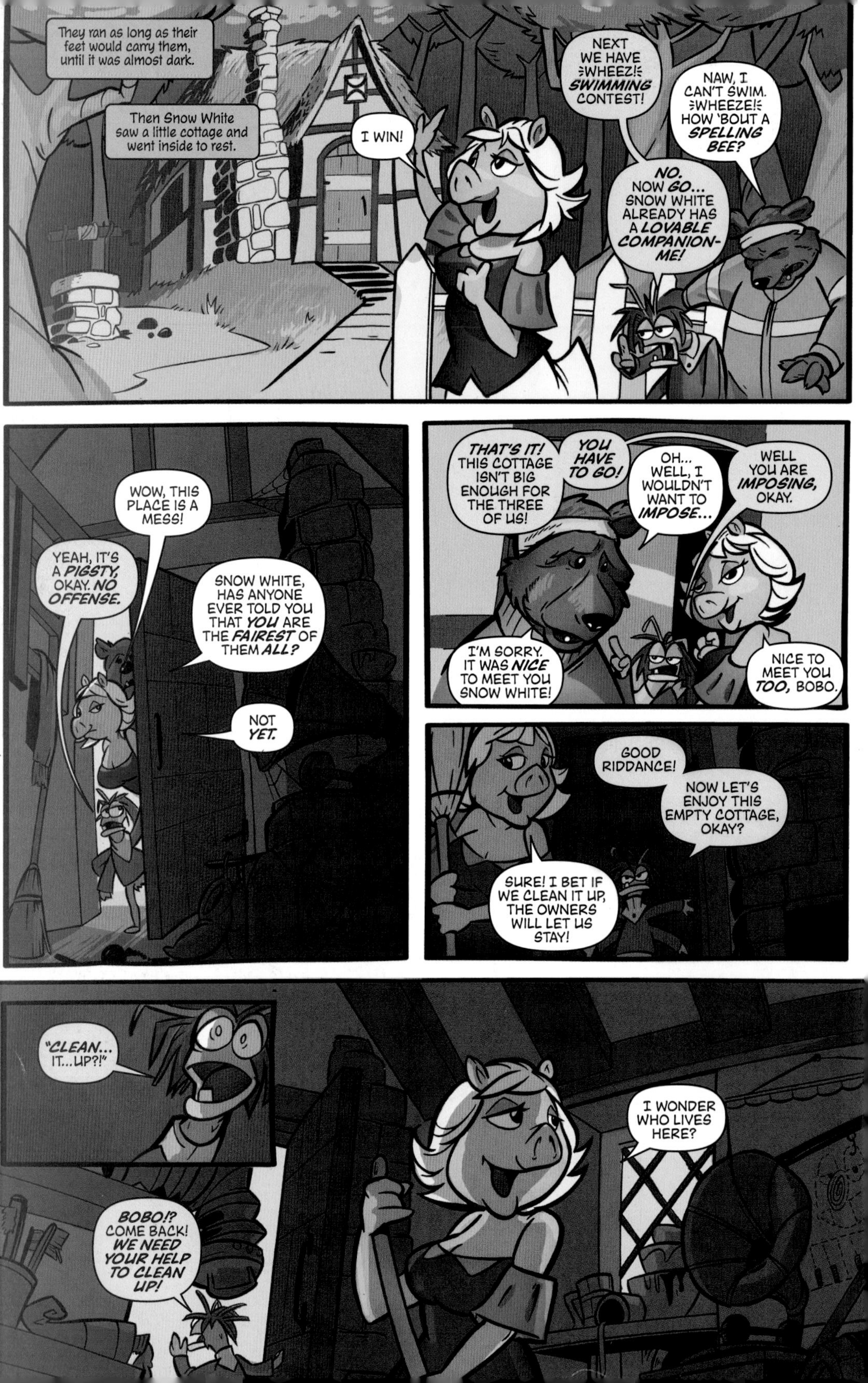

They ran as long as their feet would carry them, until it was almost dark.
Then Snow White saw a little cottage and went inside to rest.
I WIN!
NEXT WE HAVE WHEEZ! SWIMMING CONTEST!
NAW, I CAN'T SWIM. WHEEZE! HOW 'BOUT A SPELLING BEE?
NO. NOW GO... SNOW WHITE ALREADY HAS A LOVABLE COMPANION- ME!
WOW, THIS PLACE IS A MESS!
YEAH, IT'S A PIGSTY, OKAY. NO OFFENSE.
SNOW WHITE, HAS ANYONE EVER TOLD YOU THAT YOU ARE THE FAIREST OF THEM ALL?
NOT YET.
THAT'S IT! THIS COTTAGE ISN'T BIG ENOUGH FOR THE THREE OF US!
YOU HAVE TO GO!
OH... WELL, I WOULDN'T WANT TO IMPOSE...
WELL YOU ARE IMPOSING, OKAY.
I'M SORRY. IT WAS NICE TO MEET YOU SNOW WHITE!
NICE TO MEET YOU TOO, BOBO.
GOOD RIDDANCE!
NOW LET'S ENJOY THIS EMPTY COTTAGE, OKAY?
SURE! I BET IF WE CLEAN IT UP, THE OWNERS WILL LET US STAY!
"CLEAN... IT...UP?!"
I WONDER WHO LIVES HERE?
BOBO!? COME BACK! WE NEED YOUR HELP TO CLEAN UP!

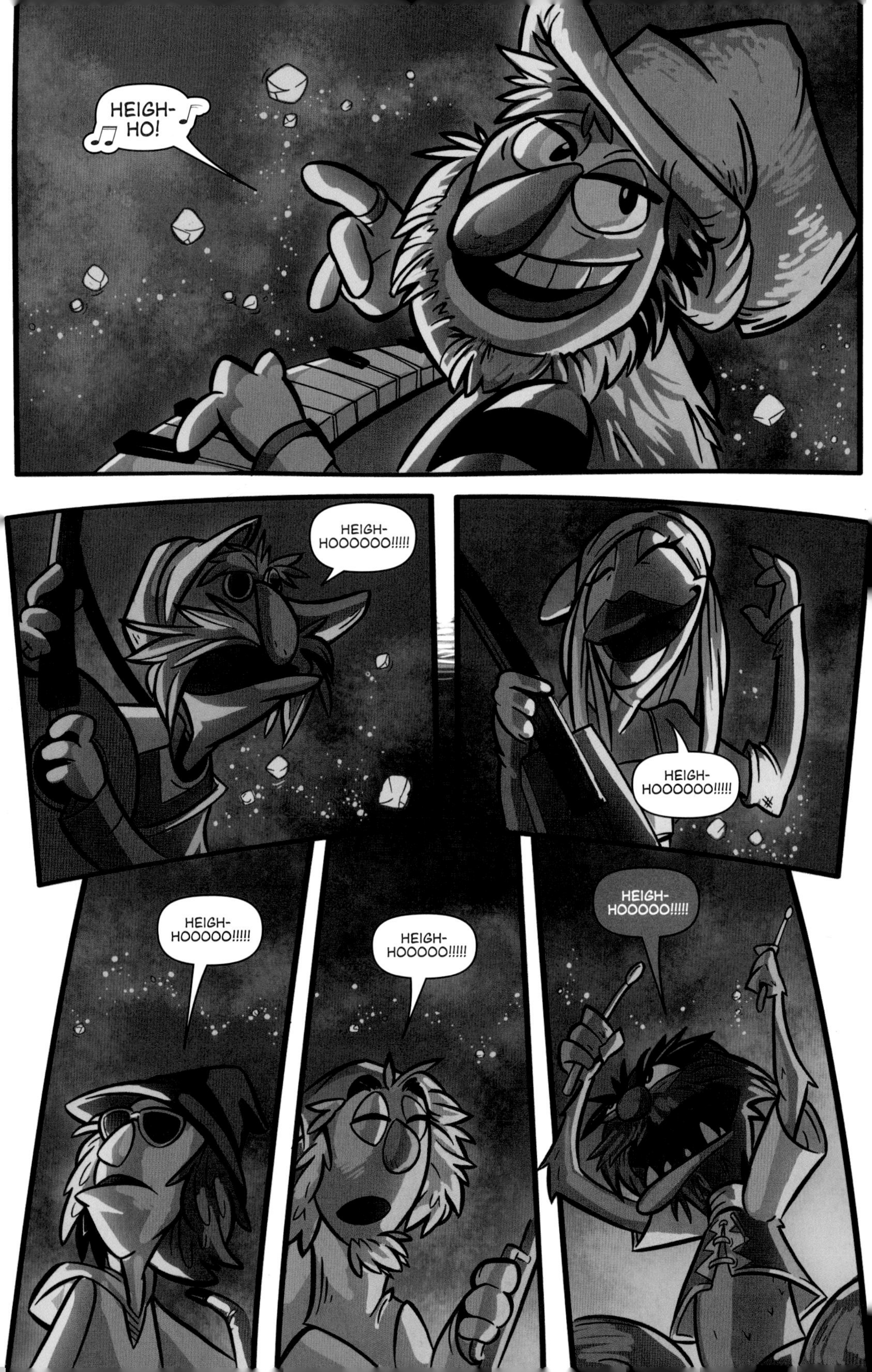
HEIGH-HO!
HEIGH-HOOOOOO!!!!!
HEIGH-HOOOOOO!!!!!
HEIGH-HOOOOO!!!!!
HEIGH-HOOOOO!!!!!
HEIGH-HOOOOO!!!!!

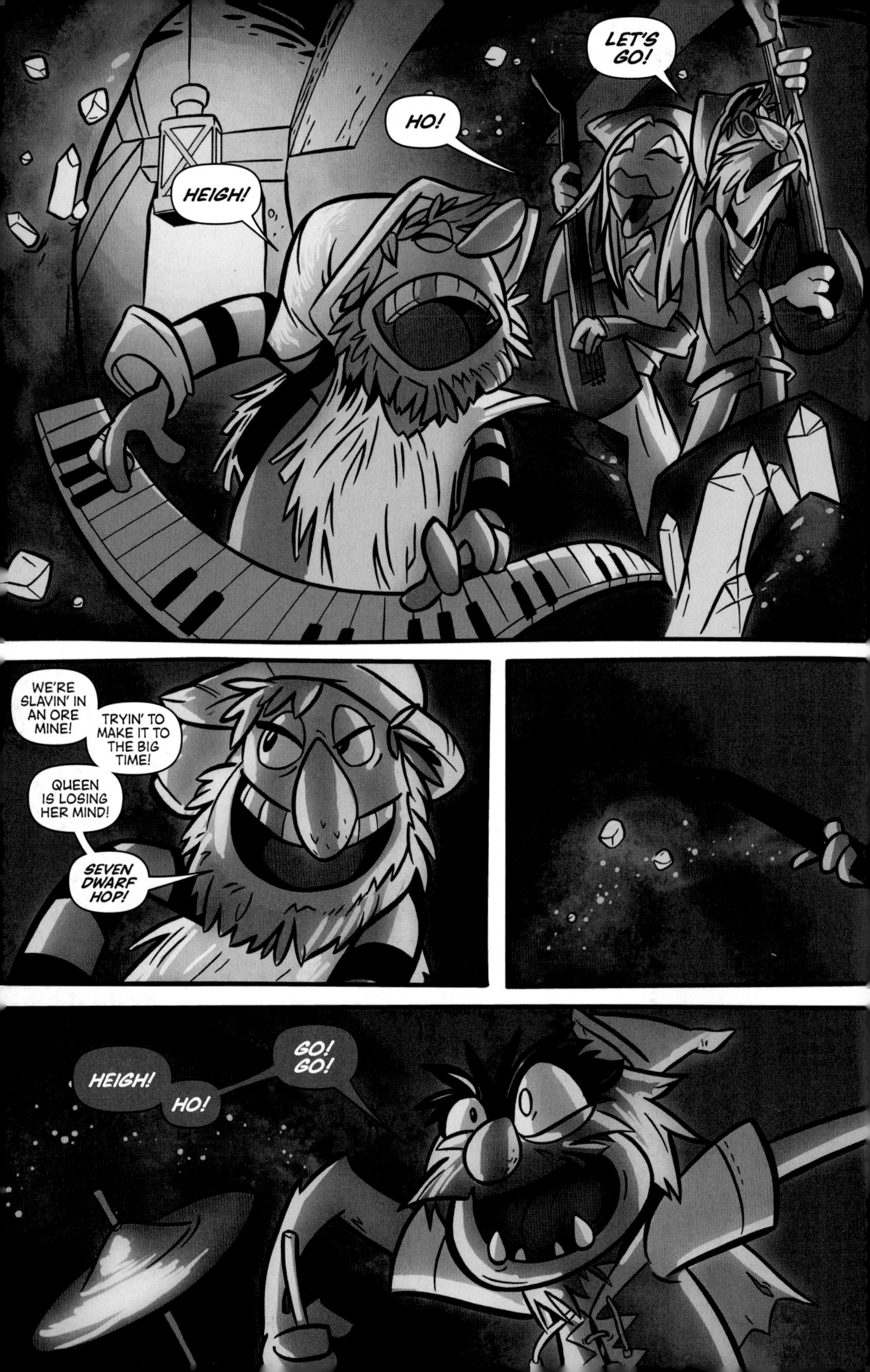
HEIGH!
HO!
LET'S GO!
WE'RE SLAVIN' IN AN ORE MINE!
TRYIN' TO MAKE IT TO THE BIG TIME!
QUEEN IS LOSING HER MIND!
SEVEN DWARF HOP!
HEIGH!
HO!
GO! GO!

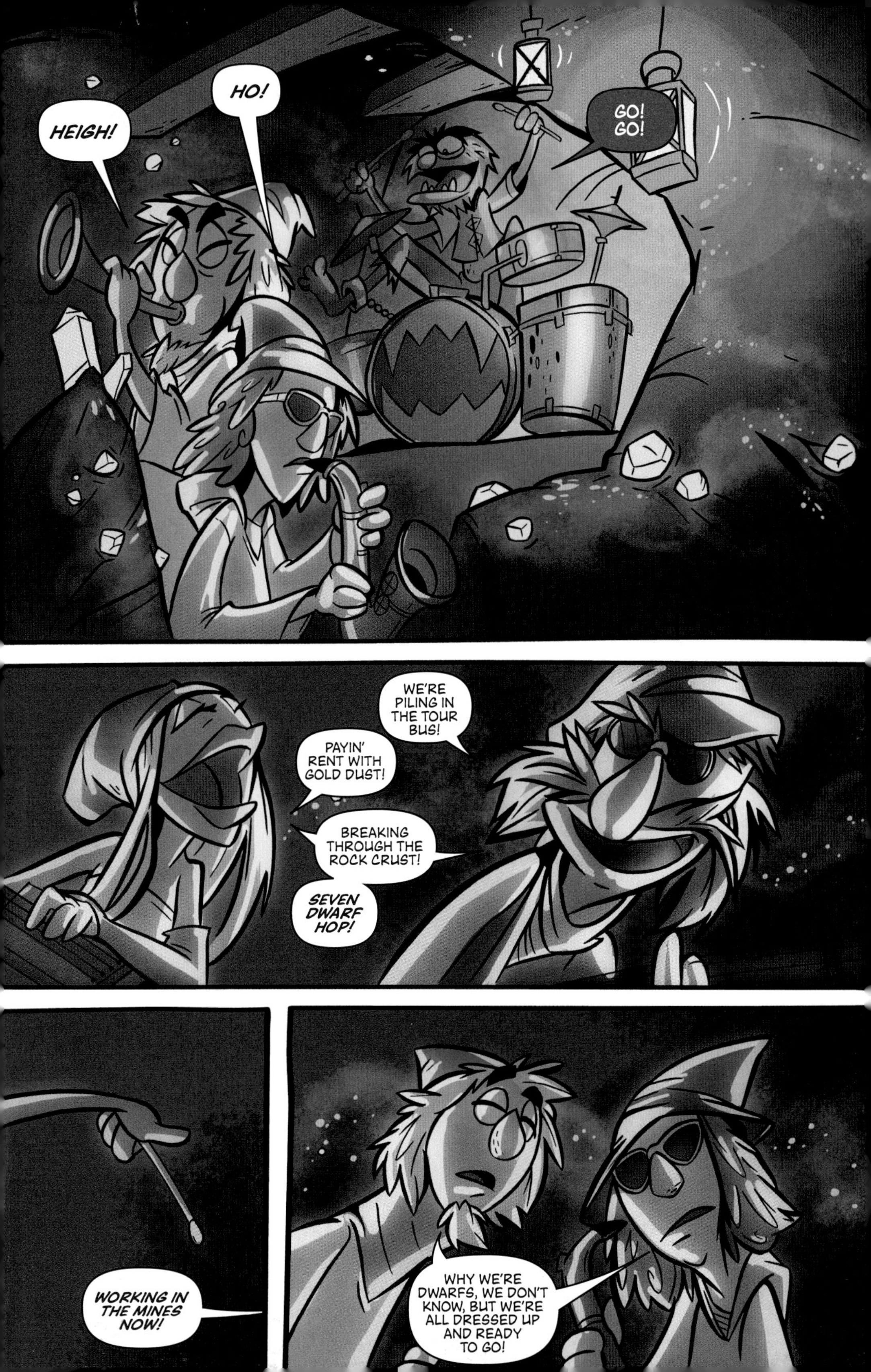
HEIGH!
HO!
GO! GO!
WE'RE PILING IN THE TOUR BUS!
PAYIN' RENT WITH GOLD DUST!
BREAKING THROUGH THE ROCK CRUST!
SEVEN DWARF HOP!
WORKING IN THE MINES NOW!
WHY WE'RE DWARFS, WE DON'T KNOW, BUT WE'RE ALL DRESSED UP AND READY TO GO!

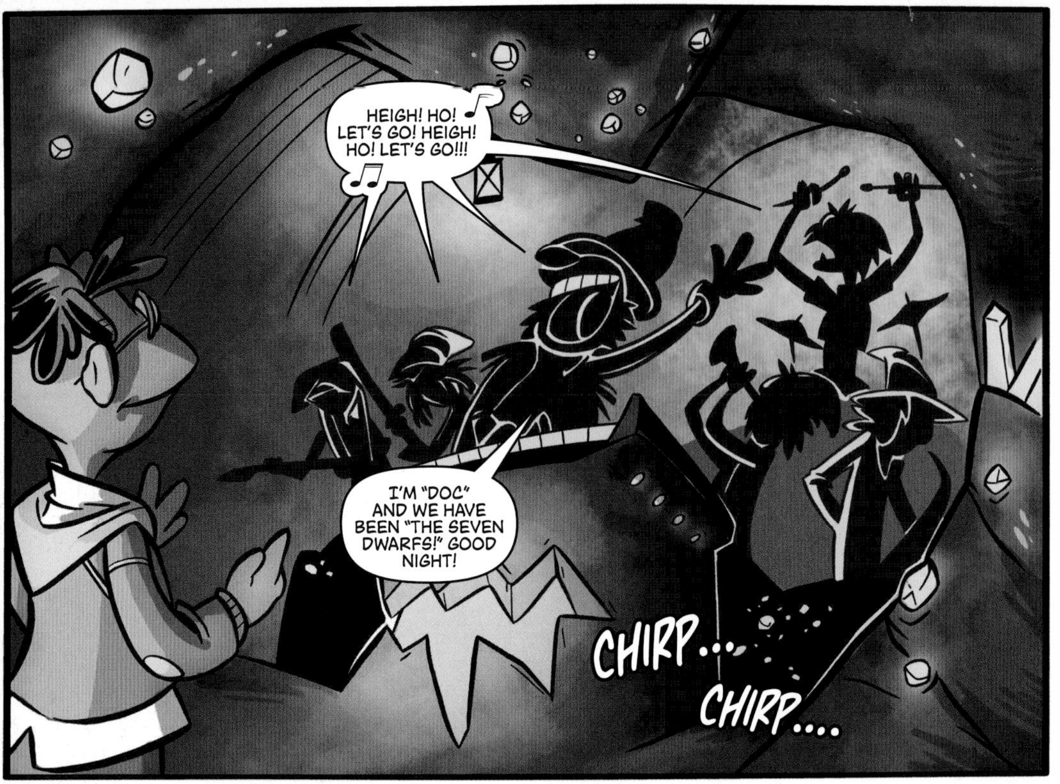
HEIGH! HO! LET'S GO! HEIGH! HO! LET'S GO!!!
I'M "DOC" AND WE HAVE BEEN "THE SEVEN DWARFS!" GOOD NIGHT!
CHIRP...
CHIRP....

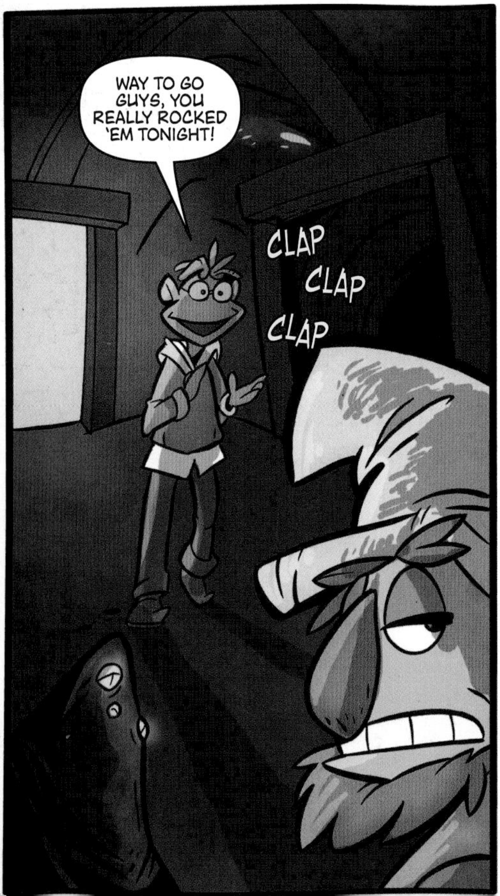
WAY TO GO GUYS, YOU REALLY ROCKED 'EM TONIGHT!
CLAP
CLAP
CLAP

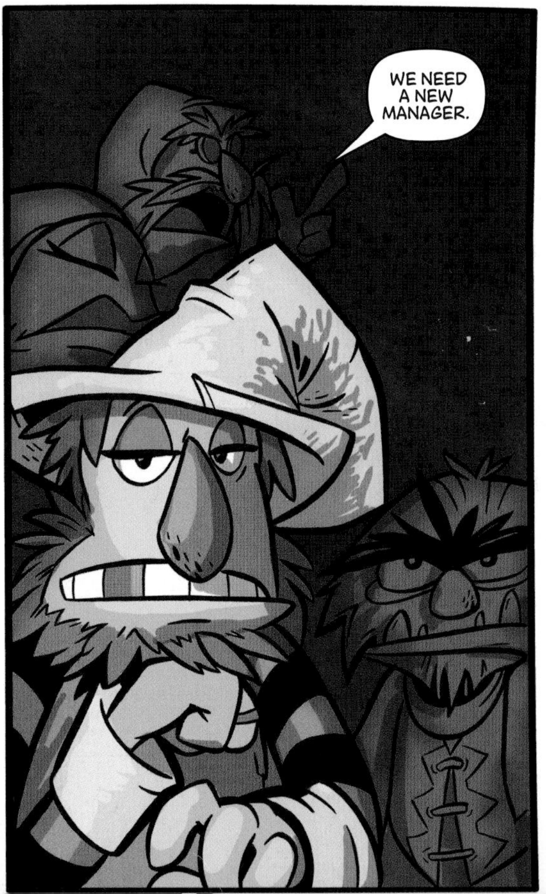
WE NEED A NEW MANAGER.

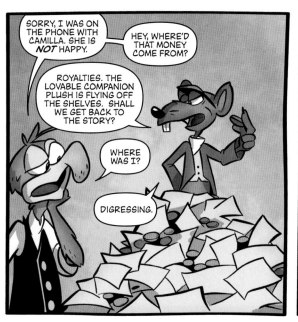

SORRY, I WAS ON THE PHONE WITH CAMILLA. SHE IS *NOT* HAPPY.

HEY, WHERE'D THAT MONEY COME FROM?

ROYALTIES. THE LOVABLE COMPANION PLUSH IS FLYING OFF THE SHELVES. SHALL WE GET BACK TO THE STORY?

WHERE WAS I?

DIGRESSING.

≡Ahem!≡ So the Queen believed Snow White was no more!

And she went to her mirror and said...

MIRROR, MIRROR, ON THE WALL, WHO IN THIS LAND IS *FAIREST* OF *ALL?*

And the mirrorglass answered...

WE'RE STILL TALKING ABOUT A 5-MILE RADIUS, RIGHT?

YES, YES, WHATEVER!

OH, QUEEN, THOU ART FAIREST OF ALL I SEE, BUT OVER THE HILLS WHERE "THE SEVEN DWARFS" PLAY, SNOW WHITE IS *STILL* LIVING: *FAIREST* IS *SHE,* AND ONLY *4.5 MILES AWAY!*

*WHAT?!* BUT I HAVE HER *HEART* RIGHT HERE IN THIS *BAG!* METAPHORICALLY SPEAKING.

SNOW WHITE IS *ALIVE,* HER *HEART* IN HER *CHEST.* YOU HAVE A TOMATO, SOME *SOUP* AT BEST!

WOCKA WOCKA!

SPLATT!

SAW *THAT* ONE COMING.

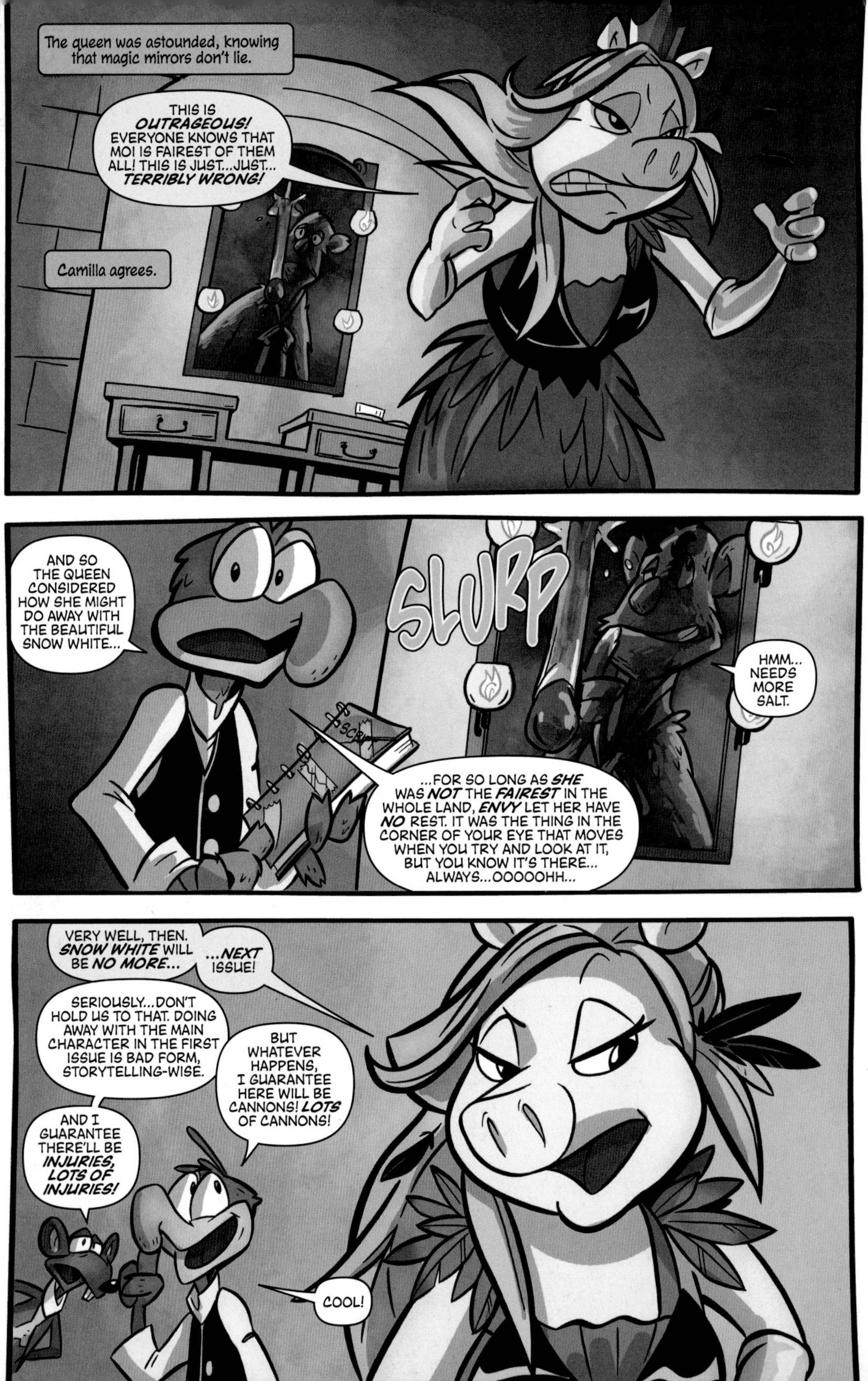
The queen was astounded, knowing that magic mirrors don't lie.
THIS IS ***OUTRAGEOUS!*** EVERYONE KNOWS THAT MOI IS FAIREST OF THEM ALL! THIS IS JUST...JUST... ***TERRIBLY WRONG!***
Camilla agrees.
AND SO THE QUEEN CONSIDERED HOW SHE MIGHT DO AWAY WITH THE BEAUTIFUL SNOW WHITE...
SLURP
HMM... NEEDS MORE SALT.
...FOR SO LONG AS ***SHE*** WAS ***NOT*** THE ***FAIREST*** IN THE WHOLE LAND, ***ENVY*** LET HER HAVE ***NO*** REST. IT WAS THE THING IN THE CORNER OF YOUR EYE THAT MOVES WHEN YOU TRY AND LOOK AT IT, BUT YOU KNOW IT'S THERE... ALWAYS...OOOOOHH...
VERY WELL, THEN. ***SNOW WHITE*** WILL BE ***NO MORE...***
***...NEXT*** ISSUE!
SERIOUSLY...DON'T HOLD US TO THAT. DOING AWAY WITH THE MAIN CHARACTER IN THE FIRST ISSUE IS BAD FORM, STORYTELLING-WISE.
BUT WHATEVER HAPPENS, I GUARANTEE HERE WILL BE CANNONS! ***LOTS*** OF CANNONS!
AND I GUARANTEE THERE'LL BE ***INJURIES, LOTS OF INJURIES!***
COOL!

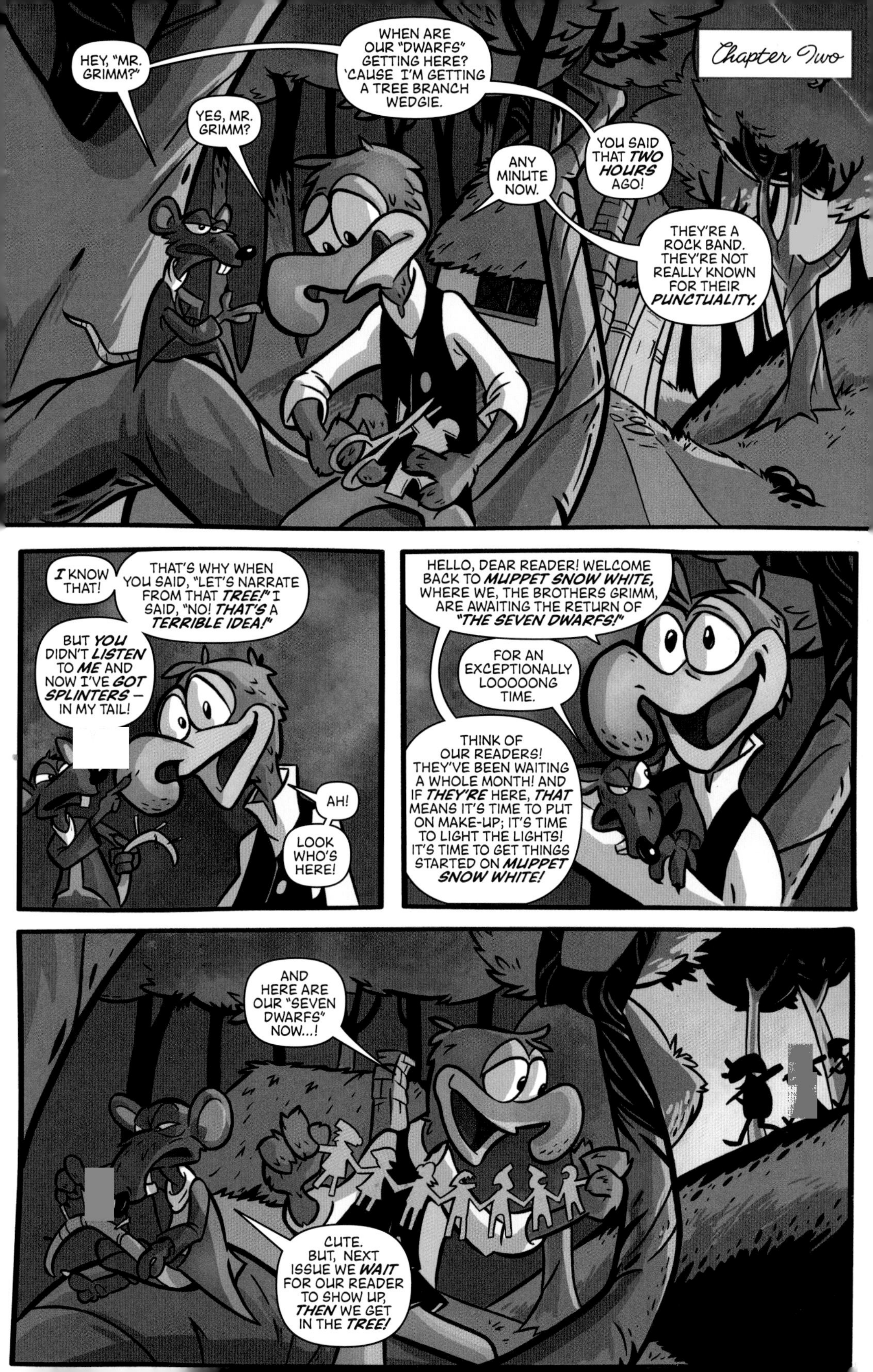

Chapter Two
HEY, "MR. GRIMM?"
YES, MR. GRIMM?
WHEN ARE OUR "DWARFS" GETTING HERE? 'CAUSE I'M GETTING A TREE BRANCH WEDGIE.
ANY MINUTE NOW.
YOU SAID THAT TWO HOURS AGO!
THEY'RE A ROCK BAND. THEY'RE NOT REALLY KNOWN FOR THEIR PUNCTUALITY.
I KNOW THAT!
THAT'S WHY WHEN YOU SAID, "LET'S NARRATE FROM THAT TREE!" I SAID, "NO! THAT'S A TERRIBLE IDEA!"
BUT YOU DIDN'T LISTEN TO ME AND NOW I'VE GOT SPLINTERS — IN MY TAIL!
AH!
LOOK WHO'S HERE!
HELLO, DEAR READER! WELCOME BACK TO MUPPET SNOW WHITE, WHERE WE, THE BROTHERS GRIMM, ARE AWAITING THE RETURN OF "THE SEVEN DWARFS!"
FOR AN EXCEPTIONALLY LOOOOONG TIME.
THINK OF OUR READERS! THEY'VE BEEN WAITING A WHOLE MONTH! AND IF THEY'RE HERE, THAT MEANS IT'S TIME TO PUT ON MAKE-UP; IT'S TIME TO LIGHT THE LIGHTS! IT'S TIME TO GET THINGS STARTED ON MUPPET SNOW WHITE!
AND HERE ARE OUR "SEVEN DWARFS" NOW...!
CUTE. BUT, NEXT ISSUE WE WAIT FOR OUR READER TO SHOW UP, THEN WE GET IN THE TREE!

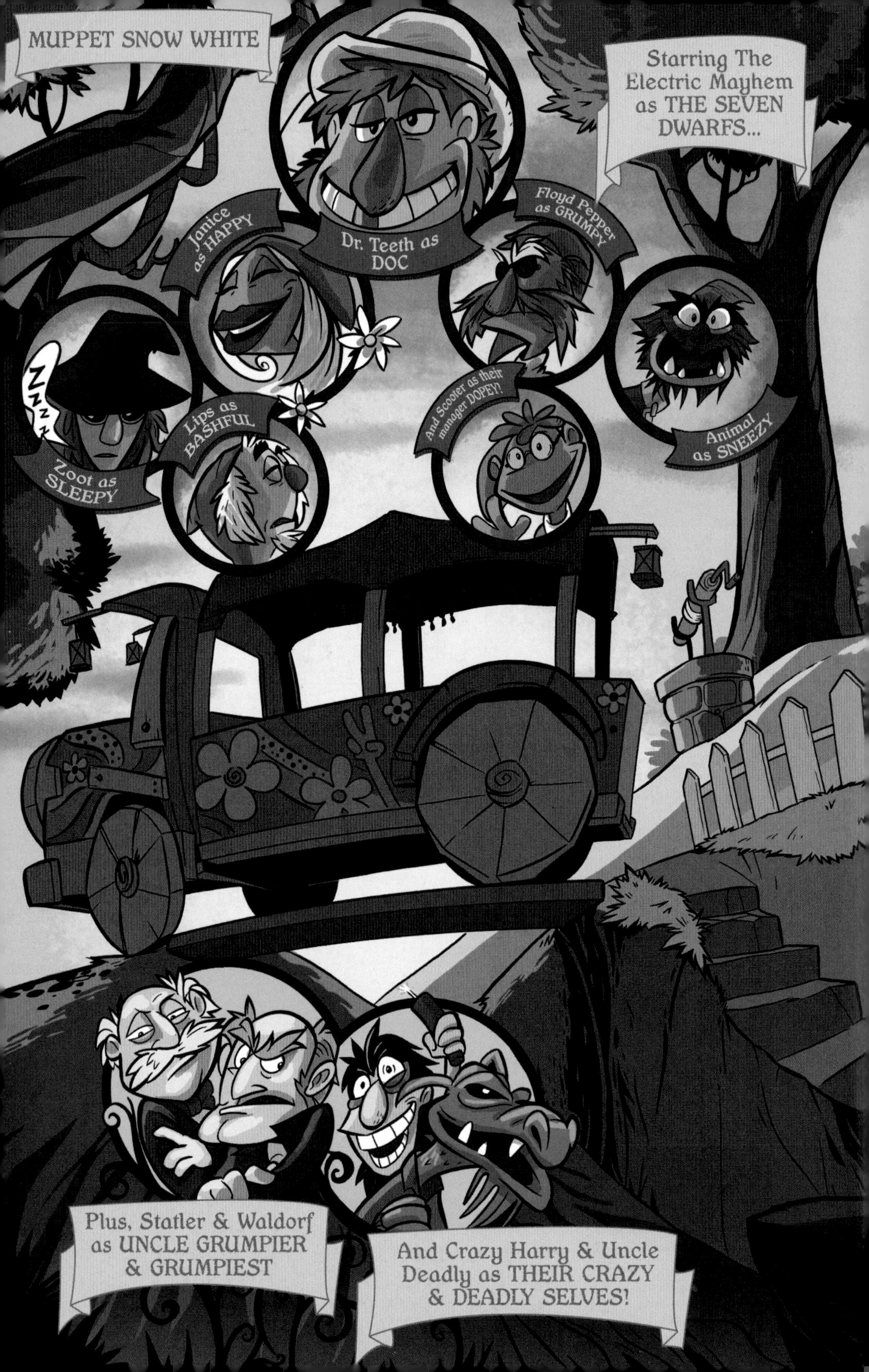
MUPPET SNOW WHITE
Starring The Electric Mayhem as THE SEVEN DWARFS...
Dr. Teeth as DOC
Janice as HAPPY
Floyd Pepper as GRUMPY
Zoot as SLEEPY
Lips as BASHFUL
And Scooter as their manager DOPEY!
Animal as SNEEZY
Plus, Statler & Waldorf as UNCLE GRUMPIER & GRUMPIEST
And Crazy Harry & Uncle Deadly as THEIR CRAZY & DEADLY SELVES!

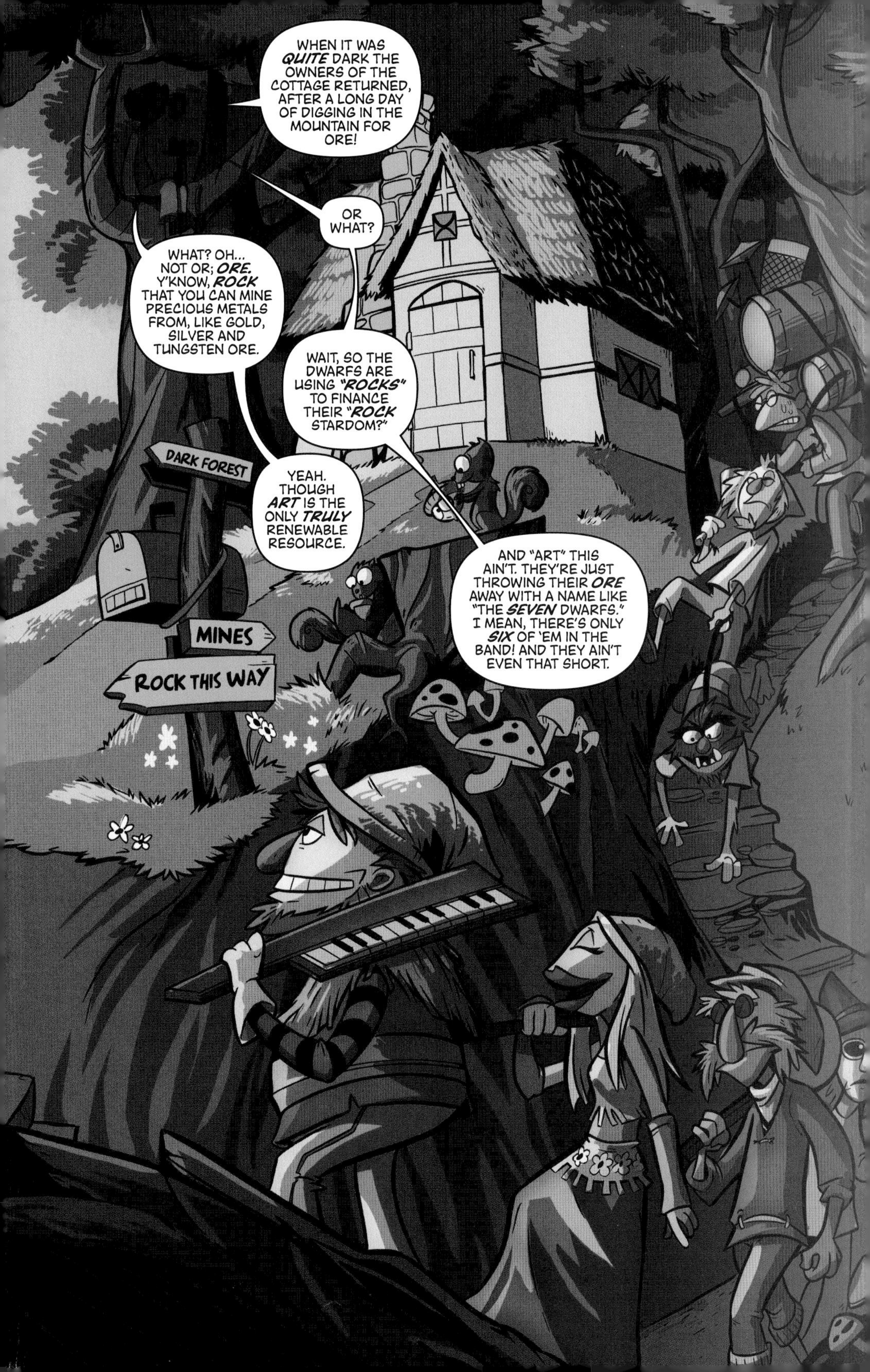
WHEN IT WAS *QUITE* DARK THE OWNERS OF THE COTTAGE RETURNED, AFTER A LONG DAY OF DIGGING IN THE MOUNTAIN FOR ORE!
OR WHAT?
WHAT? OH... NOT OR; *ORE.* Y'KNOW, *ROCK* THAT YOU CAN MINE PRECIOUS METALS FROM, LIKE GOLD, SILVER AND TUNGSTEN ORE.
WAIT, SO THE DWARFS ARE USING *"ROCKS"* TO FINANCE THEIR *"ROCK* STARDOM?"
YEAH. THOUGH *ART* IS THE ONLY *TRULY* RENEWABLE RESOURCE.
AND "ART" THIS AIN'T. THEY'RE JUST THROWING THEIR *ORE* AWAY WITH A NAME LIKE "THE *SEVEN* DWARFS." I MEAN, THERE'S ONLY *SIX* OF 'EM IN THE BAND! AND THEY AIN'T EVEN THAT SHORT.
DARK FOREST
MINES
ROCK THIS WAY

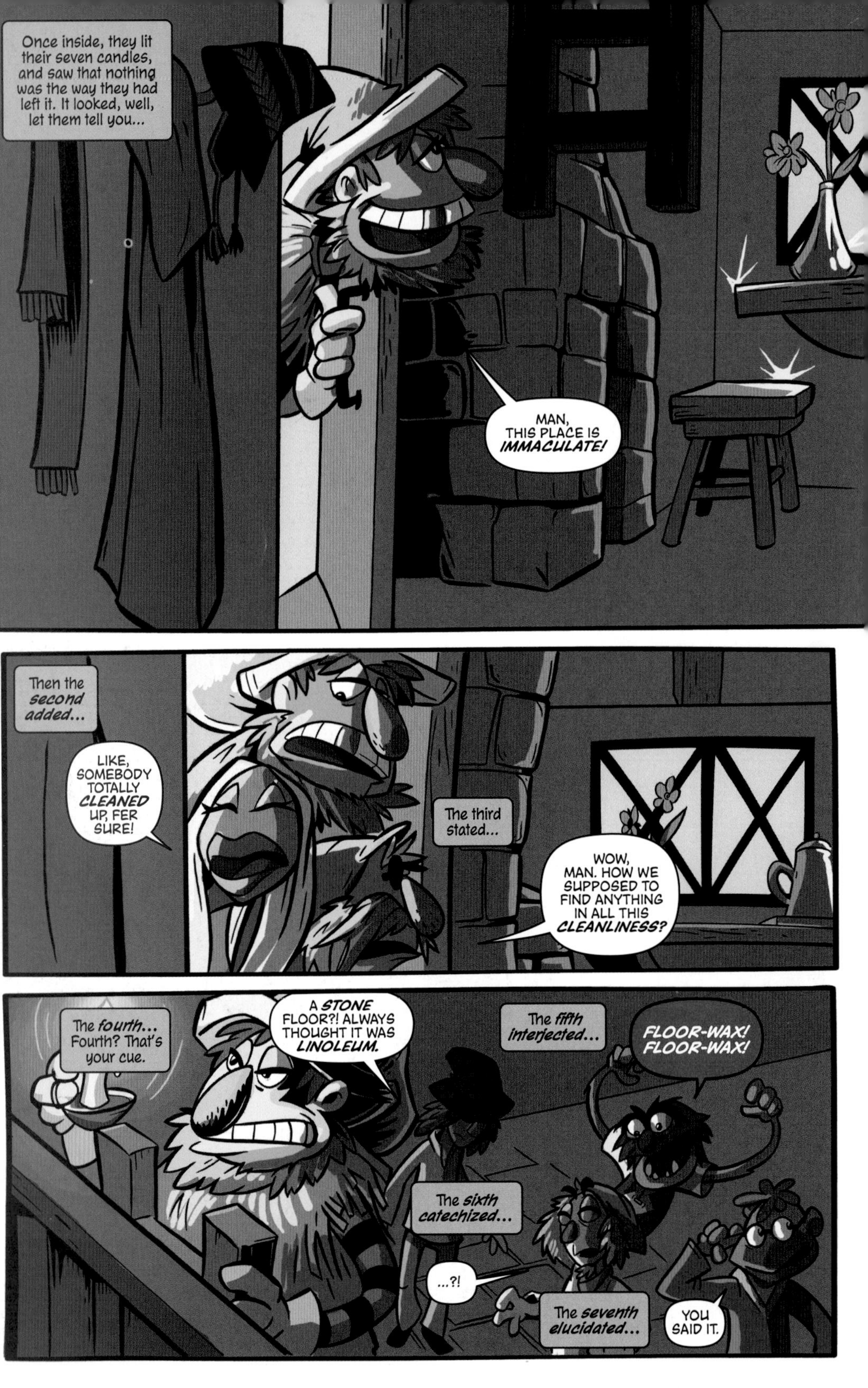
Once inside, they lit their seven candles, and saw that nothing was the way they had left it. It looked, well, let them tell you...
MAN, THIS PLACE IS IMMACULATE!
Then the second added...
LIKE, SOMEBODY TOTALLY CLEANED UP, FER SURE!
The third stated...
WOW, MAN. HOW WE SUPPOSED TO FIND ANYTHING IN ALL THIS CLEANLINESS?
The fourth... Fourth? That's your cue.
A STONE FLOOR?! ALWAYS THOUGHT IT WAS LINOLEUM.
The fifth interjected...
FLOOR-WAX! FLOOR-WAX!
The sixth catechized...
...?!
The seventh elucidated...
YOU SAID IT.

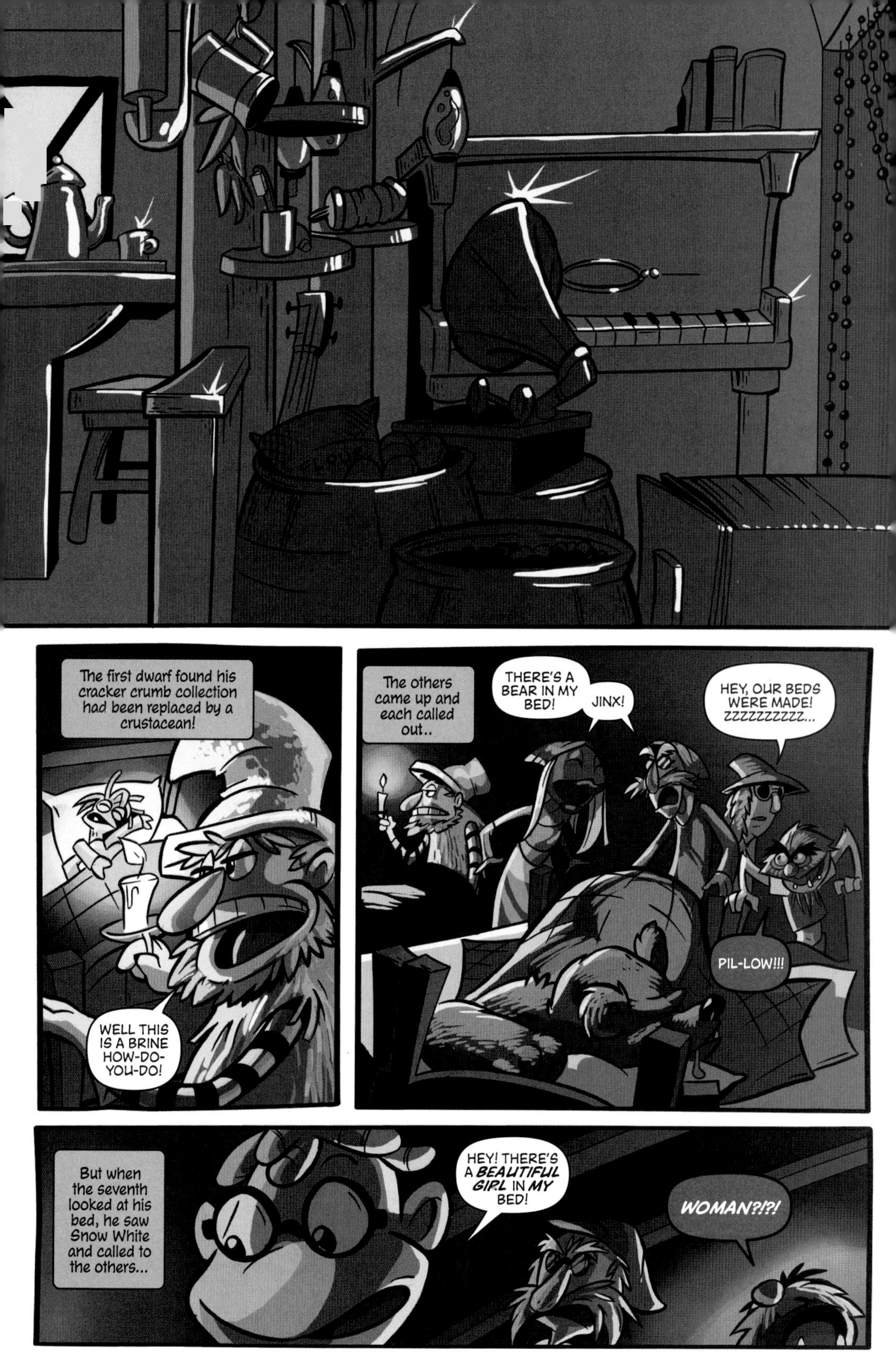

The first dwarf found his cracker crumb collection had been replaced by a crustacean!
WELL THIS IS A BRINE HOW-DO-YOU-DO!
The others came up and each called out..
THERE'S A BEAR IN MY BED!
JINX!
HEY, OUR BEDS WERE MADE! ZZZZZZZZZZ...
PIL-LOW!!!
But when the seventh looked at his bed, he saw Snow White and called to the others...
HEY! THERE'S A *BEAUTIFUL GIRL* IN *MY* BED!
*WOMAN?!?!*

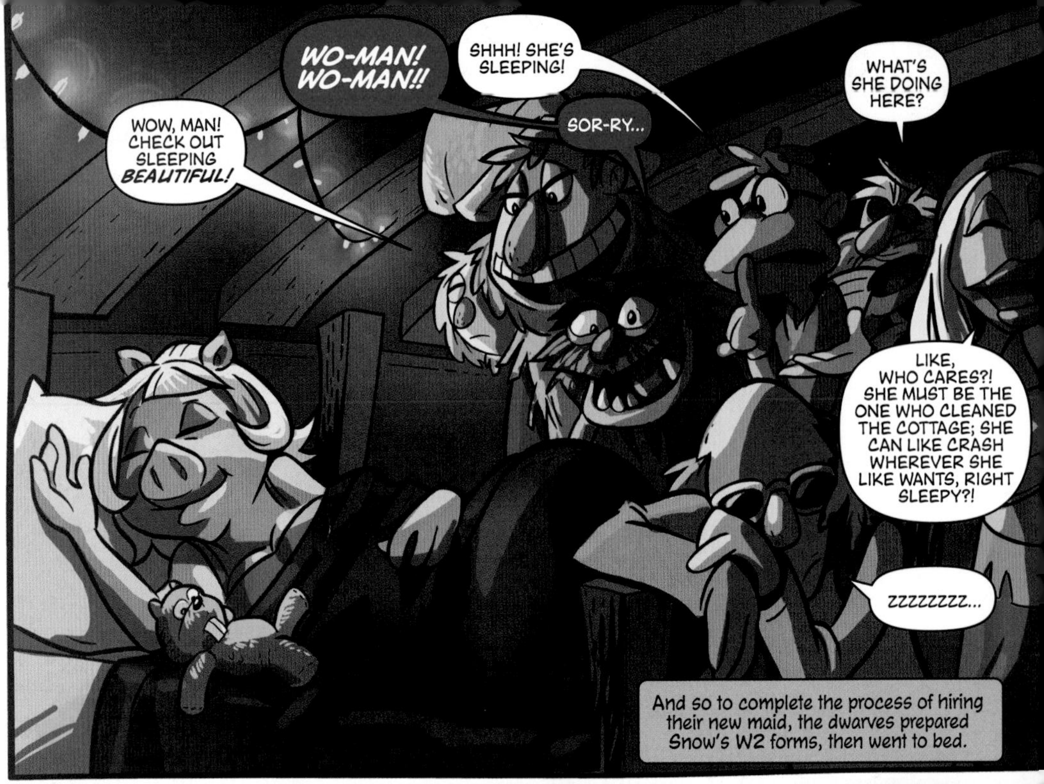
WOW, MAN! CHECK OUT SLEEPING BEAUTIFUL!
WO-MAN! WO-MAN!!
SHHH! SHE'S SLEEPING!
SOR-RY...
WHAT'S SHE DOING HERE?
LIKE, WHO CARES?! SHE MUST BE THE ONE WHO CLEANED THE COTTAGE; SHE CAN LIKE CRASH WHEREVER SHE LIKE WANTS, RIGHT SLEEPY?!
ZZZZZZZZ...
And so to complete the process of hiring their new maid, the dwarves prepared Snow's W2 forms, then went to bed.

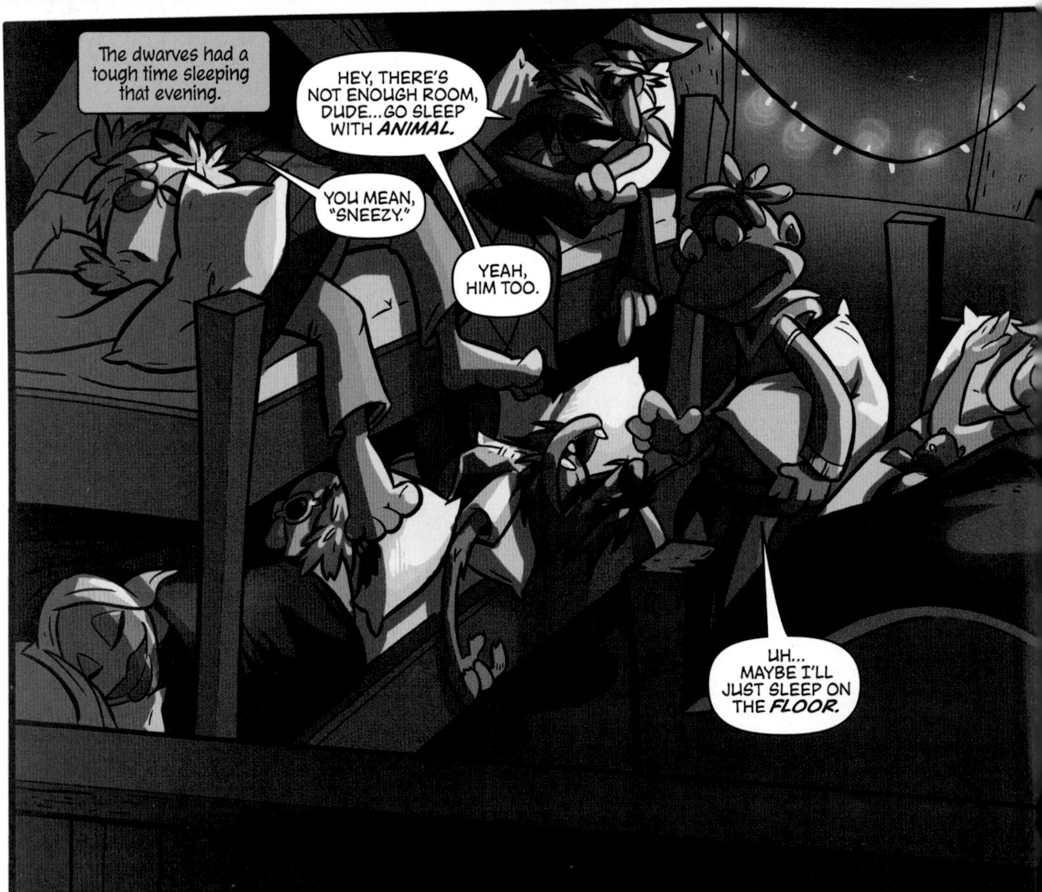
The dwarves had a tough time sleeping that evening.
HEY, THERE'S NOT ENOUGH ROOM, DUDE...GO SLEEP WITH ANIMAL.
YOU MEAN, "SNEEZY."
YEAH, HIM TOO.
UH... MAYBE I'LL JUST SLEEP ON THE FLOOR.

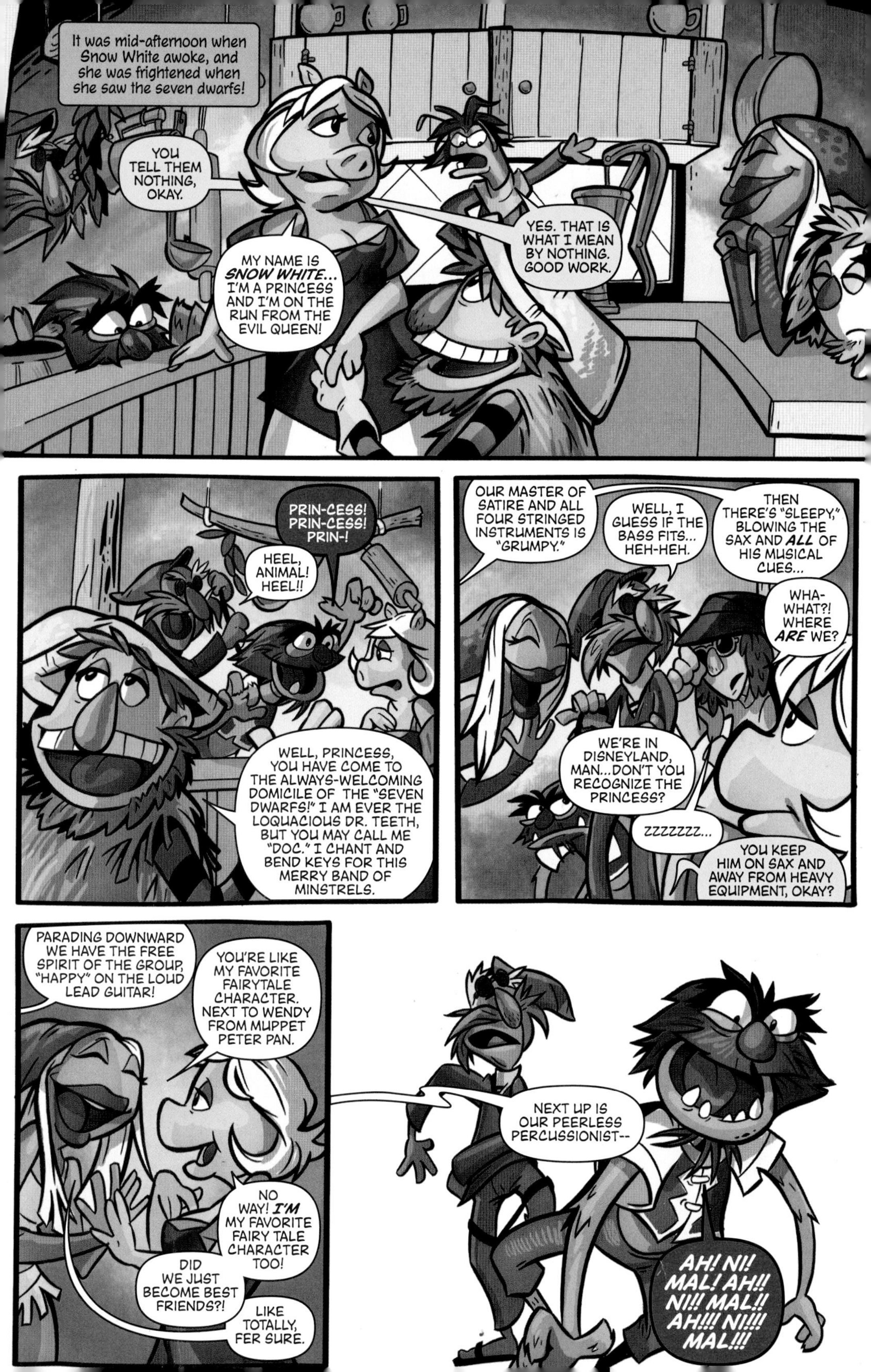
It was mid-afternoon when Snow White awoke, and she was frightened when she saw the seven dwarfs!
YOU TELL THEM NOTHING, OKAY.
MY NAME IS SNOW WHITE... I'M A PRINCESS AND I'M ON THE RUN FROM THE EVIL QUEEN!
YES. THAT IS WHAT I MEAN BY NOTHING. GOOD WORK.
PRIN-CESS! PRIN-CESS! PRIN-!
HEEL, ANIMAL! HEEL!!
WELL, PRINCESS, YOU HAVE COME TO THE ALWAYS-WELCOMING DOMICILE OF THE "SEVEN DWARFS!" I AM EVER THE LOQUACIOUS DR. TEETH, BUT YOU MAY CALL ME "DOC." I CHANT AND BEND KEYS FOR THIS MERRY BAND OF MINSTRELS.
OUR MASTER OF SATIRE AND ALL FOUR STRINGED INSTRUMENTS IS "GRUMPY."
WELL, I GUESS IF THE BASS FITS... HEH-HEH.
THEN THERE'S "SLEEPY," BLOWING THE SAX AND ALL OF HIS MUSICAL CUES...
WHA-WHAT?! WHERE ARE WE?
WE'RE IN DISNEYLAND, MAN...DON'T YOU RECOGNIZE THE PRINCESS?
ZZZZZZZ...
YOU KEEP HIM ON SAX AND AWAY FROM HEAVY EQUIPMENT, OKAY?
PARADING DOWNWARD WE HAVE THE FREE SPIRIT OF THE GROUP, "HAPPY" ON THE LOUD LEAD GUITAR!
YOU'RE LIKE MY FAVORITE FAIRYTALE CHARACTER. NEXT TO WENDY FROM MUPPET PETER PAN.
NO WAY! I'M MY FAVORITE FAIRY TALE CHARACTER TOO!
DID WE JUST BECOME BEST FRIENDS?!
LIKE TOTALLY, FER SURE.
NEXT UP IS OUR PEERLESS PERCUSSIONIST--
AH! NI! MAL! AH!! NI!! MAL!! AH!!! NI!!! MAL!!!

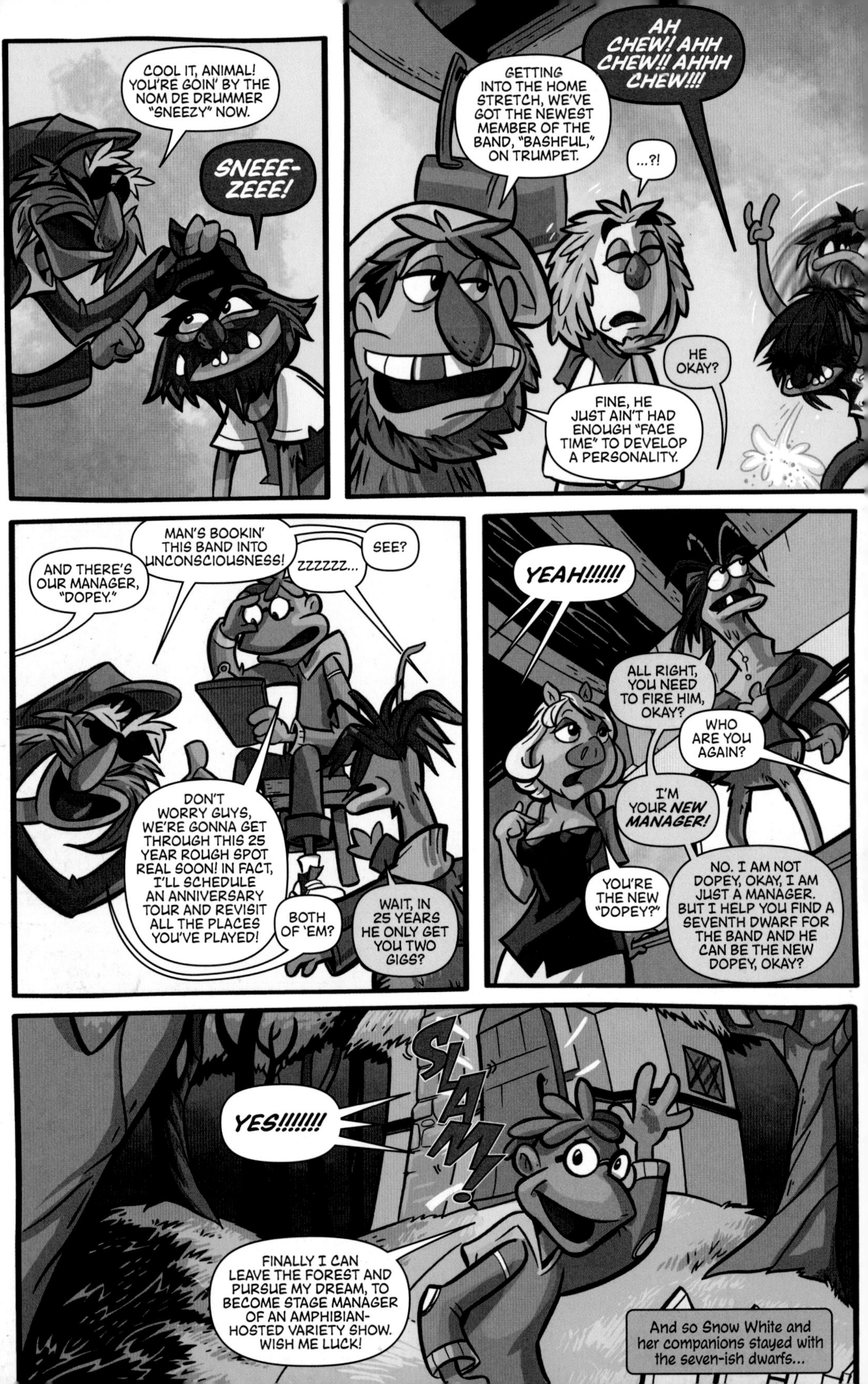
COOL IT, ANIMAL! YOU'RE GOIN' BY THE NOM DE DRUMMER "SNEEZY" NOW.
SNEEE-ZEEE!
GETTING INTO THE HOME STRETCH, WE'VE GOT THE NEWEST MEMBER OF THE BAND, "BASHFUL," ON TRUMPET.
AH CHEW! AHH CHEW!! AHHH CHEW!!!
...?!
HE OKAY?
FINE, HE JUST AIN'T HAD ENOUGH "FACE TIME" TO DEVELOP A PERSONALITY.
AND THERE'S OUR MANAGER, "DOPEY."
MAN'S BOOKIN' THIS BAND INTO UNCONSCIOUSNESS!
SEE?
ZZZZZZ...
DON'T WORRY GUYS, WE'RE GONNA GET THROUGH THIS 25 YEAR ROUGH SPOT REAL SOON! IN FACT, I'LL SCHEDULE AN ANNIVERSARY TOUR AND REVISIT ALL THE PLACES YOU'VE PLAYED!
BOTH OF 'EM?
WAIT, IN 25 YEARS HE ONLY GET YOU TWO GIGS?
YEAH!!!!!!
ALL RIGHT, YOU NEED TO FIRE HIM, OKAY?
WHO ARE YOU AGAIN?
I'M YOUR NEW MANAGER!
YOU'RE THE NEW "DOPEY?"
NO. I AM NOT DOPEY, OKAY, I AM JUST A MANAGER. BUT I HELP YOU FIND A SEVENTH DWARF FOR THE BAND AND HE CAN BE THE NEW DOPEY, OKAY?
YES!!!!!!!
SLAM!
FINALLY I CAN LEAVE THE FOREST AND PURSUE MY DREAM, TO BECOME STAGE MANAGER OF AN AMPHIBIAN-HOSTED VARIETY SHOW. WISH ME LUCK!
And so Snow White and her companions stayed with the seven-ish dwarfs...

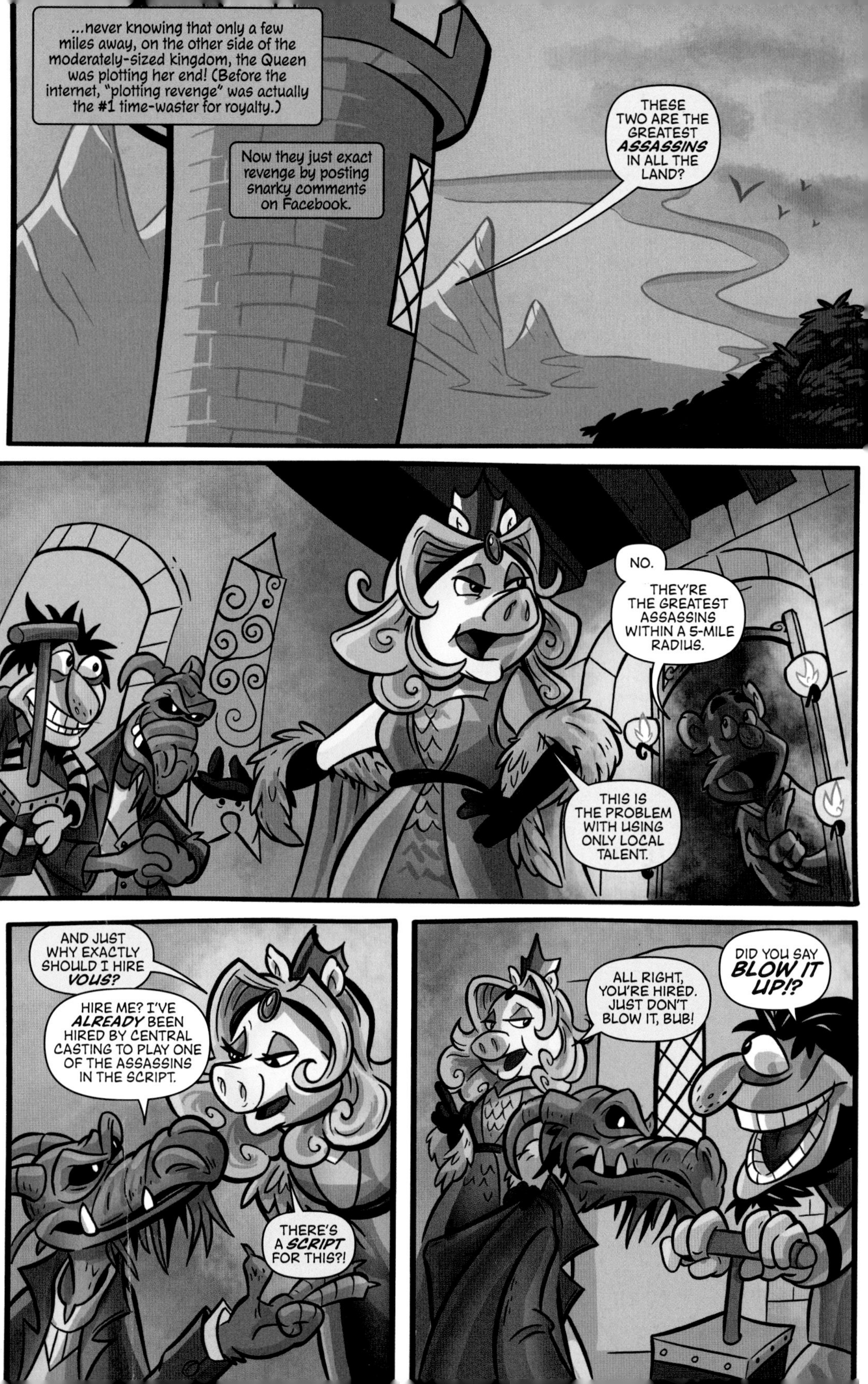
...never knowing that only a few miles away, on the other side of the moderately-sized kingdom, the Queen was plotting her end! (Before the internet, "plotting revenge" was actually the #1 time-waster for royalty.)
Now they just exact revenge by posting snarky comments on Facebook.
THESE TWO ARE THE GREATEST ASSASSINS IN ALL THE LAND?
NO.
THEY'RE THE GREATEST ASSASSINS WITHIN A 5-MILE RADIUS.
THIS IS THE PROBLEM WITH USING ONLY LOCAL TALENT.
AND JUST WHY EXACTLY SHOULD I HIRE VOUS?
HIRE ME? I'VE ALREADY BEEN HIRED BY CENTRAL CASTING TO PLAY ONE OF THE ASSASSINS IN THE SCRIPT.
THERE'S A SCRIPT FOR THIS?!
ALL RIGHT, YOU'RE HIRED. JUST DON'T BLOW IT, BUB!
DID YOU SAY BLOW IT UP!?

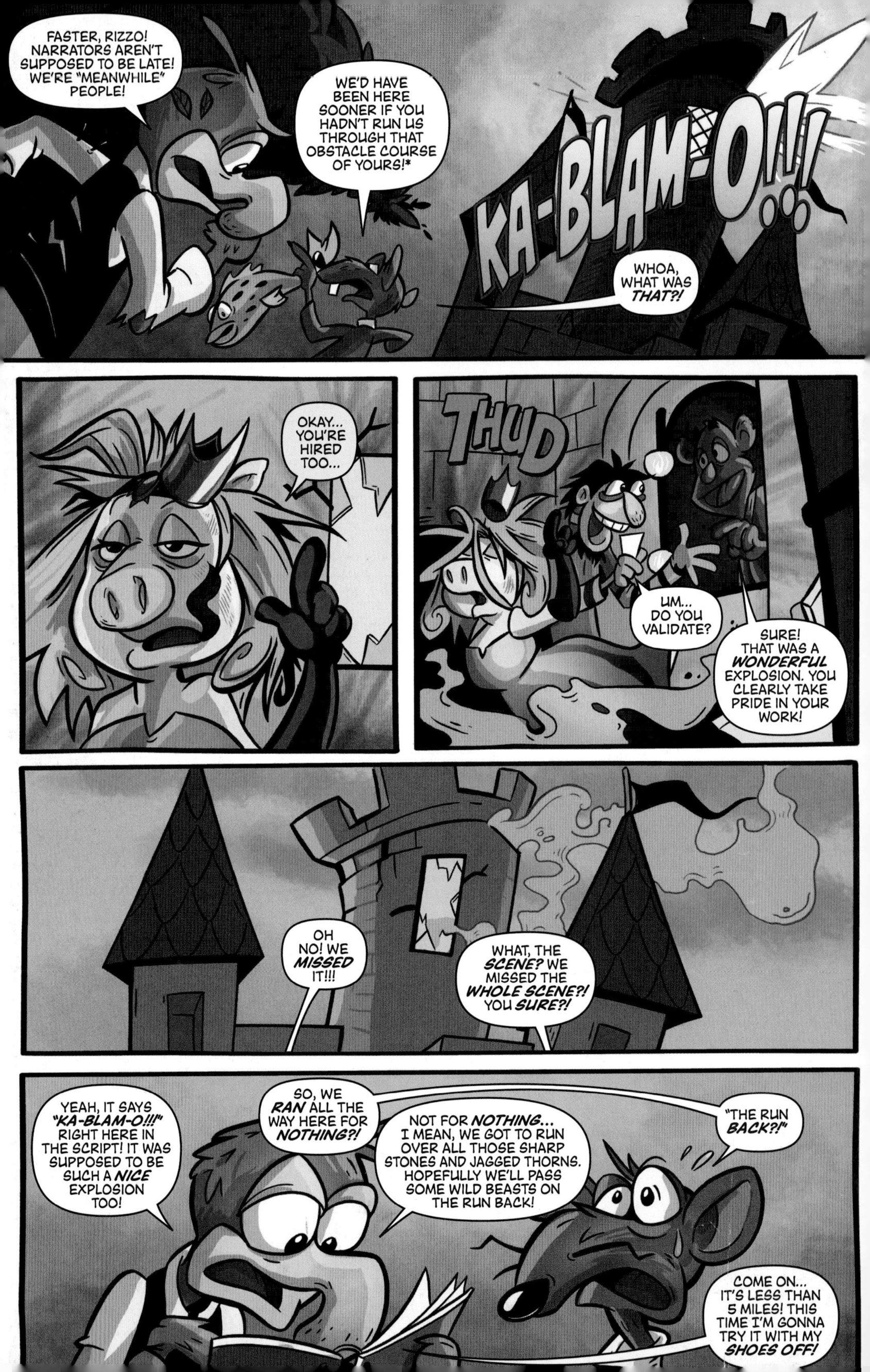

FASTER, RIZZO! NARRATORS AREN'T SUPPOSED TO BE LATE! WE'RE "MEANWHILE" PEOPLE!
WE'D HAVE BEEN HERE SOONER IF YOU HADN'T RUN US THROUGH THAT OBSTACLE COURSE OF YOURS!*
KA-BLAM-O!!!
WHOA, WHAT WAS *THAT?!*
OKAY... YOU'RE HIRED TOO...
THUD
UM... DO YOU VALIDATE?
SURE! THAT WAS A ***WONDERFUL*** EXPLOSION. YOU CLEARLY TAKE PRIDE IN YOUR WORK!
OH NO! WE ***MISSED*** IT!!!
WHAT, THE ***SCENE?*** WE MISSED THE ***WHOLE SCENE?!*** YOU ***SURE?!***
YEAH, IT SAYS ***"KA-BLAM-O!!!"*** RIGHT HERE IN THE SCRIPT! IT WAS SUPPOSED TO BE SUCH A ***NICE*** EXPLOSION TOO!
SO, WE ***RAN*** ALL THE WAY HERE FOR ***NOTHING?!***
NOT FOR ***NOTHING...*** I MEAN, WE GOT TO RUN OVER ALL THOSE SHARP STONES AND JAGGED THORNS. HOPEFULLY WE'LL PASS SOME WILD BEASTS ON THE RUN BACK!
"THE RUN ***BACK?!"***
COME ON... IT'S LESS THAN 5 MILES! THIS TIME I'M GONNA TRY IT WITH MY ***SHOES OFF!***

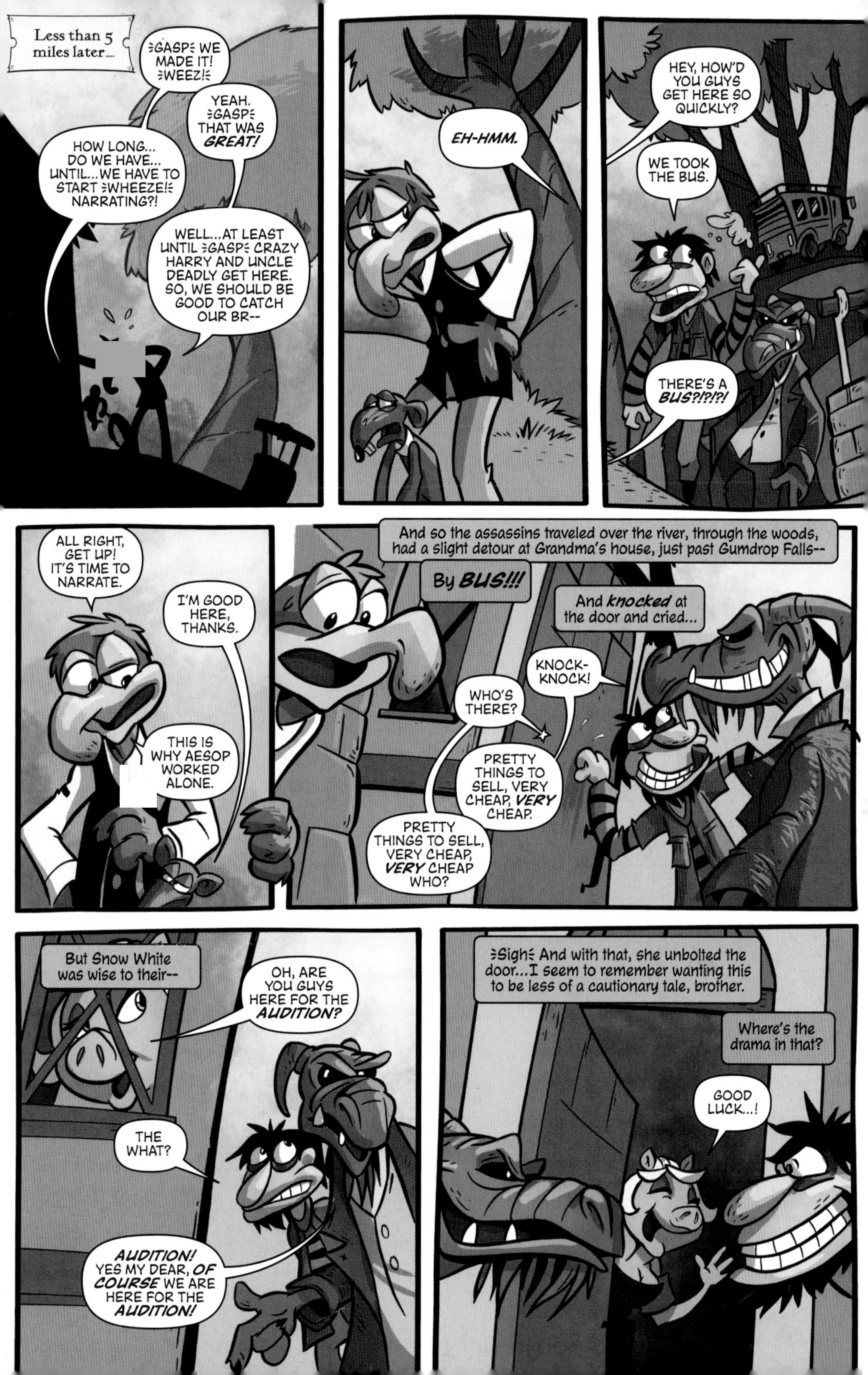
Less than 5 miles later....
=GASP= WE MADE IT! =WEEZ!=
YEAH. =GASP= THAT WAS GREAT!
HOW LONG... DO WE HAVE... UNTIL...WE HAVE TO START =WHEEZE!= NARRATING?!
WELL...AT LEAST UNTIL =GASP= CRAZY HARRY AND UNCLE DEADLY GET HERE. SO, WE SHOULD BE GOOD TO CATCH OUR BR--
EH-HMM.
HEY, HOW'D YOU GUYS GET HERE SO QUICKLY?
WE TOOK THE BUS.
THERE'S A BUS?!?!?!
ALL RIGHT, GET UP! IT'S TIME TO NARRATE.
I'M GOOD HERE, THANKS.
THIS IS WHY AESOP WORKED ALONE.
And so the assassins traveled over the river, through the woods, had a slight detour at Grandma's house, just past Gumdrop Falls--
By BUS!!!
And knocked at the door and cried...
KNOCK-KNOCK!
WHO'S THERE?
PRETTY THINGS TO SELL, VERY CHEAP, VERY CHEAP.
PRETTY THINGS TO SELL, VERY CHEAP, VERY CHEAP WHO?
But Snow White was wise to their--
OH, ARE YOU GUYS HERE FOR THE AUDITION?
THE WHAT?
AUDITION! YES MY DEAR, OF COURSE WE ARE HERE FOR THE AUDITION!
=Sigh= And with that, she unbolted the door...I seem to remember wanting this to be less of a cautionary tale, brother.
Where's the drama in that?
GOOD LUCK...!

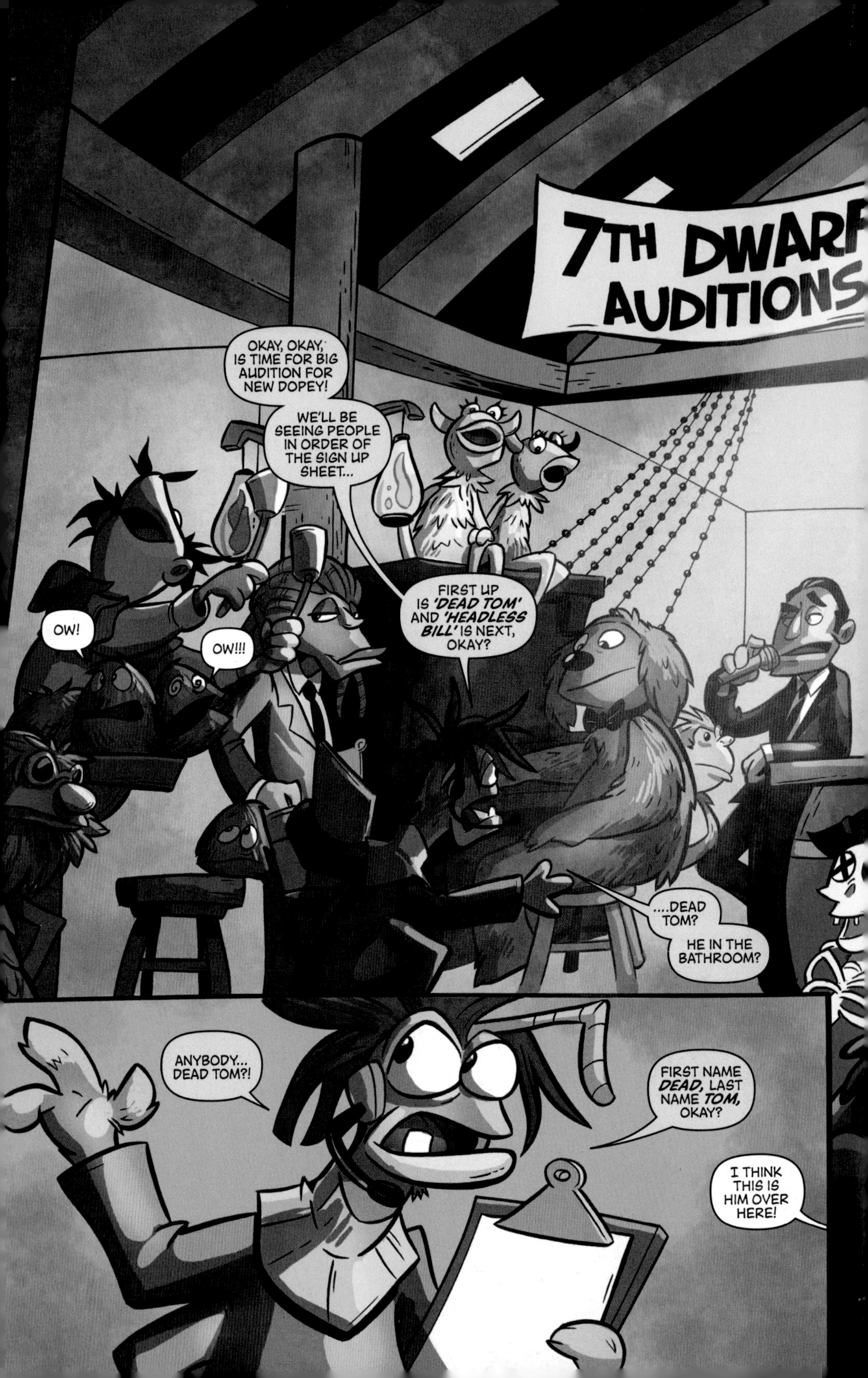
7TH DWARF AUDITIONS
OKAY, OKAY, IS TIME FOR BIG AUDITION FOR NEW DOPEY!
WE'LL BE SEEING PEOPLE IN ORDER OF THE SIGN UP SHEET...
FIRST UP IS 'DEAD TOM' AND 'HEADLESS BILL' IS NEXT, OKAY?
OW!
OW!!!
....DEAD TOM?
HE IN THE BATHROOM?
ANYBODY... DEAD TOM?!
FIRST NAME DEAD, LAST NAME TOM, OKAY?
I THINK THIS IS HIM OVER HERE!

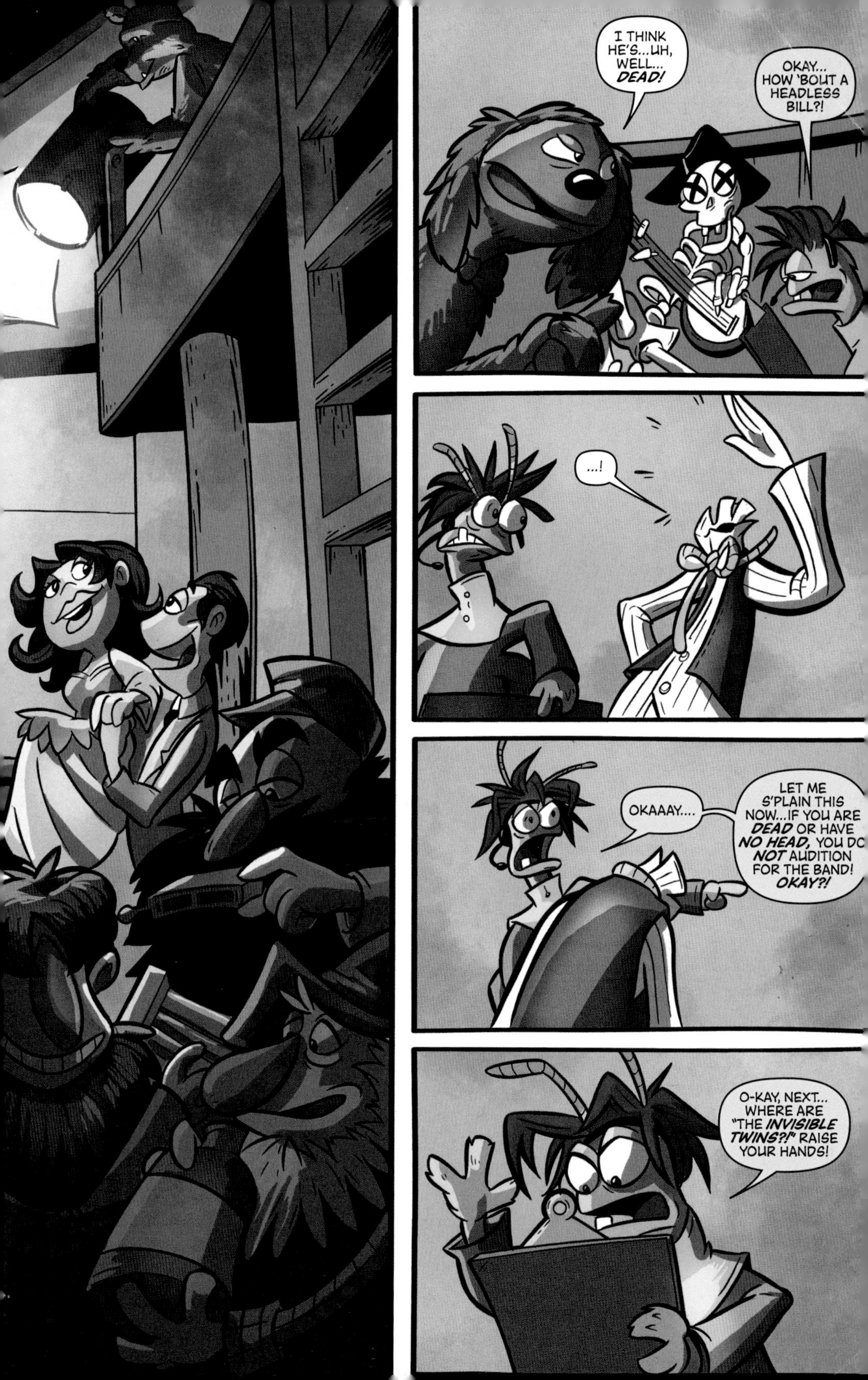
I THINK HE'S...UH, WELL... DEAD!
OKAY... HOW 'BOUT A HEADLESS BILL?!
...!
OKAAAY....
LET ME S'PLAIN THIS NOW...IF YOU ARE DEAD OR HAVE NO HEAD, YOU DO NOT AUDITION FOR THE BAND! OKAY?!
O-KAY, NEXT... WHERE ARE "THE INVISIBLE TWINS?!" RAISE YOUR HANDS!

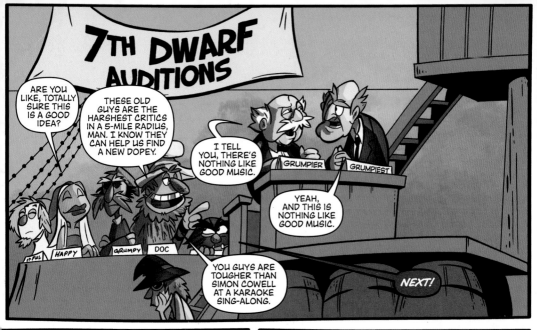

**7TH DWARF AUDITIONS**

ARE YOU LIKE, TOTALLY SURE THIS IS A GOOD IDEA?

THESE OLD GUYS ARE THE HARSHEST CRITICS IN A 5-MILE RADIUS, MAN. I KNOW THEY CAN HELP US FIND A NEW DOPEY.

I TELL YOU, THERE'S NOTHING LIKE GOOD MUSIC.

GRUMPIER

GRUMPIEST

YEAH, AND THIS IS NOTHING LIKE GOOD MUSIC.

BASHFUL

HAPPY

GRUMPY

DOC

YOU GUYS ARE TOUGHER THAN SIMON COWELL AT A KARAOKE SING-ALONG.

NEXT!

ZZZ...

SO SORRY, BUT HALF OF MY MUPPAPHONE HAS BEGUN TO GO FLAT. THEY JUST A NEED A FEW DAYS TO HEAL.

OWWW... PLEASE DON'T LET HIM HIT ME AGAIN...

THAT MUST HURT!

SHE'S RIGHT... MY EARS ARE KILLING ME! OH HO HO HO!

HEY, WHAT'S WITH THE SLEEPING BEAR?

I DON'T KNOW, BUT IF HE WAKES UP AND STARTS TELLING JOKES I'M OUTTA HERE!

≈GARGLE-- GARGLE-- GARGLE!!!≈

NEXT!

WHAT'S HE DOING?

IT SOUNDS LIKE HE'S *GARGLING* GERSHWIN TUNES.

I PREFER *MOUTHWASH.*

BRING 'EM BACK WHEN THEY'RE OLDER.

BETTER YET, PUT 'EM UP FOR ADOPTION!

NEXT.

AFTER ALL THESE YEARS, THEY HAVEN'T LOST A STEP!

YEAH...THEY'RE STILL TERRIBLE!

NEXT!

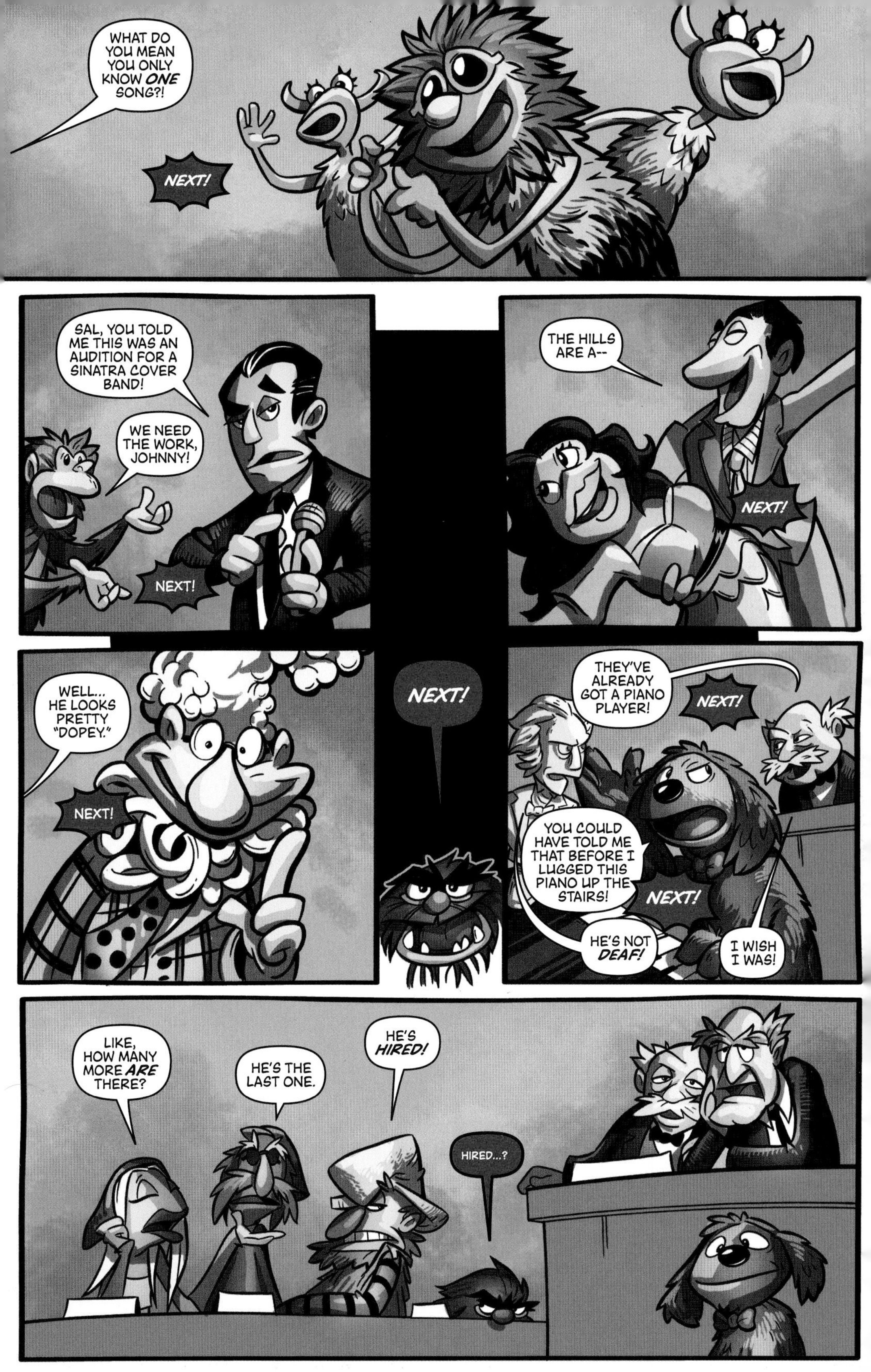
WHAT DO YOU MEAN YOU ONLY KNOW ONE SONG?!
NEXT!
SAL, YOU TOLD ME THIS WAS AN AUDITION FOR A SINATRA COVER BAND!
WE NEED THE WORK, JOHNNY!
NEXT!
THE HILLS ARE A--
NEXT!
WELL... HE LOOKS PRETTY "DOPEY."
NEXT!
NEXT!
THEY'VE ALREADY GOT A PIANO PLAYER!
NEXT!
YOU COULD HAVE TOLD ME THAT BEFORE I LUGGED THIS PIANO UP THE STAIRS!
NEXT!
HE'S NOT DEAF!
I WISH I WAS!
LIKE, HOW MANY MORE ARE THERE?
HE'S THE LAST ONE.
HE'S HIRED!
HIRED...?

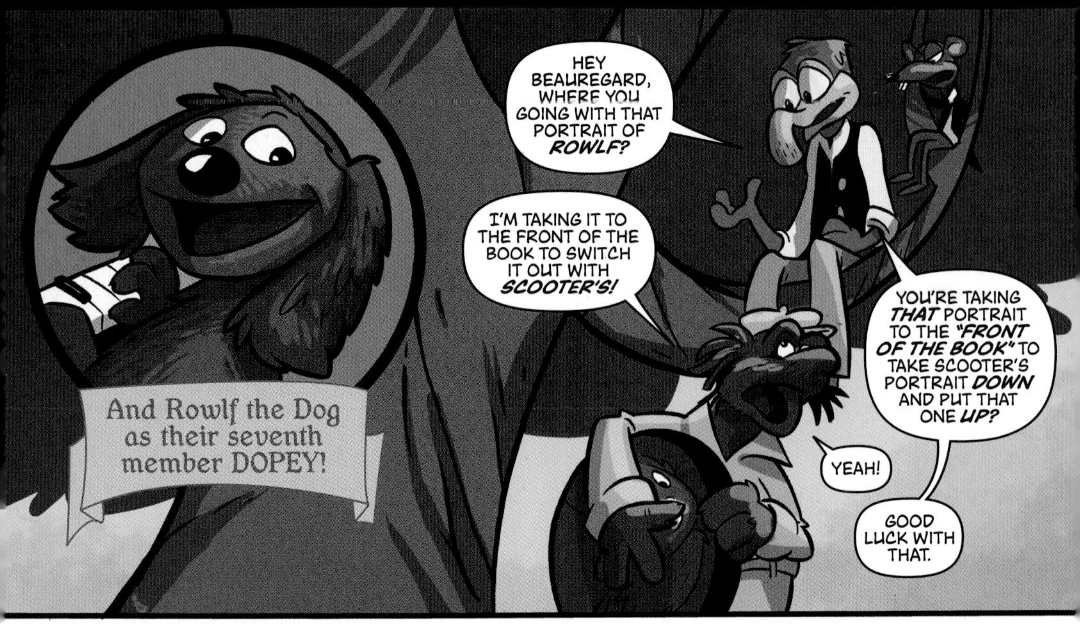
And Rowlf the Dog as their seventh member DOPEY!
HEY BEAUREGARD, WHERE YOU GOING WITH THAT PORTRAIT OF *ROWLF?*
I'M TAKING IT TO THE FRONT OF THE BOOK TO SWITCH IT OUT WITH *SCOOTER'S!*
YOU'RE TAKING *THAT* PORTRAIT TO THE *"FRONT OF THE BOOK"* TO TAKE SCOOTER'S PORTRAIT *DOWN* AND PUT THAT ONE *UP?*
YEAH!
GOOD LUCK WITH THAT.

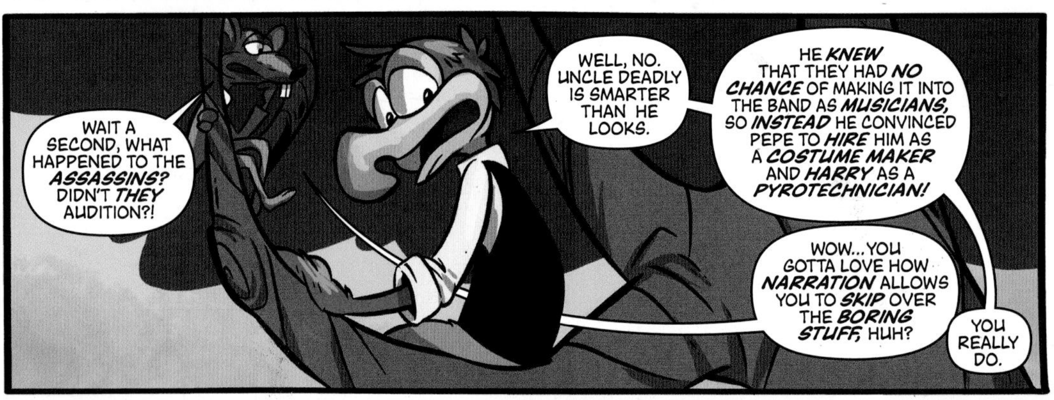
WAIT A SECOND, WHAT HAPPENED TO THE *ASSASSINS?* DIDN'T *THEY* AUDITION?!
WELL, NO. UNCLE DEADLY IS SMARTER THAN HE LOOKS.
HE *KNEW* THAT THEY HAD *NO CHANCE* OF MAKING IT INTO THE BAND AS *MUSICIANS,* SO *INSTEAD* HE CONVINCED PEPE TO *HIRE* HIM AS A *COSTUME MAKER* AND *HARRY* AS A *PYROTECHNICIAN!*
WOW...YOU GOTTA LOVE HOW *NARRATION* ALLOWS YOU TO *SKIP* OVER THE *BORING STUFF,* HUH?
YOU REALLY DO.

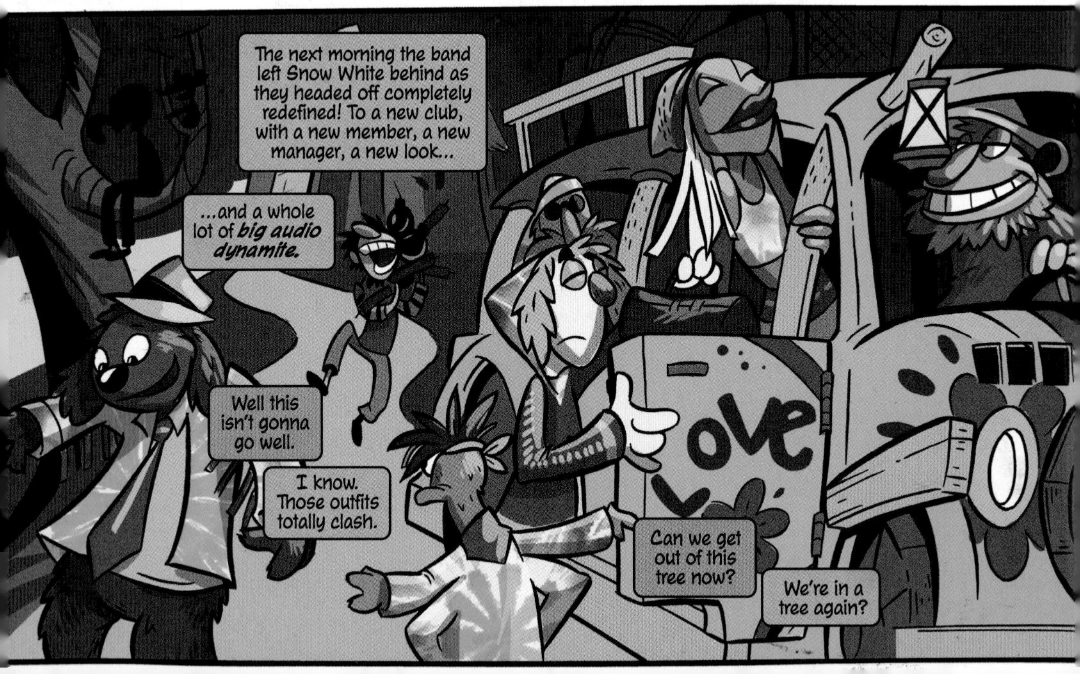
The next morning the band left Snow White behind as they headed off completely redefined! To a new club, with a new member, a new manager, a new look...
...and a whole lot of *big audio dynamite.*
Well this isn't gonna go well.
I know. Those outfits totally clash.
Can we get out of this tree now?
We're in a tree again?
Love

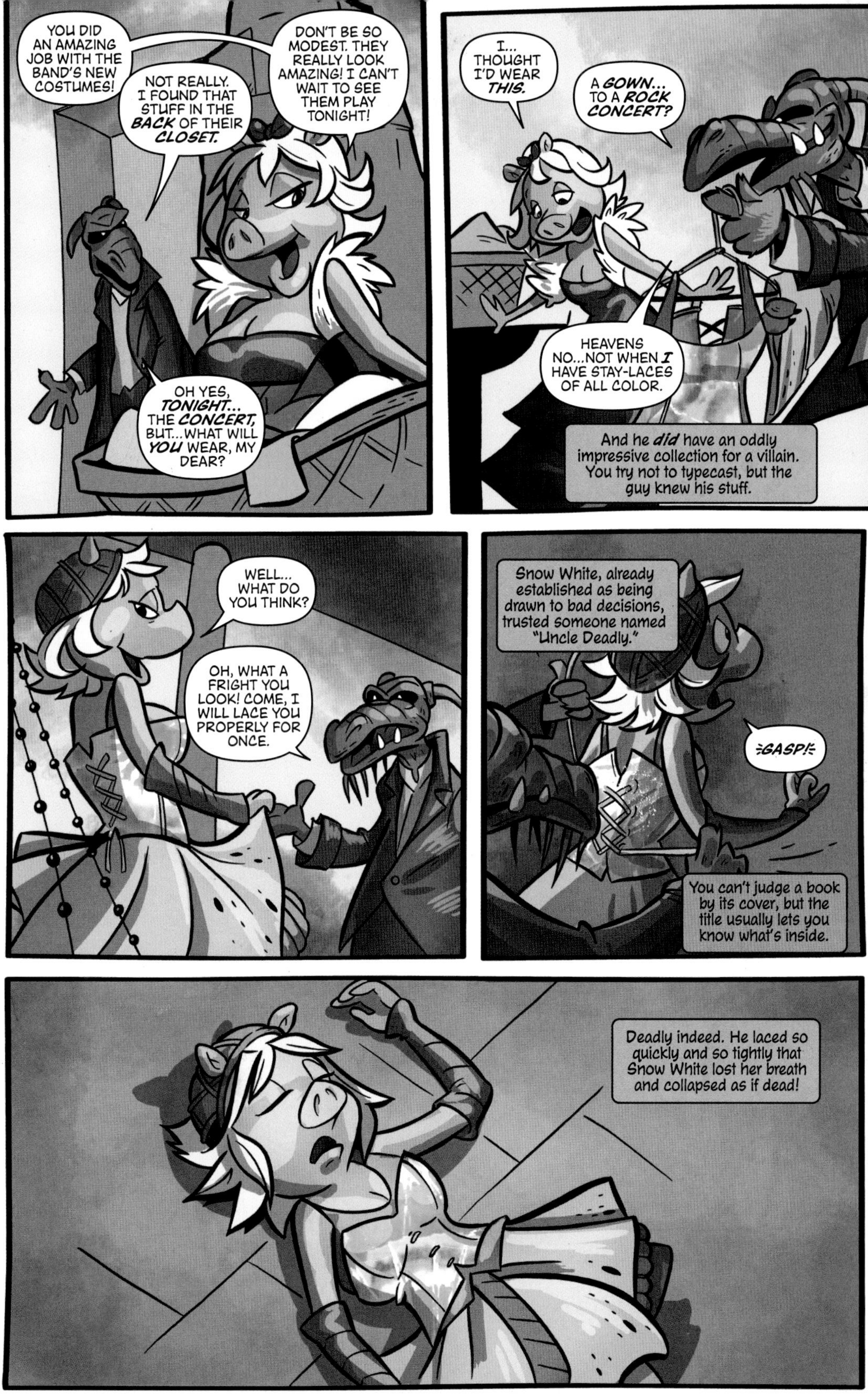
YOU DID AN AMAZING JOB WITH THE BAND'S NEW COSTUMES!
NOT REALLY. I FOUND THAT STUFF IN THE BACK OF THEIR CLOSET.
DON'T BE SO MODEST. THEY REALLY LOOK AMAZING! I CAN'T WAIT TO SEE THEM PLAY TONIGHT!
OH YES, TONIGHT... THE CONCERT, BUT...WHAT WILL YOU WEAR, MY DEAR?
I... THOUGHT I'D WEAR THIS.
A GOWN... TO A ROCK CONCERT?
HEAVENS NO...NOT WHEN I HAVE STAY-LACES OF ALL COLOR.
And he did have an oddly impressive collection for a villain. You try not to typecast, but the guy knew his stuff.
WELL... WHAT DO YOU THINK?
OH, WHAT A FRIGHT YOU LOOK! COME, I WILL LACE YOU PROPERLY FOR ONCE.
Snow White, already established as being drawn to bad decisions, trusted someone named "Uncle Deadly."
GASP!
You can't judge a book by its cover, but the title usually lets you know what's inside.
Deadly indeed. He laced so quickly and so tightly that Snow White lost her breath and collapsed as if dead!

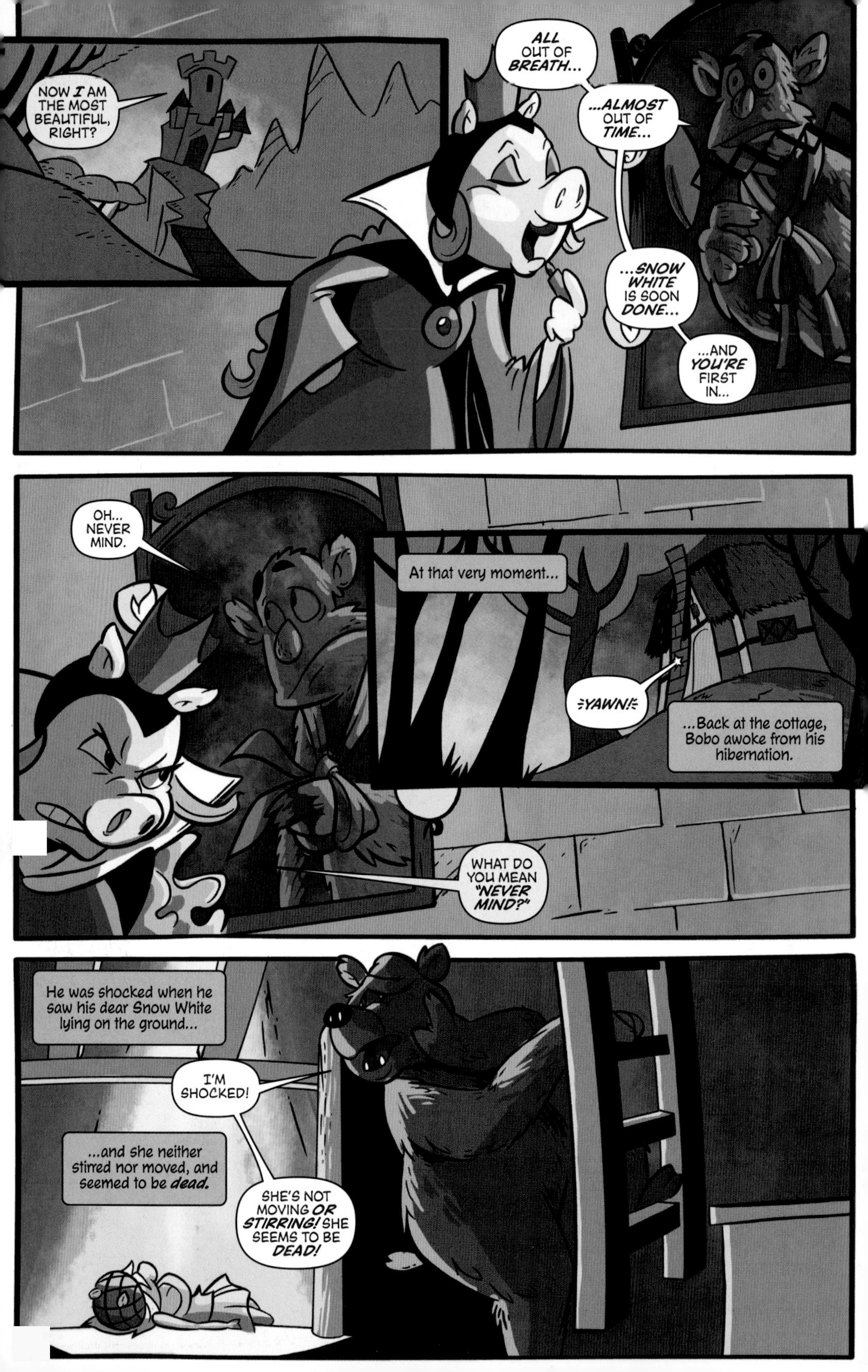
NOW I AM THE MOST BEAUTIFUL, RIGHT?
ALL OUT OF BREATH...
...ALMOST OUT OF TIME...
...SNOW WHITE IS SOON DONE...
...AND YOU'RE FIRST IN...
OH... NEVER MIND.
At that very moment...
YAWN!
...Back at the cottage, Bobo awoke from his hibernation.
WHAT DO YOU MEAN "NEVER MIND?"
He was shocked when he saw his dear Snow White lying on the ground...
I'M SHOCKED!
...and she neither stirred nor moved, and seemed to be dead.
SHE'S NOT MOVING OR STIRRING! SHE SEEMS TO BE DEAD!

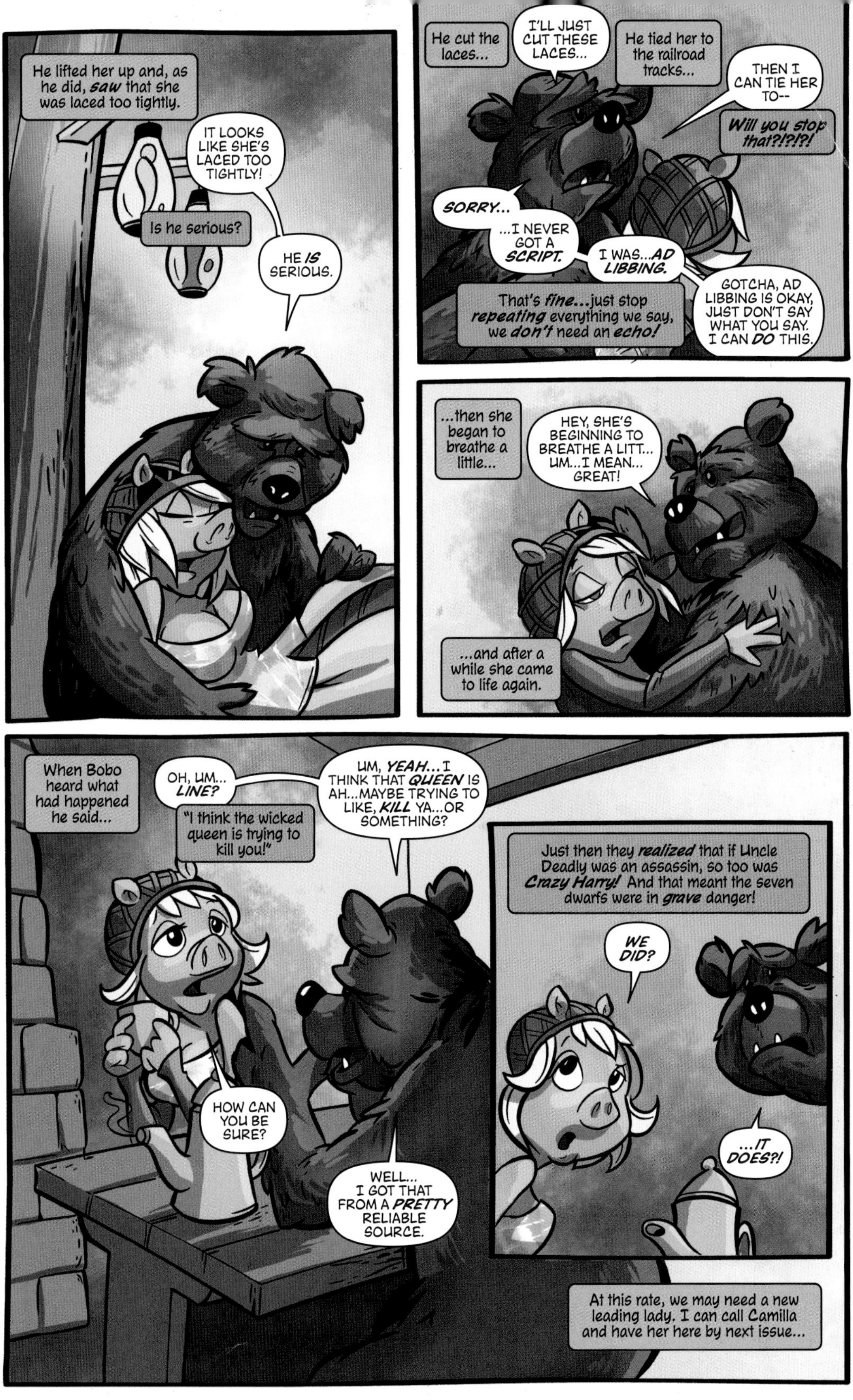
He lifted her up and, as he did, *saw* that she was laced too tightly.
IT LOOKS LIKE SHE'S LACED TOO TIGHTLY!
Is he serious?
HE *IS* SERIOUS.
He cut the laces...
I'LL JUST CUT THESE LACES...
He tied her to the railroad tracks...
THEN I CAN TIE HER TO--
*Will you stop that?!?!?!*
*SORRY...*
...I NEVER GOT A *SCRIPT.*
I WAS...*AD LIBBING.*
That's *fine...*just stop *repeating* everything we say, we *don't* need an *echo!*
GOTCHA, AD LIBBING IS OKAY, JUST DON'T SAY WHAT YOU SAY. I CAN *DO* THIS.
...then she began to breathe a little...
HEY, SHE'S BEGINNING TO BREATHE A LITT... UM...I MEAN... GREAT!
...and after a while she came to life again.
When Bobo heard what had happened he said...
OH, UM... *LINE?*
"I think the wicked queen is trying to kill you!"
UM, *YEAH...* I THINK THAT *QUEEN* IS AH...MAYBE TRYING TO LIKE, *KILL* YA...OR SOMETHING?
HOW CAN YOU BE SURE?
WELL... I GOT THAT FROM A *PRETTY* RELIABLE SOURCE.
Just then they *realized* that if Uncle Deadly was an assassin, so too was *Crazy Harry!* And that meant the seven dwarfs were in *grave* danger!
*WE DID?*
*...IT DOES?!*
At this rate, we may need a new leading lady. I can call Camilla and have her here by next issue...

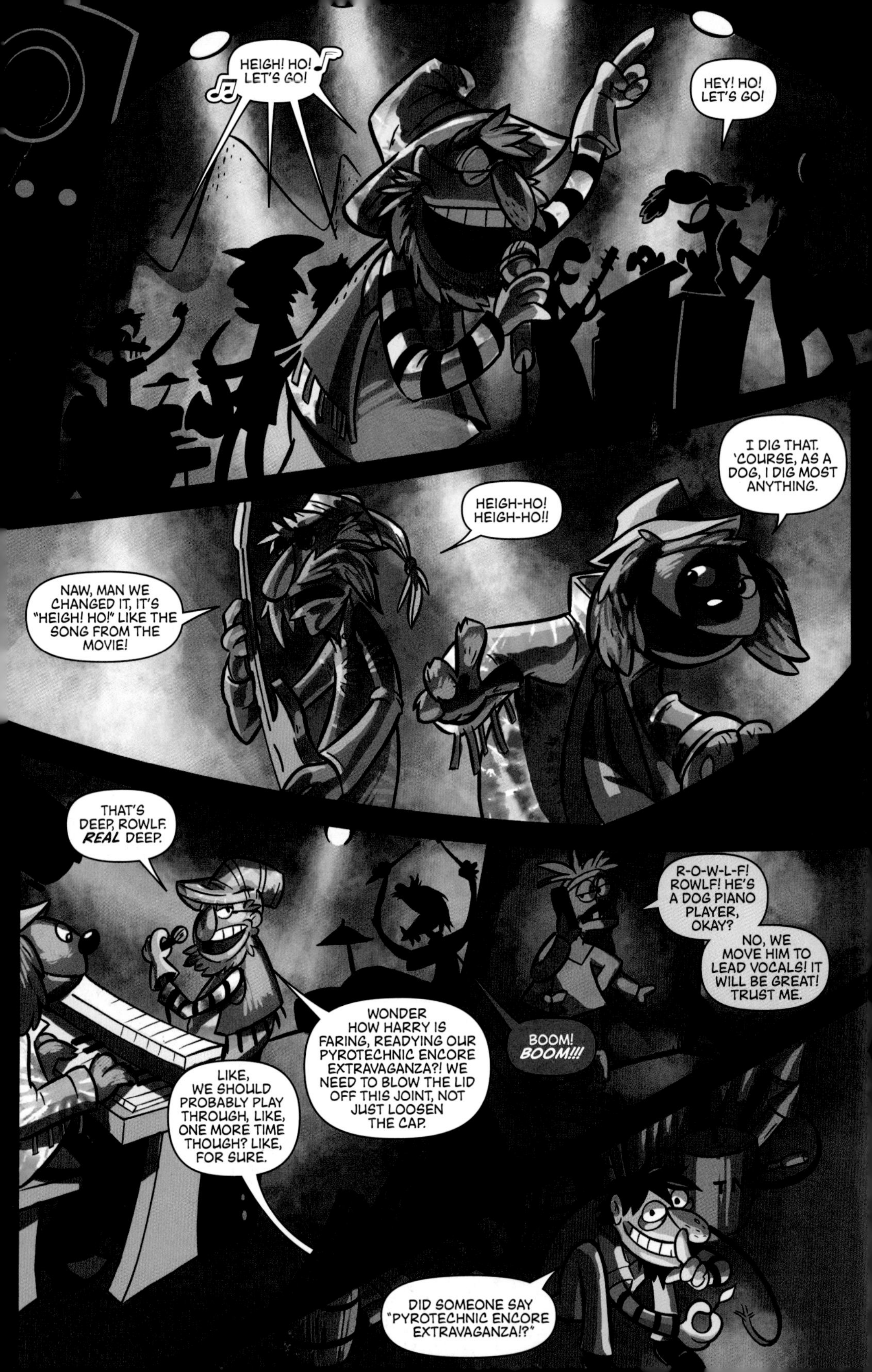
HEIGH! HO! LET'S GO!
HEY! HO! LET'S GO!
HEIGH-HO! HEIGH-HO!!
I DIG THAT. 'COURSE, AS A DOG, I DIG MOST ANYTHING.
NAW, MAN WE CHANGED IT, IT'S "HEIGH! HO!" LIKE THE SONG FROM THE MOVIE!
THAT'S DEEP, ROWLF. *REAL* DEEP.
R-O-W-L-F! ROWLF! HE'S A DOG PIANO PLAYER, OKAY?
NO, WE MOVE HIM TO LEAD VOCALS! IT WILL BE GREAT! TRUST ME.
BOOM! *BOOM!!!*
WONDER HOW HARRY IS FARING, READYING OUR PYROTECHNIC ENCORE EXTRAVAGANZA?! WE NEED TO BLOW THE LID OFF THIS JOINT, NOT JUST LOOSEN THE CAP.
LIKE, WE SHOULD PROBABLY PLAY THROUGH, LIKE, ONE MORE TIME THOUGH? LIKE, FOR SURE.
DID SOMEONE SAY "PYROTECHNIC ENCORE EXTRAVAGANZA!?"

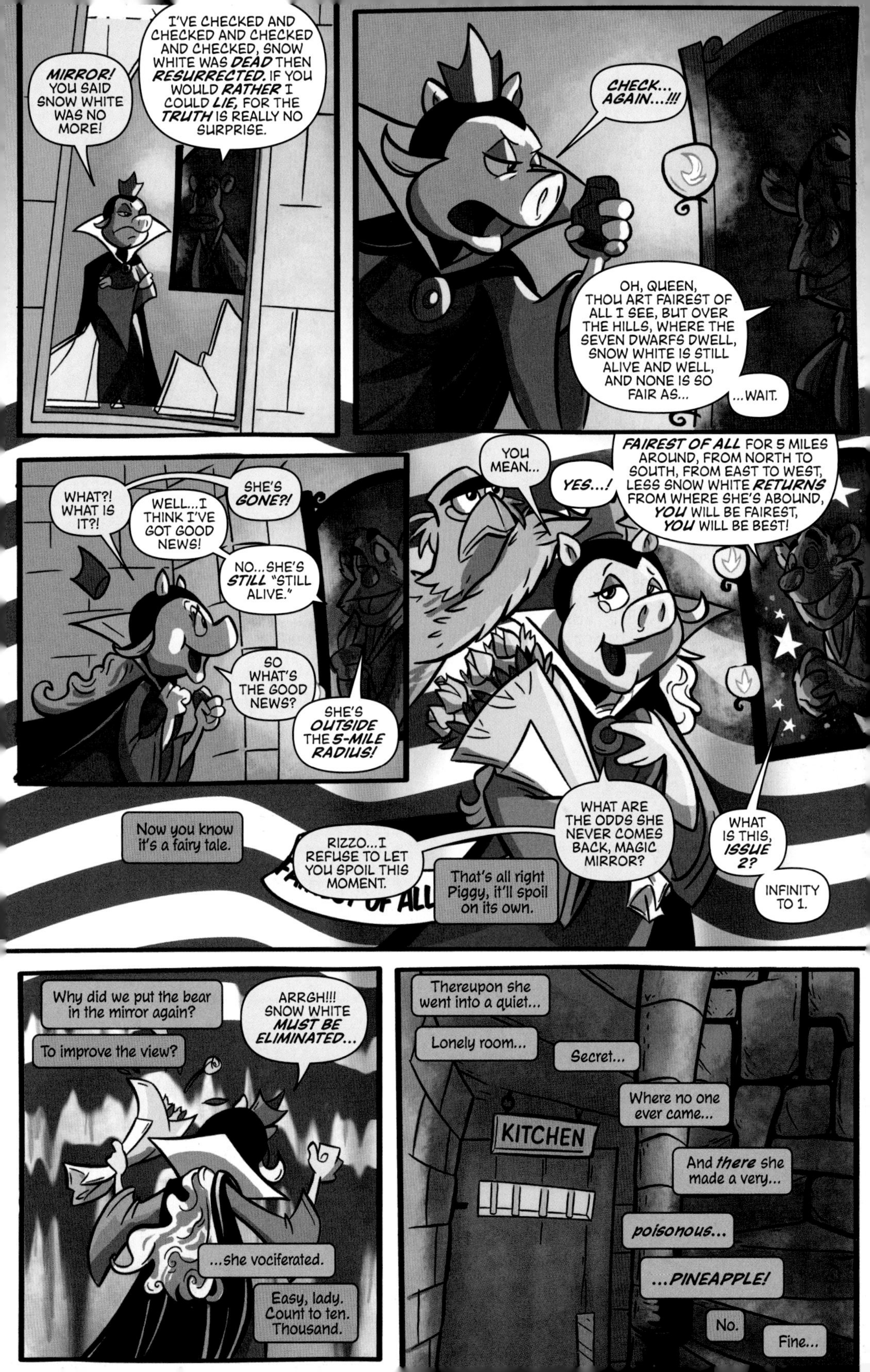
MIRROR! YOU SAID SNOW WHITE WAS NO MORE!
I'VE CHECKED AND CHECKED AND CHECKED AND CHECKED, SNOW WHITE WAS DEAD THEN RESURRECTED. IF YOU WOULD RATHER I COULD LIE, FOR THE TRUTH IS REALLY NO SURPRISE.
CHECK... AGAIN...!!!
OH, QUEEN, THOU ART FAIREST OF ALL I SEE, BUT OVER THE HILLS, WHERE THE SEVEN DWARFS DWELL, SNOW WHITE IS STILL ALIVE AND WELL, AND NONE IS SO FAIR AS...
...WAIT.
WHAT?! WHAT IS IT?!
WELL...I THINK I'VE GOT GOOD NEWS!
SHE'S GONE?!
NO...SHE'S STILL "STILL ALIVE."
SO WHAT'S THE GOOD NEWS?
SHE'S OUTSIDE THE 5-MILE RADIUS!
YOU MEAN...
YES...!
FAIREST OF ALL FOR 5 MILES AROUND, FROM NORTH TO SOUTH, FROM EAST TO WEST, LESS SNOW WHITE RETURNS FROM WHERE SHE'S ABOUND, YOU WILL BE FAIREST, YOU WILL BE BEST!
Now you know it's a fairy tale.
RIZZO...I REFUSE TO LET YOU SPOIL THIS MOMENT.
That's all right Piggy, it'll spoil on its own.
WHAT ARE THE ODDS SHE NEVER COMES BACK, MAGIC MIRROR?
WHAT IS THIS, ISSUE 2?
INFINITY TO 1.
Why did we put the bear in the mirror again?
To improve the view?
ARRGH!!! SNOW WHITE MUST BE ELIMINATED...
...she vociferated.
Easy, lady. Count to ten. Thousand.
Thereupon she went into a quiet...
Lonely room...
Secret...
Where no one ever came...
KITCHEN
And there she made a very...
poisonous...
...PINEAPPLE!
No.
Fine...

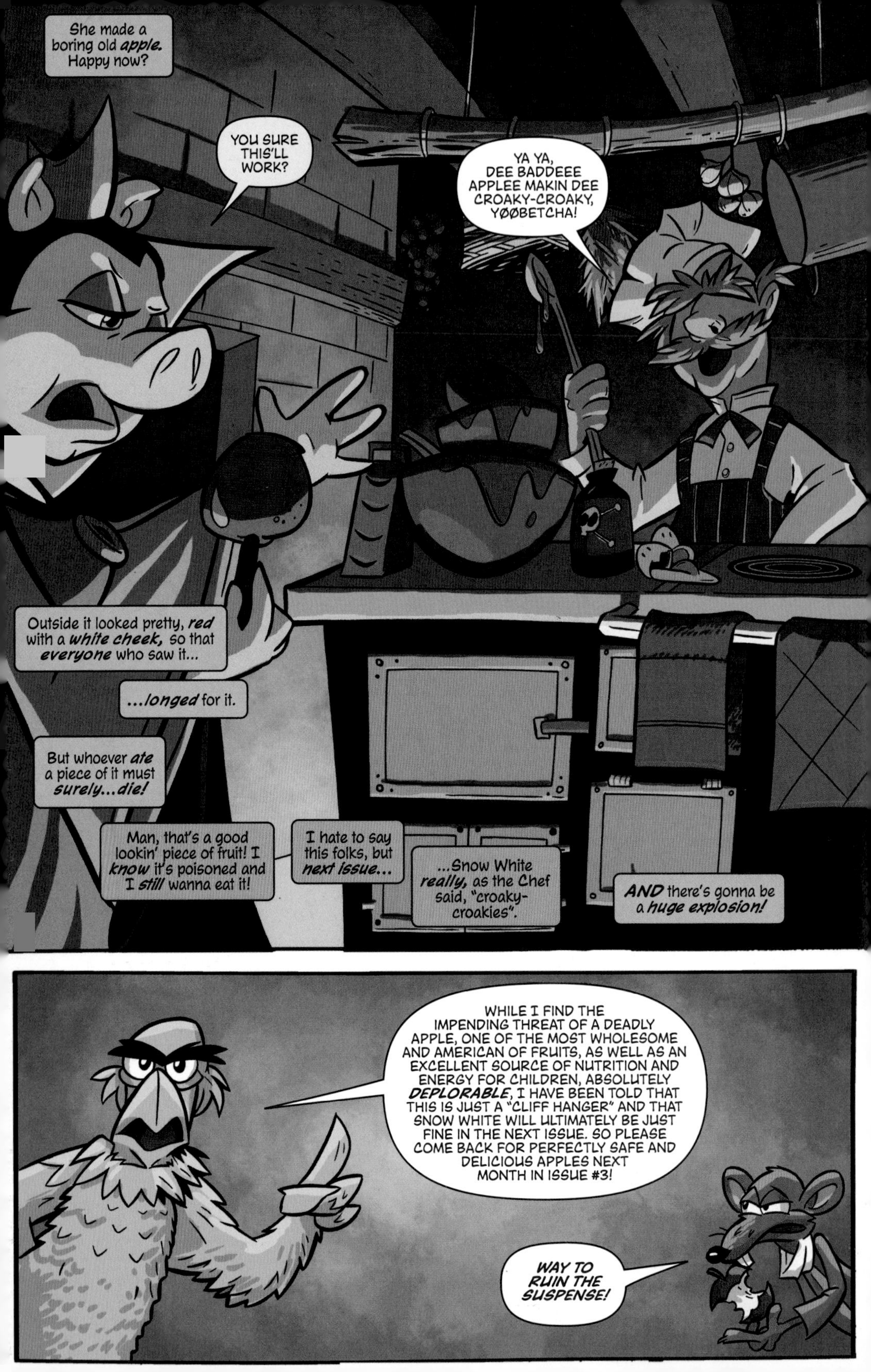
She made a boring old *apple.* Happy now?
YOU SURE THIS'LL WORK?
YA YA, DEE BADDEEE APPLEE MAKIN DEE CROAKY-CROAKY, YØØBETCHA!
Outside it looked pretty, *red* with a *white cheek,* so that *everyone* who saw it...
*...longed* for it.
But whoever *ate* a piece of it must *surely...die!*
Man, that's a good lookin' piece of fruit! I *know* it's poisoned and I *still* wanna eat it!
I hate to say this folks, but *next issue...*
...Snow White *really,* as the Chef said, "croaky-croakies".
*AND* there's gonna be a *huge explosion!*
WHILE I FIND THE IMPENDING THREAT OF A DEADLY APPLE, ONE OF THE MOST WHOLESOME AND AMERICAN OF FRUITS, AS WELL AS AN EXCELLENT SOURCE OF NUTRITION AND ENERGY FOR CHILDREN, ABSOLUTELY *DEPLORABLE*, I HAVE BEEN TOLD THAT THIS IS JUST A "CLIFF HANGER" AND THAT SNOW WHITE WILL ULTIMATELY BE JUST FINE IN THE NEXT ISSUE. SO PLEASE COME BACK FOR PERFECTLY SAFE AND DELICIOUS APPLES NEXT MONTH IN ISSUE #3!
*WAY TO RUIN THE SUSPENSE!*

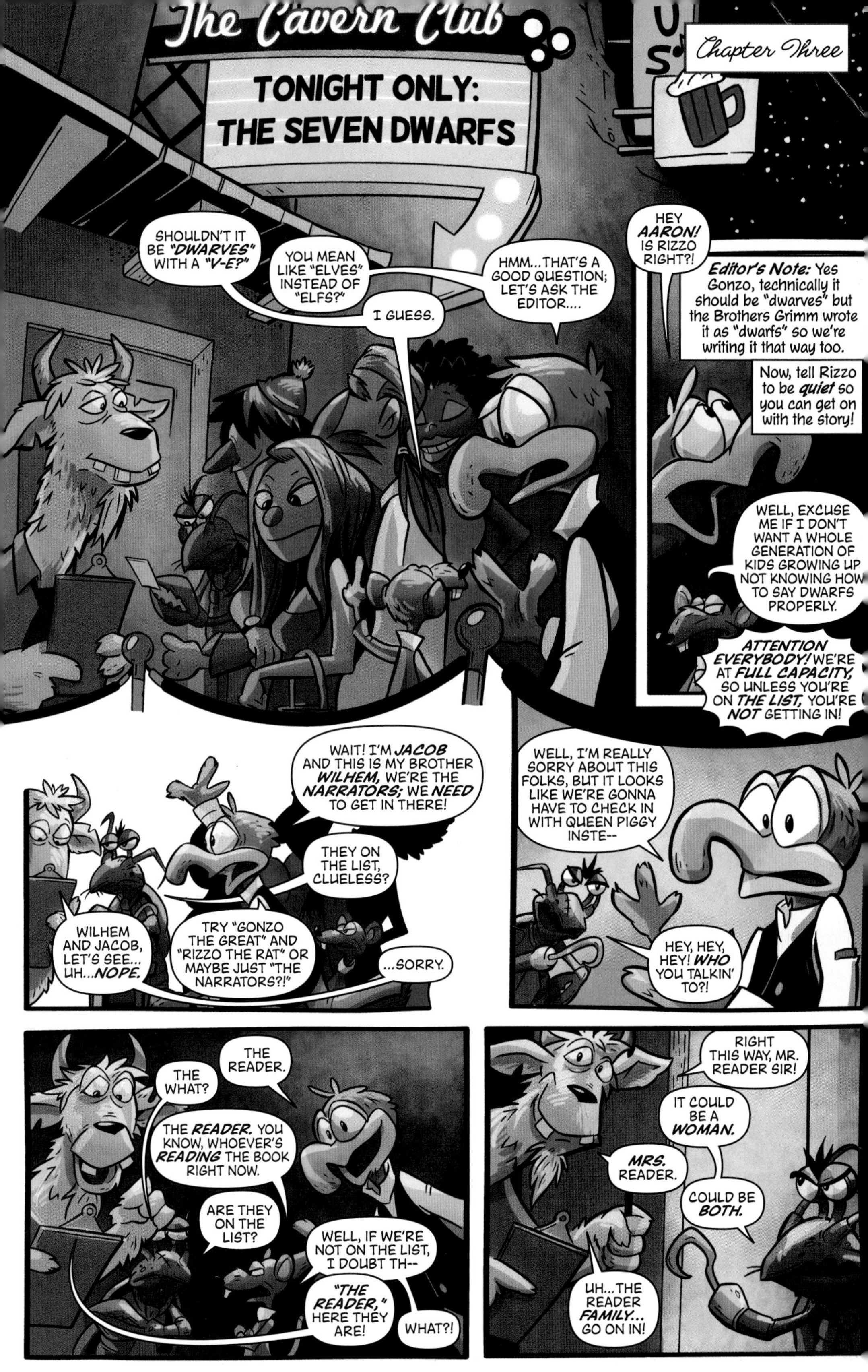
The Cavern Club
TONIGHT ONLY: THE SEVEN DWARFS
Chapter Three
SHOULDN'T IT BE "DWARVES" WITH A "V-E?"
YOU MEAN LIKE "ELVES" INSTEAD OF "ELFS?"
I GUESS.
HMM...THAT'S A GOOD QUESTION; LET'S ASK THE EDITOR....
HEY AARON! IS RIZZO RIGHT?!
Editor's Note: Yes Gonzo, technically it should be "dwarves" but the Brothers Grimm wrote it as "dwarfs" so we're writing it that way too.
Now, tell Rizzo to be quiet so you can get on with the story!
WELL, EXCUSE ME IF I DON'T WANT A WHOLE GENERATION OF KIDS GROWING UP NOT KNOWING HOW TO SAY DWARFS PROPERLY.
ATTENTION EVERYBODY! WE'RE AT FULL CAPACITY, SO UNLESS YOU'RE ON THE LIST, YOU'RE NOT GETTING IN!
WAIT! I'M JACOB AND THIS IS MY BROTHER WILHEM, WE'RE THE NARRATORS; WE NEED TO GET IN THERE!
THEY ON THE LIST, CLUELESS?
WILHEM AND JACOB, LET'S SEE... UH...NOPE.
TRY "GONZO THE GREAT" AND "RIZZO THE RAT" OR MAYBE JUST "THE NARRATORS?!"
...SORRY.
WELL, I'M REALLY SORRY ABOUT THIS FOLKS, BUT IT LOOKS LIKE WE'RE GONNA HAVE TO CHECK IN WITH QUEEN PIGGY INSTE--
HEY, HEY, HEY! WHO YOU TALKIN' TO?!
THE READER.
THE WHAT?
THE READER. YOU KNOW, WHOEVER'S READING THE BOOK RIGHT NOW.
ARE THEY ON THE LIST?
WELL, IF WE'RE NOT ON THE LIST, I DOUBT TH--
"THE READER," HERE THEY ARE!
WHAT?!
RIGHT THIS WAY, MR. READER SIR!
IT COULD BE A WOMAN.
MRS. READER.
COULD BE BOTH.
UH...THE READER FAMILY... GO ON IN!

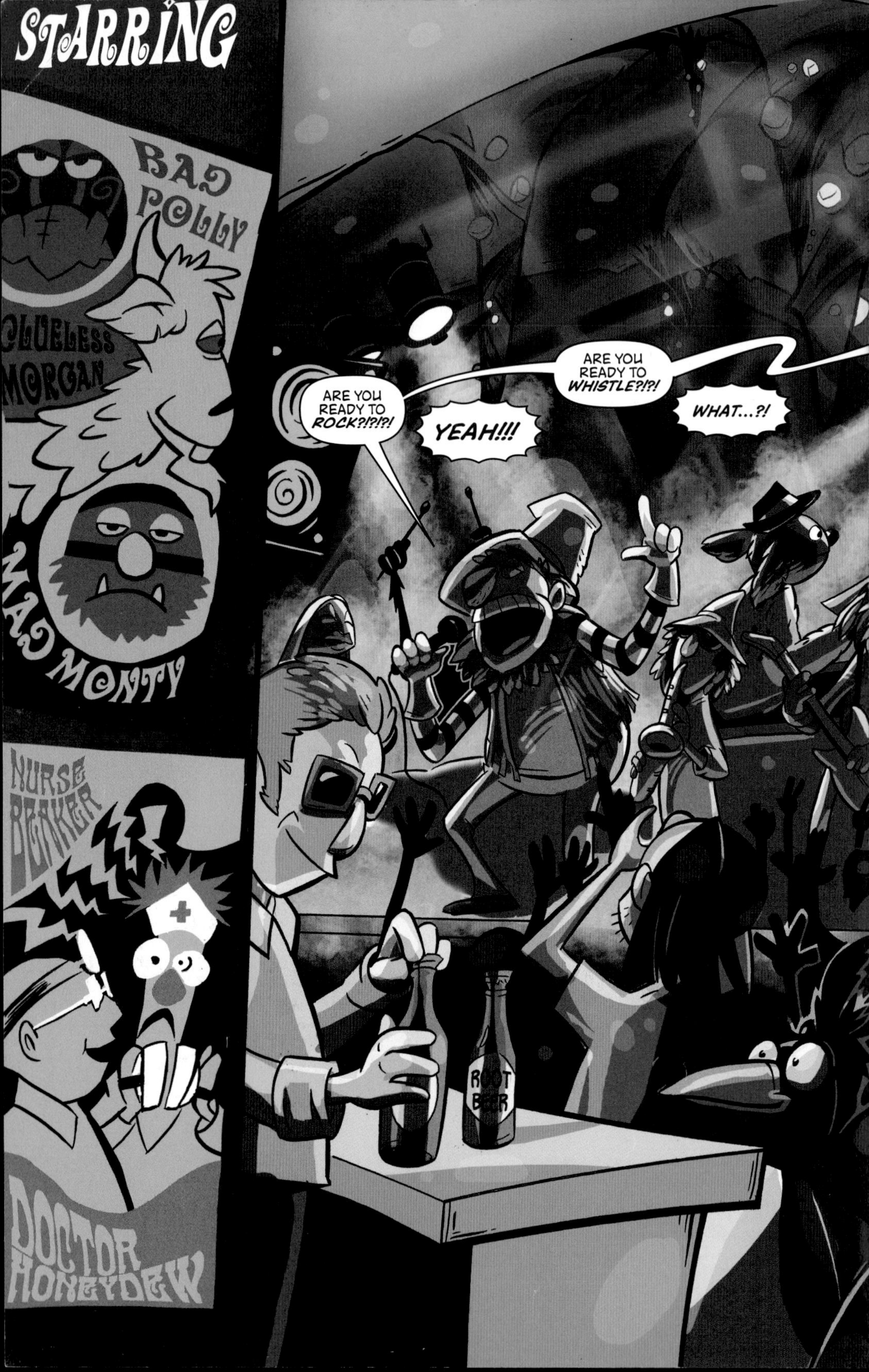
STARRING
BAD POLLY
CLUELESS MORGAN
MAD MONTY
NURSE BEAKER
DOCTOR HONEYDEW
ARE YOU READY TO ROCK?!?!?!
YEAH!!!
ARE YOU READY TO WHISTLE?!?!
WHAT...?!
ROOT BEER

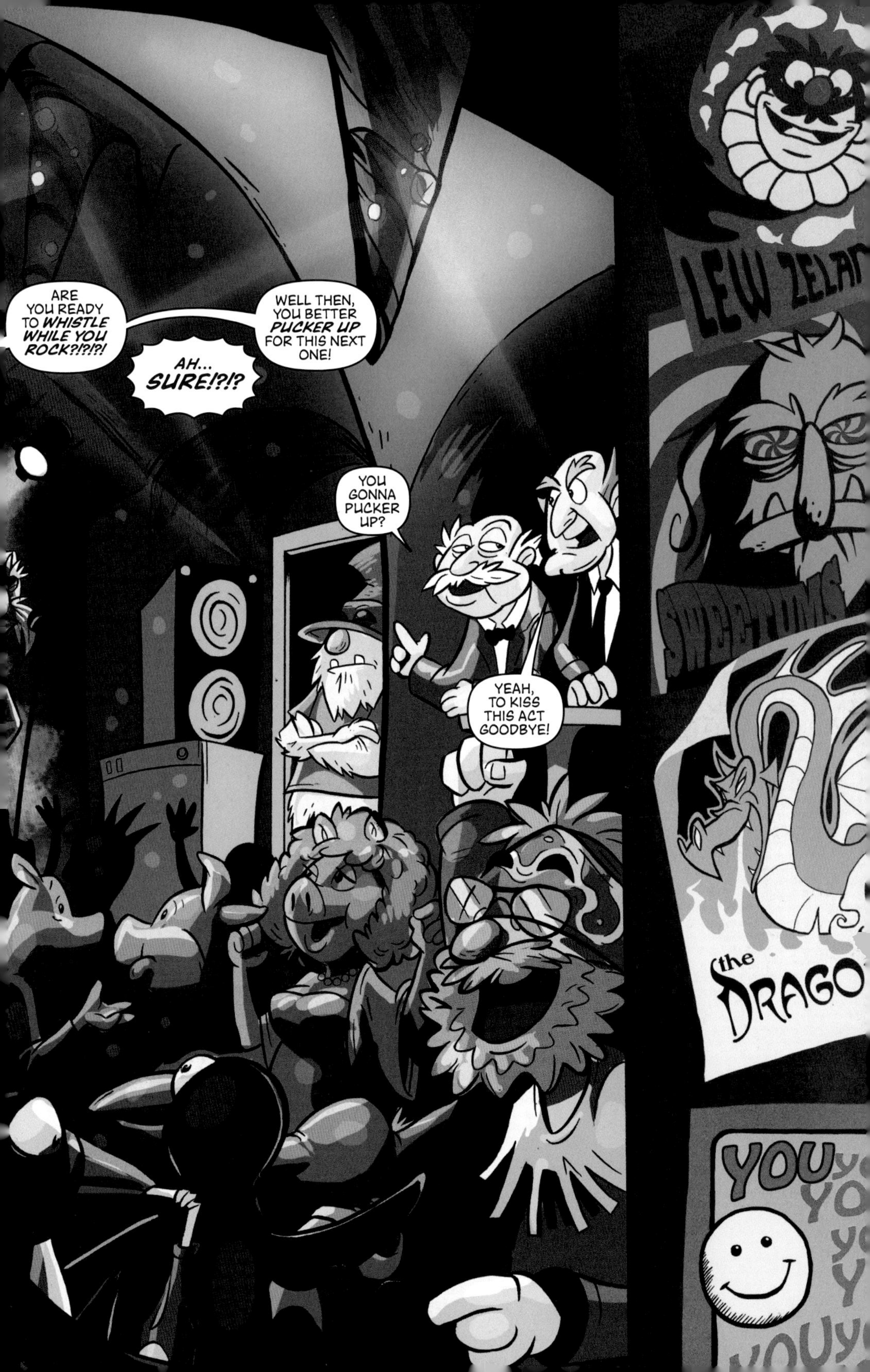
ARE YOU READY TO WHISTLE WHILE YOU ROCK?!?!?!
AH... SURE!?!?
WELL THEN, YOU BETTER PUCKER UP FOR THIS NEXT ONE!
YOU GONNA PUCKER UP?
YEAH, TO KISS THIS ACT GOODBYE!
LEW ZELA
SWEETUMS
the DRAGO
YOU

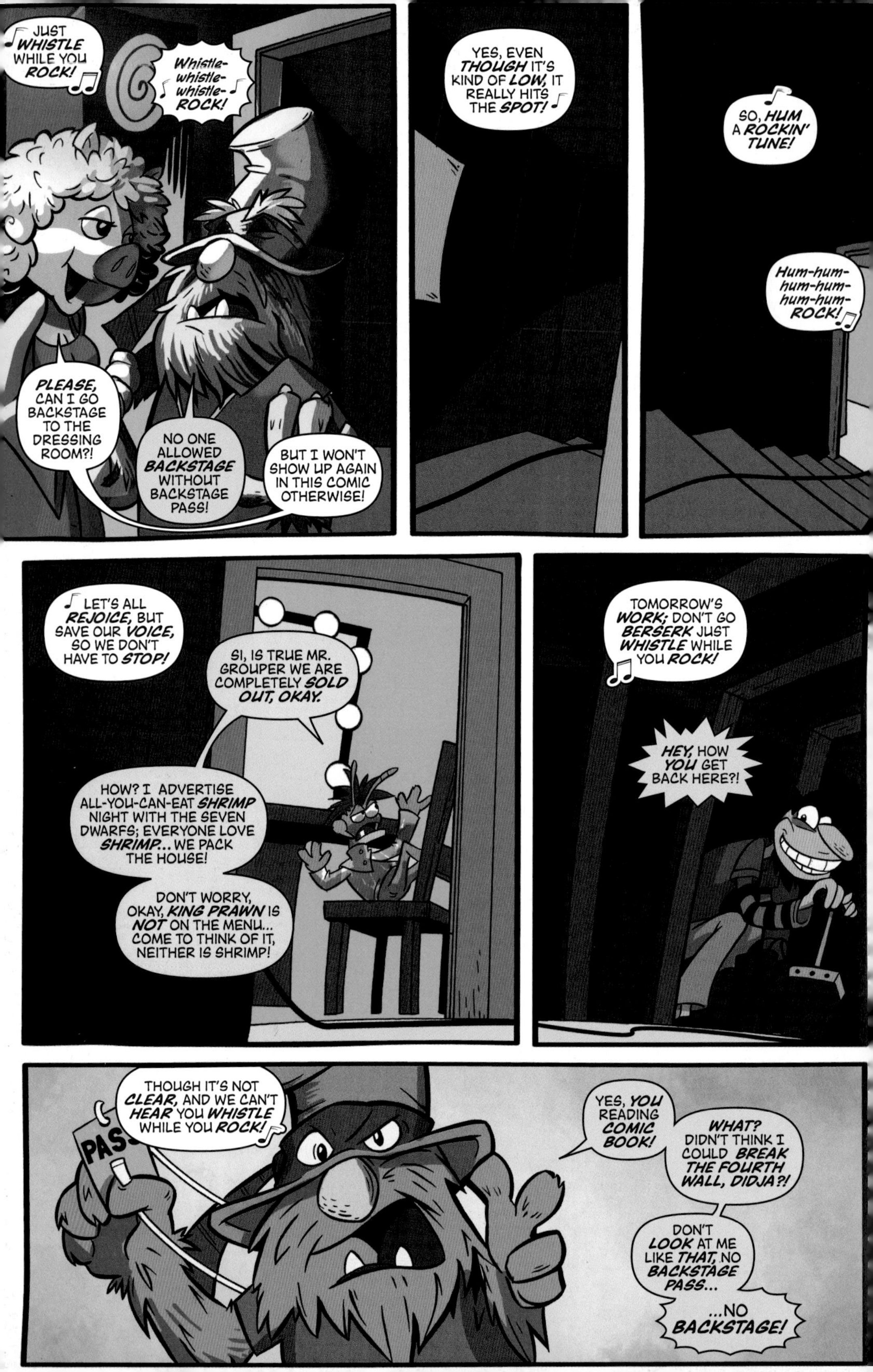

JUST WHISTLE WHILE YOU ROCK!
Whistle-whistle-whistle-ROCK!
PLEASE, CAN I GO BACKSTAGE TO THE DRESSING ROOM?!
NO ONE ALLOWED BACKSTAGE WITHOUT BACKSTAGE PASS!
BUT I WON'T SHOW UP AGAIN IN THIS COMIC OTHERWISE!
YES, EVEN THOUGH IT'S KIND OF LOW, IT REALLY HITS THE SPOT!
SO, HUM A ROCKIN' TUNE!
Hum-hum-hum-hum-hum-hum-ROCK!
LET'S ALL REJOICE, BUT SAVE OUR VOICE, SO WE DON'T HAVE TO STOP!
SI, IS TRUE MR. GROUPER WE ARE COMPLETELY SOLD OUT, OKAY.
HOW? I ADVERTISE ALL-YOU-CAN-EAT SHRIMP NIGHT WITH THE SEVEN DWARFS; EVERYONE LOVE SHRIMP... WE PACK THE HOUSE!
DON'T WORRY, OKAY, KING PRAWN IS NOT ON THE MENU... COME TO THINK OF IT, NEITHER IS SHRIMP!
TOMORROW'S WORK; DON'T GO BERSERK JUST WHISTLE WHILE YOU ROCK!
HEY, HOW YOU GET BACK HERE?!
THOUGH IT'S NOT CLEAR, AND WE CAN'T HEAR YOU WHISTLE WHILE YOU ROCK!
PASS
YES, YOU READING COMIC BOOK!
WHAT? DIDN'T THINK I COULD BREAK THE FOURTH WALL, DIDJA?!
DON'T LOOK AT ME LIKE THAT, NO BACKSTAGE PASS...
...NO BACKSTAGE!

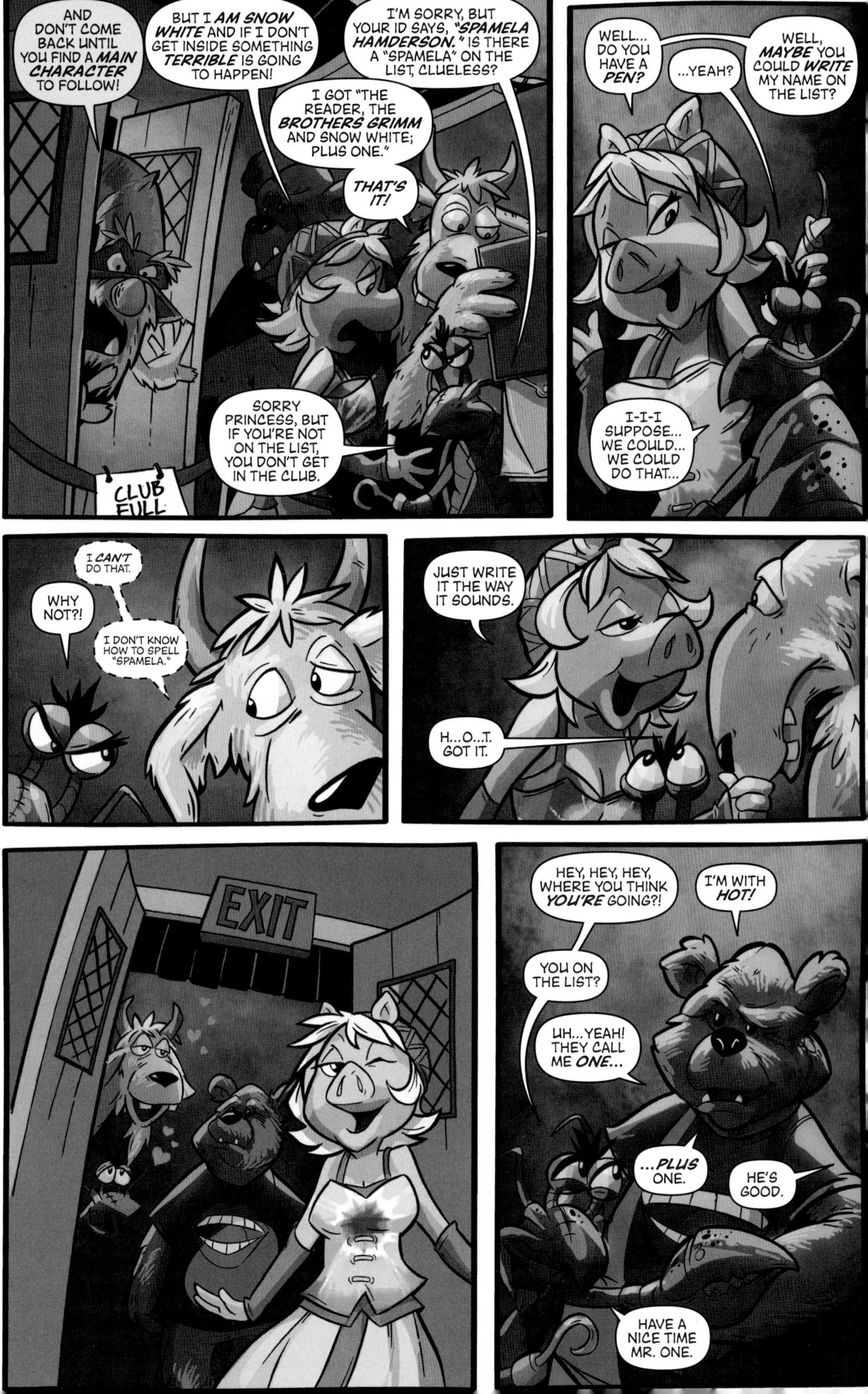

AND DON'T COME BACK UNTIL YOU FIND A MAIN CHARACTER TO FOLLOW!
BUT I AM SNOW WHITE AND IF I DON'T GET INSIDE SOMETHING TERRIBLE IS GOING TO HAPPEN!
I'M SORRY, BUT YOUR ID SAYS, "SPAMELA HAMDERSON." IS THERE A "SPAMELA" ON THE LIST, CLUELESS?
I GOT "THE READER, THE BROTHERS GRIMM AND SNOW WHITE; PLUS ONE."
THAT'S IT!
SORRY PRINCESS, BUT IF YOU'RE NOT ON THE LIST, YOU DON'T GET IN THE CLUB.
CLUB FULL
WELL... DO YOU HAVE A PEN?
...YEAH?
WELL, MAYBE YOU COULD WRITE MY NAME ON THE LIST?
I-I-I SUPPOSE... WE COULD... WE COULD DO THAT...
I CAN'T DO THAT.
WHY NOT?!
I DON'T KNOW HOW TO SPELL "SPAMELA."
JUST WRITE IT THE WAY IT SOUNDS.
H...O...T. GOT IT.
EXIT
HEY, HEY, HEY, WHERE YOU THINK YOU'RE GOING?!
I'M WITH HOT!
YOU ON THE LIST?
UH...YEAH! THEY CALL ME ONE...
...PLUS ONE.
HE'S GOOD.
HAVE A NICE TIME MR. ONE.

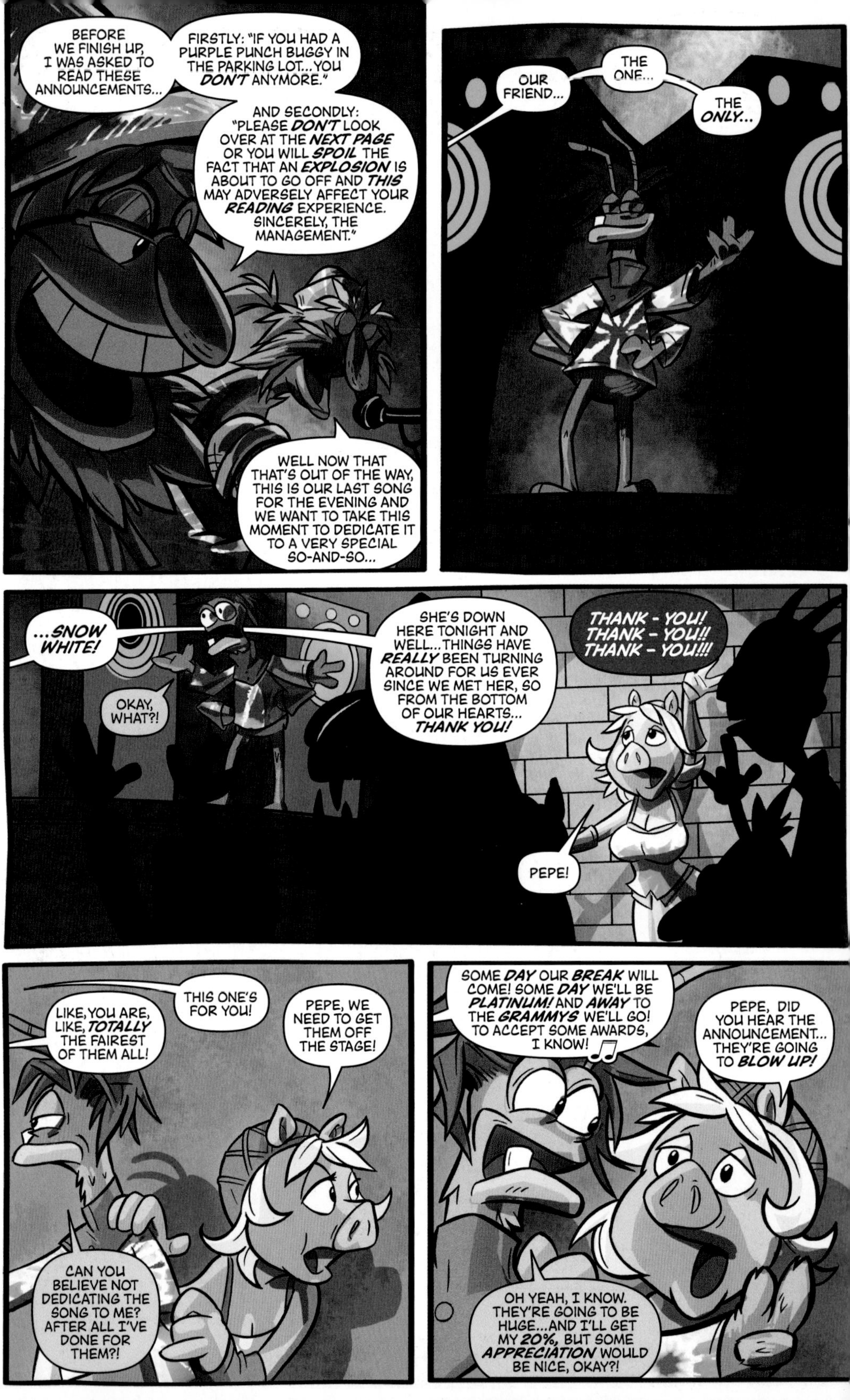
BEFORE WE FINISH UP, I WAS ASKED TO READ THESE ANNOUNCEMENTS...
FIRSTLY: "IF YOU HAD A PURPLE PUNCH BUGGY IN THE PARKING LOT...YOU DON'T ANYMORE."
AND SECONDLY: "PLEASE DON'T LOOK OVER AT THE NEXT PAGE OR YOU WILL SPOIL THE FACT THAT AN EXPLOSION IS ABOUT TO GO OFF AND THIS MAY ADVERSELY AFFECT YOUR READING EXPERIENCE. SINCERELY, THE MANAGEMENT."
WELL NOW THAT THAT'S OUT OF THE WAY, THIS IS OUR LAST SONG FOR THE EVENING AND WE WANT TO TAKE THIS MOMENT TO DEDICATE IT TO A VERY SPECIAL SO-AND-SO...
OUR FRIEND...
THE ONE...
THE ONLY...
...SNOW WHITE!
OKAY, WHAT?!
SHE'S DOWN HERE TONIGHT AND WELL...THINGS HAVE REALLY BEEN TURNING AROUND FOR US EVER SINCE WE MET HER, SO FROM THE BOTTOM OF OUR HEARTS... THANK YOU!
THANK - YOU! THANK - YOU!! THANK - YOU!!!
PEPE!
LIKE, YOU ARE, LIKE, TOTALLY THE FAIREST OF THEM ALL!
THIS ONE'S FOR YOU!
PEPE, WE NEED TO GET THEM OFF THE STAGE!
CAN YOU BELIEVE NOT DEDICATING THE SONG TO ME? AFTER ALL I'VE DONE FOR THEM?!
SOME DAY OUR BREAK WILL COME! SOME DAY WE'LL BE PLATINUM! AND AWAY TO THE GRAMMYS WE'LL GO! TO ACCEPT SOME AWARDS, I KNOW!
PEPE, DID YOU HEAR THE ANNOUNCEMENT... THEY'RE GOING TO BLOW UP!
OH YEAH, I KNOW. THEY'RE GOING TO BE HUGE...AND I'LL GET MY 20%, BUT SOME APPRECIATION WOULD BE NICE, OKAY?!

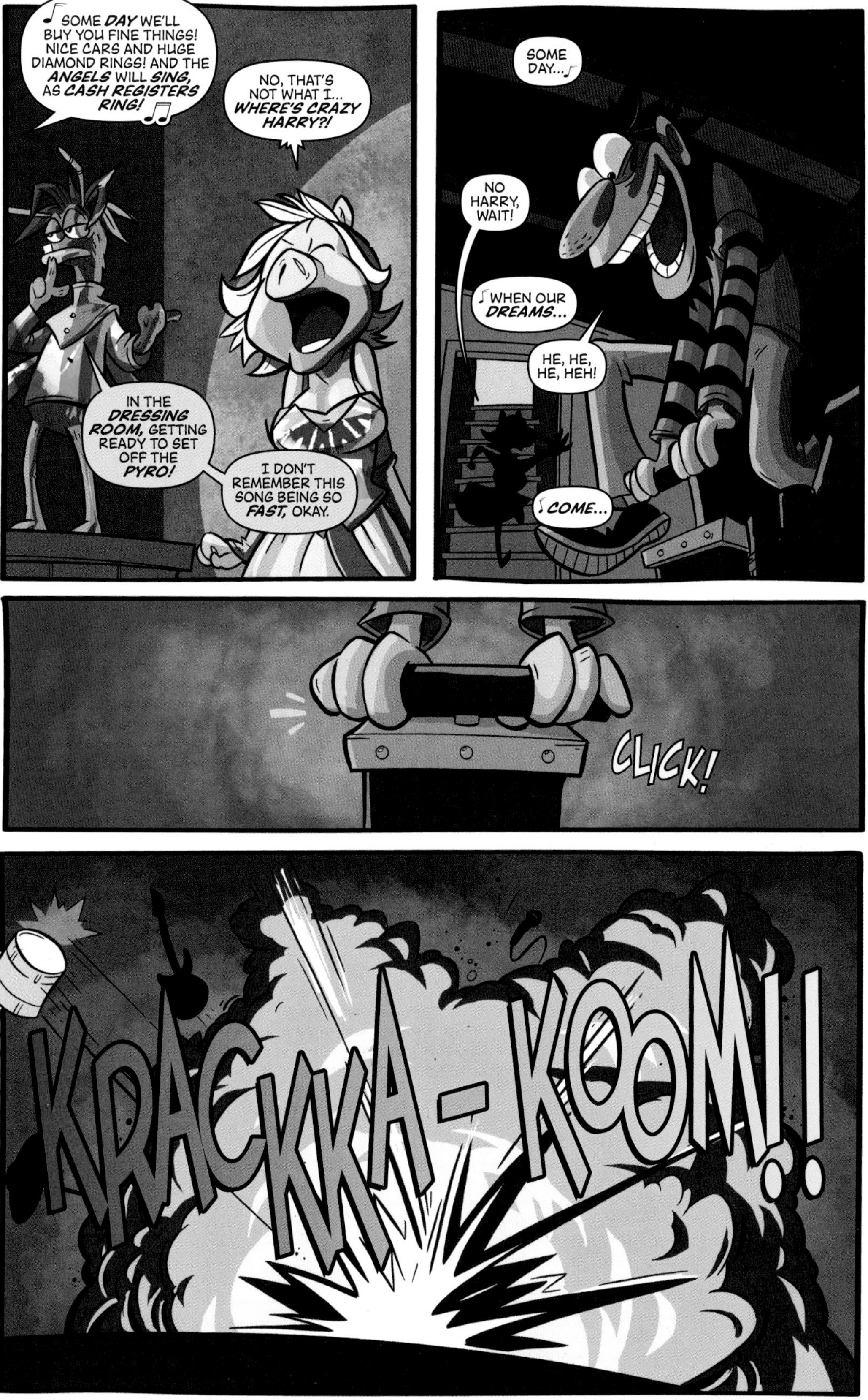
SOME DAY WE'LL BUY YOU FINE THINGS! NICE CARS AND HUGE DIAMOND RINGS! AND THE ANGELS WILL SING, AS CASH REGISTERS RING!
NO, THAT'S NOT WHAT I... WHERE'S CRAZY HARRY?!
IN THE DRESSING ROOM, GETTING READY TO SET OFF THE PYRO!
I DON'T REMEMBER THIS SONG BEING SO FAST, OKAY.
SOME DAY...
NO HARRY, WAIT!
WHEN OUR DREAMS...
HE, HE, HE, HEH!
COME...
CLICK!
KRACKKA-KOOM!!!

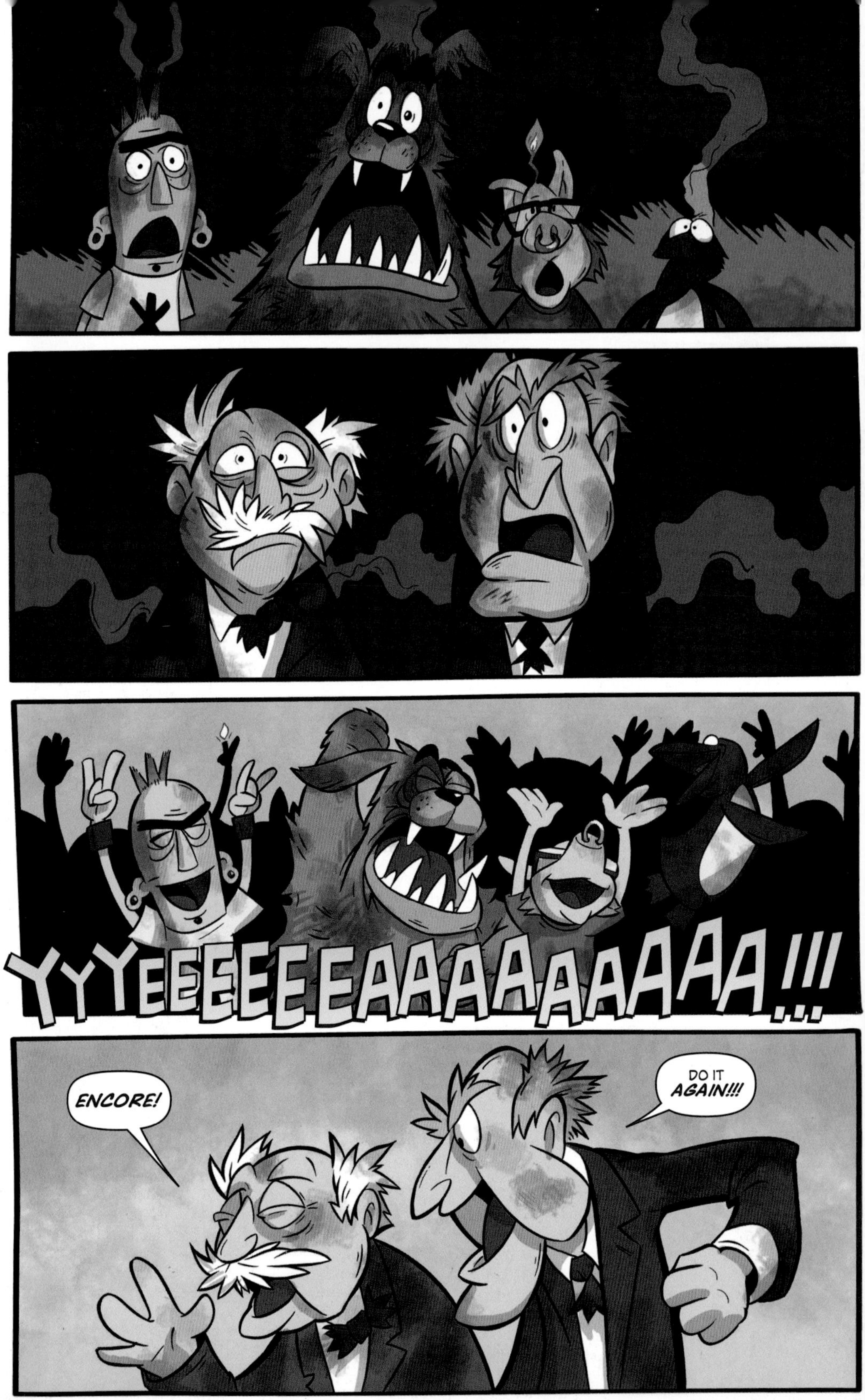

YYYEEEEEEAAAAAAAAAA!!!
ENCORE!
DO IT AGAIN!!!

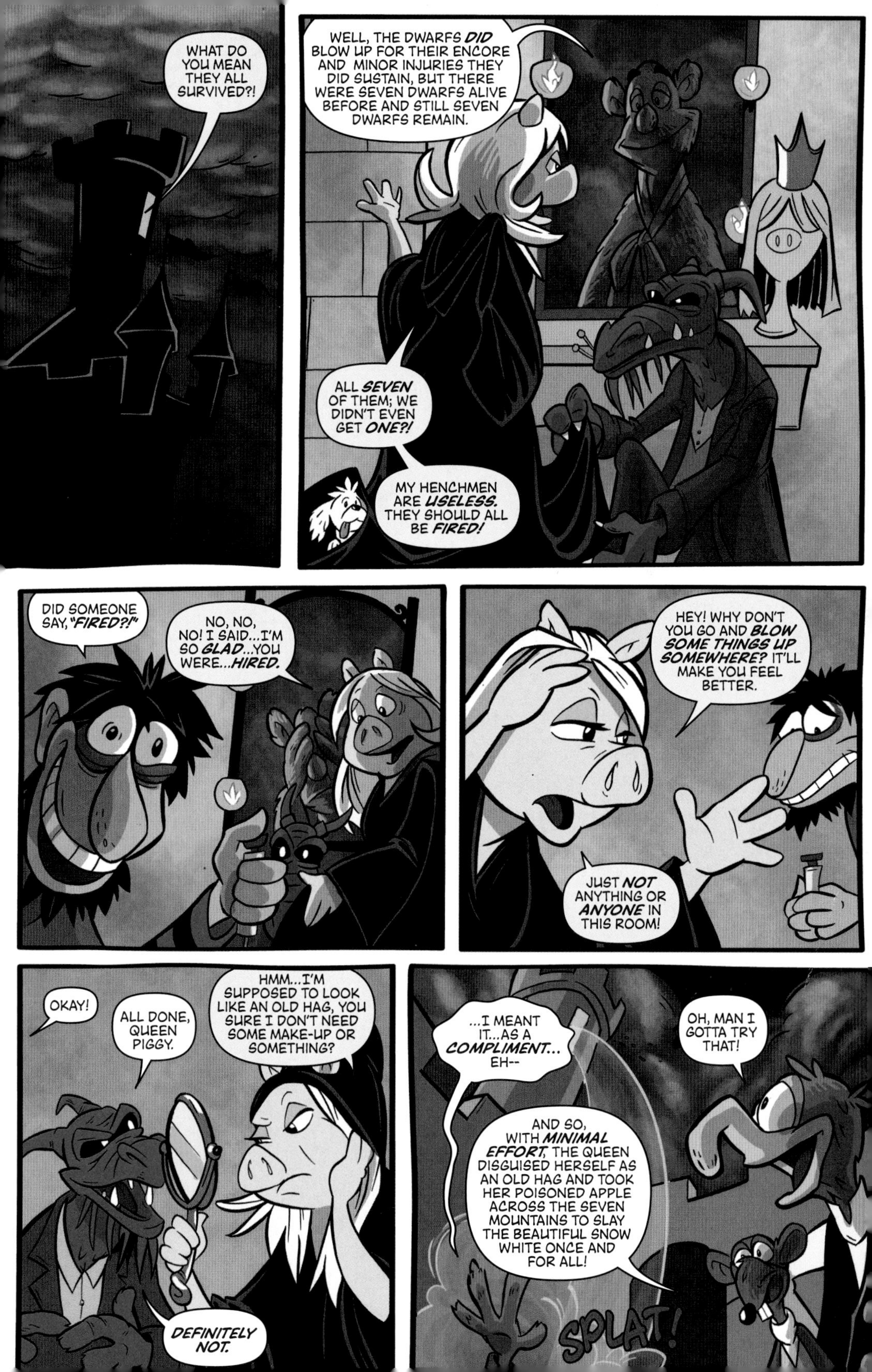

WHAT DO YOU MEAN THEY ALL SURVIVED?!
WELL, THE DWARFS DID BLOW UP FOR THEIR ENCORE AND MINOR INJURIES THEY DID SUSTAIN, BUT THERE WERE SEVEN DWARFS ALIVE BEFORE AND STILL SEVEN DWARFS REMAIN.
ALL SEVEN OF THEM; WE DIDN'T EVEN GET ONE?!
MY HENCHMEN ARE USELESS. THEY SHOULD ALL BE FIRED!
DID SOMEONE SAY, "FIRED?!"
NO, NO, NO! I SAID...I'M SO GLAD...YOU WERE...HIRED.
HEY! WHY DON'T YOU GO AND BLOW SOME THINGS UP SOMEWHERE? IT'LL MAKE YOU FEEL BETTER.
JUST NOT ANYTHING OR ANYONE IN THIS ROOM!
OKAY!
ALL DONE, QUEEN PIGGY.
HMM...I'M SUPPOSED TO LOOK LIKE AN OLD HAG, YOU SURE I DON'T NEED SOME MAKE-UP OR SOMETHING?
DEFINITELY NOT.
...I MEANT IT...AS A COMPLIMENT... EH--
OH, MAN I GOTTA TRY THAT!
AND SO, WITH MINIMAL EFFORT, THE QUEEN DISGUISED HERSELF AS AN OLD HAG AND TOOK HER POISONED APPLE ACROSS THE SEVEN MOUNTAINS TO SLAY THE BEAUTIFUL SNOW WHITE ONCE AND FOR ALL!
SPLAT!

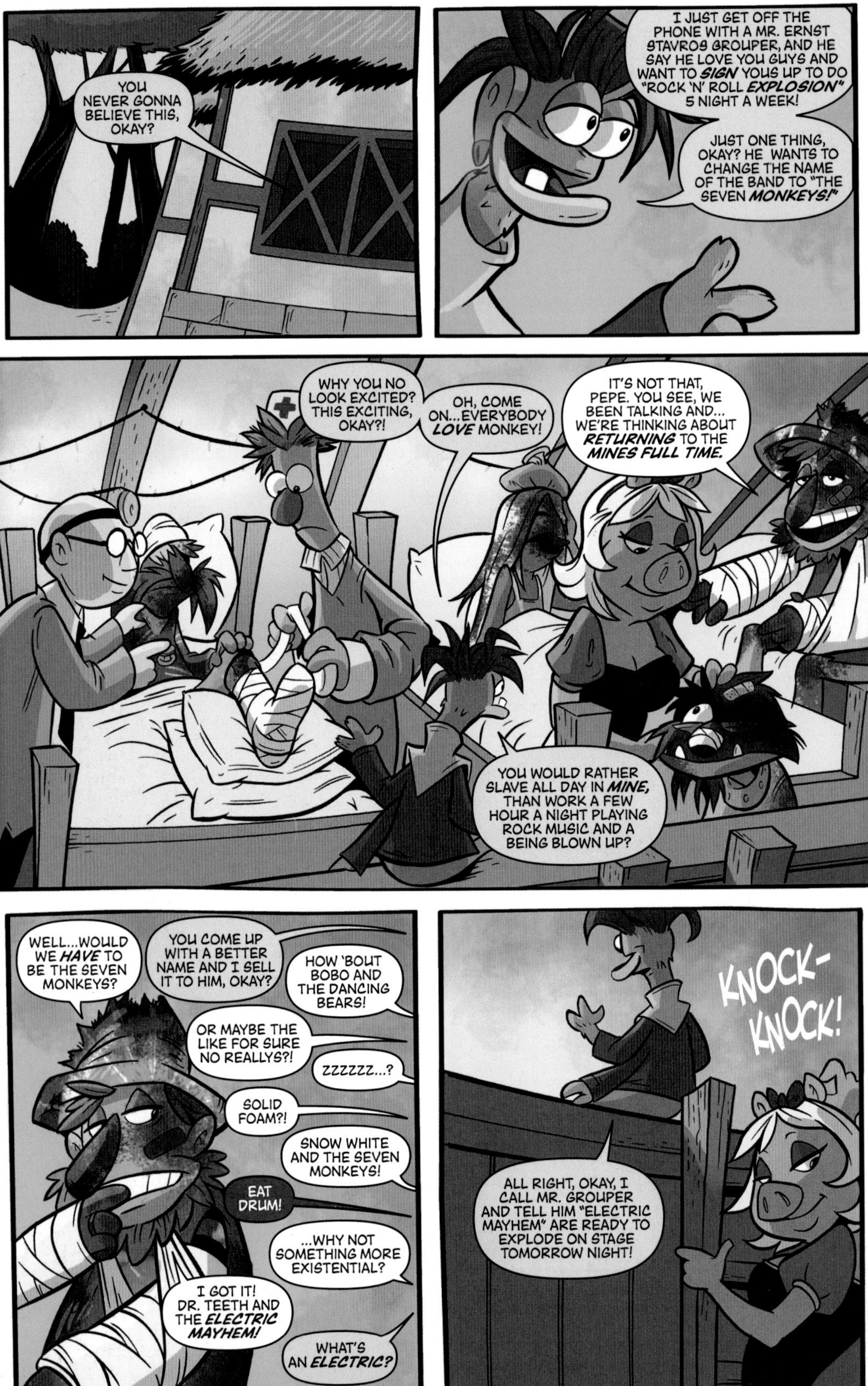
YOU NEVER GONNA BELIEVE THIS, OKAY?
I JUST GET OFF THE PHONE WITH A MR. ERNST STAVROS GROUPER, AND HE SAY HE LOVE YOU GUYS AND WANT TO SIGN YOUS UP TO DO "ROCK 'N' ROLL EXPLOSION" 5 NIGHT A WEEK!
JUST ONE THING, OKAY? HE WANTS TO CHANGE THE NAME OF THE BAND TO "THE SEVEN MONKEYS!"
WHY YOU NO LOOK EXCITED? THIS EXCITING, OKAY?!
OH, COME ON...EVERYBODY LOVE MONKEY!
IT'S NOT THAT, PEPE. YOU SEE, WE BEEN TALKING AND... WE'RE THINKING ABOUT RETURNING TO THE MINES FULL TIME.
YOU WOULD RATHER SLAVE ALL DAY IN MINE, THAN WORK A FEW HOUR A NIGHT PLAYING ROCK MUSIC AND A BEING BLOWN UP?
WELL...WOULD WE HAVE TO BE THE SEVEN MONKEYS?
YOU COME UP WITH A BETTER NAME AND I SELL IT TO HIM, OKAY?
HOW 'BOUT BOBO AND THE DANCING BEARS!
OR MAYBE THE LIKE FOR SURE NO REALLYS?!
ZZZZZZ...?
SOLID FOAM?!
SNOW WHITE AND THE SEVEN MONKEYS!
EAT DRUM!
...WHY NOT SOMETHING MORE EXISTENTIAL?
I GOT IT! DR. TEETH AND THE ELECTRIC MAYHEM!
WHAT'S AN ELECTRIC?
KNOCK-KNOCK!
ALL RIGHT, OKAY, I CALL MR. GROUPER AND TELL HIM "ELECTRIC MAYHEM" ARE READY TO EXPLODE ON STAGE TOMORROW NIGHT!

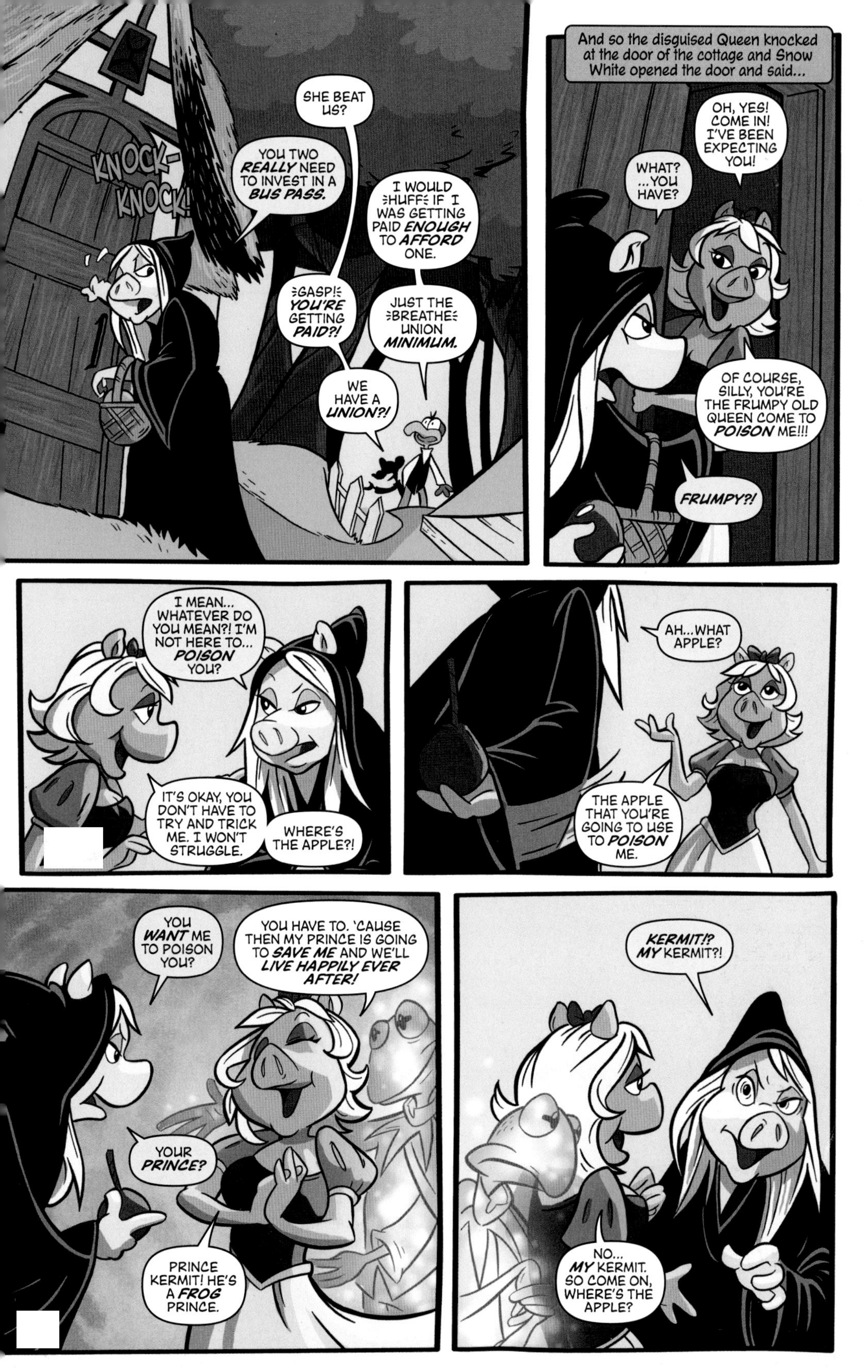
KNOCK-KNOCK!
SHE BEAT US?
YOU TWO REALLY NEED TO INVEST IN A BUS PASS.
I WOULD ≡HUFF≡ IF I WAS GETTING PAID ENOUGH TO AFFORD ONE.
≡GASP!≡ YOU'RE GETTING PAID?!
JUST THE ≡BREATHE≡ UNION MINIMUM.
WE HAVE A UNION?!
And so the disguised Queen knocked at the door of the cottage and Snow White opened the door and said...
OH, YES! COME IN! I'VE BEEN EXPECTING YOU!
WHAT? ...YOU HAVE?
OF COURSE, SILLY, YOU'RE THE FRUMPY OLD QUEEN COME TO POISON ME!!!
FRUMPY?!
I MEAN... WHATEVER DO YOU MEAN?! I'M NOT HERE TO... POISON YOU?
IT'S OKAY, YOU DON'T HAVE TO TRY AND TRICK ME. I WON'T STRUGGLE.
WHERE'S THE APPLE?!
AH...WHAT APPLE?
THE APPLE THAT YOU'RE GOING TO USE TO POISON ME.
YOU WANT ME TO POISON YOU?
YOU HAVE TO. 'CAUSE THEN MY PRINCE IS GOING TO SAVE ME AND WE'LL LIVE HAPPILY EVER AFTER!
YOUR PRINCE?
PRINCE KERMIT! HE'S A FROG PRINCE.
KERMIT!? MY KERMIT?!
NO... MY KERMIT. SO COME ON, WHERE'S THE APPLE?

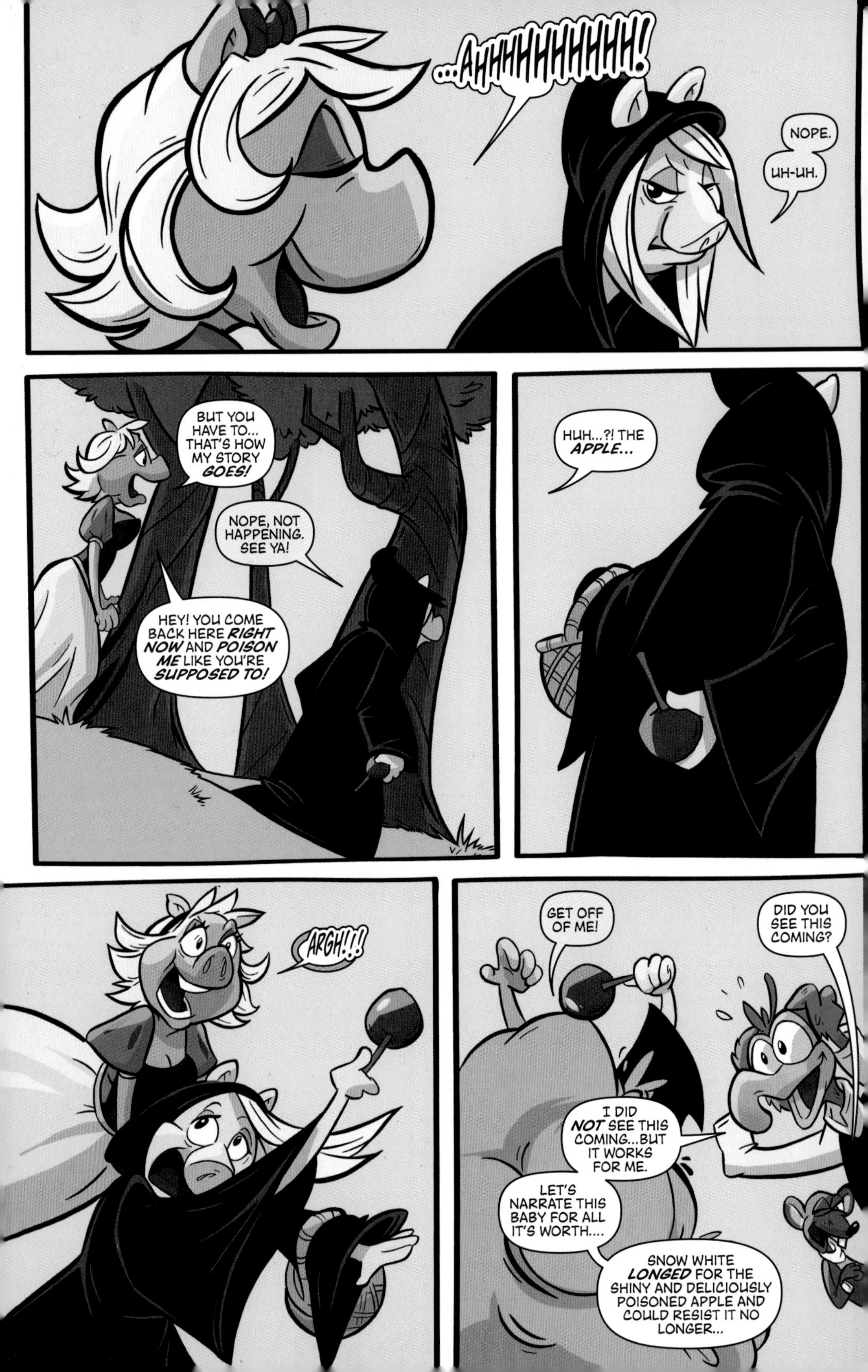
...AHHHHHHHHHH!
NOPE.
UH-UH.
BUT YOU HAVE TO... THAT'S HOW MY STORY *GOES!*
NOPE, NOT HAPPENING. SEE YA!
HEY! YOU COME BACK HERE *RIGHT NOW* AND *POISON ME* LIKE YOU'RE *SUPPOSED TO!*
HUH...?! THE *APPLE...*
ARGH!!!
GET OFF OF ME!
DID YOU SEE THIS COMING?
I DID *NOT* SEE THIS COMING...BUT IT WORKS FOR ME.
LET'S NARRATE THIS BABY FOR ALL IT'S WORTH....
SNOW WHITE *LONGED* FOR THE SHINY AND DELICIOUSLY POISONED APPLE AND COULD RESIST IT NO LONGER...

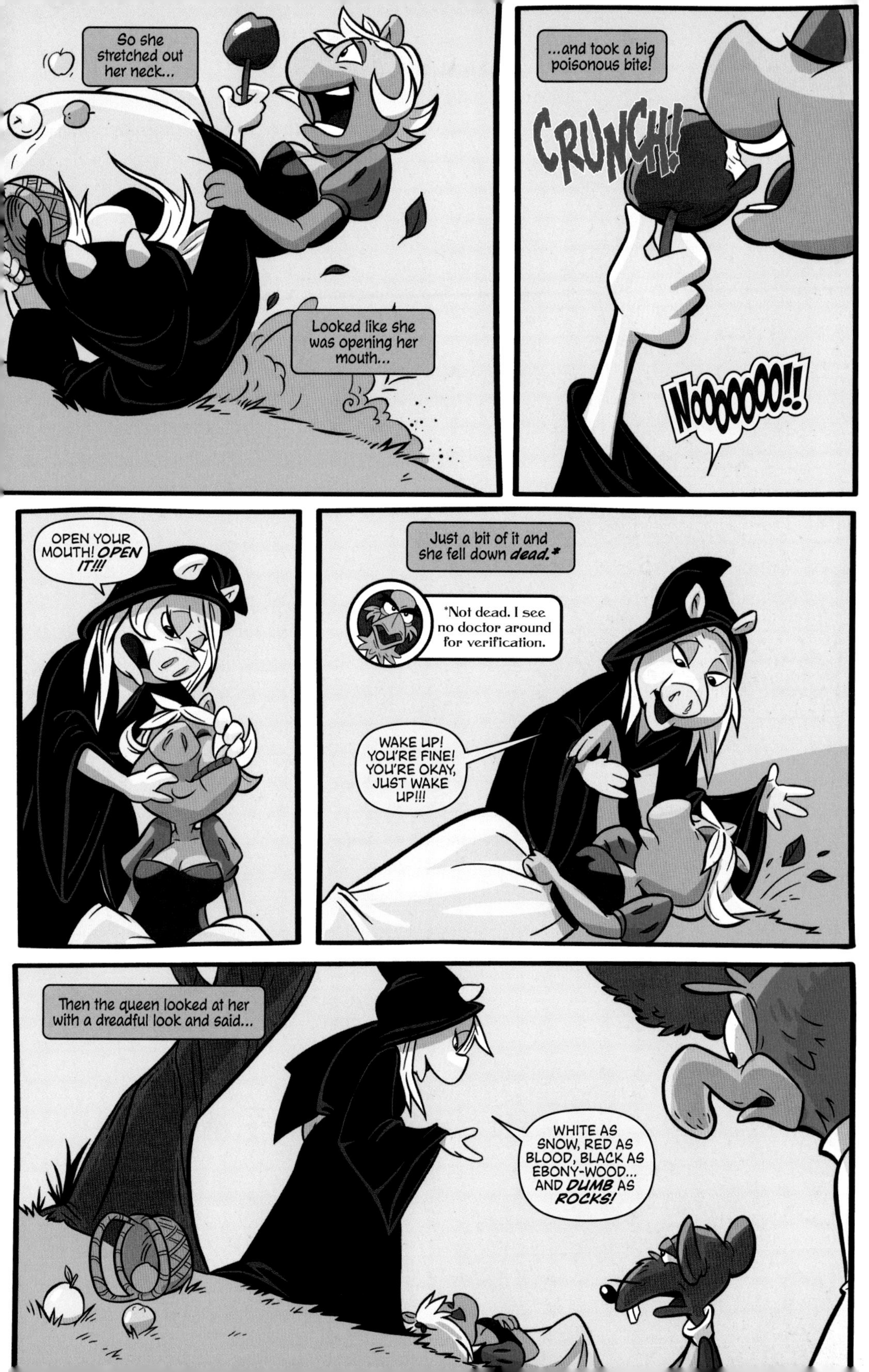

So she stretched out her neck...
Looked like she was opening her mouth...
...and took a big poisonous bite!
CRUNCH!
NOOOOOOO!!
OPEN YOUR MOUTH! OPEN IT!!!
Just a bit of it and she fell down dead.*
*Not dead. I see no doctor around for verification.
WAKE UP! YOU'RE FINE! YOU'RE OKAY, JUST WAKE UP!!!
Then the queen looked at her with a dreadful look and said...
WHITE AS SNOW, RED AS BLOOD, BLACK AS EBONY-WOOD... AND DUMB AS ROCKS!

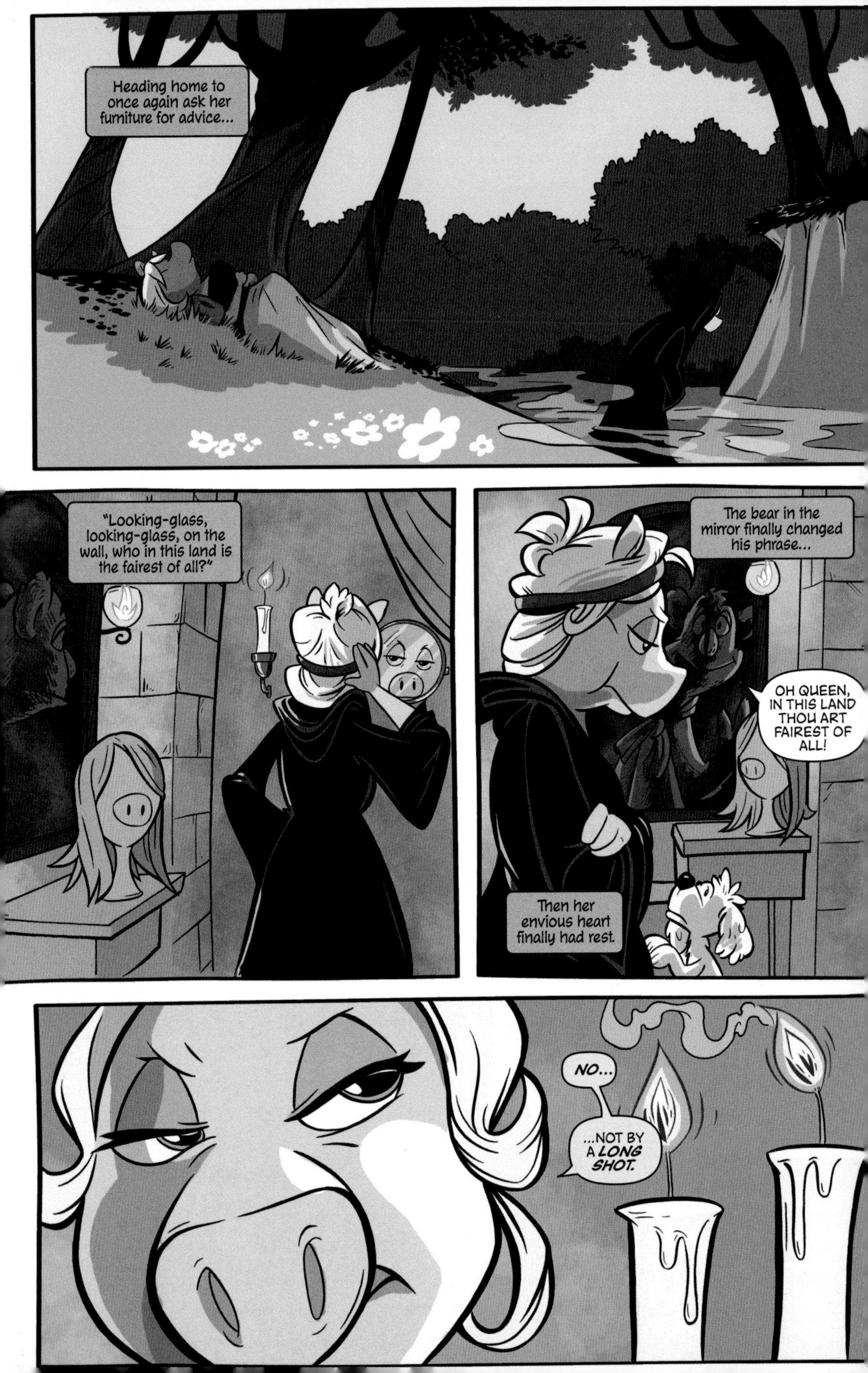

Heading home to once again ask her furniture for advice...
"Looking-glass, looking-glass, on the wall, who in this land is the fairest of all?"
The bear in the mirror finally changed his phrase...
OH QUEEN, IN THIS LAND THOU ART FAIREST OF ALL!
Then her envious heart finally had rest.
NO...
...NOT BY A LONG SHOT.

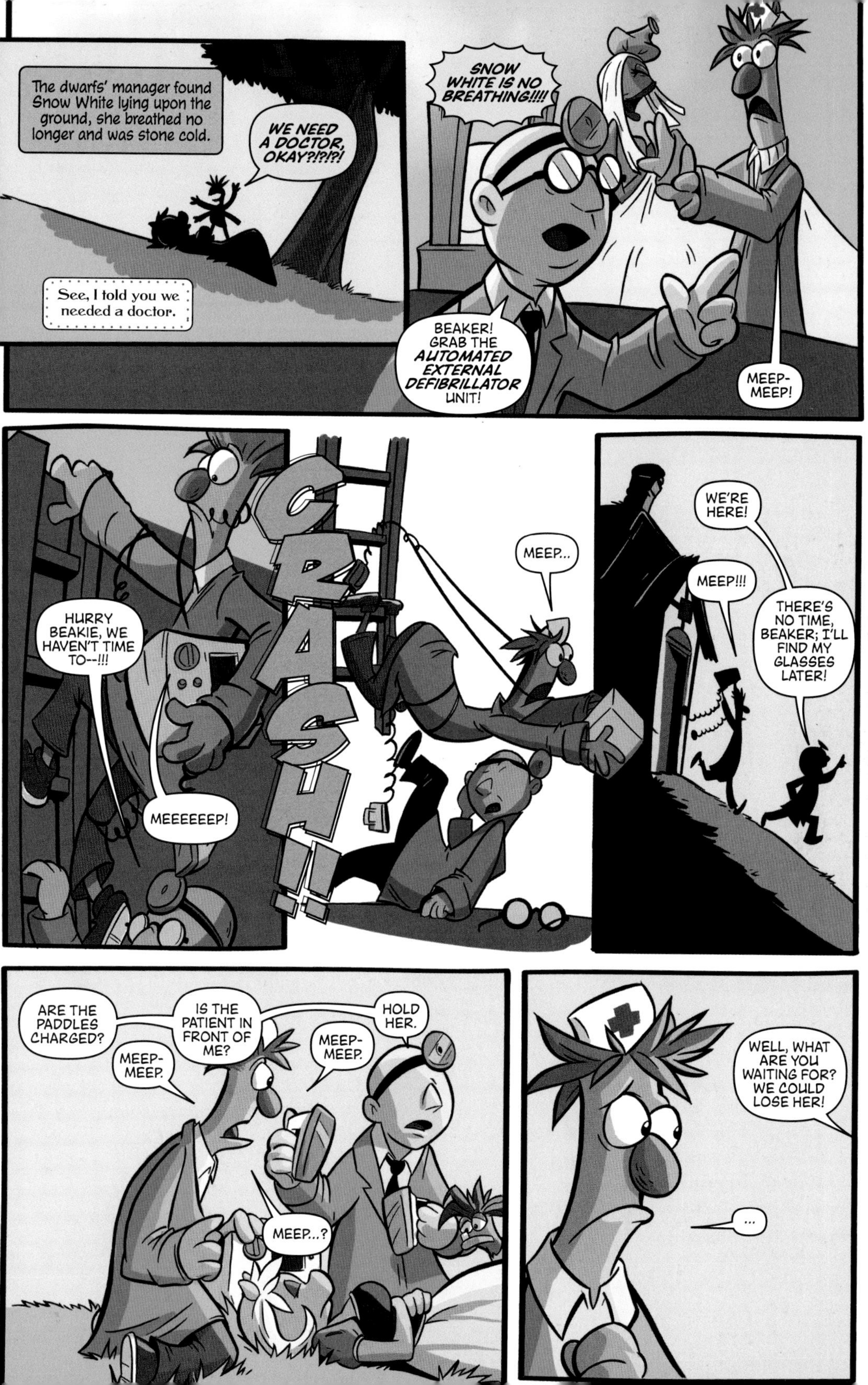

The dwarfs' manager found Snow White lying upon the ground, she breathed no longer and was stone cold.
WE NEED A DOCTOR, OKAY?!?!?!
See, I told you we needed a doctor.
SNOW WHITE IS NO BREATHING!!!!
BEAKER! GRAB THE AUTOMATED EXTERNAL DEFIBRILLATOR UNIT!
MEEP-MEEP!
HURRY BEAKIE, WE HAVEN'T TIME TO--!!!
MEEEEEEP!
CRASH!!
MEEP...
WE'RE HERE!
MEEP!!!
THERE'S NO TIME, BEAKER; I'LL FIND MY GLASSES LATER!
ARE THE PADDLES CHARGED?
MEEP-MEEP.
IS THE PATIENT IN FRONT OF ME?
MEEP-MEEP.
HOLD HER.
MEEP...?
WELL, WHAT ARE YOU WAITING FOR? WE COULD LOSE HER!
...

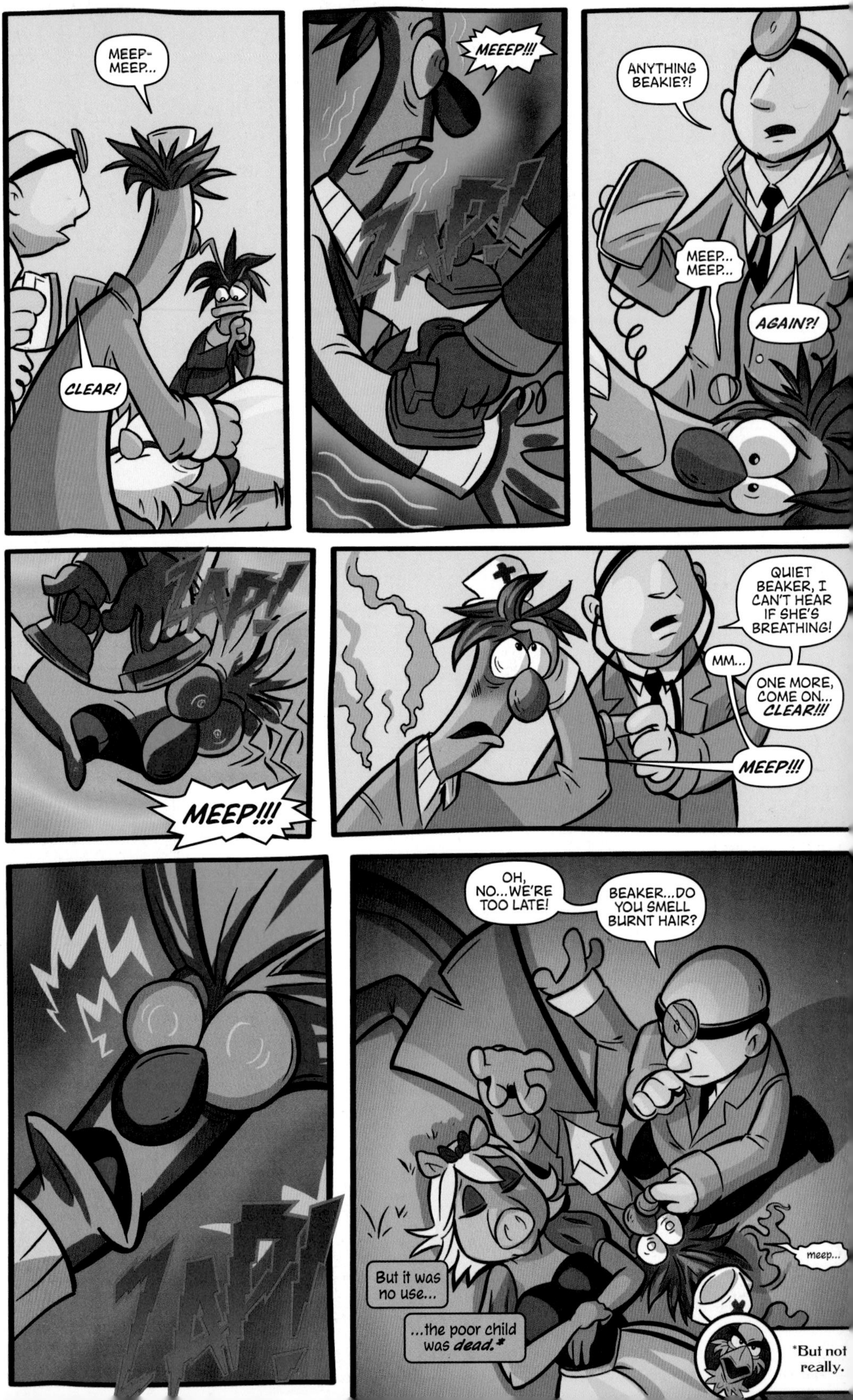
MEEP-MEEP...
CLEAR!
MEEEP!!!
ZAP!
ANYTHING BEAKIE?!
MEEP... MEEP...
AGAIN?!
ZAP!
MEEP!!!
QUIET BEAKER, I CAN'T HEAR IF SHE'S BREATHING!
MM...
ONE MORE, COME ON... CLEAR!!!
MEEP!!!
ZAP!
OH, NO...WE'RE TOO LATE!
BEAKER...DO YOU SMELL BURNT HAIR?
meep...
But it was no use...
...the poor child was dead.*
*But not really.

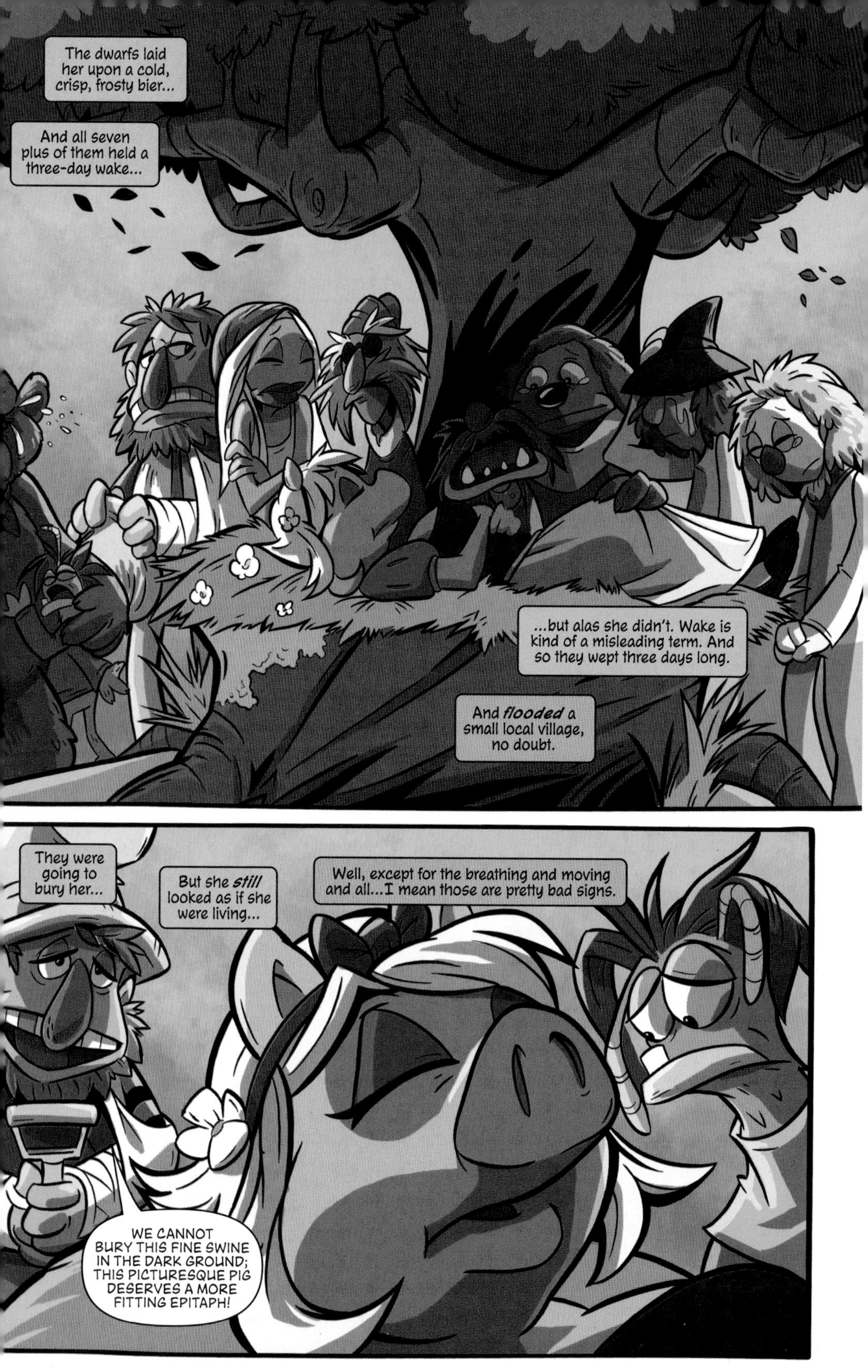
The dwarfs laid her upon a cold, crisp, frosty bier...
And all seven plus of them held a three-day wake...
...but alas she didn't. Wake is kind of a misleading term. And so they wept three days long.
And *flooded* a small local village, no doubt.
They were going to bury her...
But she *still* looked as if she were living...
Well, except for the breathing and moving and all...I mean those are pretty bad signs.
WE CANNOT BURY THIS FINE SWINE IN THE DARK GROUND; THIS PICTURESQUE PIG DESERVES A MORE FITTING EPITAPH!

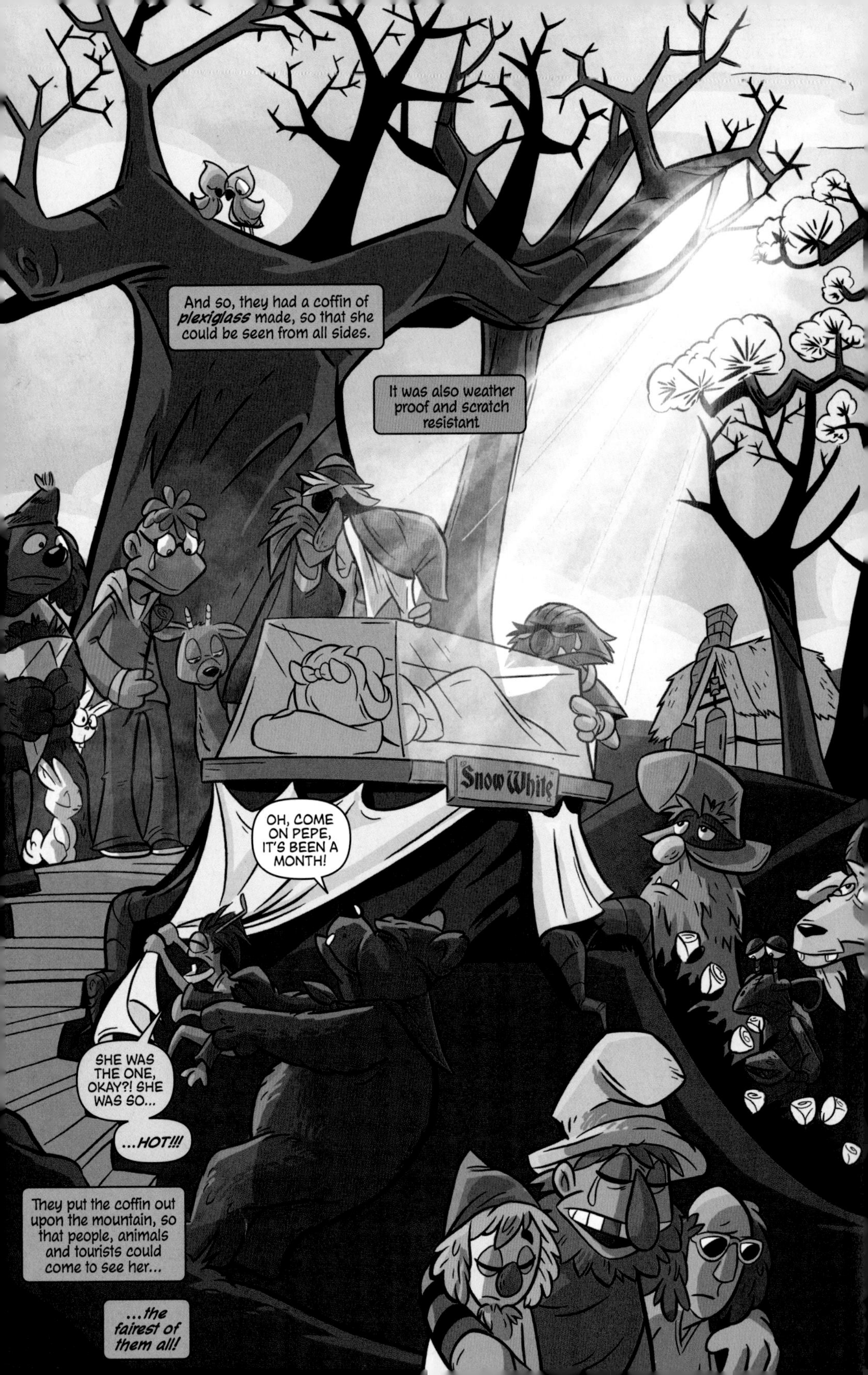
And so, they had a coffin of *plexiglass* made, so that she could be seen from all sides.
It was also weather proof and scratch resistant.
Snow White
OH, COME ON PEPE, IT'S BEEN A MONTH!
SHE WAS THE ONE, OKAY?! SHE WAS SO...
...HOT!!!
They put the coffin out upon the mountain, so that people, animals and tourists could come to see her...
...the fairest of them all!

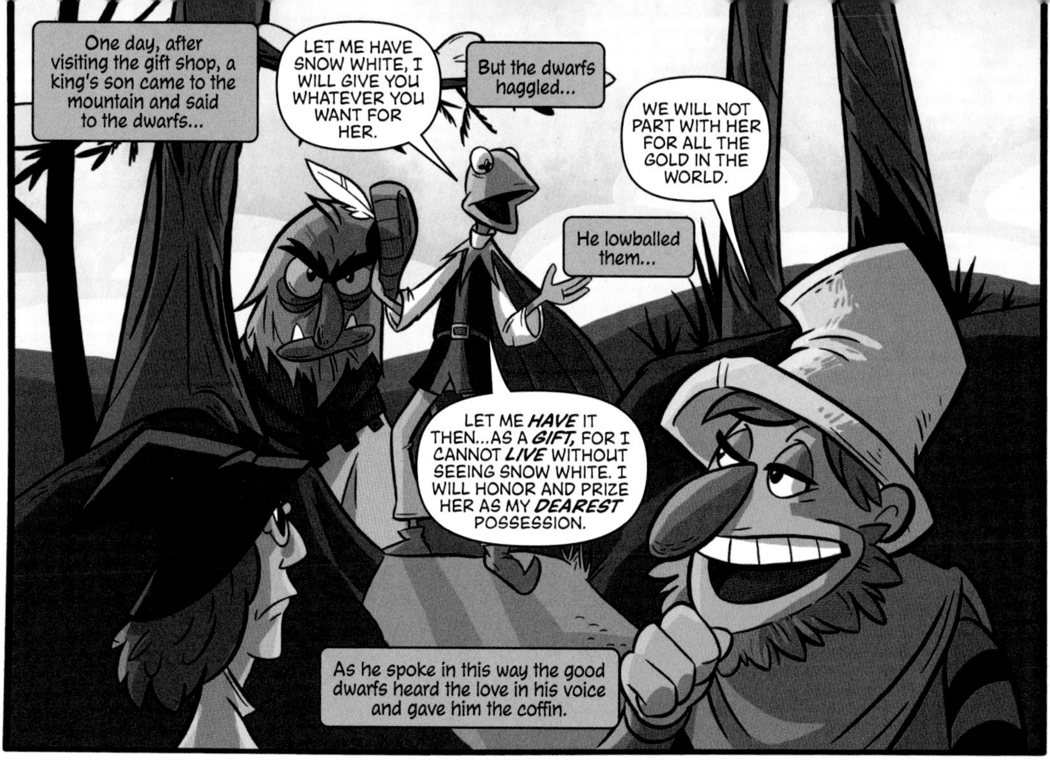
One day, after visiting the gift shop, a king's son came to the mountain and said to the dwarfs...
LET ME HAVE SNOW WHITE, I WILL GIVE YOU WHATEVER YOU WANT FOR HER.
But the dwarfs haggled...
WE WILL NOT PART WITH HER FOR ALL THE GOLD IN THE WORLD.
He lowballed them...
LET ME HAVE IT THEN...AS A GIFT, FOR I CANNOT LIVE WITHOUT SEEING SNOW WHITE. I WILL HONOR AND PRIZE HER AS MY DEAREST POSSESSION.
As he spoke in this way the good dwarfs heard the love in his voice and gave him the coffin.

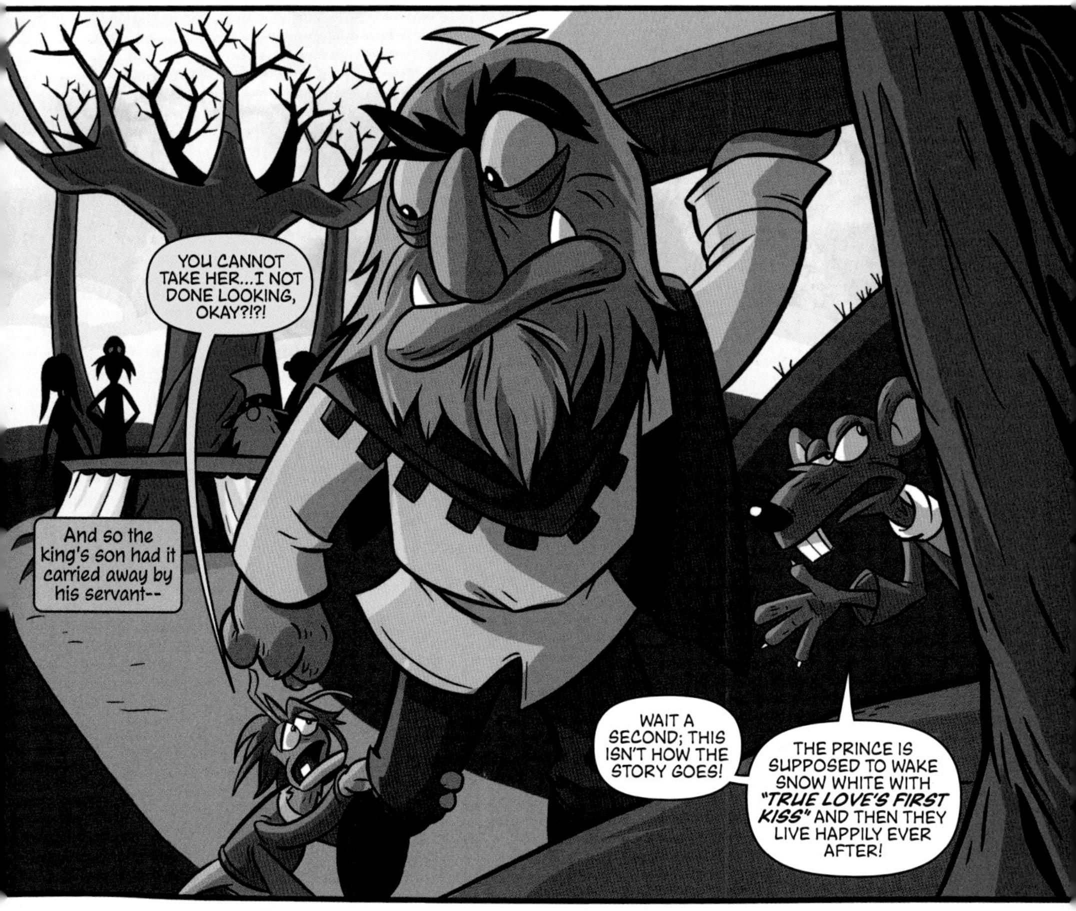
YOU CANNOT TAKE HER...I NOT DONE LOOKING, OKAY?!?!
And so the king's son had it carried away by his servant--
WAIT A SECOND; THIS ISN'T HOW THE STORY GOES!
THE PRINCE IS SUPPOSED TO WAKE SNOW WHITE WITH "TRUE LOVE'S FIRST KISS" AND THEN THEY LIVE HAPPILY EVER AFTER!

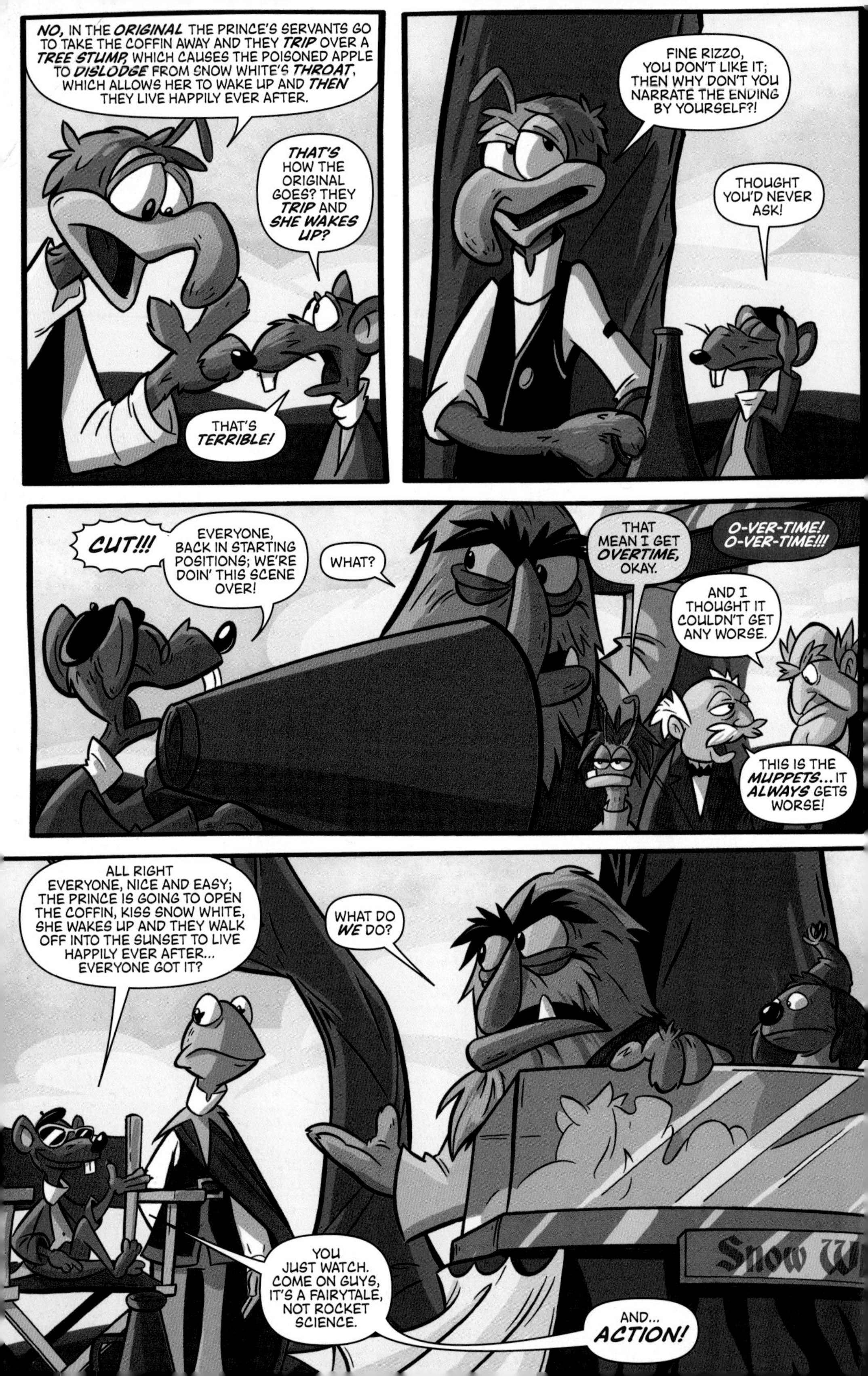
NO, IN THE ORIGINAL THE PRINCE'S SERVANTS GO TO TAKE THE COFFIN AWAY AND THEY TRIP OVER A TREE STUMP, WHICH CAUSES THE POISONED APPLE TO DISLODGE FROM SNOW WHITE'S THROAT, WHICH ALLOWS HER TO WAKE UP AND THEN THEY LIVE HAPPILY EVER AFTER.
THAT'S HOW THE ORIGINAL GOES? THEY TRIP AND SHE WAKES UP?
THAT'S TERRIBLE!
FINE RIZZO, YOU DON'T LIKE IT; THEN WHY DON'T YOU NARRATE THE ENDING BY YOURSELF?!
THOUGHT YOU'D NEVER ASK!
CUT!!!
EVERYONE, BACK IN STARTING POSITIONS; WE'RE DOIN' THIS SCENE OVER!
WHAT?
THAT MEAN I GET OVERTIME, OKAY.
O-VER-TIME! O-VER-TIME!!!
AND I THOUGHT IT COULDN'T GET ANY WORSE.
THIS IS THE MUPPETS... IT ALWAYS GETS WORSE!
ALL RIGHT EVERYONE, NICE AND EASY; THE PRINCE IS GOING TO OPEN THE COFFIN, KISS SNOW WHITE, SHE WAKES UP AND THEY WALK OFF INTO THE SUNSET TO LIVE HAPPILY EVER AFTER... EVERYONE GOT IT?
WHAT DO WE DO?
YOU JUST WATCH. COME ON GUYS, IT'S A FAIRYTALE, NOT ROCKET SCIENCE.
AND... ACTION!

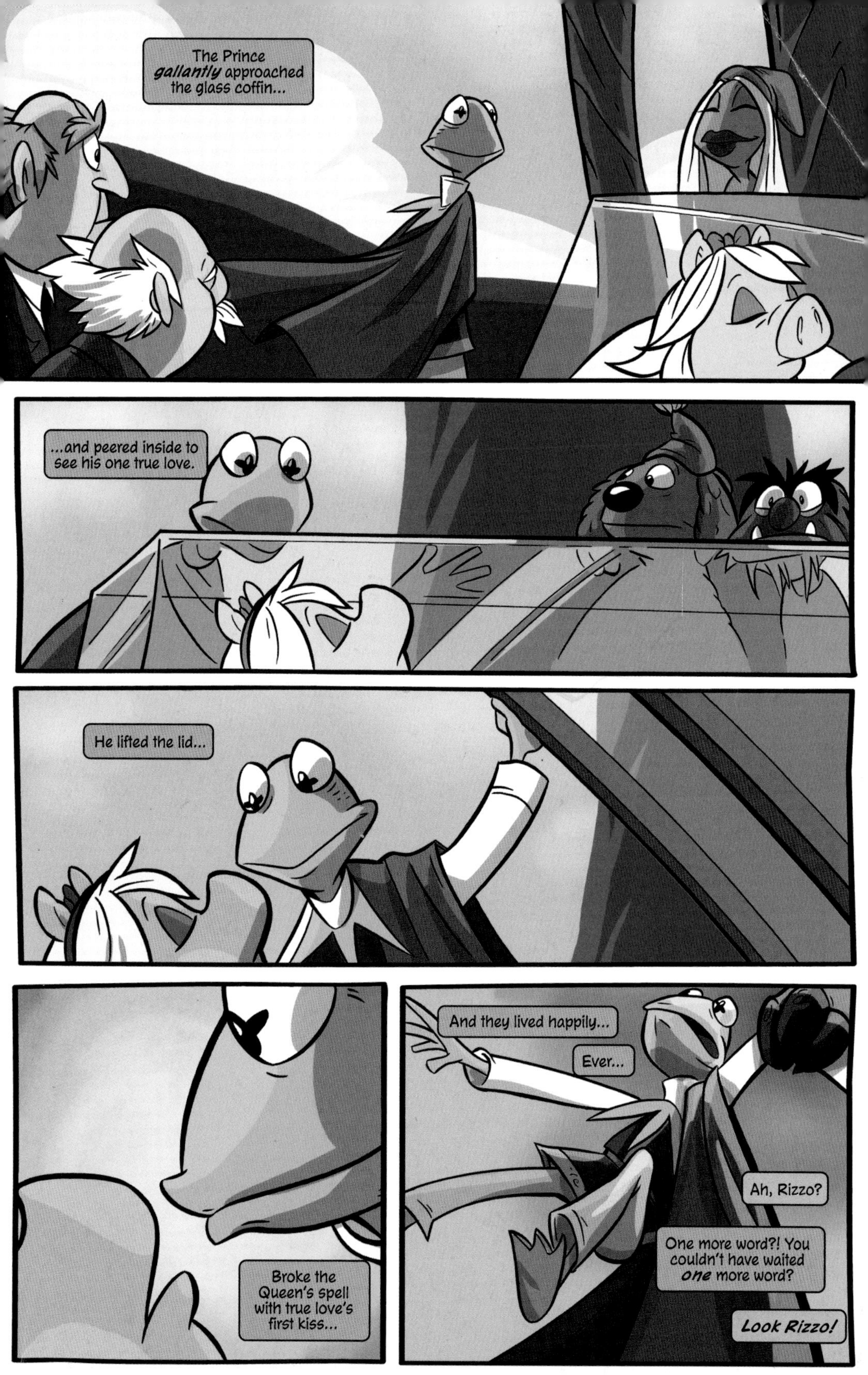
The Prince *gallantly* approached the glass coffin...
...and peered inside to see his one true love.
He lifted the lid...
Broke the Queen's spell with true love's first kiss...
And they lived happily...
Ever...
Ah, Rizzo?
One more word?! You couldn't have waited *one* more word?
Look Rizzo!

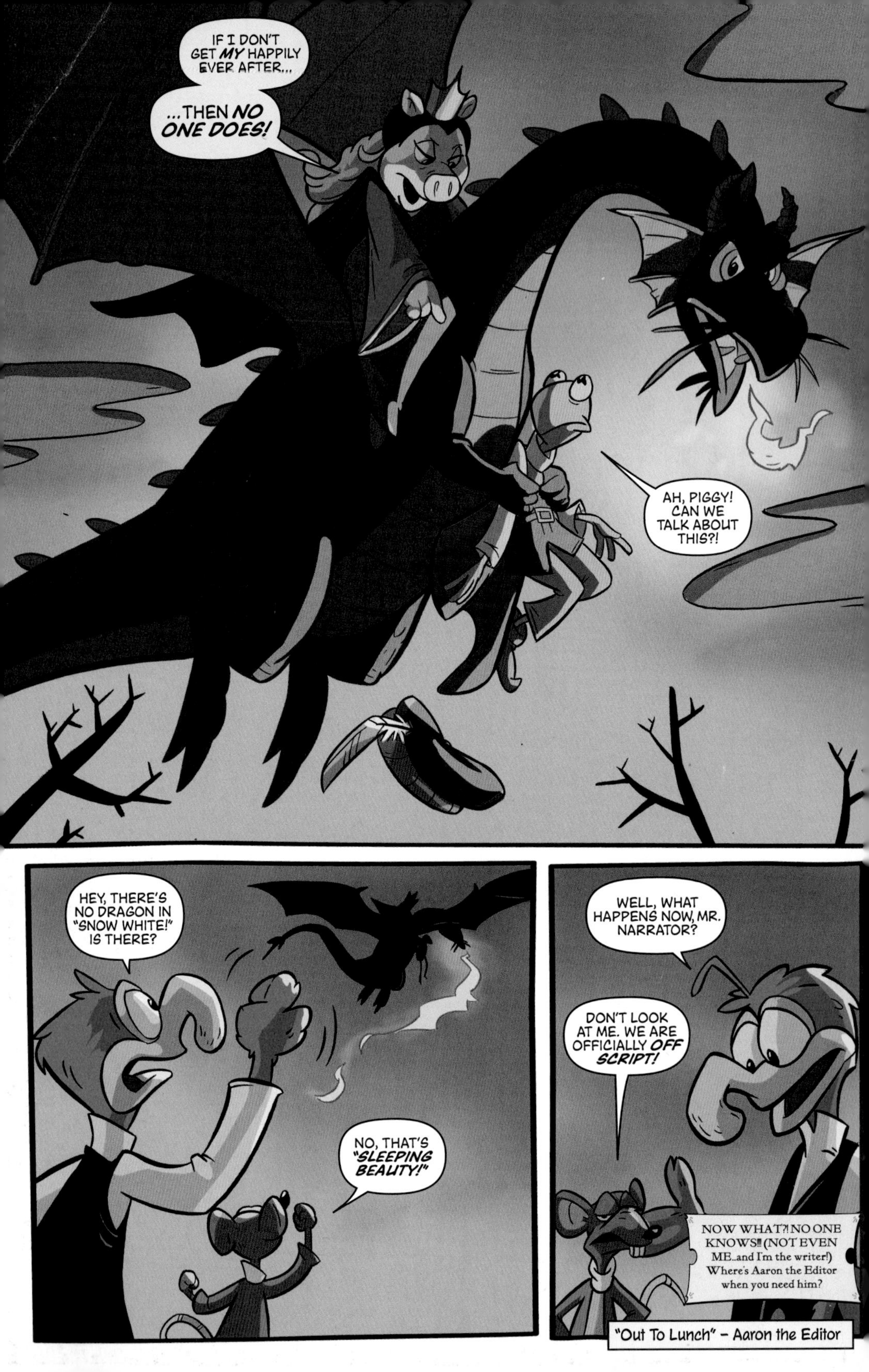
IF I DON'T GET *MY* HAPPILY EVER AFTER...
...THEN *NO ONE DOES!*
AH, PIGGY! CAN WE TALK ABOUT THIS?!
HEY, THERE'S NO DRAGON IN "SNOW WHITE!" IS THERE?
NO, THAT'S *"SLEEPING BEAUTY!"*
WELL, WHAT HAPPENS NOW, MR. NARRATOR?
DON'T LOOK AT ME. WE ARE OFFICIALLY *OFF SCRIPT!*
NOW WHAT?! NO ONE KNOWS!!! (NOT EVEN ME...and I'm the writer!) Where's Aaron the Editor when you need him?
"Out To Lunch" - Aaron the Editor

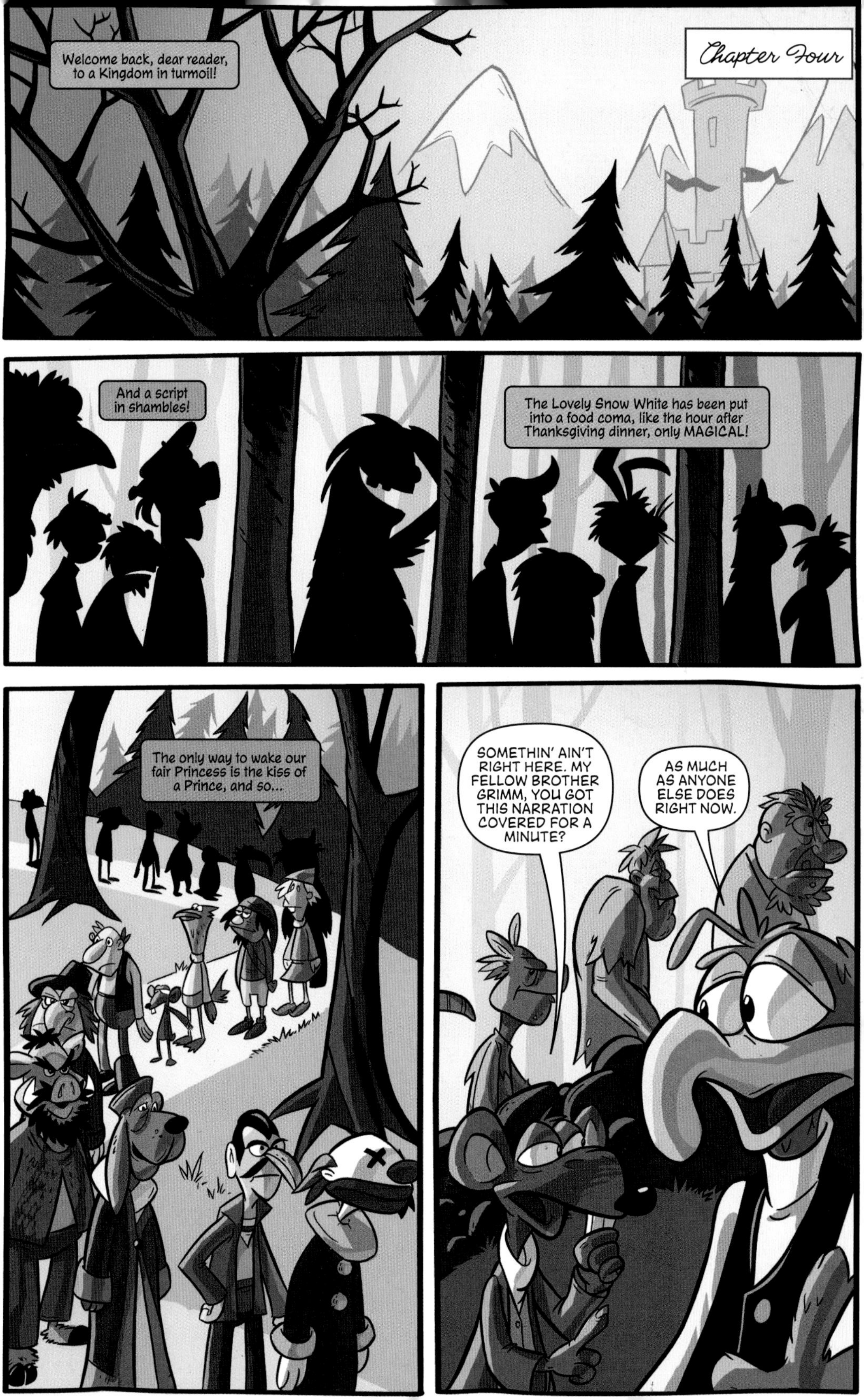
Welcome back, dear reader, to a Kingdom in turmoil!
Chapter Four
And a script in shambles!
The Lovely Snow White has been put into a food coma, like the hour after Thanksgiving dinner, only MAGICAL!
The only way to wake our fair Princess is the kiss of a Prince, and so...
SOMETHIN' AIN'T RIGHT HERE. MY FELLOW BROTHER GRIMM, YOU GOT THIS NARRATION COVERED FOR A MINUTE?
AS MUCH AS ANYONE ELSE DOES RIGHT NOW.

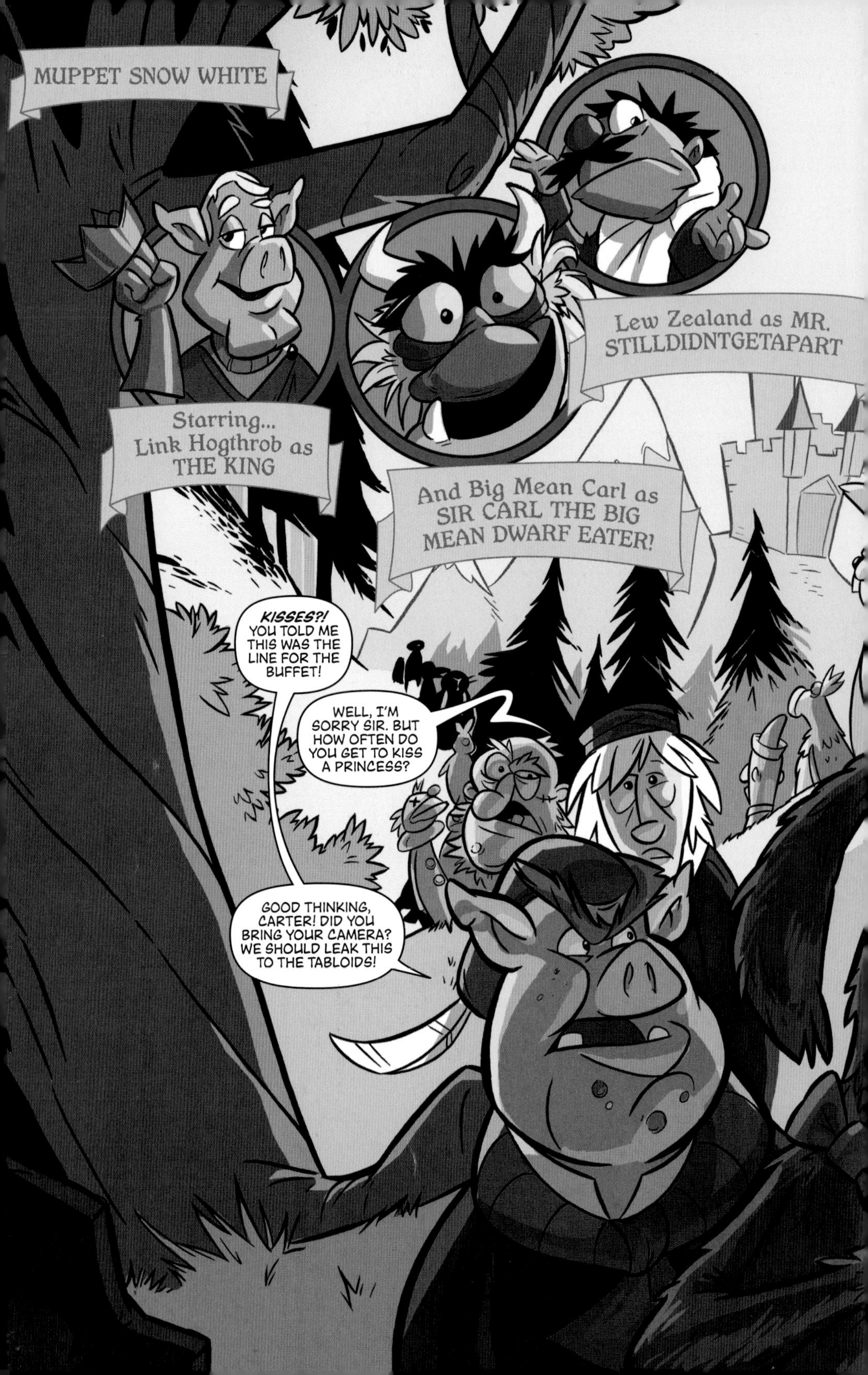
MUPPET SNOW WHITE
Lew Zealand as MR. STILLDIDNTGETAPART
Starring... Link Hogthrob as THE KING
And Big Mean Carl as SIR CARL THE BIG MEAN DWARF EATER!
KISSES?! YOU TOLD ME THIS WAS THE LINE FOR THE BUFFET!
WELL, I'M SORRY SIR. BUT HOW OFTEN DO YOU GET TO KISS A PRINCESS?
GOOD THINKING, CARTER! DID YOU BRING YOUR CAMERA? WE SHOULD LEAK THIS TO THE TABLOIDS!

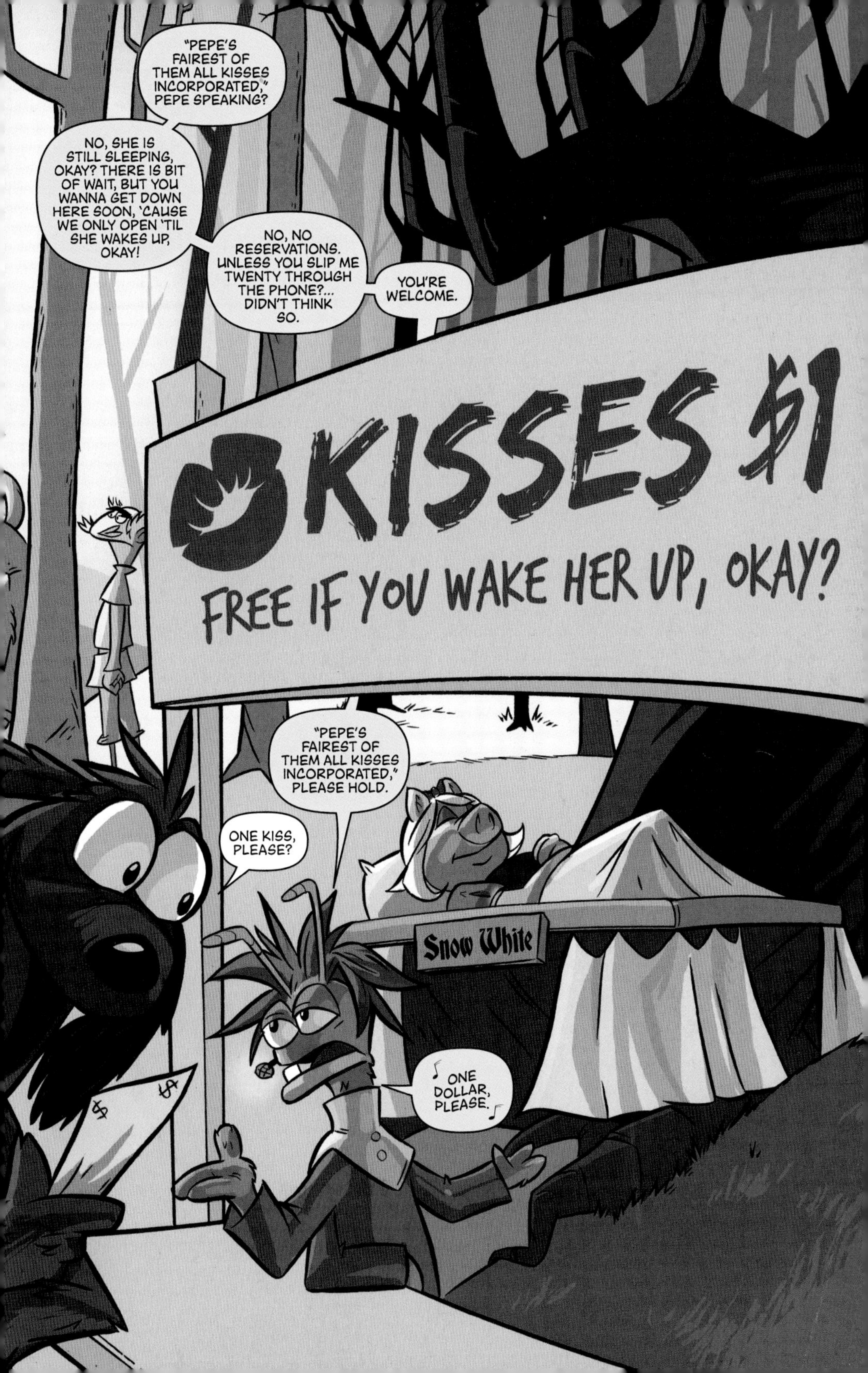
"PEPE'S FAIREST OF THEM ALL KISSES INCORPORATED," PEPE SPEAKING?
NO, SHE IS STILL SLEEPING, OKAY? THERE IS BIT OF WAIT, BUT YOU WANNA GET DOWN HERE SOON, 'CAUSE WE ONLY OPEN 'TIL SHE WAKES UP, OKAY!
NO, NO RESERVATIONS. UNLESS YOU SLIP ME TWENTY THROUGH THE PHONE?... DIDN'T THINK SO.
YOU'RE WELCOME.
KISSES $1
FREE IF YOU WAKE HER UP, OKAY?
"PEPE'S FAIREST OF THEM ALL KISSES INCORPORATED," PLEASE HOLD.
ONE KISS, PLEASE?
Snow White
ONE DOLLAR, PLEASE.

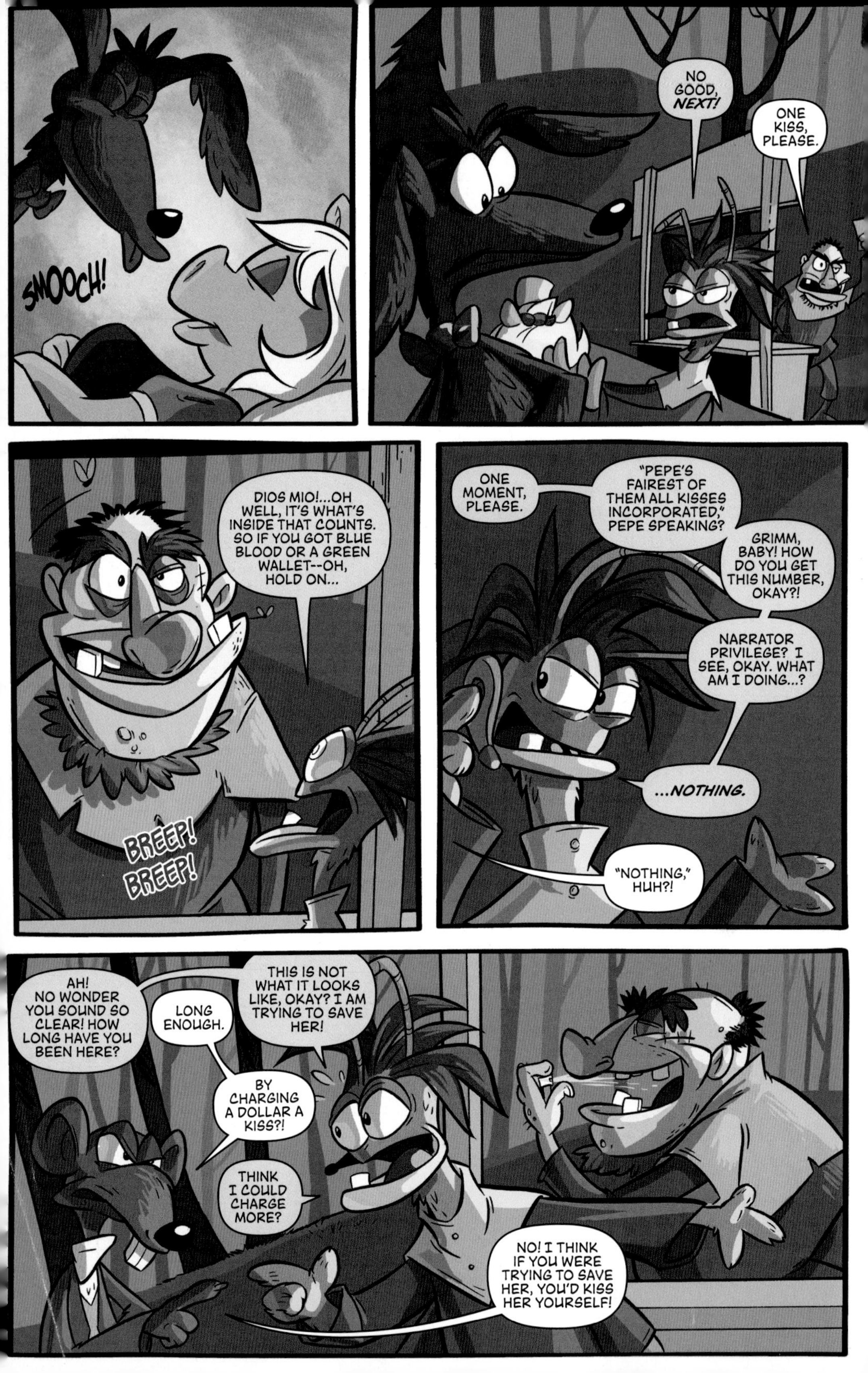
SMOOCH!
NO GOOD, NEXT!
ONE KISS, PLEASE.
DIOS MIO!...OH WELL, IT'S WHAT'S INSIDE THAT COUNTS. SO IF YOU GOT BLUE BLOOD OR A GREEN WALLET--OH, HOLD ON...
BREEP! BREEP!
ONE MOMENT, PLEASE.
"PEPE'S FAIREST OF THEM ALL KISSES INCORPORATED," PEPE SPEAKING?
GRIMM, BABY! HOW DO YOU GET THIS NUMBER, OKAY?!
NARRATOR PRIVILEGE? I SEE, OKAY. WHAT AM I DOING...?
...NOTHING.
"NOTHING," HUH?!
AH! NO WONDER YOU SOUND SO CLEAR! HOW LONG HAVE YOU BEEN HERE?
LONG ENOUGH.
THIS IS NOT WHAT IT LOOKS LIKE, OKAY? I AM TRYING TO SAVE HER!
BY CHARGING A DOLLAR A KISS?!
THINK I COULD CHARGE MORE?
NO! I THINK IF YOU WERE TRYING TO SAVE HER, YOU'D KISS HER YOURSELF!

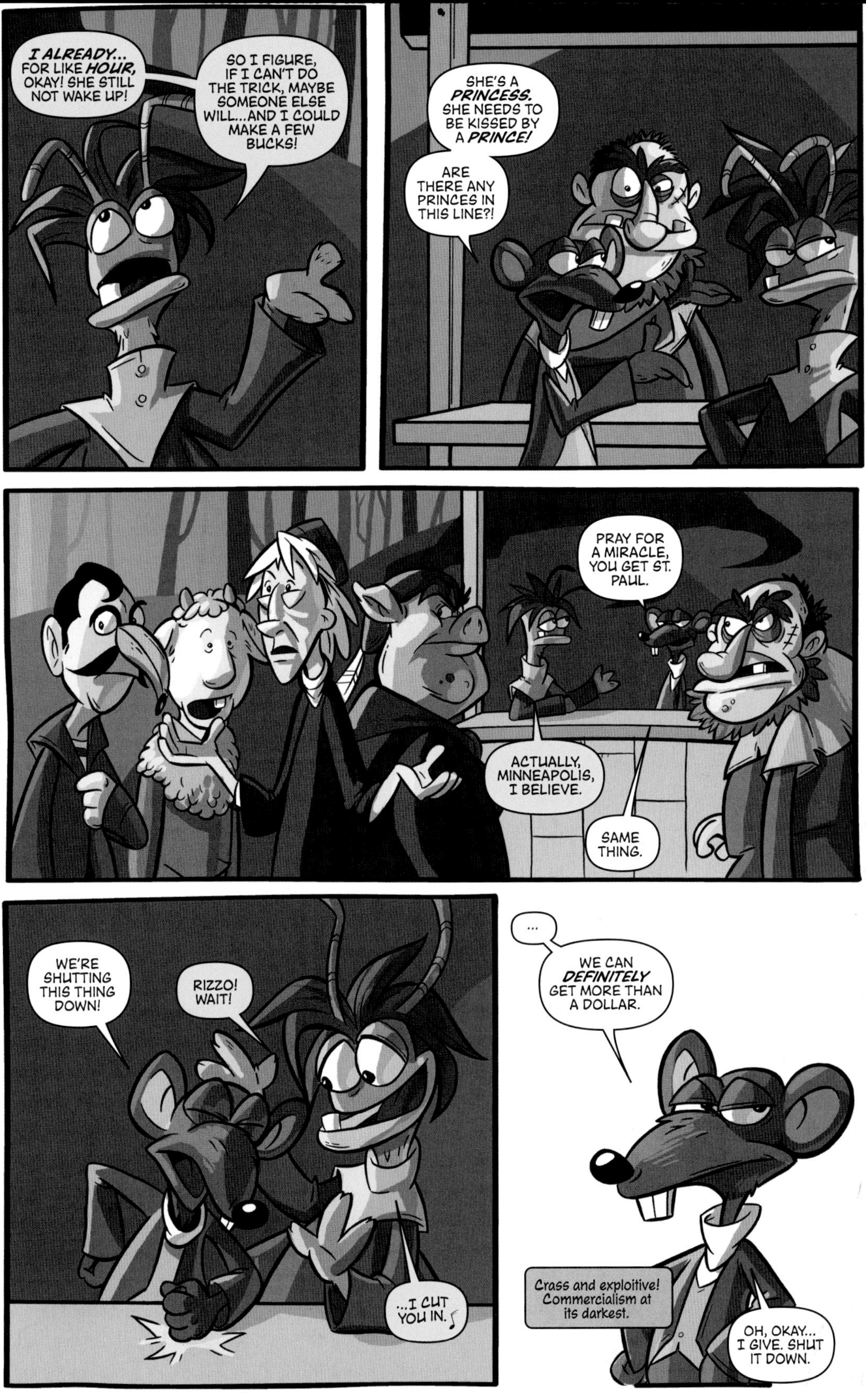

I ALREADY... FOR LIKE HOUR, OKAY! SHE STILL NOT WAKE UP!
SO I FIGURE, IF I CAN'T DO THE TRICK, MAYBE SOMEONE ELSE WILL...AND I COULD MAKE A FEW BUCKS!
SHE'S A PRINCESS. SHE NEEDS TO BE KISSED BY A PRINCE!
ARE THERE ANY PRINCES IN THIS LINE?!
PRAY FOR A MIRACLE, YOU GET ST. PAUL.
ACTUALLY, MINNEAPOLIS, I BELIEVE.
SAME THING.
WE'RE SHUTTING THIS THING DOWN!
RIZZO! WAIT!
...I CUT YOU IN.
...
WE CAN DEFINITELY GET MORE THAN A DOLLAR.
Crass and exploitive! Commercialism at its darkest.
OH, OKAY... I GIVE. SHUT IT DOWN.

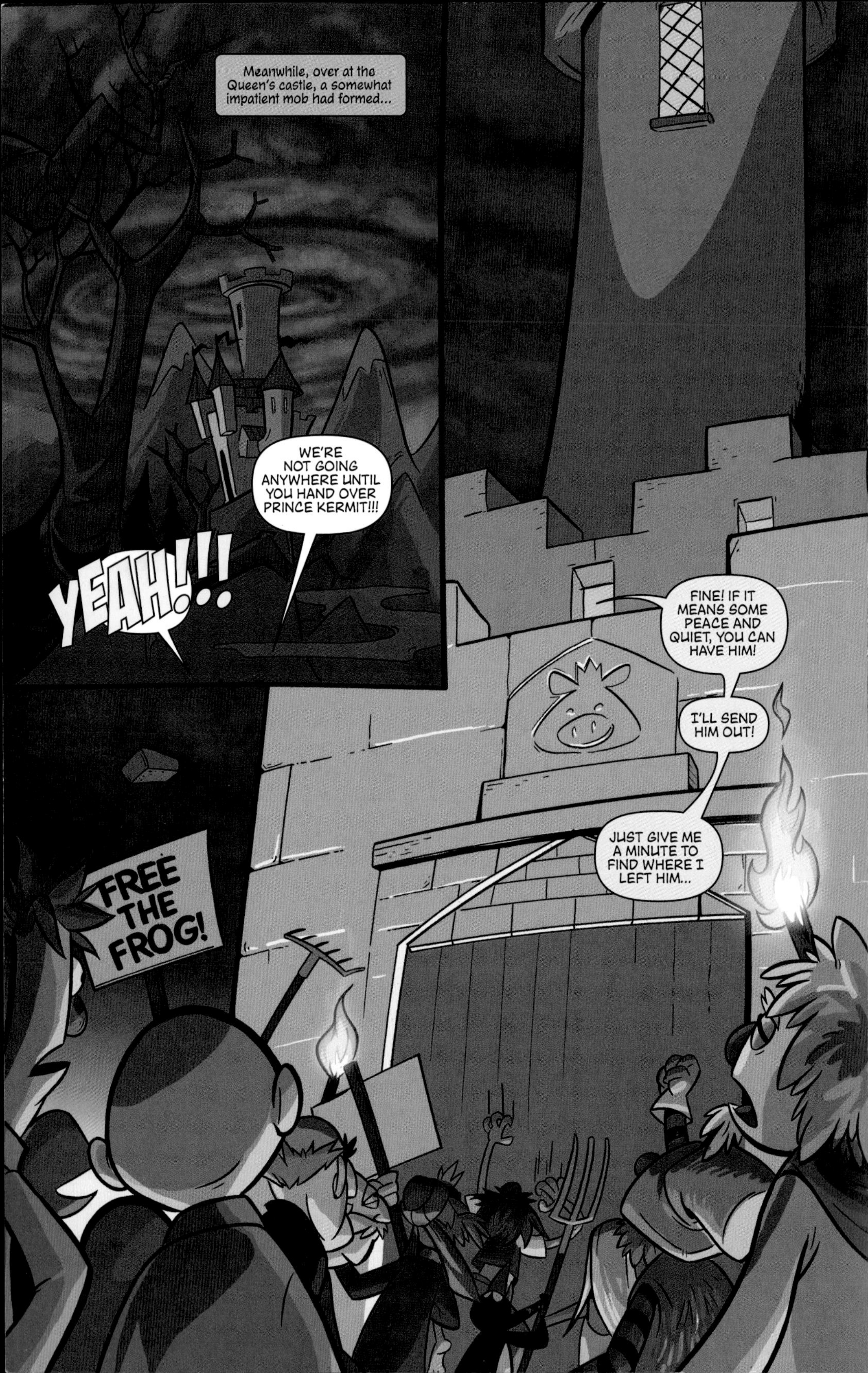

Meanwhile, over at the Queen's castle, a somewhat impatient mob had formed...
WE'RE NOT GOING ANYWHERE UNTIL YOU HAND OVER PRINCE KERMIT!!!
YEAH!!!
FINE! IF IT MEANS SOME PEACE AND QUIET, YOU CAN HAVE HIM!
I'LL SEND HIM OUT!
JUST GIVE ME A MINUTE TO FIND WHERE I LEFT HIM...
FREE THE FROG!

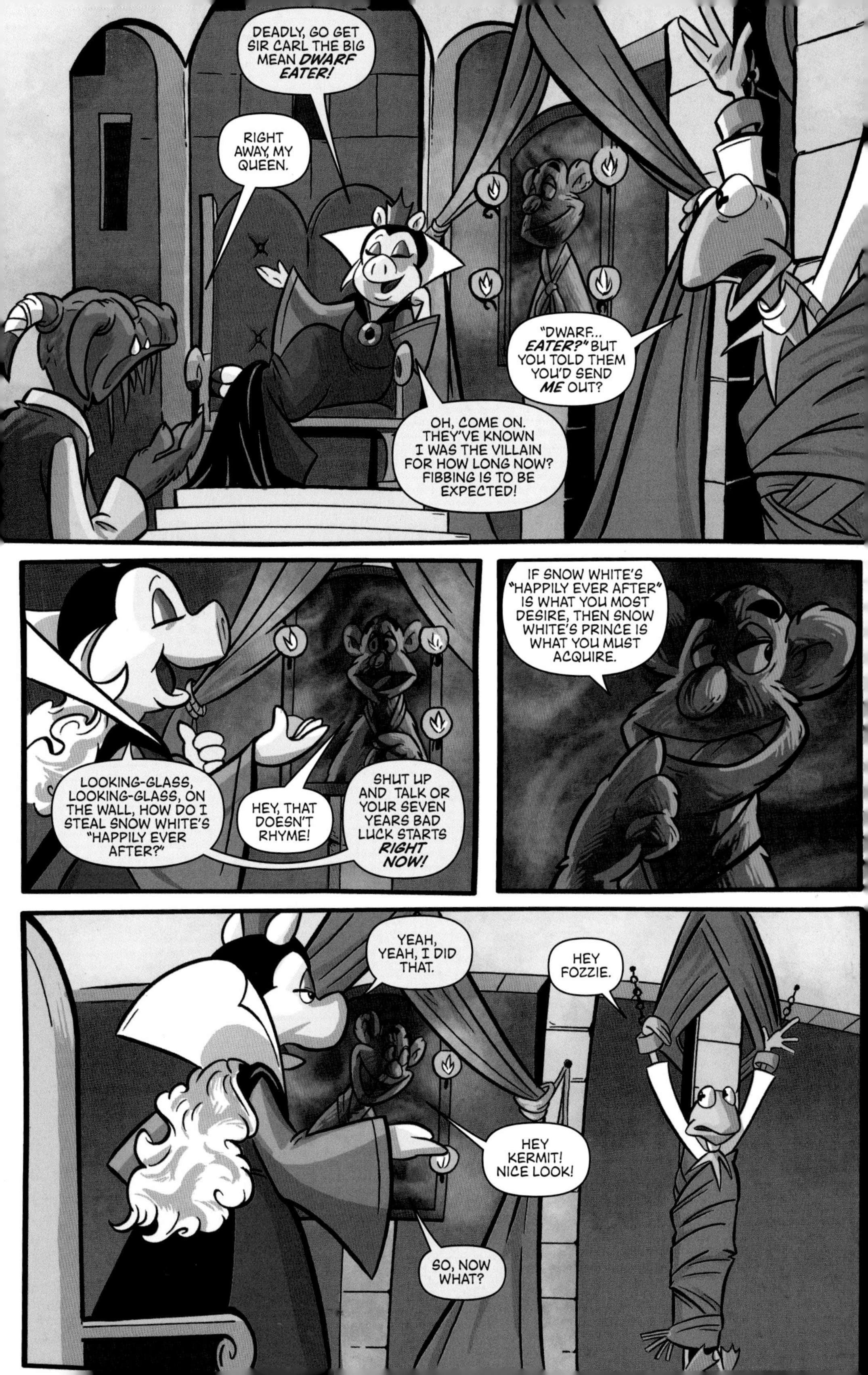
DEADLY, GO GET SIR CARL THE BIG MEAN DWARF EATER!
RIGHT AWAY, MY QUEEN.
"DWARF... EATER?" BUT YOU TOLD THEM YOU'D SEND ME OUT?
OH, COME ON. THEY'VE KNOWN I WAS THE VILLAIN FOR HOW LONG NOW? FIBBING IS TO BE EXPECTED!
LOOKING-GLASS, LOOKING-GLASS, ON THE WALL, HOW DO I STEAL SNOW WHITE'S "HAPPILY EVER AFTER?"
HEY, THAT DOESN'T RHYME!
SHUT UP AND TALK OR YOUR SEVEN YEARS BAD LUCK STARTS RIGHT NOW!
IF SNOW WHITE'S "HAPPILY EVER AFTER" IS WHAT YOU MOST DESIRE, THEN SNOW WHITE'S PRINCE IS WHAT YOU MUST ACQUIRE.
YEAH, YEAH, I DID THAT.
HEY FOZZIE.
HEY KERMIT! NICE LOOK!
SO, NOW WHAT?

WELL, NOW YOU MUST WALK DOWN THE AISLE AND CONVINCE HER PRINCE TO SAY "I DO", BUT THIS MIGHT TAKE A LITTLE WHILE, AS YOU WAIT FOR YOUR DIVORCE TO GO THROUGH.

DIVORCE? I'M MARRIED?!

TO WHO?! IS HE GOOD LOOKING?

OF COURSE, YOU'RE MARRIED; YOU'RE A QUEEN, WHO'S MARRIED TO A KING UNSEEN. WEIRD YOU HAVEN'T MET THE MAN, WHO'S SNOW WHITE'S DAD AND YOUR HUSBAND.

UGH, I HATE GETTING BACKSTORY IN THE FINAL ACT! KERMIE, WHY HAVEN'T I MET MY HUSBAND?

BECAUSE HE DIDN'T HAVE A PART IN THE ORIGINAL SCRIPT, SO WE NEVER BOTHERED TO CAST SOMEONE TO PLAY HIM.

WELL, YOU BETTER CAST SOMEONE QUICK, 'CAUSE I'VE GOT TO DIVORCE HIM!

AND KERMIE... MAKE SURE HE'S *REALLY* GOOD LOOKING.

HELLO... CENTRAL CASTING, I'M GONNA NEED A GOOD-LOOKING KING.

*REALLY* GOOD-LOOKING!

*REALLY* GOOD-LOOKING KING. NOT SO MUCH LOUIS XVI, A LITTLE MORE XIII, WITH A HINT OF XV. ALL OUT?

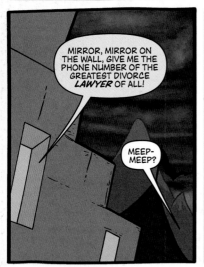

MIRROR, MIRROR ON THE WALL, GIVE ME THE PHONE NUMBER OF THE GREATEST DIVORCE *LAWYER* OF ALL!

MEEP-MEEP?

TOO TRUE, TOO TRUE, BUT IF *WE* DON'T GIVE SNOW WHITE HER "HAPPILY EVER AFTER," THIS STORY MAY *NEVER END!*

GAK!

NEVER... END...?

WHAT'S WRONG GRUMPIER?!

THIS STORY MAY NOT END, BUT THAT WON'T STOP HIM FROM CHECKING OUT ANY WAY HE CAN.

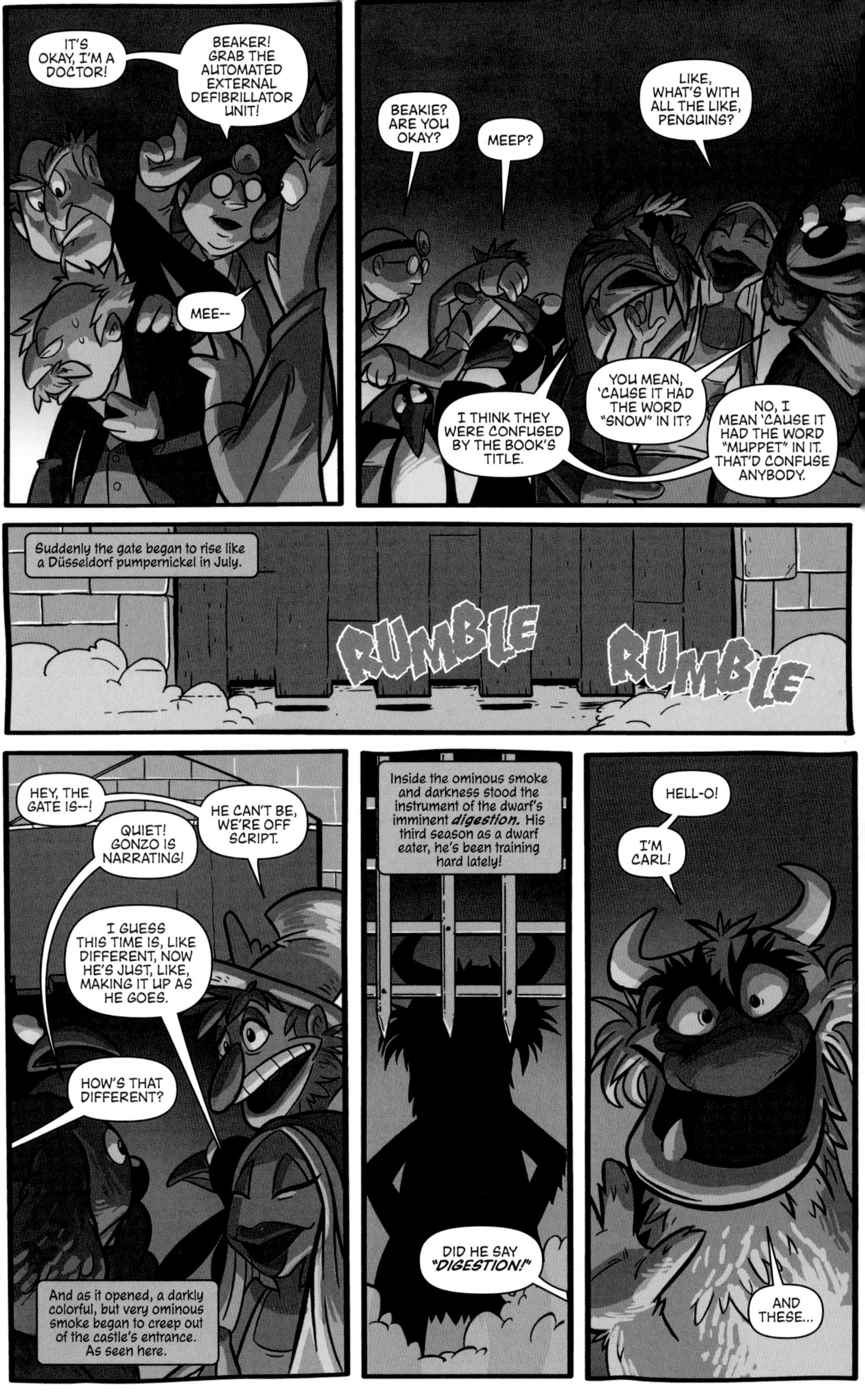
IT'S OKAY, I'M A DOCTOR!
BEAKER! GRAB THE AUTOMATED EXTERNAL DEFIBRILLATOR UNIT!
MEE--
BEAKIE? ARE YOU OKAY?
MEEP?
LIKE, WHAT'S WITH ALL THE LIKE, PENGUINS?
I THINK THEY WERE CONFUSED BY THE BOOK'S TITLE.
YOU MEAN, 'CAUSE IT HAD THE WORD "SNOW" IN IT?
NO, I MEAN 'CAUSE IT HAD THE WORD "MUPPET" IN IT. THAT'D CONFUSE ANYBODY.
Suddenly the gate began to rise like a Düsseldorf pumpernickel in July.
RUMBLE
RUMBLE
HEY, THE GATE IS--!
HE CAN'T BE, WE'RE OFF SCRIPT.
QUIET! GONZO IS NARRATING!
I GUESS THIS TIME IS, LIKE DIFFERENT, NOW HE'S JUST, LIKE, MAKING IT UP AS HE GOES.
HOW'S THAT DIFFERENT?
And as it opened, a darkly colorful, but very ominous smoke began to creep out of the castle's entrance. As seen here.
Inside the ominous smoke and darkness stood the instrument of the dwarf's imminent *digestion.* His third season as a dwarf eater, he's been training hard lately!
DID HE SAY *"DIGESTION!"*
HELL-O!
I'M CARL!
AND THESE...

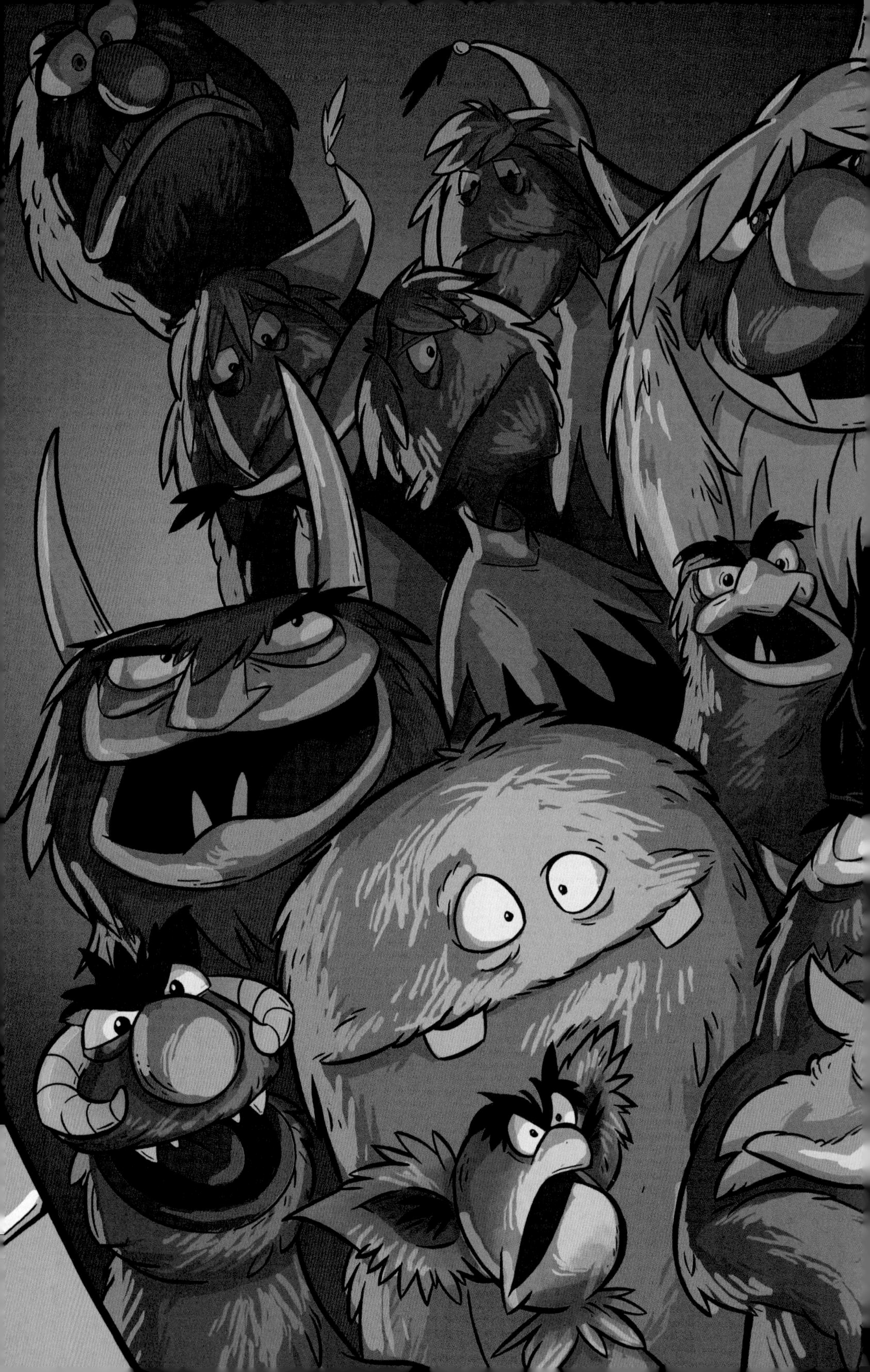

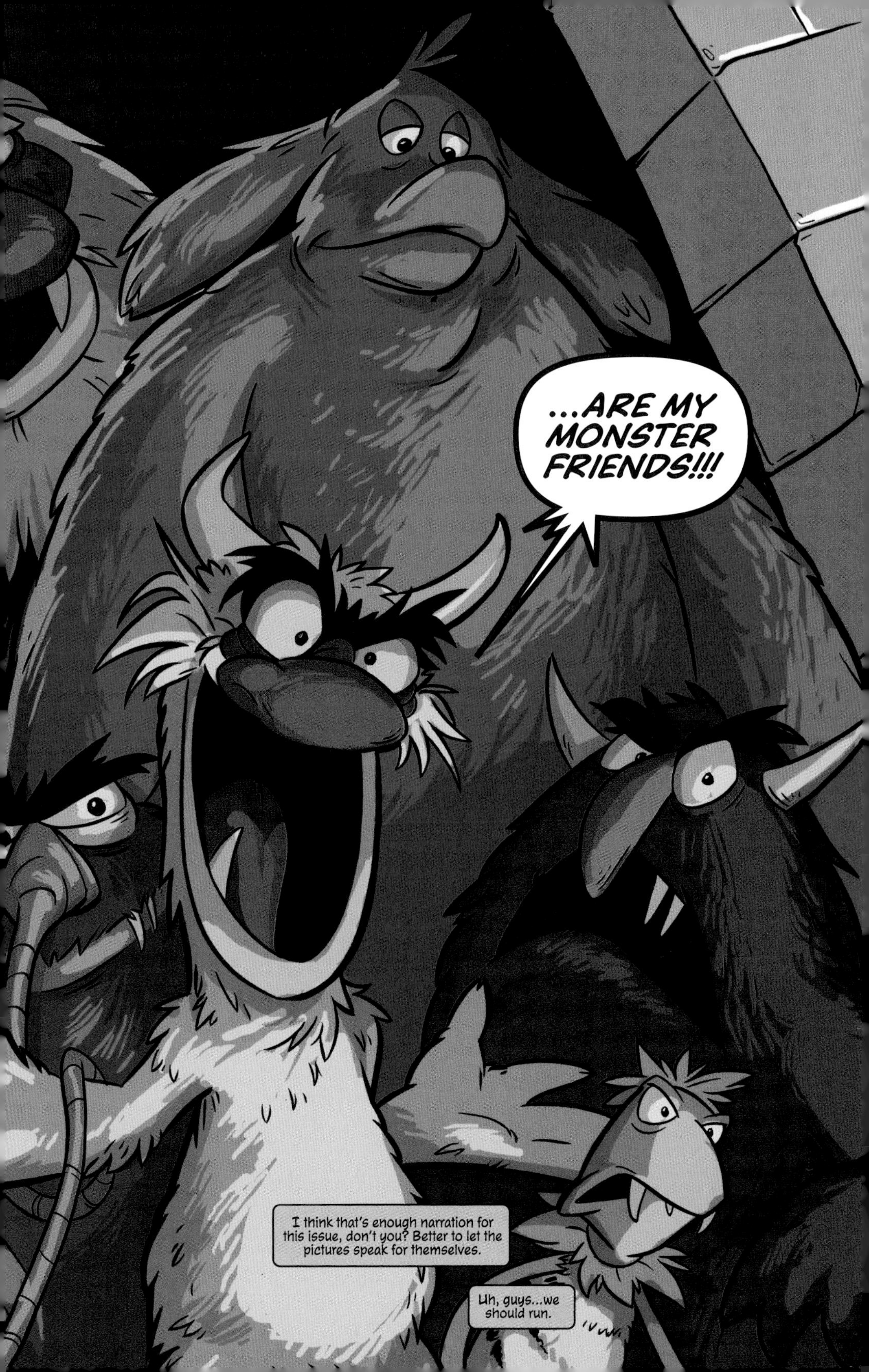
...ARE MY MONSTER FRIENDS!!!
I think that's enough narration for this issue, don't you? Better to let the pictures speak for themselves.
Uh, guys...we should run.

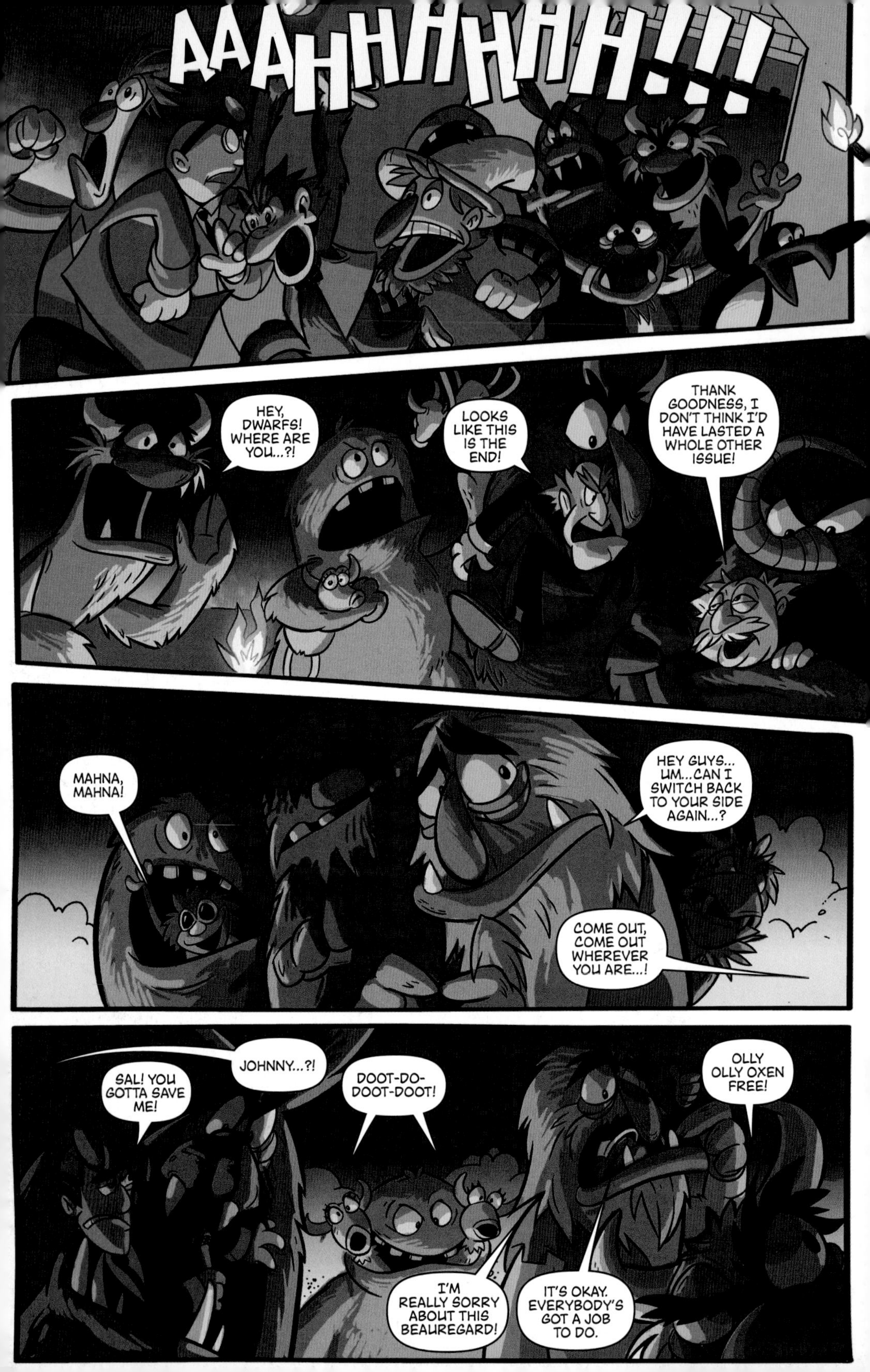
AAAHHHHHHH!!!
HEY, DWARFS! WHERE ARE YOU...?!
LOOKS LIKE THIS IS THE END!
THANK GOODNESS, I DON'T THINK I'D HAVE LASTED A WHOLE OTHER ISSUE!
MAHNA, MAHNA!
HEY GUYS... UM...CAN I SWITCH BACK TO YOUR SIDE AGAIN...?
COME OUT, COME OUT WHEREVER YOU ARE...!
SAL! YOU GOTTA SAVE ME!
JOHNNY...?!
DOOT-DO-DOOT-DOOT!
OLLY OLLY OXEN FREE!
I'M REALLY SORRY ABOUT THIS BEAUREGARD!
IT'S OKAY. EVERYBODY'S GOT A JOB TO DO.

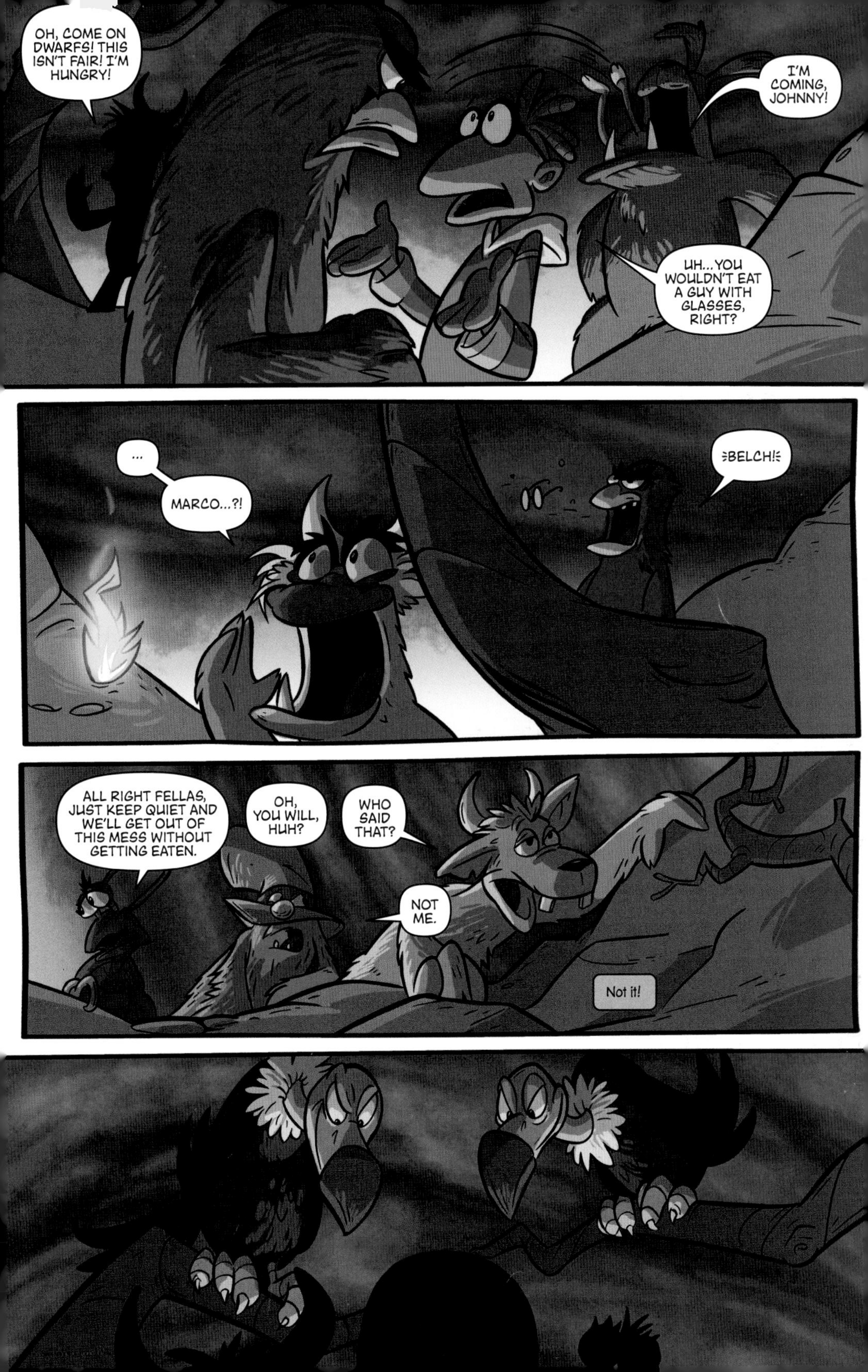
OH, COME ON DWARFS! THIS ISN'T FAIR! I'M HUNGRY!
I'M COMING, JOHNNY!
UH... YOU WOULDN'T EAT A GUY WITH GLASSES, RIGHT?
...
MARCO...?!
BELCH!
ALL RIGHT FELLAS, JUST KEEP QUIET AND WE'LL GET OUT OF THIS MESS WITHOUT GETTING EATEN.
OH, YOU WILL, HUH?
WHO SAID THAT?
NOT ME.
Not it!

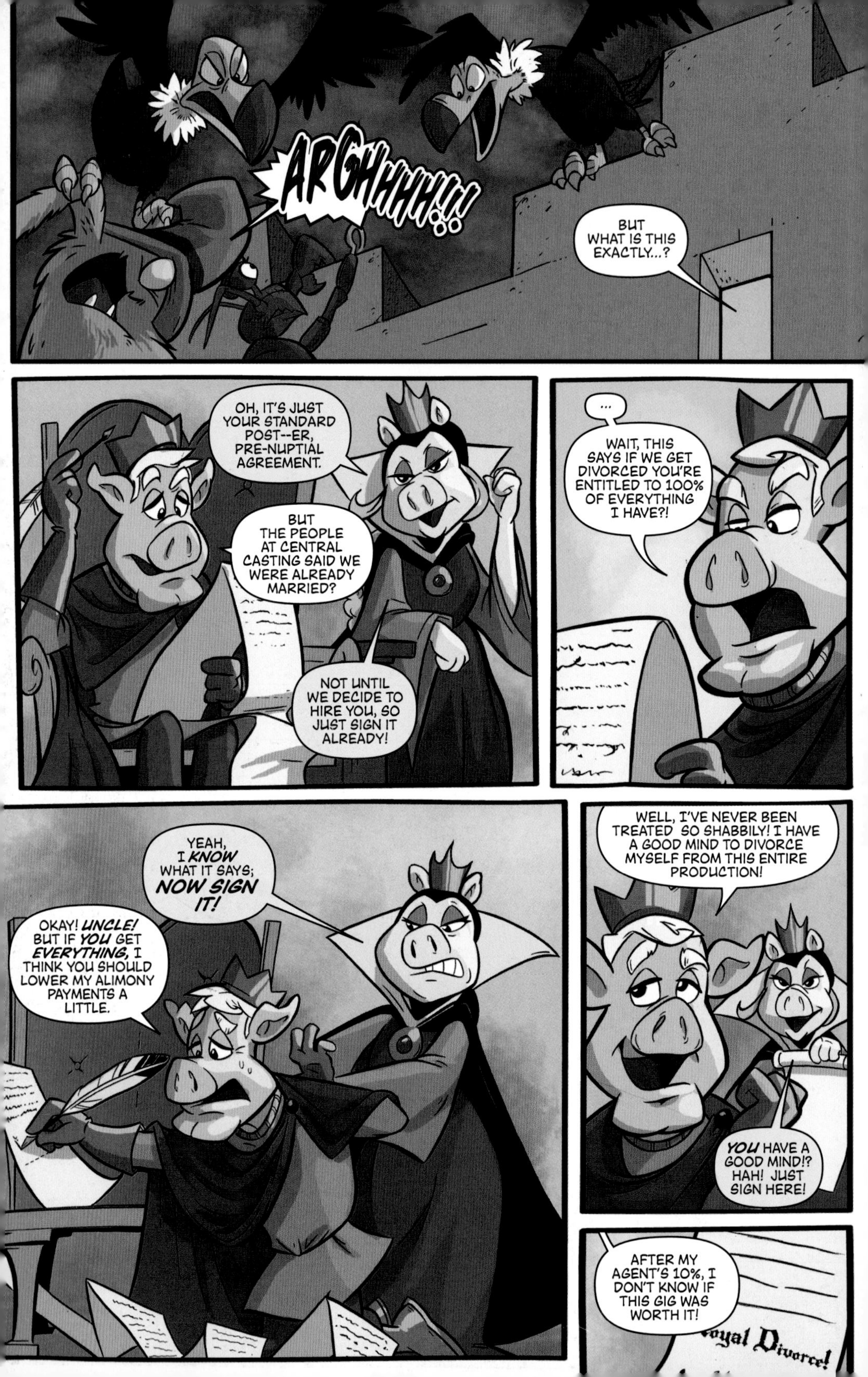
ARGHHHHH!!!
BUT WHAT IS THIS EXACTLY...?
OH, IT'S JUST YOUR STANDARD POST--ER, PRE-NUPTIAL AGREEMENT.
BUT THE PEOPLE AT CENTRAL CASTING SAID WE WERE ALREADY MARRIED?
NOT UNTIL WE DECIDE TO HIRE YOU, SO JUST SIGN IT ALREADY!
...
WAIT, THIS SAYS IF WE GET DIVORCED YOU'RE ENTITLED TO 100% OF EVERYTHING I HAVE?!
YEAH, I *KNOW* WHAT IT SAYS; ***NOW SIGN IT!***
OKAY! ***UNCLE!*** BUT IF ***YOU*** GET ***EVERYTHING,*** I THINK YOU SHOULD LOWER MY ALIMONY PAYMENTS A LITTLE.
WELL, I'VE NEVER BEEN TREATED SO SHABBILY! I HAVE A GOOD MIND TO DIVORCE MYSELF FROM THIS ENTIRE PRODUCTION!
***YOU*** HAVE A GOOD MIND!? HAH! JUST SIGN HERE!
AFTER MY AGENT'S 10%, I DON'T KNOW IF THIS GIG WAS WORTH IT!
...oyal Divorce!

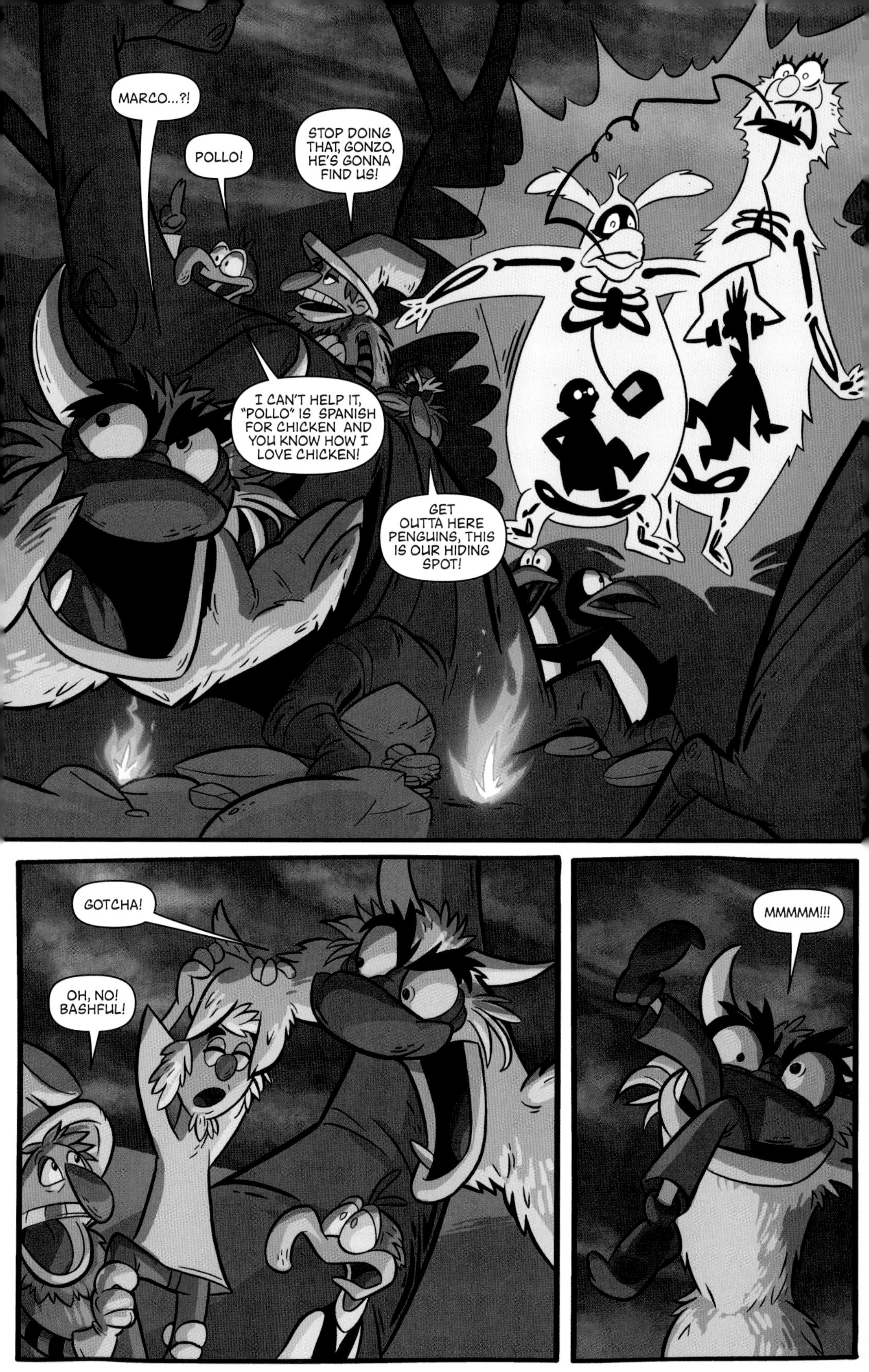
MARCO...?!
POLLO!
STOP DOING THAT, GONZO, HE'S GONNA FIND US!
I CAN'T HELP IT, "POLLO" IS SPANISH FOR CHICKEN AND YOU KNOW HOW I LOVE CHICKEN!
GET OUTTA HERE PENGUINS, THIS IS OUR HIDING SPOT!
GOTCHA!
OH, NO! BASHFUL!
MMMMM!!!

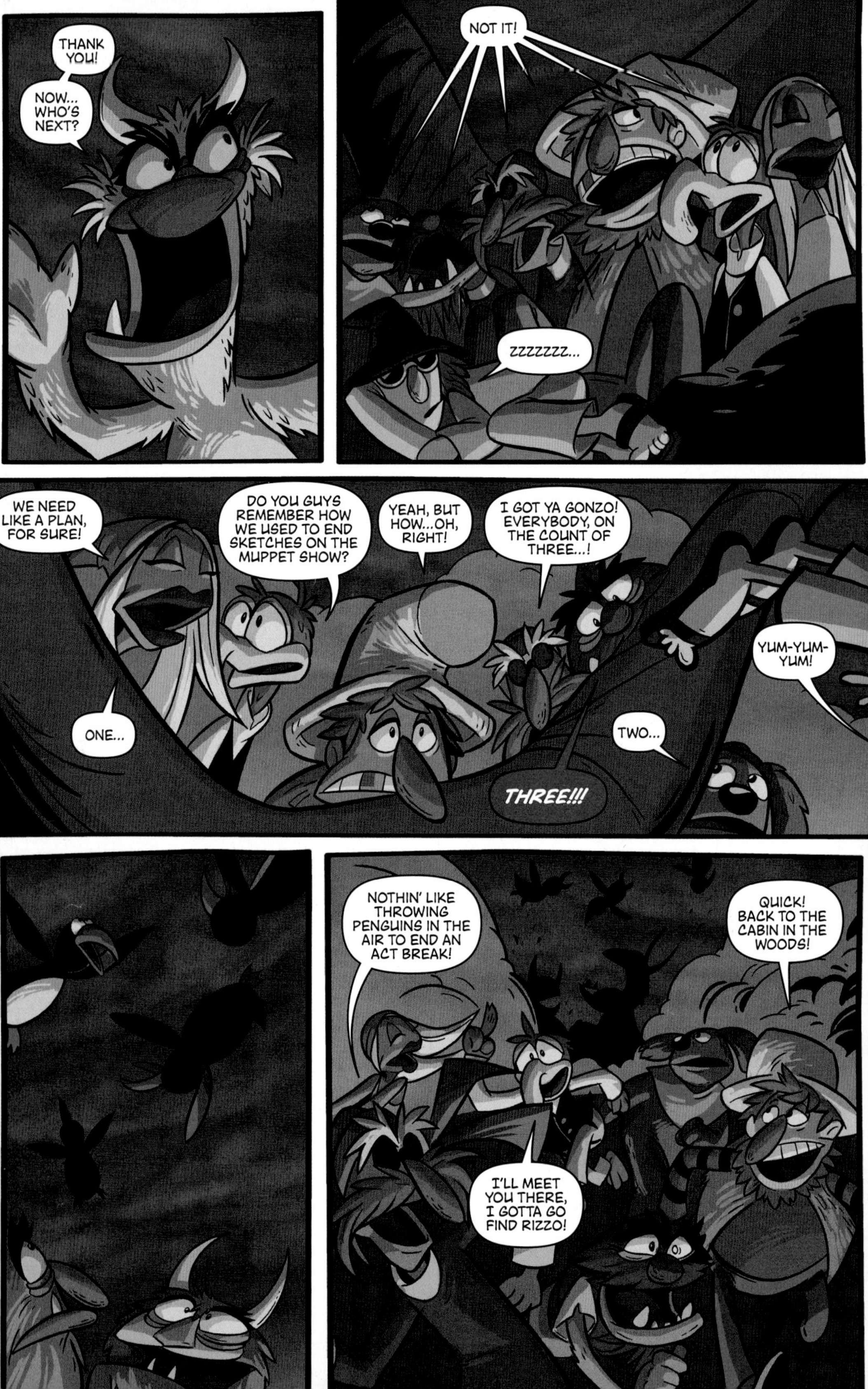
THANK YOU!
NOW... WHO'S NEXT?
NOT IT!
ZZZZZZZ...
WE NEED LIKE A PLAN, FOR SURE!
DO YOU GUYS REMEMBER HOW WE USED TO END SKETCHES ON THE MUPPET SHOW?
YEAH, BUT HOW...OH, RIGHT!
I GOT YA GONZO! EVERYBODY, ON THE COUNT OF THREE...!
ONE...
TWO...
YUM-YUM-YUM!
THREE!!!
NOTHIN' LIKE THROWING PENGUINS IN THE AIR TO END AN ACT BREAK!
QUICK! BACK TO THE CABIN IN THE WOODS!
I'LL MEET YOU THERE, I GOTTA GO FIND RIZZO!

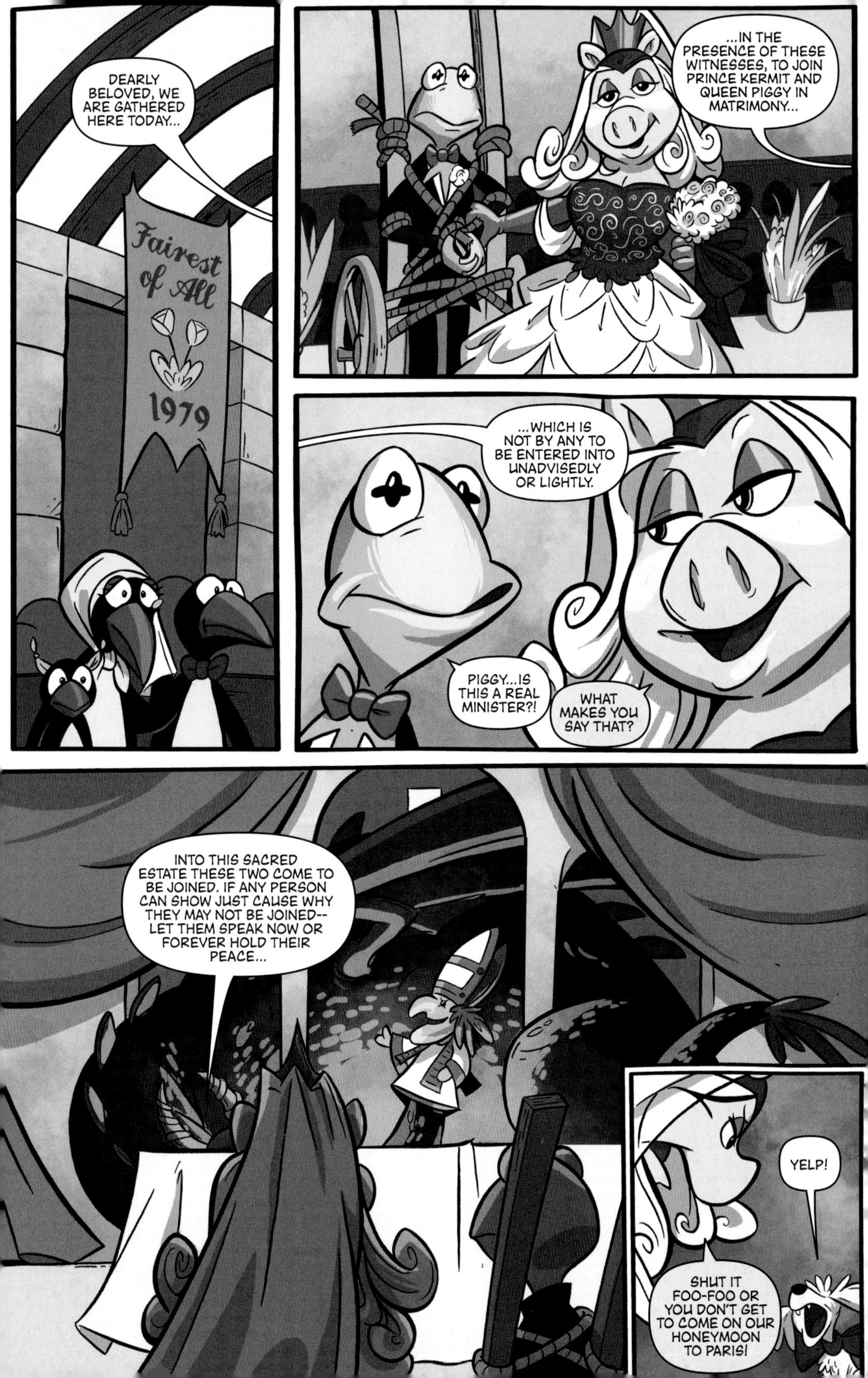
DEARLY BELOVED, WE ARE GATHERED HERE TODAY...
Fairest of All
1979
...IN THE PRESENCE OF THESE WITNESSES, TO JOIN PRINCE KERMIT AND QUEEN PIGGY IN MATRIMONY...
...WHICH IS NOT BY ANY TO BE ENTERED INTO UNADVISEDLY OR LIGHTLY.
PIGGY...IS THIS A REAL MINISTER?!
WHAT MAKES YOU SAY THAT?
INTO THIS SACRED ESTATE THESE TWO COME TO BE JOINED. IF ANY PERSON CAN SHOW JUST CAUSE WHY THEY MAY NOT BE JOINED-- LET THEM SPEAK NOW OR FOREVER HOLD THEIR PEACE...
YELP!
SHUT IT FOO-FOO OR YOU DON'T GET TO COME ON OUR HONEYMOON TO PARIS!

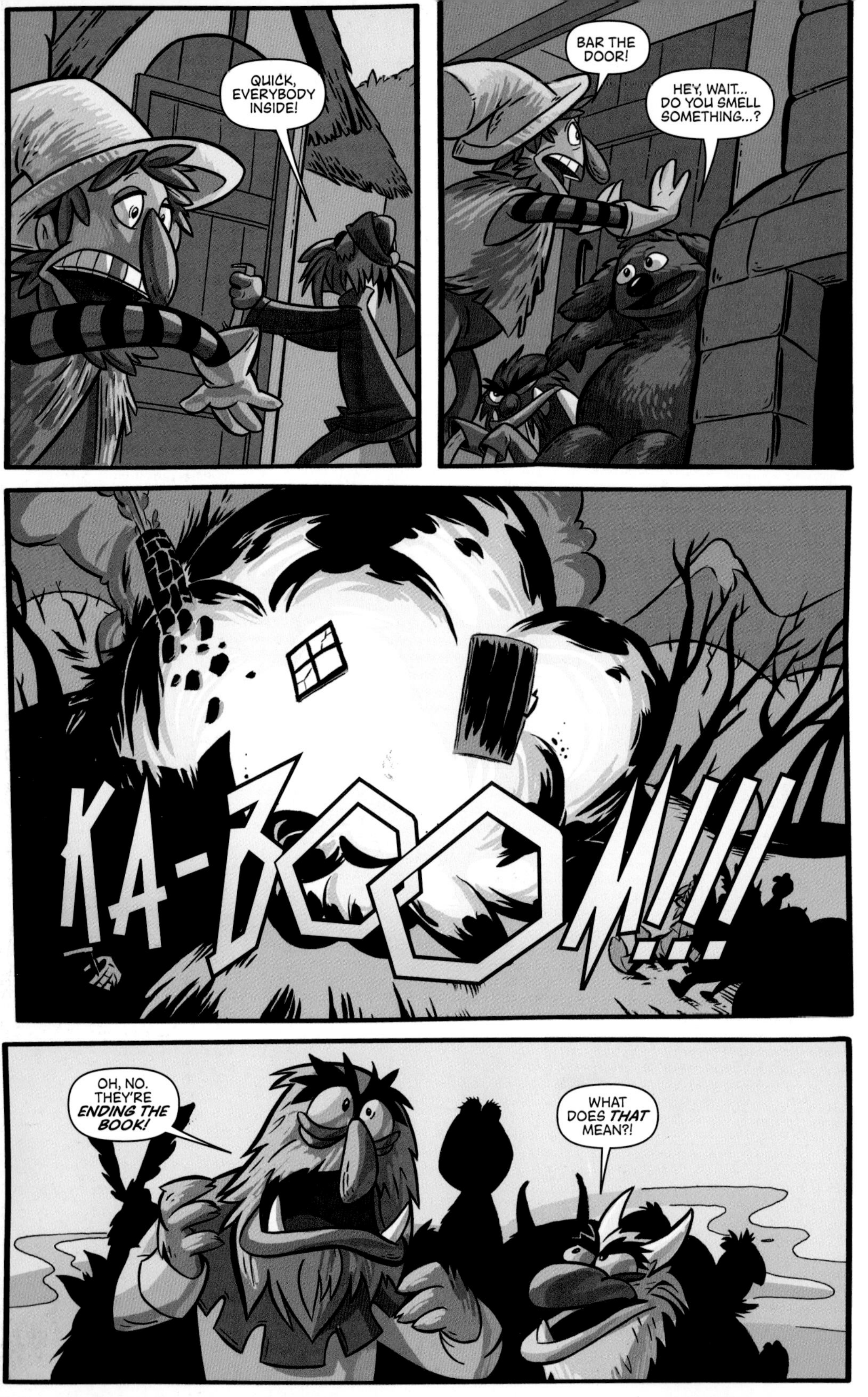
QUICK, EVERYBODY INSIDE!
BAR THE DOOR!
HEY, WAIT... DO YOU SMELL SOMETHING...?
KA-BOOM!!!
OH, NO. THEY'RE *ENDING THE BOOK!*
WHAT DOES *THAT* MEAN?!

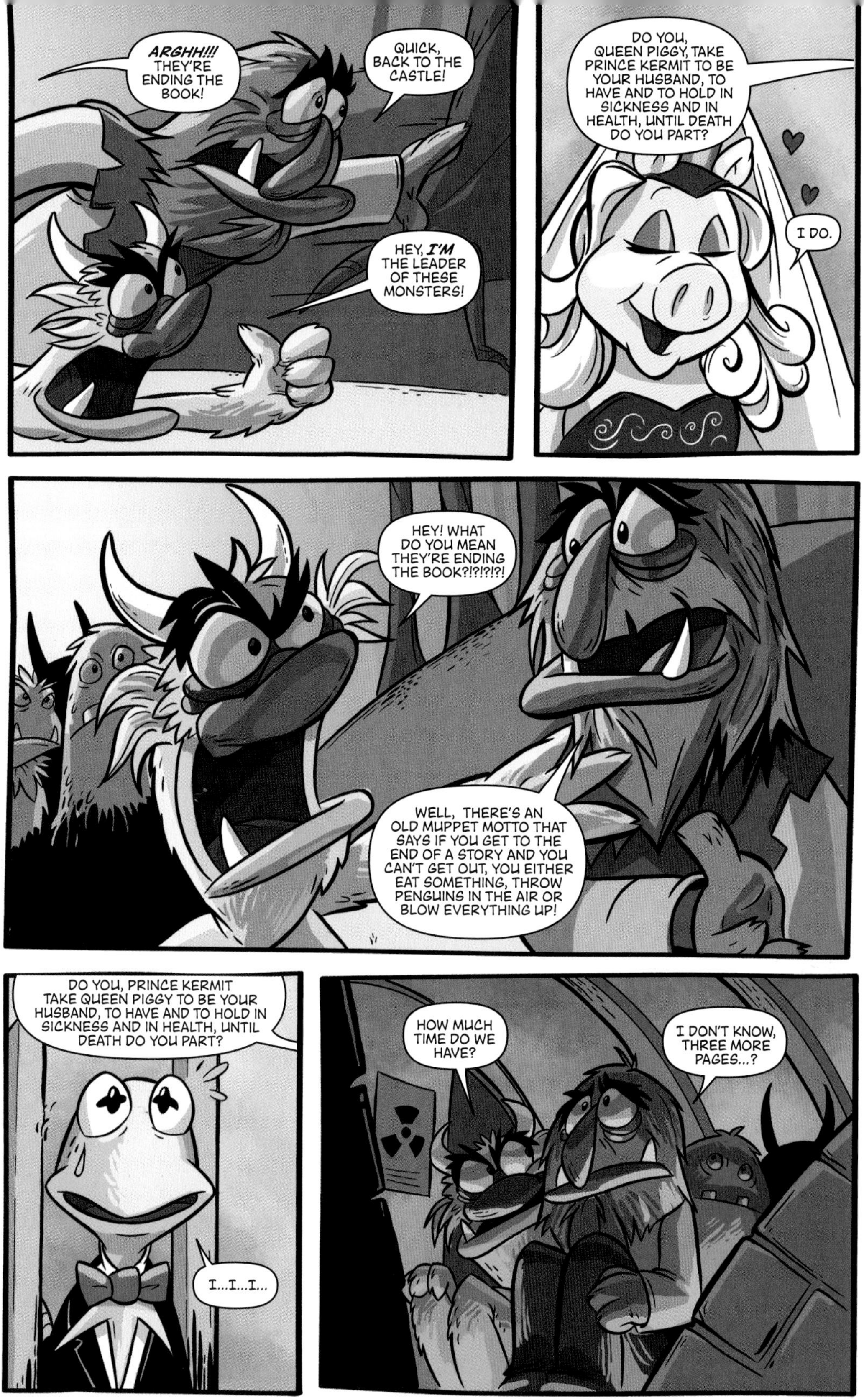
ARGHH!!! THEY'RE ENDING THE BOOK!
QUICK, BACK TO THE CASTLE!
HEY, I'M THE LEADER OF THESE MONSTERS!
DO YOU, QUEEN PIGGY, TAKE PRINCE KERMIT TO BE YOUR HUSBAND, TO HAVE AND TO HOLD IN SICKNESS AND IN HEALTH, UNTIL DEATH DO YOU PART?
I DO.
HEY! WHAT DO YOU MEAN THEY'RE ENDING THE BOOK?!?!?!?!
WELL, THERE'S AN OLD MUPPET MOTTO THAT SAYS IF YOU GET TO THE END OF A STORY AND YOU CAN'T GET OUT, YOU EITHER EAT SOMETHING, THROW PENGUINS IN THE AIR OR BLOW EVERYTHING UP!
DO YOU, PRINCE KERMIT TAKE QUEEN PIGGY TO BE YOUR HUSBAND, TO HAVE AND TO HOLD IN SICKNESS AND IN HEALTH, UNTIL DEATH DO YOU PART?
I...I...I...
HOW MUCH TIME DO WE HAVE?
I DON'T KNOW, THREE MORE PAGES...?

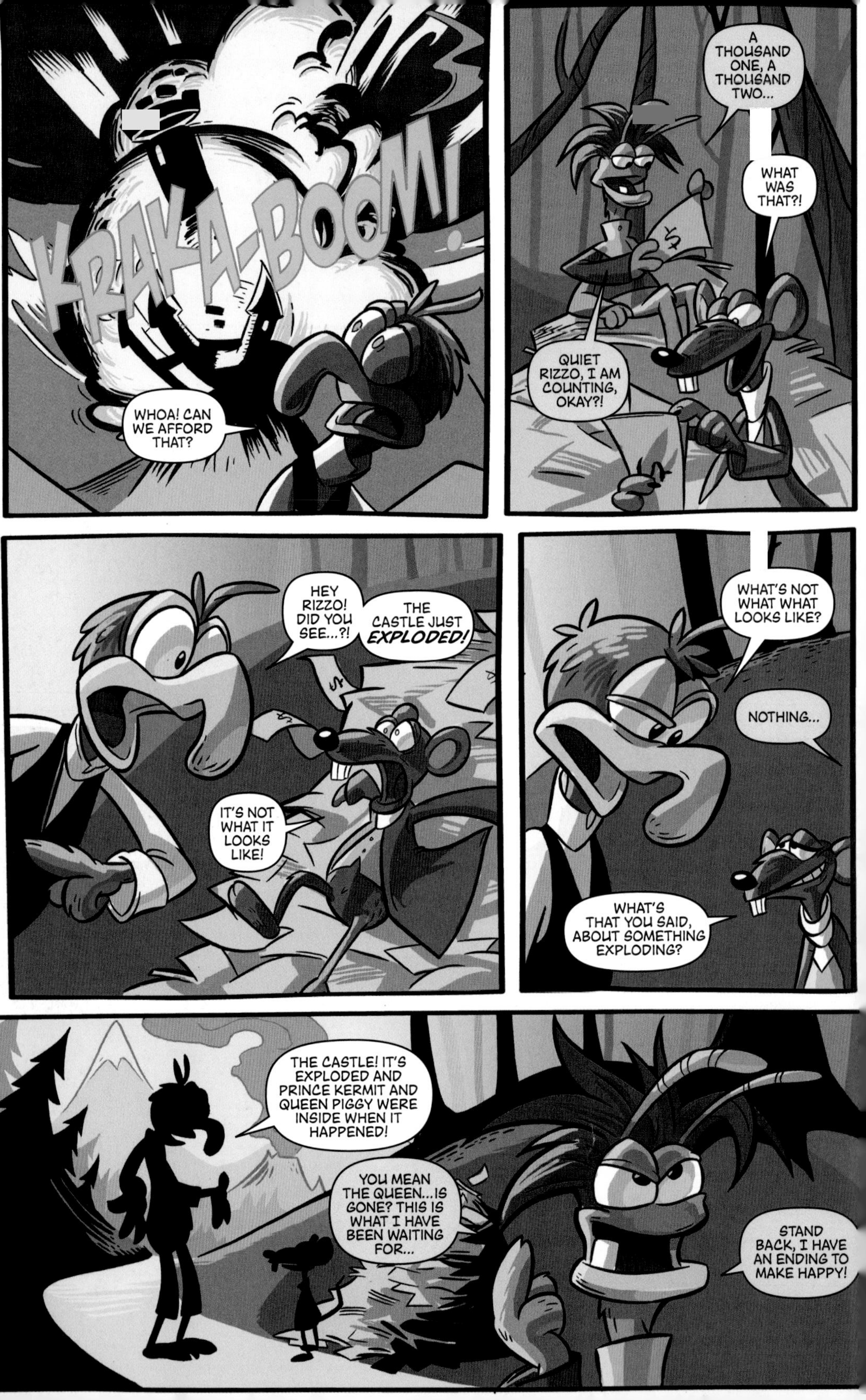
KRAKA-BOOM!
WHOA! CAN WE AFFORD THAT?
A THOUSAND ONE, A THOUSAND TWO...
WHAT WAS THAT?!
QUIET RIZZO, I AM COUNTING, OKAY?!
HEY RIZZO! DID YOU SEE...?!
THE CASTLE JUST *EXPLODED!*
IT'S NOT WHAT IT LOOKS LIKE!
WHAT'S NOT WHAT WHAT LOOKS LIKE?
NOTHING...
WHAT'S THAT YOU SAID, ABOUT SOMETHING EXPLODING?
THE CASTLE! IT'S EXPLODED AND PRINCE KERMIT AND QUEEN PIGGY WERE INSIDE WHEN IT HAPPENED!
YOU MEAN THE QUEEN...IS GONE? THIS IS WHAT I HAVE BEEN WAITING FOR...
STAND BACK, I HAVE AN ENDING TO MAKE HAPPY!

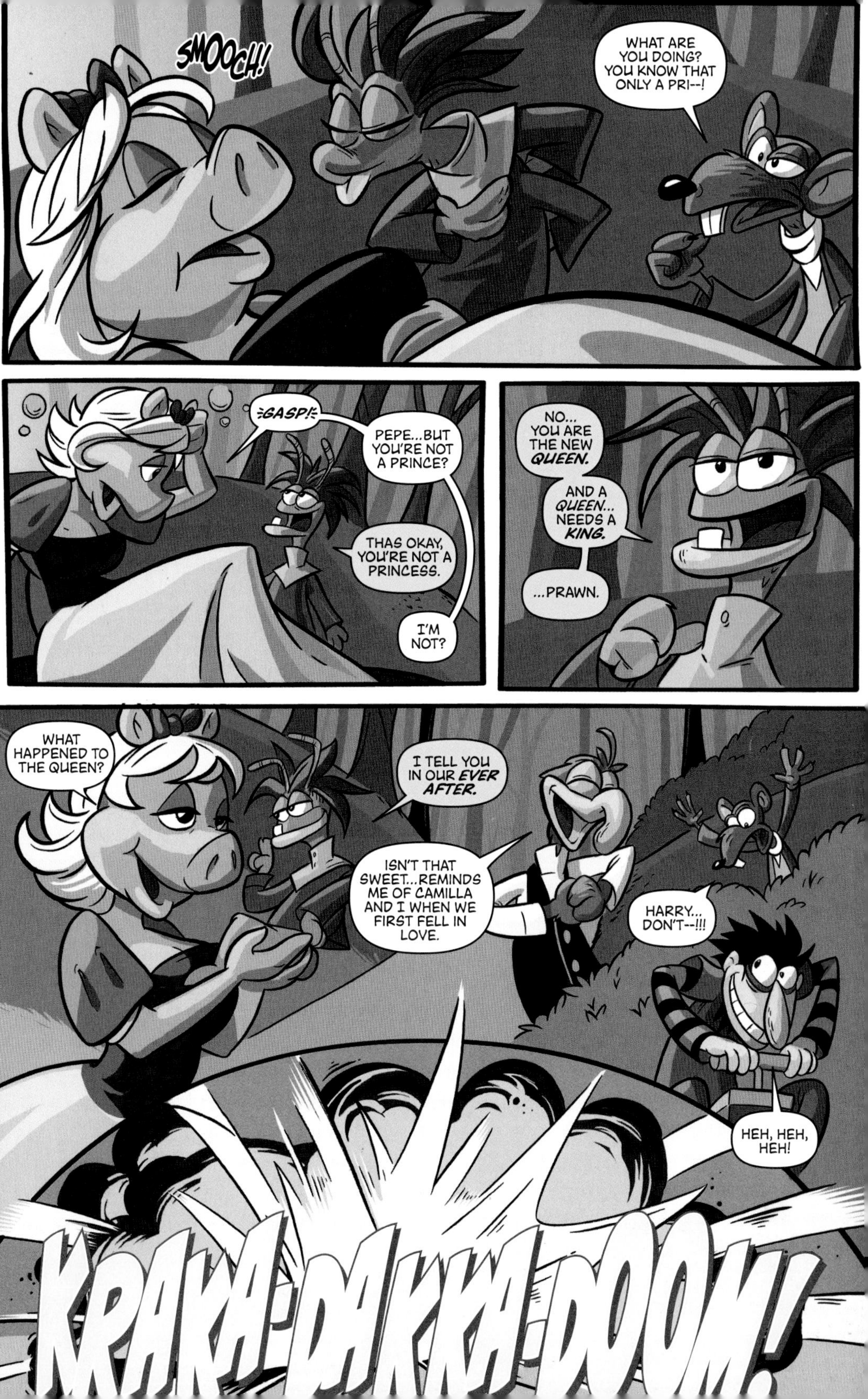
SMOOCH!
WHAT ARE YOU DOING? YOU KNOW THAT ONLY A PRI--!
GASP!
PEPE...BUT YOU'RE NOT A PRINCE?
THAS OKAY, YOU'RE NOT A PRINCESS.
I'M NOT?
NO... YOU ARE THE NEW QUEEN.
AND A QUEEN... NEEDS A KING.
...PRAWN.
WHAT HAPPENED TO THE QUEEN?
I TELL YOU IN OUR EVER AFTER.
ISN'T THAT SWEET...REMINDS ME OF CAMILLA AND I WHEN WE FIRST FELL IN LOVE.
HARRY... DON'T--!!!
HEH, HEH, HEH!
KRAKA-DAKKA-DOOM!

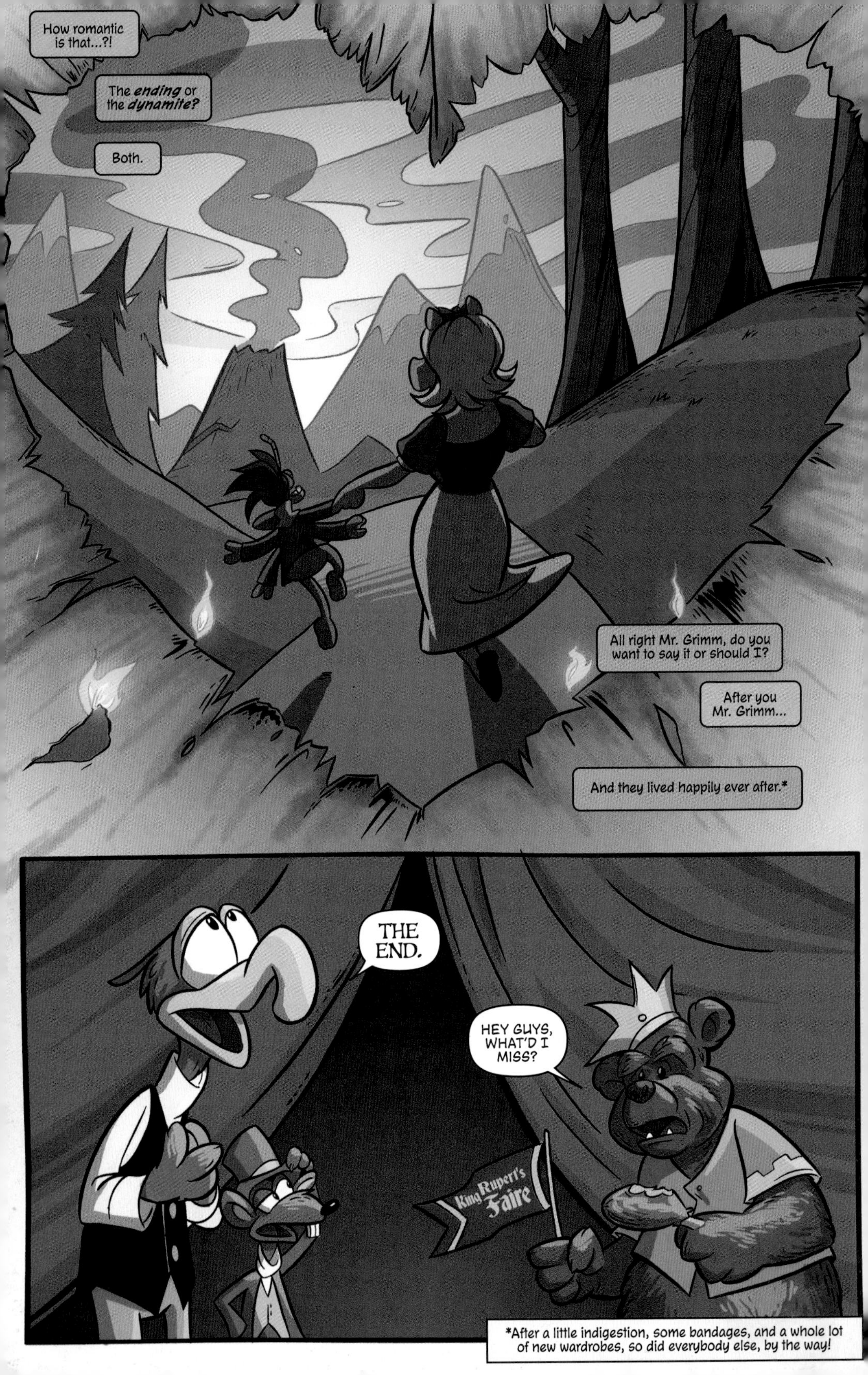
How romantic is that...?!
The *ending* or the *dynamite?*
Both.
All right Mr. Grimm, do you want to say it or should I?
After you Mr. Grimm...
And they lived happily ever after.*
THE END.
HEY GUYS, WHAT'D I MISS?
King Rupert's Faire
*After a little indigestion, some bandages, and a whole lot of new wardrobes, so did everybody else, by the way!

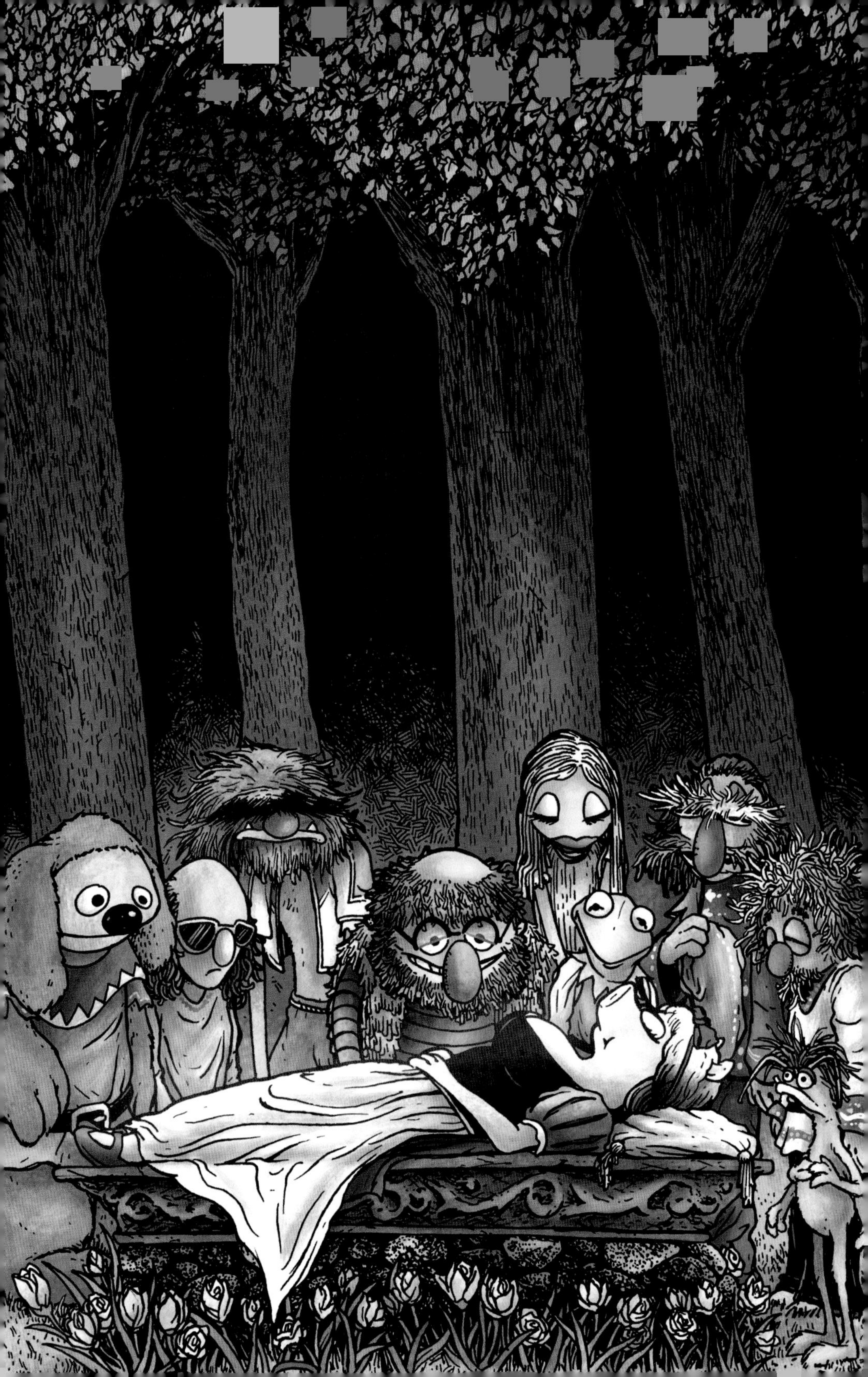

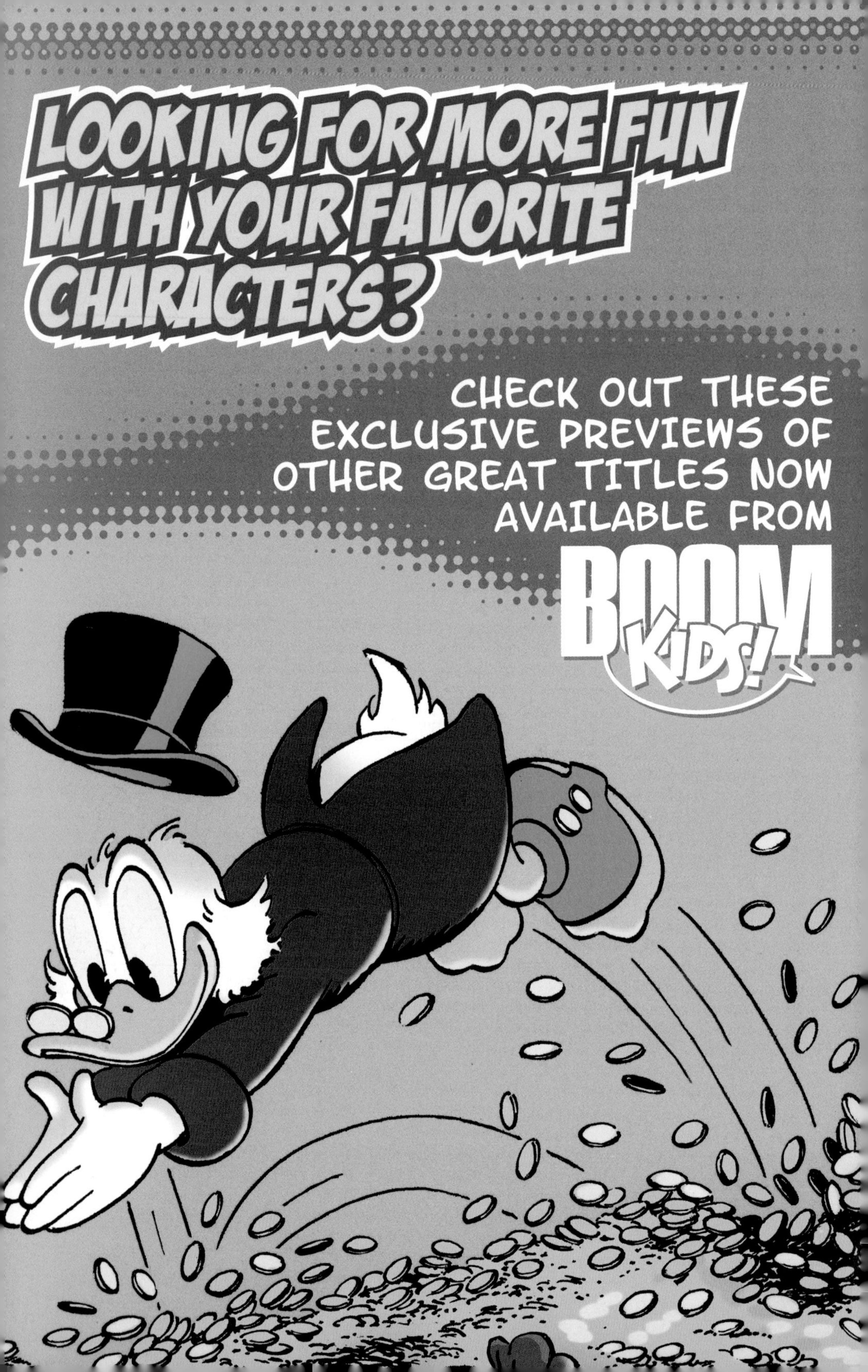
LOOKING FOR MORE FUN WITH YOUR FAVORITE CHARACTERS?
CHECK OUT THESE EXCLUSIVE PREVIEWS OF OTHER GREAT TITLES NOW AVAILABLE FROM
BOOM KIDS!

It's time to meet the Muppets once again! Join Kermit, Fozzie, Gonzo, Miss Piggy and the rest of the gang for a hilarious collection of madcap skits and gags perfect for new and old fans alike!

THE MUPPET SHOW: MEET THE MUPPETS
DIAMOND CODE: MAY090750
SC $9.99 ISBN 9781934506851
HC $24.99 ISBN 9781608865277

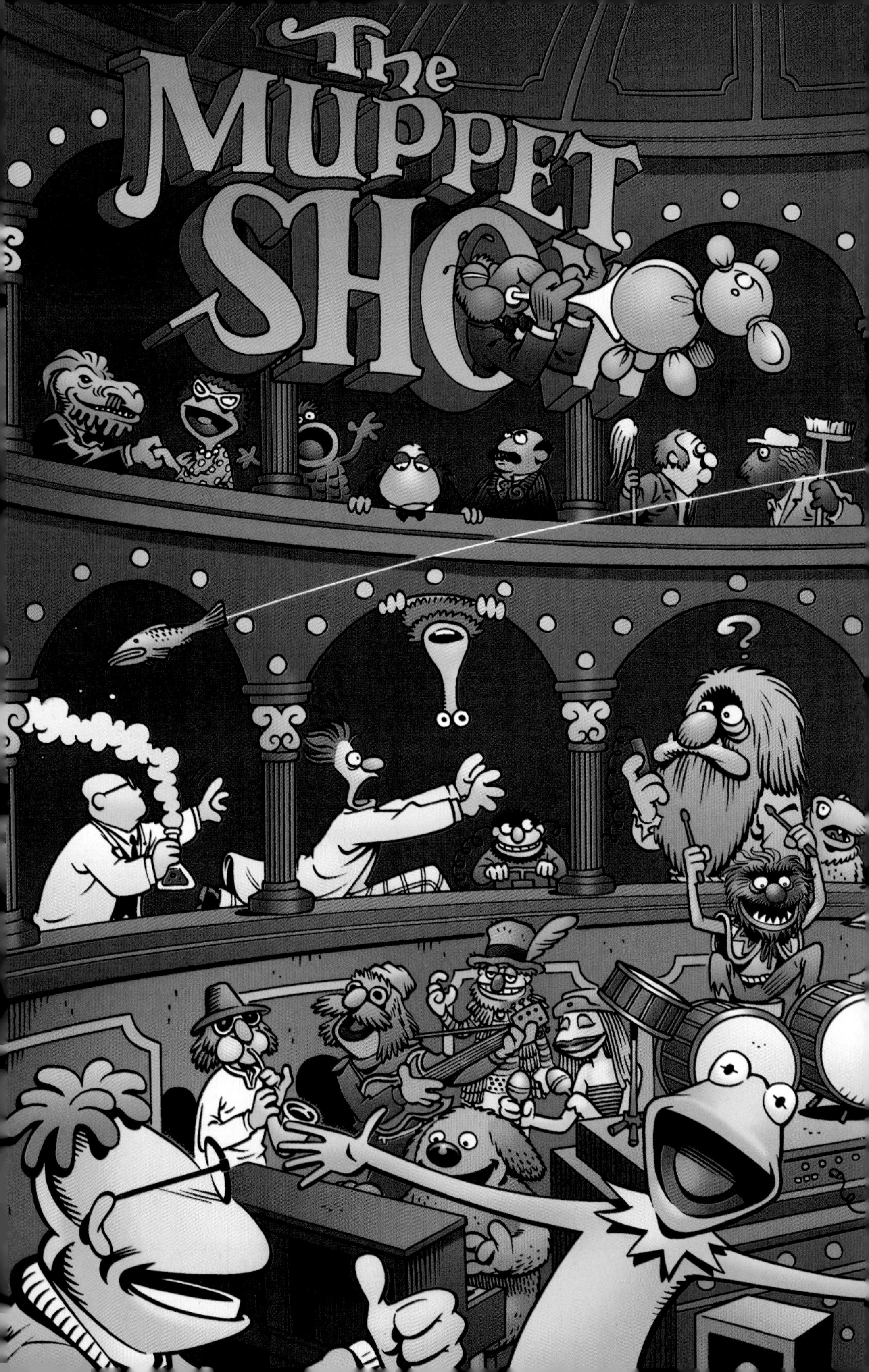

The
MUPPET
SHO
?

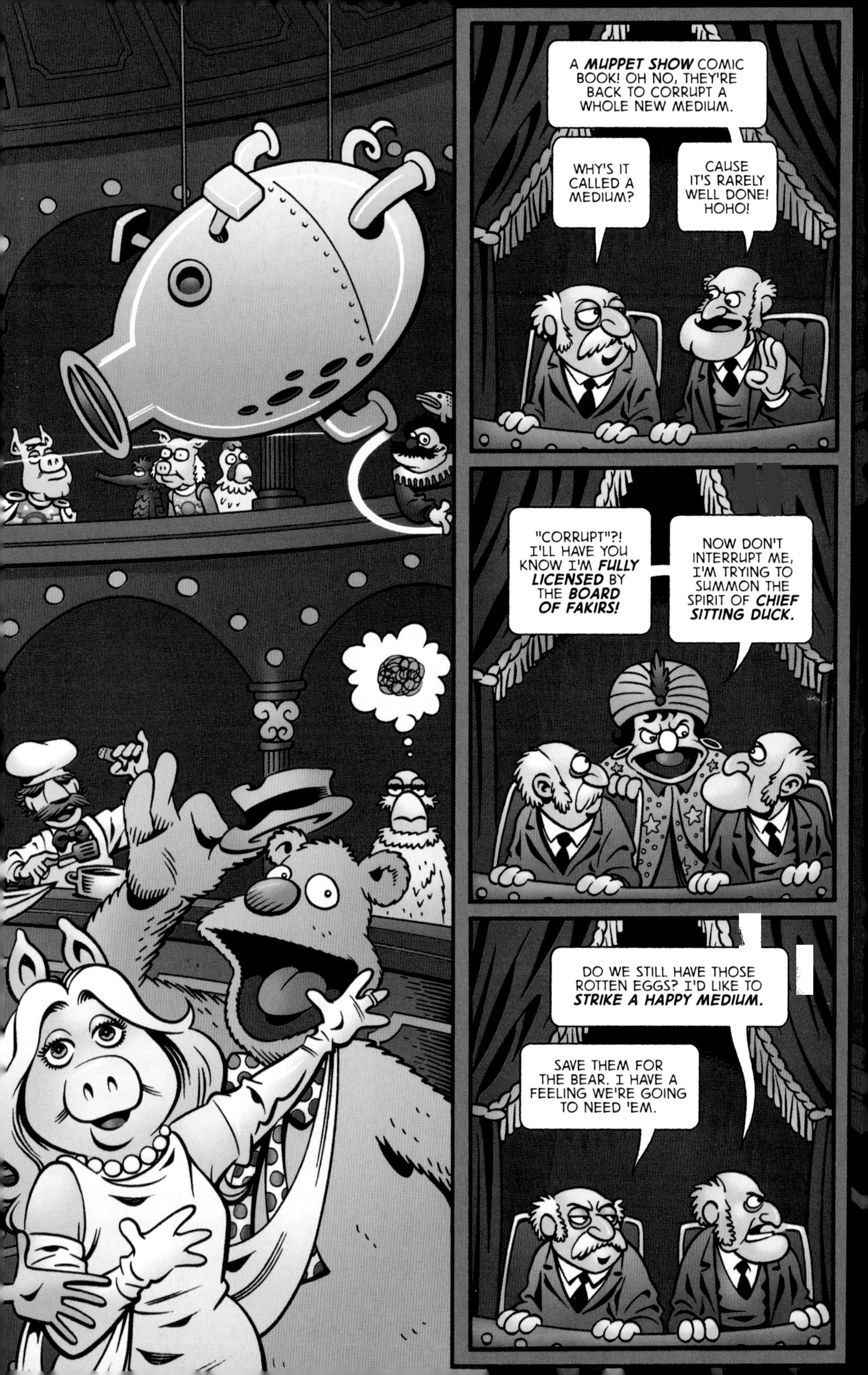
A ***MUPPET SHOW*** COMIC BOOK! OH NO, THEY'RE BACK TO CORRUPT A WHOLE NEW MEDIUM.
WHY'S IT CALLED A MEDIUM?
CAUSE IT'S RARELY WELL DONE! HOHO!
"CORRUPT"?! I'LL HAVE YOU KNOW I'M ***FULLY LICENSED*** BY THE ***BOARD OF FAKIRS!***
NOW DON'T INTERRUPT ME, I'M TRYING TO SUMMON THE SPIRIT OF ***CHIEF SITTING DUCK.***
DO WE STILL HAVE THOSE ROTTEN EGGS? I'D LIKE TO ***STRIKE A HAPPY MEDIUM.***
SAVE THEM FOR THE BEAR. I HAVE A FEELING WE'RE GOING TO NEED 'EM.

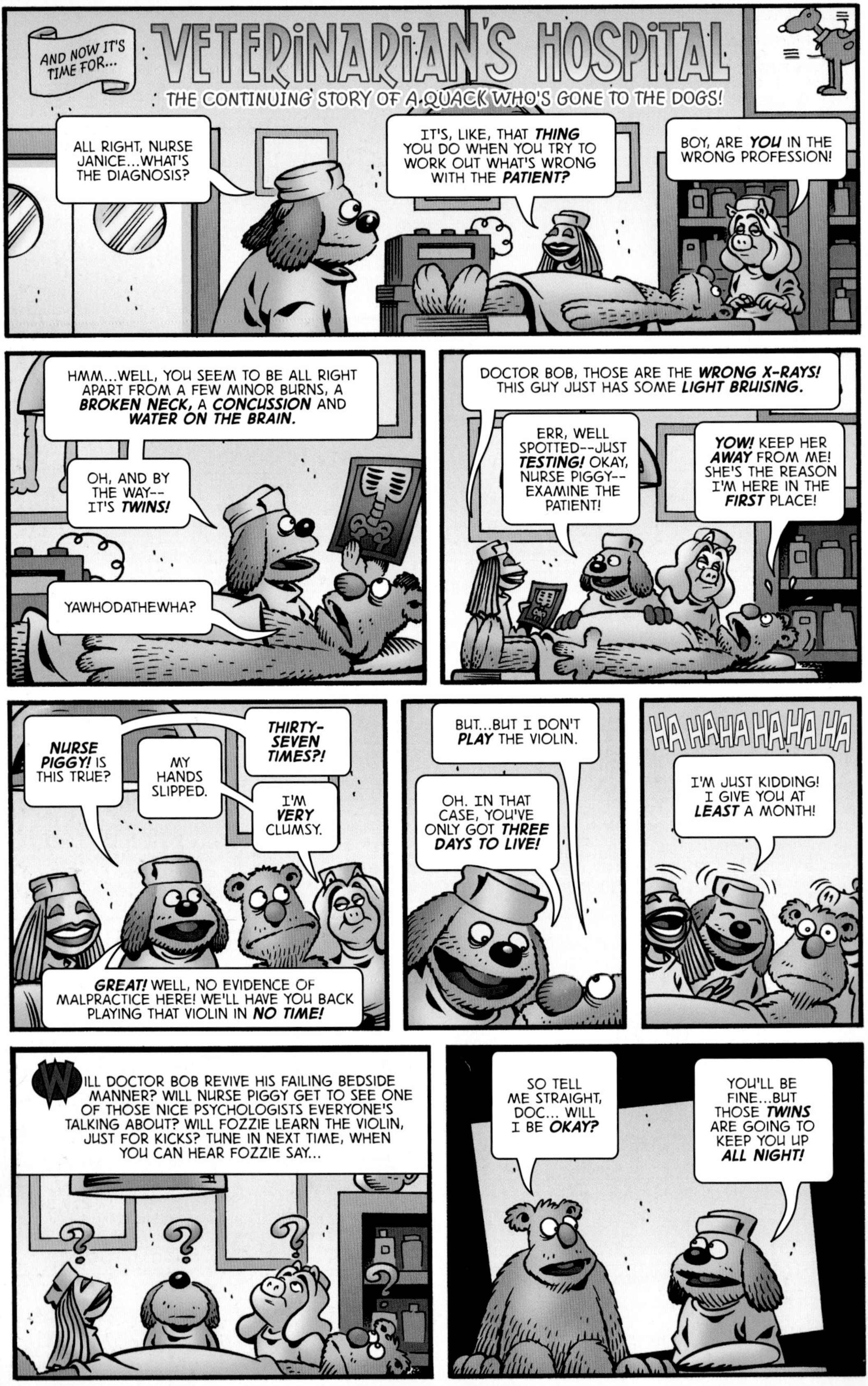

AND NOW IT'S TIME FOR...
VETERINARIAN'S HOSPITAL
THE CONTINUING STORY OF A QUACK WHO'S GONE TO THE DOGS!
ALL RIGHT, NURSE JANICE...WHAT'S THE DIAGNOSIS?
IT'S, LIKE, THAT THING YOU DO WHEN YOU TRY TO WORK OUT WHAT'S WRONG WITH THE PATIENT?
BOY, ARE YOU IN THE WRONG PROFESSION!
HMM...WELL, YOU SEEM TO BE ALL RIGHT APART FROM A FEW MINOR BURNS, A BROKEN NECK, A CONCUSSION AND WATER ON THE BRAIN.
OH, AND BY THE WAY-- IT'S TWINS!
YAWHODATHEWHA?
DOCTOR BOB, THOSE ARE THE WRONG X-RAYS! THIS GUY JUST HAS SOME LIGHT BRUISING.
ERR, WELL SPOTTED--JUST TESTING! OKAY, NURSE PIGGY-- EXAMINE THE PATIENT!
YOW! KEEP HER AWAY FROM ME! SHE'S THE REASON I'M HERE IN THE FIRST PLACE!
NURSE PIGGY! IS THIS TRUE?
MY HANDS SLIPPED.
THIRTY-SEVEN TIMES?!
I'M VERY CLUMSY.
GREAT! WELL, NO EVIDENCE OF MALPRACTICE HERE! WE'LL HAVE YOU BACK PLAYING THAT VIOLIN IN NO TIME!
BUT...BUT I DON'T PLAY THE VIOLIN.
OH. IN THAT CASE, YOU'VE ONLY GOT THREE DAYS TO LIVE!
HA HAHA HAHAHA HA
I'M JUST KIDDING! I GIVE YOU AT LEAST A MONTH!
WILL DOCTOR BOB REVIVE HIS FAILING BEDSIDE MANNER? WILL NURSE PIGGY GET TO SEE ONE OF THOSE NICE PSYCHOLOGISTS EVERYONE'S TALKING ABOUT? WILL FOZZIE LEARN THE VIOLIN, JUST FOR KICKS? TUNE IN NEXT TIME, WHEN YOU CAN HEAR FOZZIE SAY...
SO TELL ME STRAIGHT, DOC... WILL I BE OKAY?
YOU'LL BE FINE...BUT THOSE TWINS ARE GOING TO KEEP YOU UP ALL NIGHT!

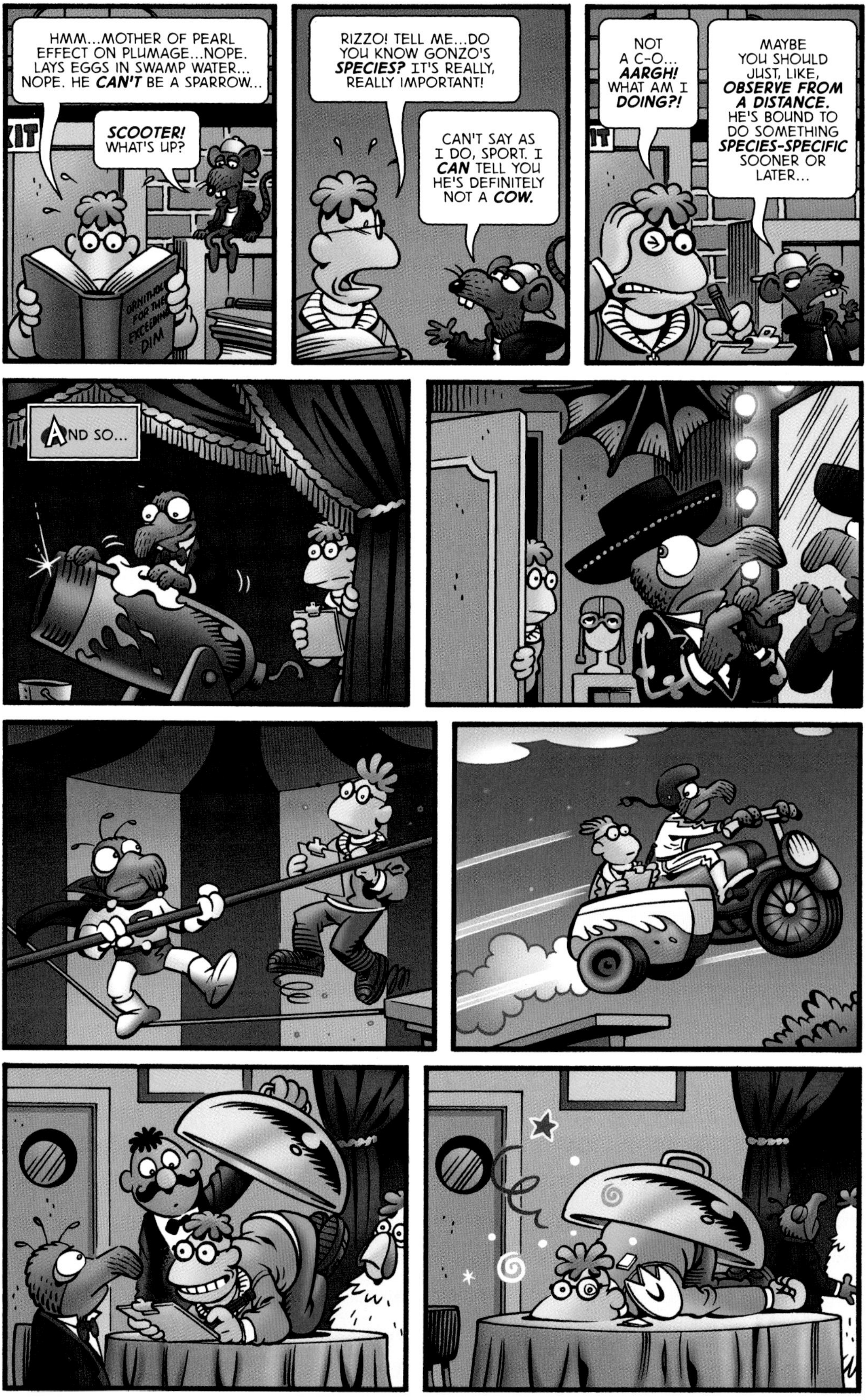

HMM...MOTHER OF PEARL EFFECT ON PLUMAGE...NOPE. LAYS EGGS IN SWAMP WATER... NOPE. HE CAN'T BE A SPARROW...
SCOOTER! WHAT'S UP?
ORNITHOL... FOR THE EXCEEDING... DIM
RIZZO! TELL ME...DO YOU KNOW GONZO'S SPECIES? IT'S REALLY, REALLY IMPORTANT!
CAN'T SAY AS I DO, SPORT. I CAN TELL YOU HE'S DEFINITELY NOT A COW.
NOT A C-O... AARGH! WHAT AM I DOING?!
MAYBE YOU SHOULD JUST, LIKE, OBSERVE FROM A DISTANCE. HE'S BOUND TO DO SOMETHING SPECIES-SPECIFIC SOONER OR LATER...
AND SO...

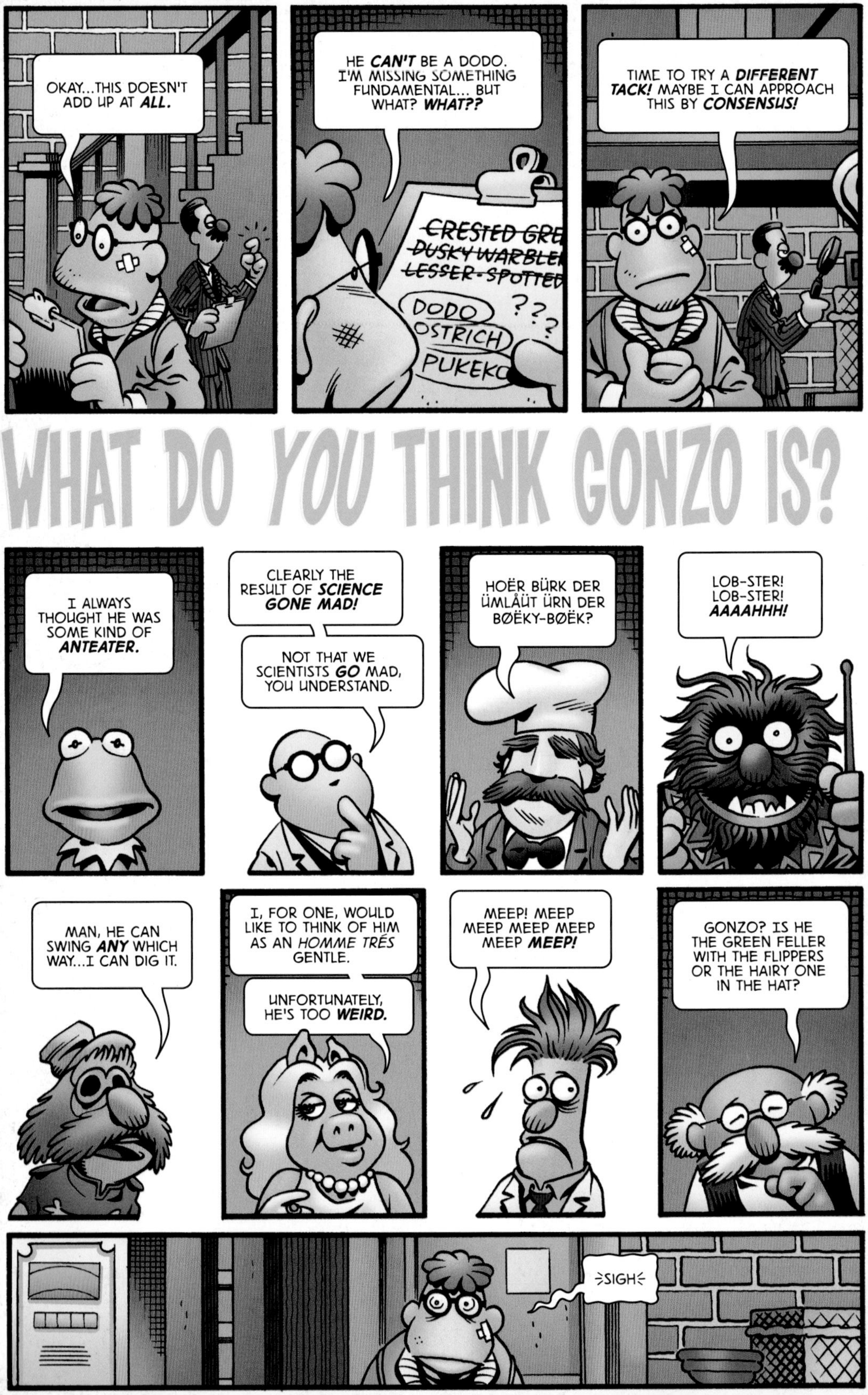
OKAY...THIS DOESN'T ADD UP AT ALL.
HE CAN'T BE A DODO. I'M MISSING SOMETHING FUNDAMENTAL... BUT WHAT? WHAT??
CRESTED GRE
DUSKY WARBLER
LESSER-SPOTTED
DODO
OSTRICH
PUKEKO
???
TIME TO TRY A DIFFERENT TACK! MAYBE I CAN APPROACH THIS BY CONSENSUS!
WHAT DO YOU THINK GONZO IS?
I ALWAYS THOUGHT HE WAS SOME KIND OF ANTEATER.
CLEARLY THE RESULT OF SCIENCE GONE MAD!
NOT THAT WE SCIENTISTS GO MAD, YOU UNDERSTAND.
HOËR BÜRK DER ÜMLÅÜT ÜRN DER BØËKY-BØËK?
LOB-STER! LOB-STER! AAAAHHH!
MAN, HE CAN SWING ANY WHICH WAY...I CAN DIG IT.
I, FOR ONE, WOULD LIKE TO THINK OF HIM AS AN HOMME TRÉS GENTLE.
UNFORTUNATELY, HE'S TOO WEIRD.
MEEP! MEEP MEEP MEEP MEEP MEEP MEEP!
GONZO? IS HE THE GREEN FELLER WITH THE FLIPPERS OR THE HAIRY ONE IN THE HAT?
SIGH

DISNEY · PIXAR

# WALL•E

## OUT THERE

A brand-new story set before the hit film! When a
mysterious spaceship crash-lands on Earth, WALL•E
makes a new friend...but can the adventurous pair
triumph over the robot's tyrannical boss, BULL•E?

WALL•E: OUT THERE
DIAMOND CODE: MAY100900
SC $9.99 ISBN 9781608865680

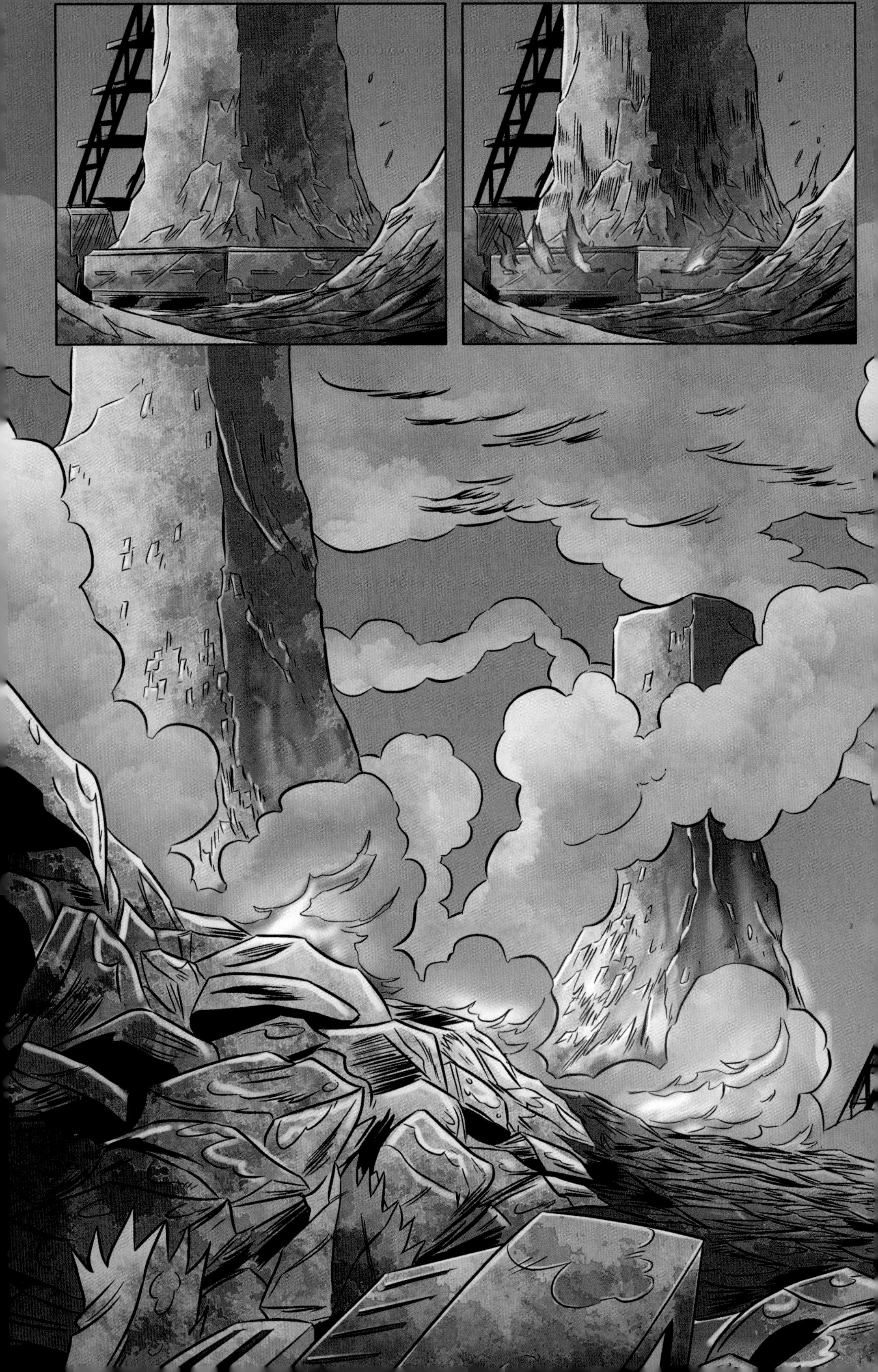

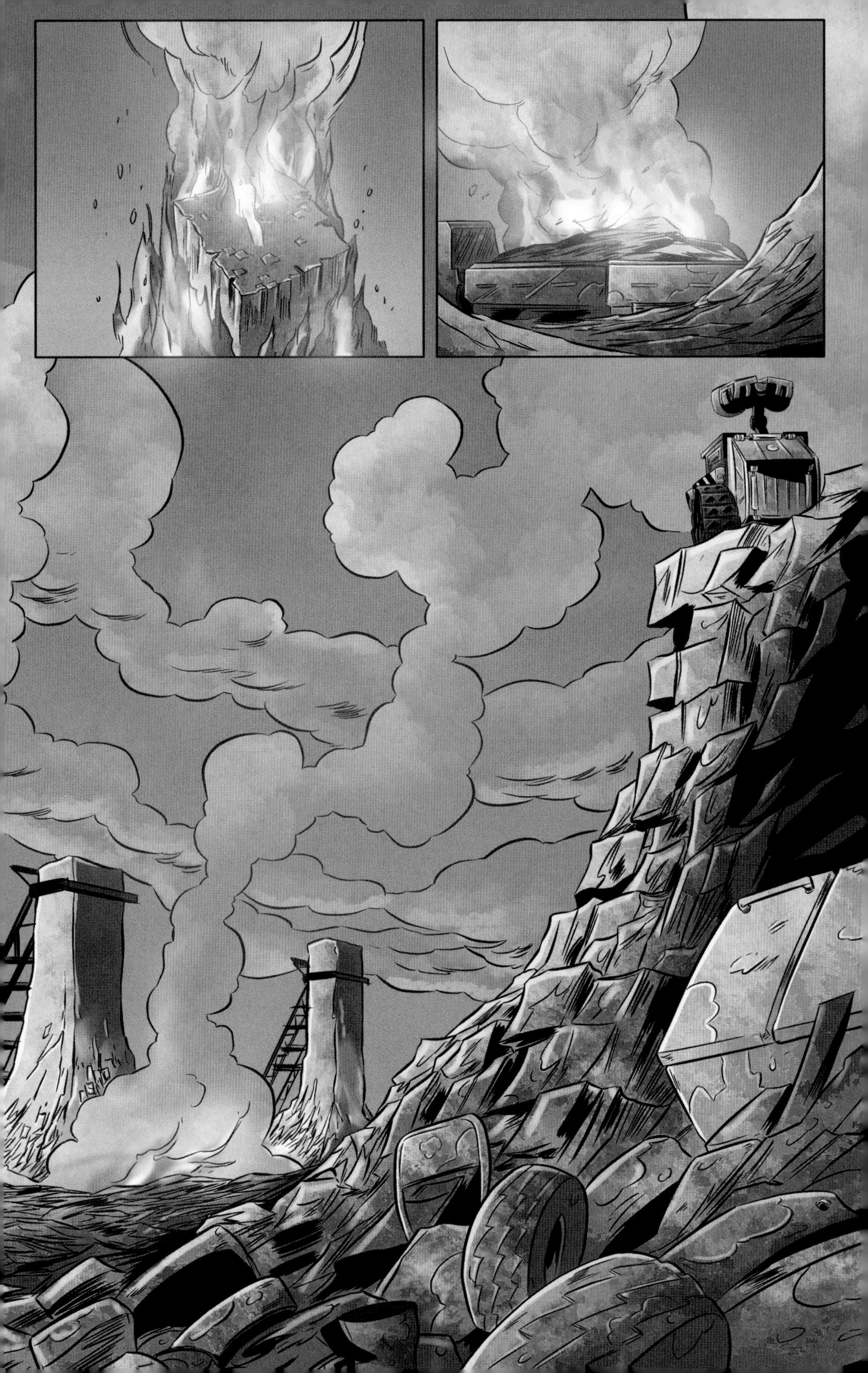

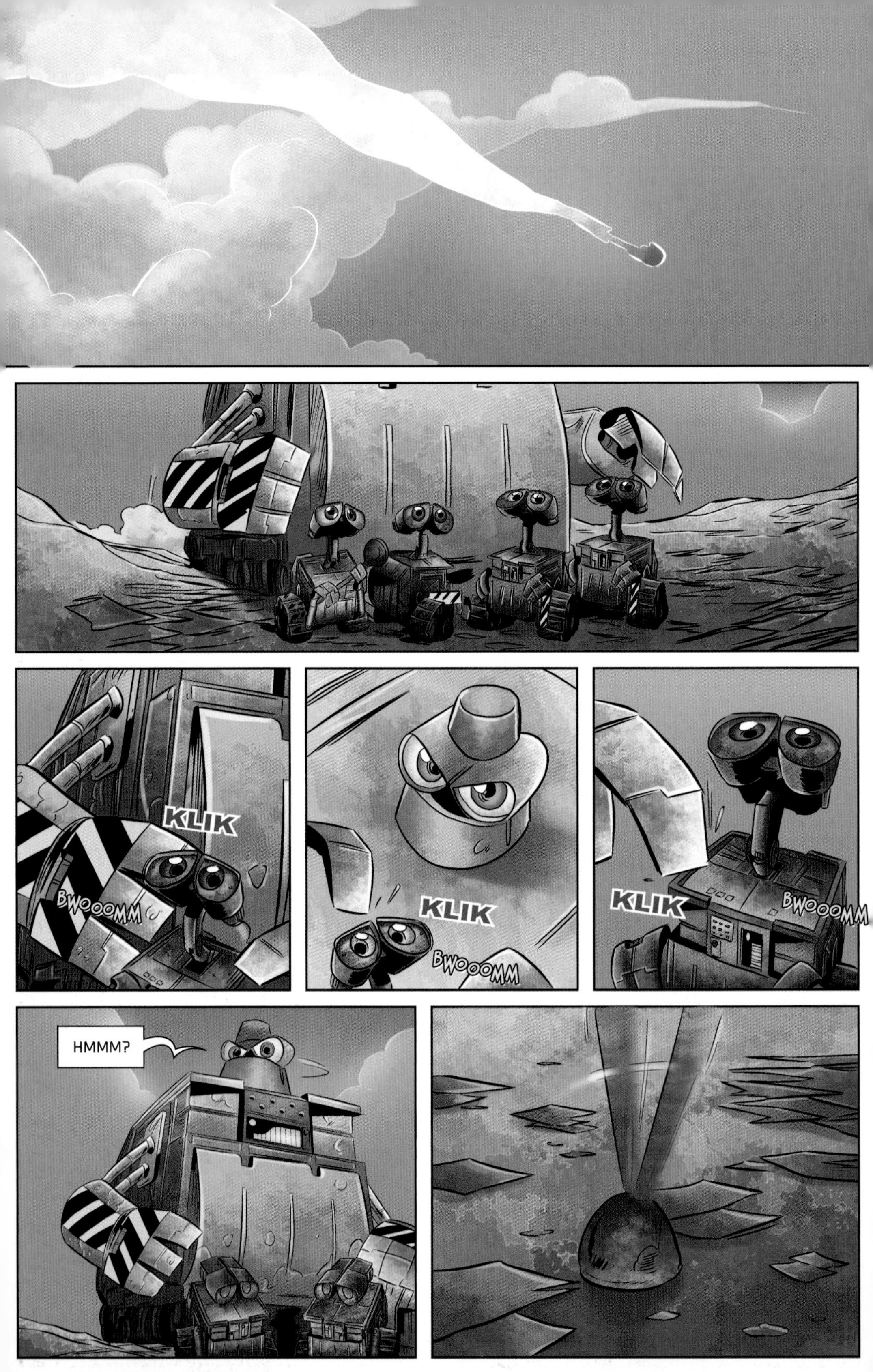
KLIK
BWOOOMM
KLIK
BWOOOMM
KLIK
BWOOOMM
HMMM?

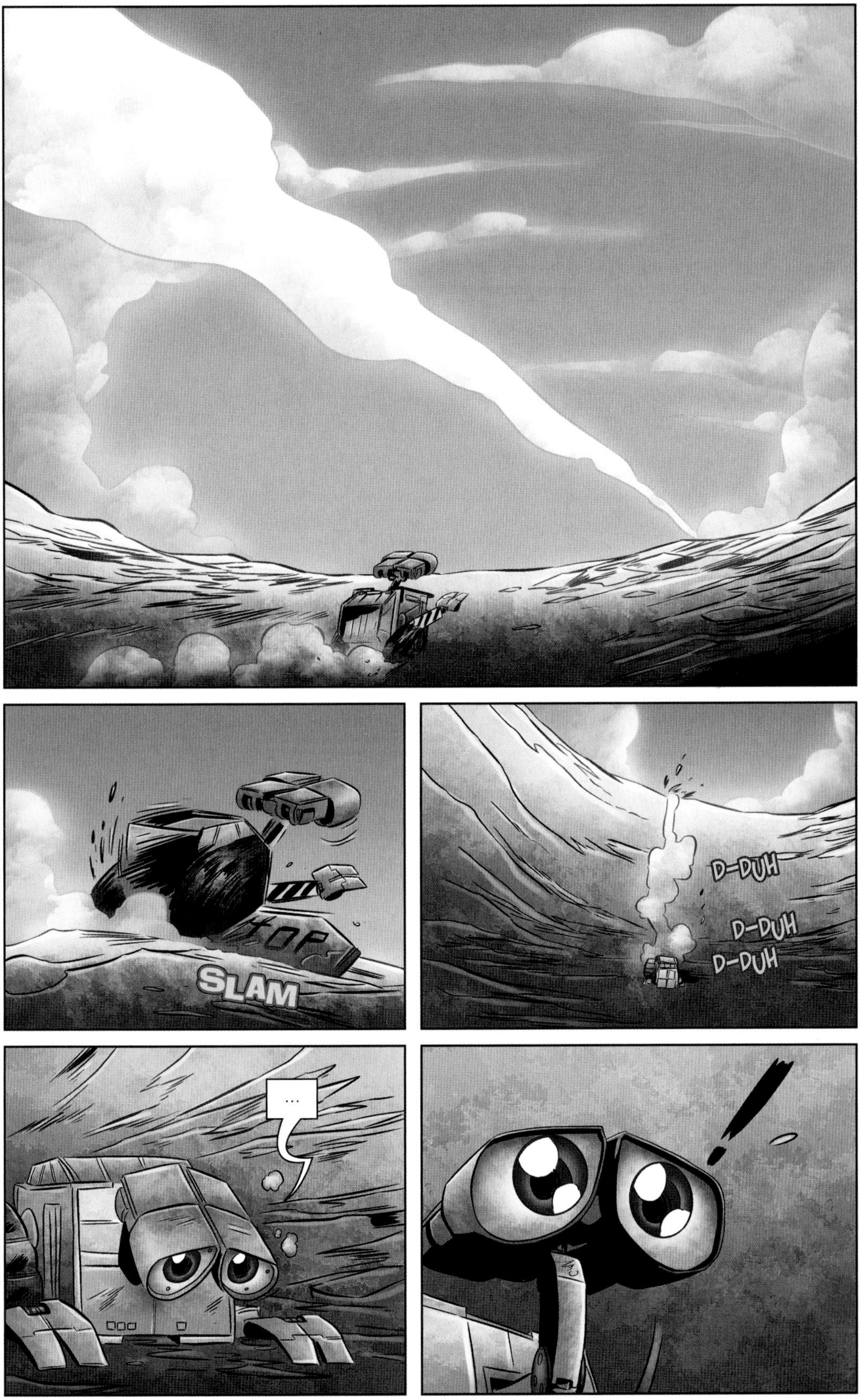
SLAM
D-DUH
D-DUH
D-DUH
...

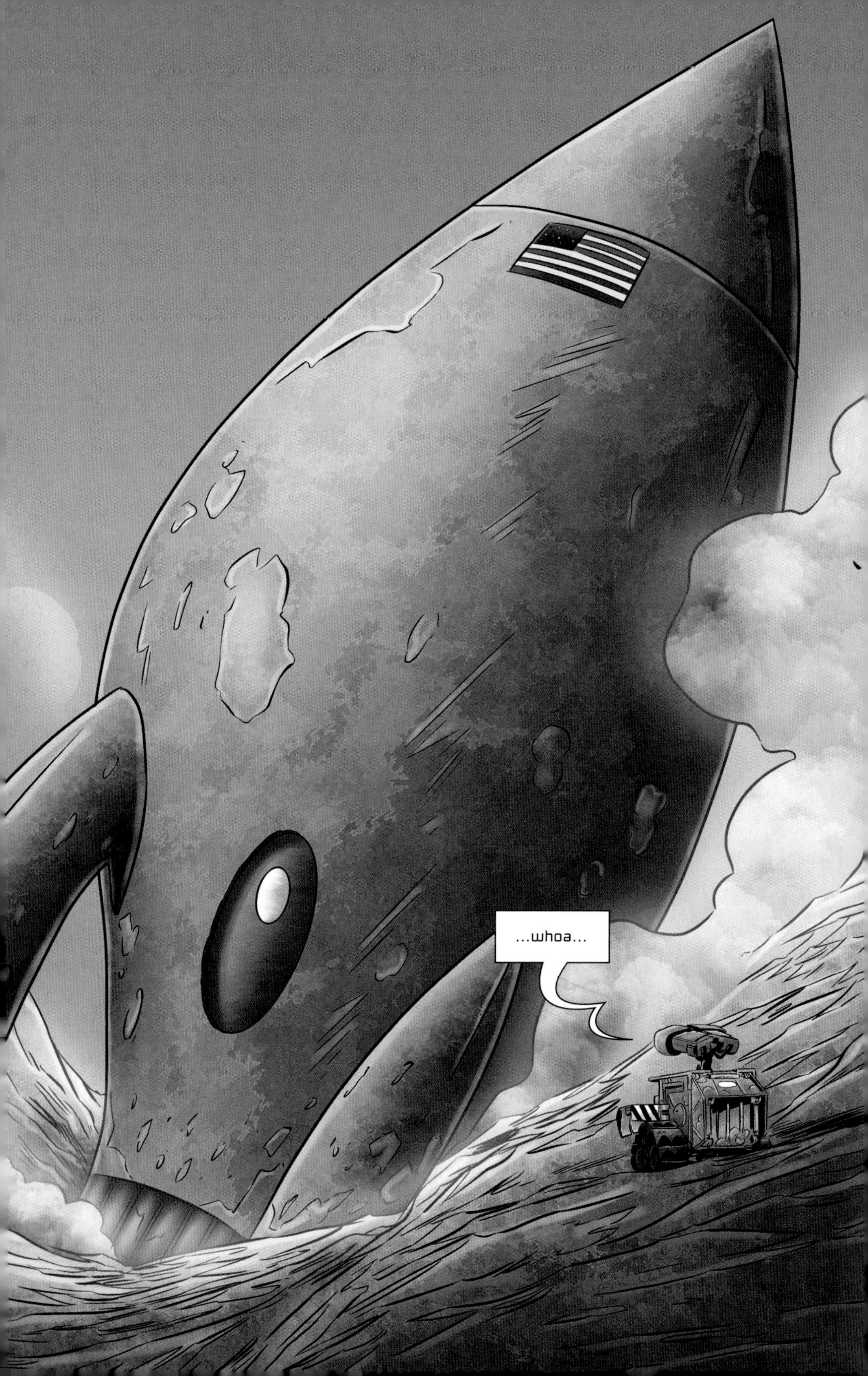
...whoa...

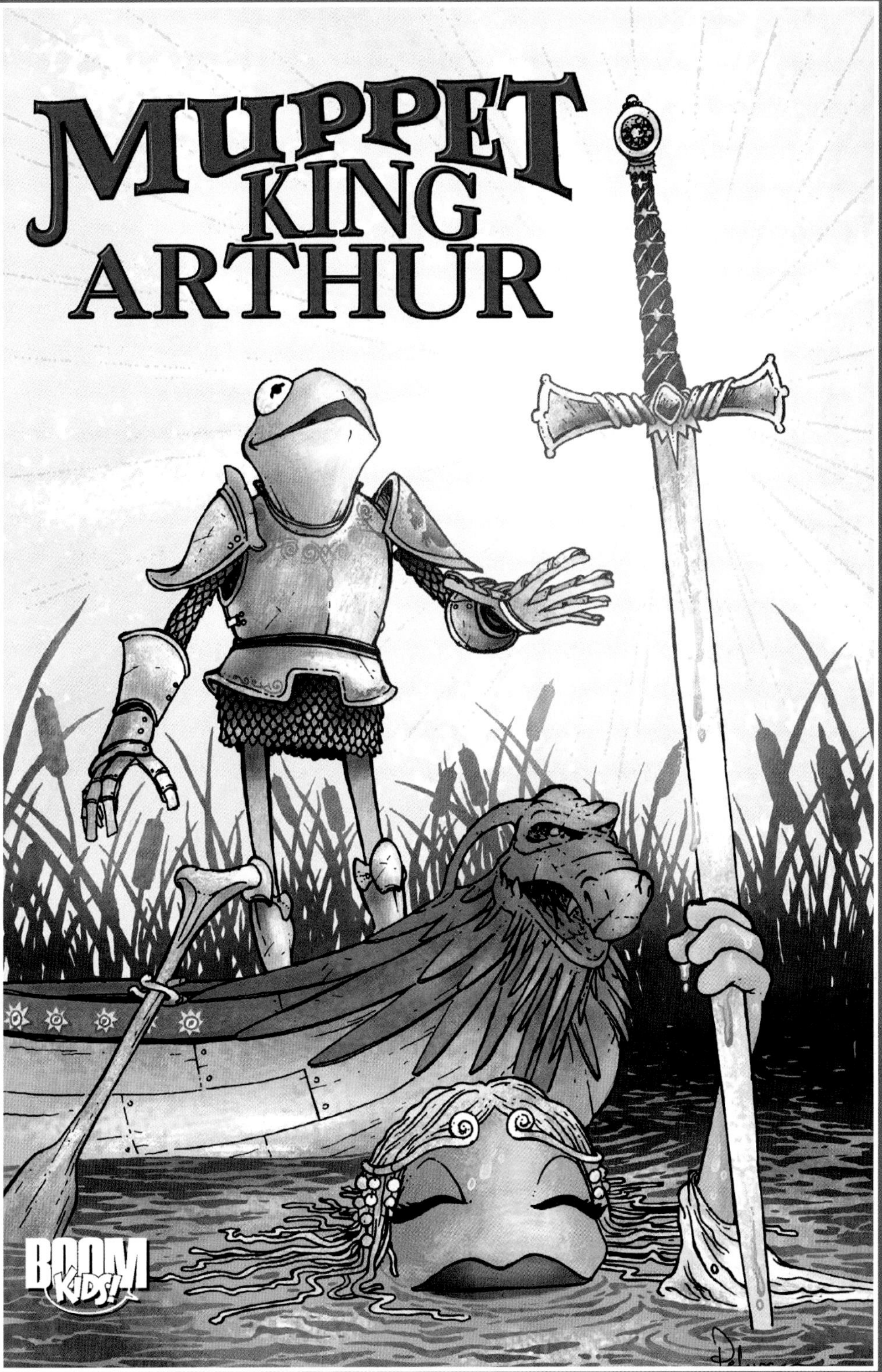
MUPPET
KING
ARTHUR
BOOM KIDS!

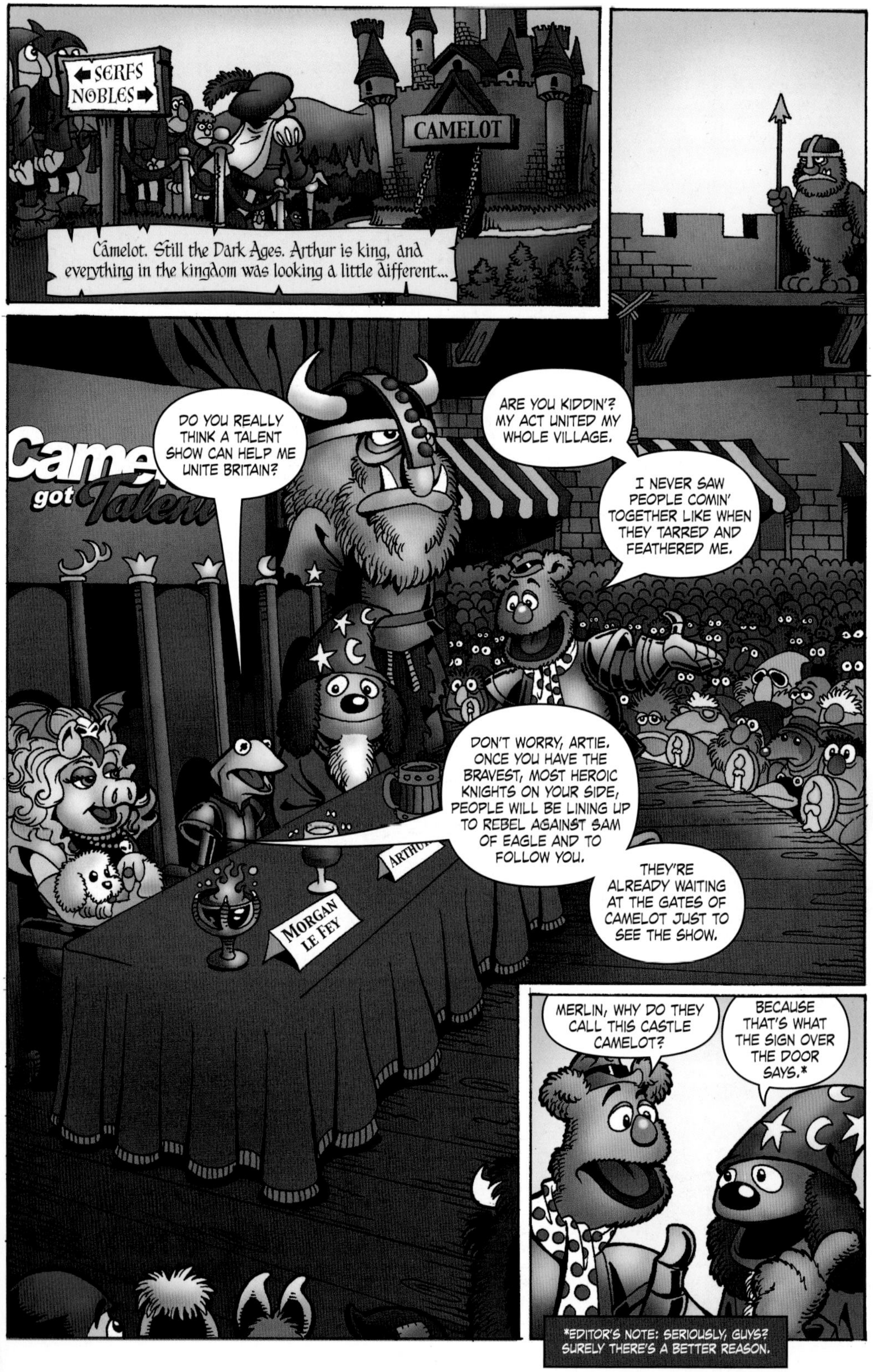

SERFS
NOBLES
CAMELOT
Camelot. Still the Dark Ages. Arthur is king, and everything in the kingdom was looking a little different...
DO YOU REALLY THINK A TALENT SHOW CAN HELP ME UNITE BRITAIN?
ARE YOU KIDDIN'? MY ACT UNITED MY WHOLE VILLAGE.
I NEVER SAW PEOPLE COMIN' TOGETHER LIKE WHEN THEY TARRED AND FEATHERED ME.
DON'T WORRY, ARTIE. ONCE YOU HAVE THE BRAVEST, MOST HEROIC KNIGHTS ON YOUR SIDE, PEOPLE WILL BE LINING UP TO REBEL AGAINST SAM OF EAGLE AND TO FOLLOW YOU.
THEY'RE ALREADY WAITING AT THE GATES OF CAMELOT JUST TO SEE THE SHOW.
MORGAN LE FEY
MERLIN, WHY DO THEY CALL THIS CASTLE CAMELOT?
BECAUSE THAT'S WHAT THE SIGN OVER THE DOOR SAYS.*
*EDITOR'S NOTE: SERIOUSLY, GUYS? SURELY THERE'S A BETTER REASON.

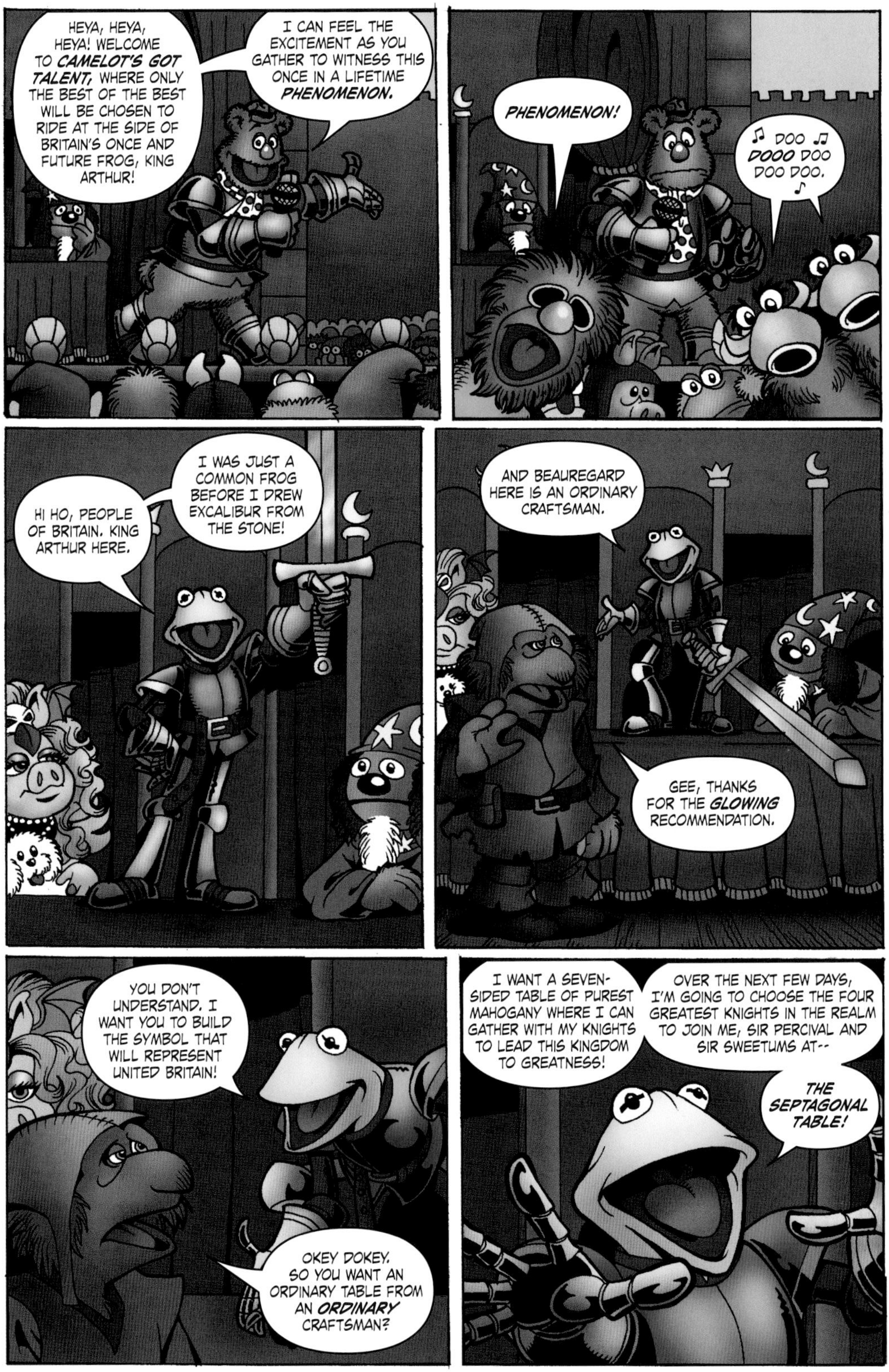
HEYA, HEYA, HEYA! WELCOME TO CAMELOT'S GOT TALENT, WHERE ONLY THE BEST OF THE BEST WILL BE CHOSEN TO RIDE AT THE SIDE OF BRITAIN'S ONCE AND FUTURE FROG, KING ARTHUR!
I CAN FEEL THE EXCITEMENT AS YOU GATHER TO WITNESS THIS ONCE IN A LIFETIME PHENOMENON.
PHENOMENON!
♫ DOO ♫ DOOO DOO DOO DOO. ♪
HI HO, PEOPLE OF BRITAIN. KING ARTHUR HERE.
I WAS JUST A COMMON FROG BEFORE I DREW EXCALIBUR FROM THE STONE!
AND BEAUREGARD HERE IS AN ORDINARY CRAFTSMAN.
GEE, THANKS FOR THE GLOWING RECOMMENDATION.
YOU DON'T UNDERSTAND. I WANT YOU TO BUILD THE SYMBOL THAT WILL REPRESENT UNITED BRITAIN!
OKEY DOKEY. SO YOU WANT AN ORDINARY TABLE FROM AN ORDINARY CRAFTSMAN?
I WANT A SEVEN-SIDED TABLE OF PUREST MAHOGANY WHERE I CAN GATHER WITH MY KNIGHTS TO LEAD THIS KINGDOM TO GREATNESS!
OVER THE NEXT FEW DAYS, I'M GOING TO CHOOSE THE FOUR GREATEST KNIGHTS IN THE REALM TO JOIN ME, SIR PERCIVAL AND SIR SWEETUMS AT--
THE SEPTAGONAL TABLE!

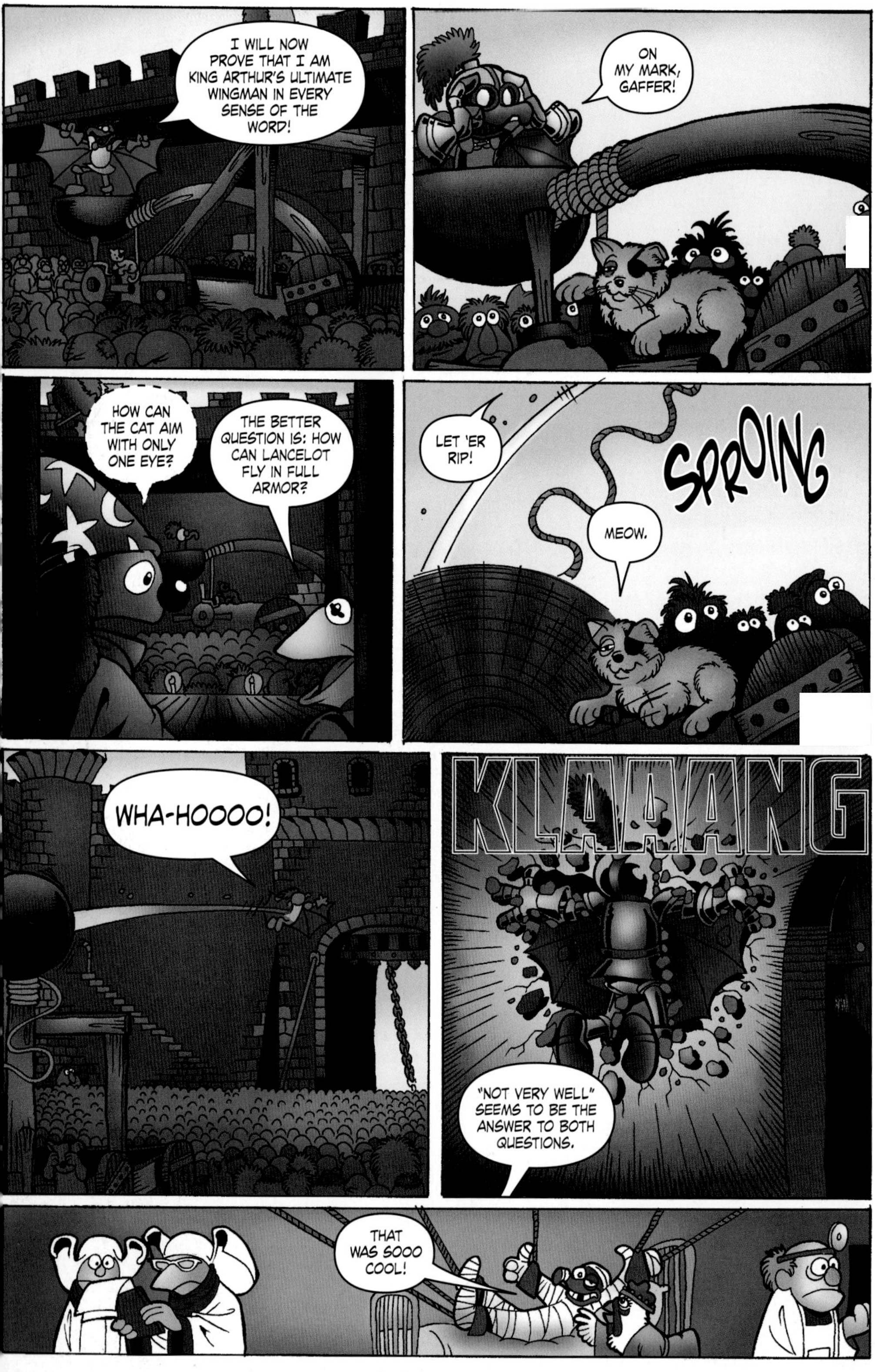
I WILL NOW PROVE THAT I AM KING ARTHUR'S ULTIMATE WINGMAN IN EVERY SENSE OF THE WORD!
ON MY MARK, GAFFER!
HOW CAN THE CAT AIM WITH ONLY ONE EYE?
THE BETTER QUESTION IS: HOW CAN LANCELOT FLY IN FULL ARMOR?
LET 'ER RIP!
SPROING
MEOW.
WHA-HOOOO!
KLAAAANG
"NOT VERY WELL" SEEMS TO BE THE ANSWER TO BOTH QUESTIONS.
THAT WAS SOOO COOL!

**DISNEY · PIXAR**

# MONSTERS, INC.

## LAUGH FACTORY

Someone is stealing comedy props from the other employees, making it hard for them to harvest the laughter they need to power Monstropolis...and all evidence points to Sulley's best friend, Mike Wazowski!

MONSTERS, INC.: LAUGH FACTORY
DIAMOND CODE: OCT090801
SC $9.99 ISBN 9781608865086
HC $24.99 ISBN 9781608865338

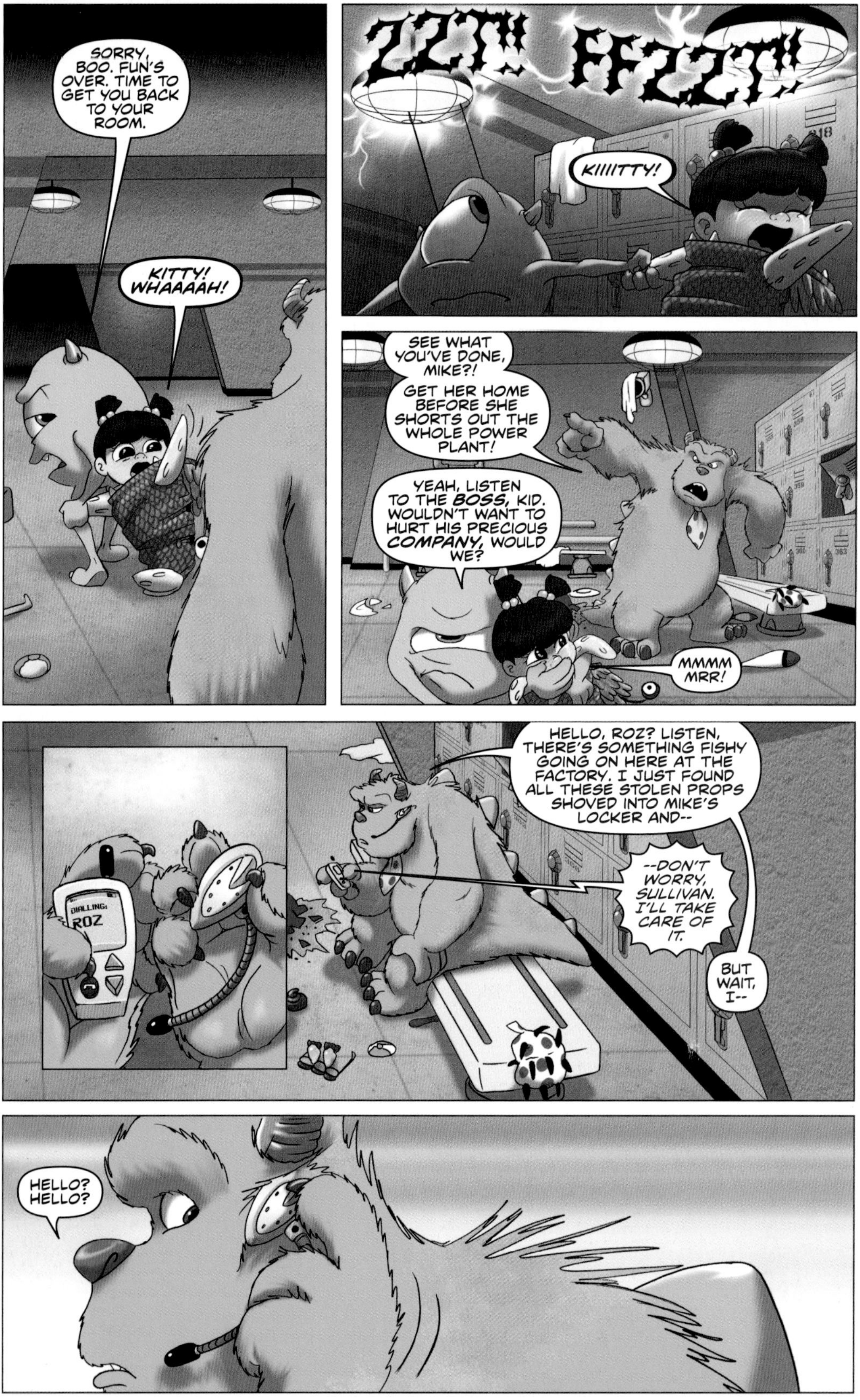
SORRY, BOO. FUN'S OVER. TIME TO GET YOU BACK TO YOUR ROOM.
KITTY! WHAAAAH!
ZZZT!! FFZZZT!!
KIIIITTY!
SEE WHAT YOU'VE DONE, MIKE?!
GET HER HOME BEFORE SHE SHORTS OUT THE WHOLE POWER PLANT!
YEAH, LISTEN TO THE BOSS, KID. WOULDN'T WANT TO HURT HIS PRECIOUS COMPANY, WOULD WE?
MMMM MRR!
DIALLING: ROZ
HELLO, ROZ? LISTEN, THERE'S SOMETHING FISHY GOING ON HERE AT THE FACTORY. I JUST FOUND ALL THESE STOLEN PROPS SHOVED INTO MIKE'S LOCKER AND--
--DON'T WORRY, SULLIVAN. I'LL TAKE CARE OF IT.
BUT WAIT, I--
HELLO? HELLO?

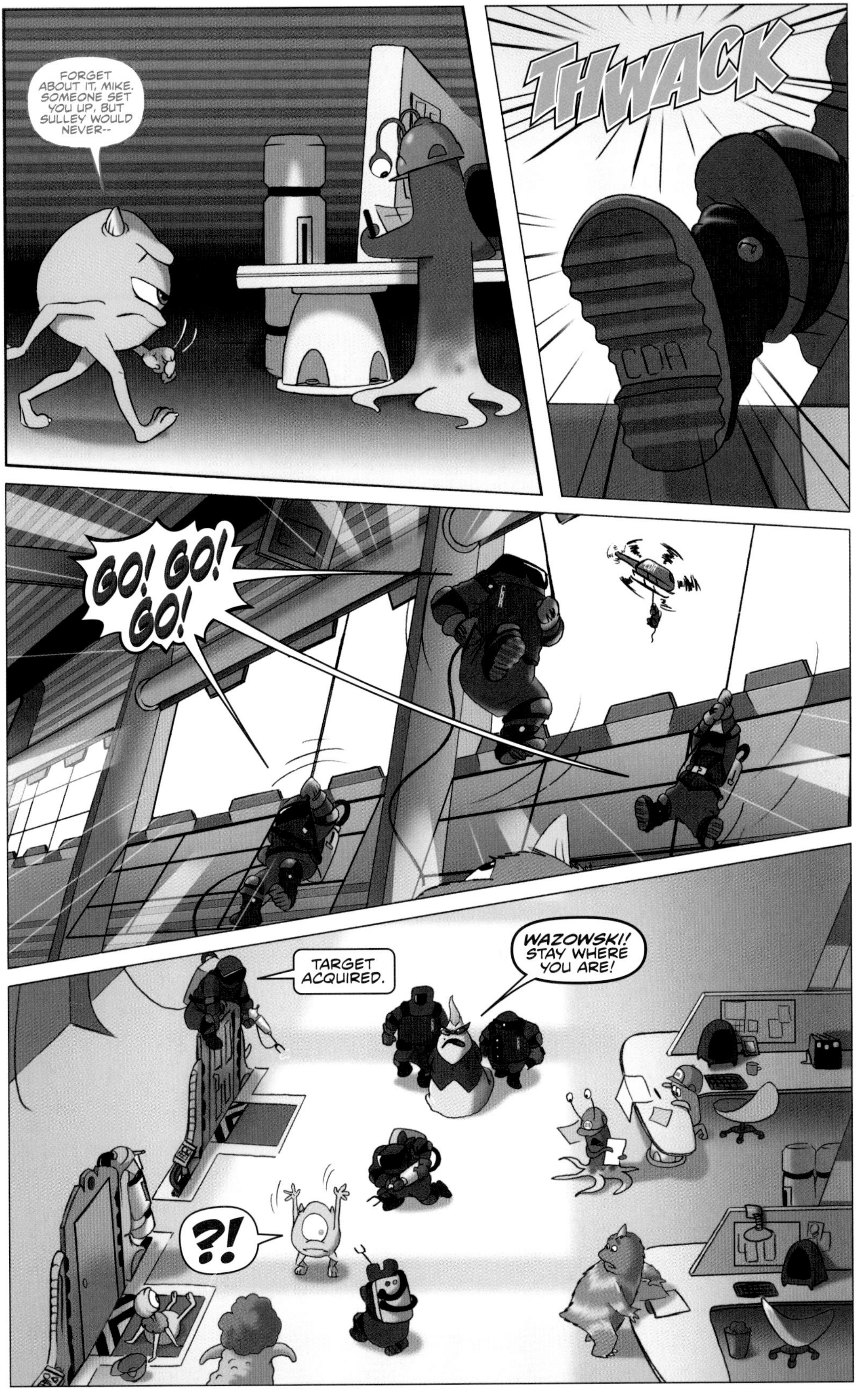

FORGET ABOUT IT, MIKE. SOMEONE SET YOU UP, BUT SULLEY WOULD NEVER--
THWACK
CDA
GO! GO! GO!
TARGET ACQUIRED.
WAZOWSKI! STAY WHERE YOU ARE!
?!

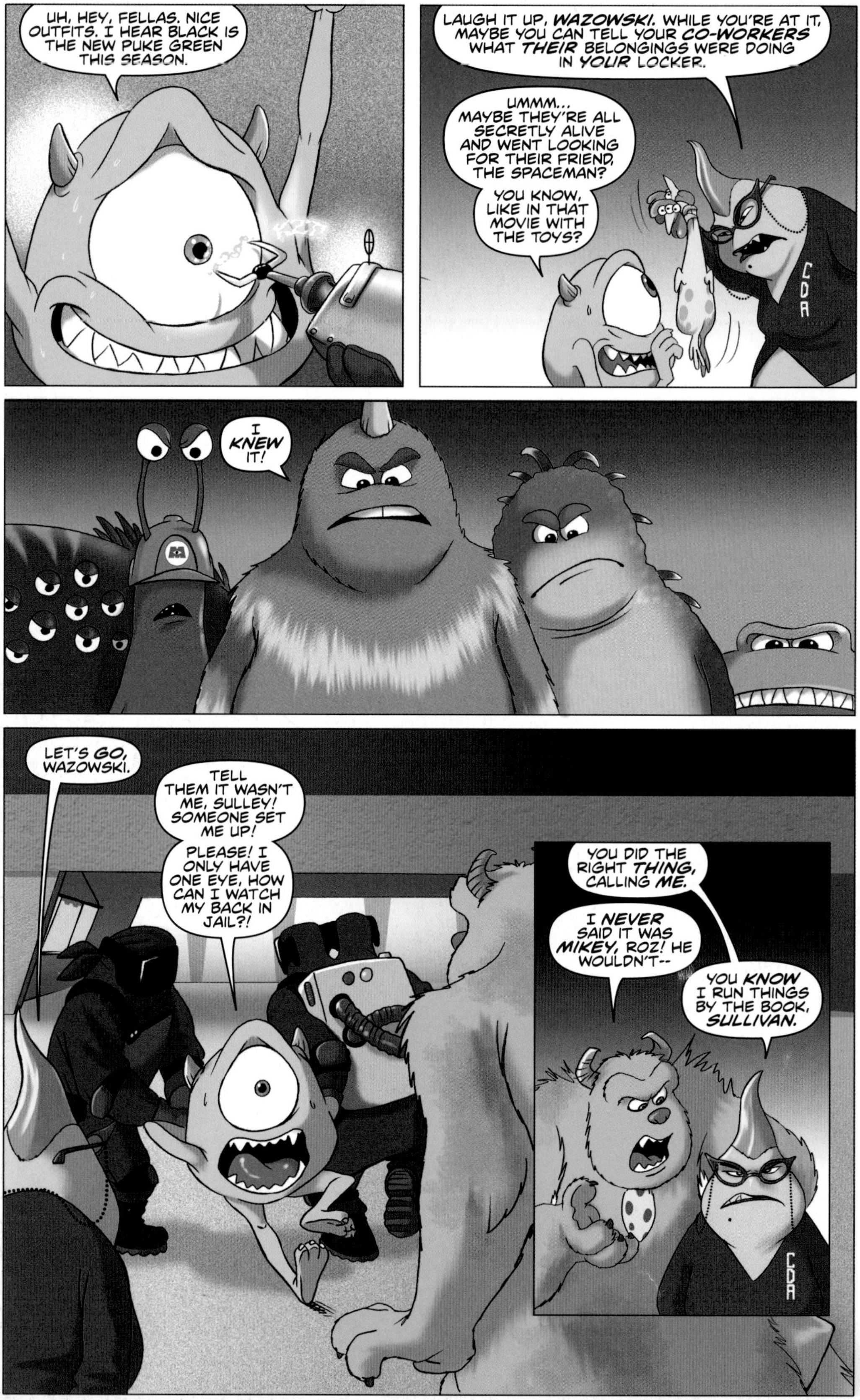

UH, HEY, FELLAS. NICE OUTFITS. I HEAR BLACK IS THE NEW PUKE GREEN THIS SEASON.
KZT
LAUGH IT UP, WAZOWSKI. WHILE YOU'RE AT IT, MAYBE YOU CAN TELL YOUR CO-WORKERS WHAT THEIR BELONGINGS WERE DOING IN YOUR LOCKER.
UMMM... MAYBE THEY'RE ALL SECRETLY ALIVE AND WENT LOOKING FOR THEIR FRIEND, THE SPACEMAN?
YOU KNOW, LIKE IN THAT MOVIE WITH THE TOYS?
CDA
I KNEW IT!
LET'S GO, WAZOWSKI.
TELL THEM IT WASN'T ME, SULLEY! SOMEONE SET ME UP!
PLEASE! I ONLY HAVE ONE EYE, HOW CAN I WATCH MY BACK IN JAIL?!
YOU DID THE RIGHT THING, CALLING ME.
I NEVER SAID IT WAS MIKEY, ROZ! HE WOULDN'T--
YOU KNOW I RUN THINGS BY THE BOOK, SULLIVAN.
CDA

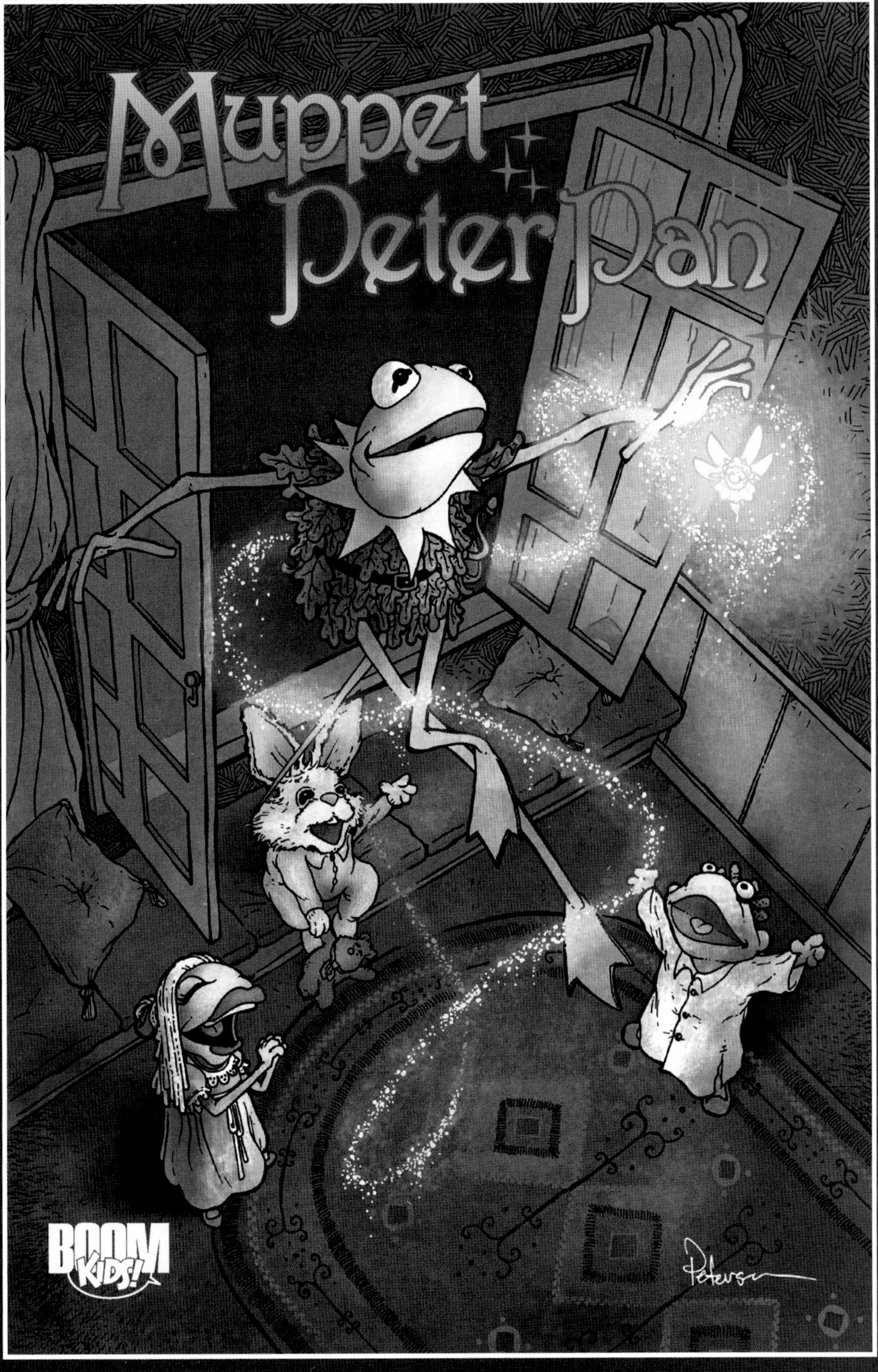

Muppet Peter Pan
BOOM KIDS!
Petersen


Peter Pan (Kermit) whisks Wendy (Janice) and her brothers to the magical realm of Neverswamp! Also starring Captain Hook (Gonzo) and Piggytink (Miss Piggy), this hilarious spin on the timeless tale is one that you'll never forget!

MUPPET PETER PAN
DIAMOND CODE: OCT090802

SC $9.99 ISBN 9781608865079
HC $24.99 ISBN 9781608865314

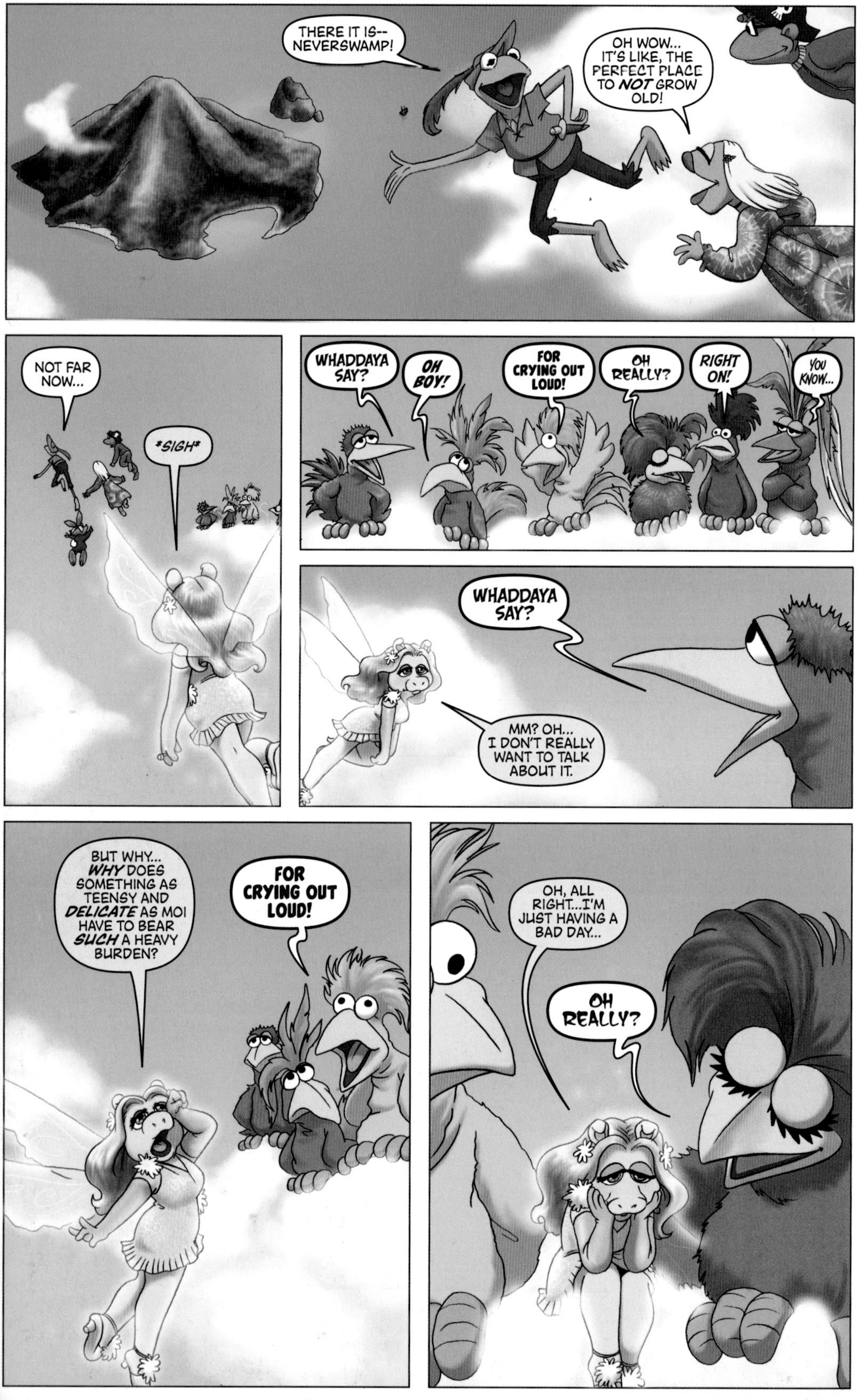
THERE IT IS-- NEVERSWAMP!
OH WOW... IT'S LIKE, THE PERFECT PLACE TO NOT GROW OLD!
NOT FAR NOW...
*SIGH*
WHADDAYA SAY?
OH BOY!
FOR CRYING OUT LOUD!
OH REALLY?
RIGHT ON!
YOU KNOW...
WHADDAYA SAY?
MM? OH... I DON'T REALLY WANT TO TALK ABOUT IT.
BUT WHY... WHY DOES SOMETHING AS TEENSY AND DELICATE AS MOI HAVE TO BEAR SUCH A HEAVY BURDEN?
FOR CRYING OUT LOUD!
OH, ALL RIGHT...I'M JUST HAVING A BAD DAY...
OH REALLY?

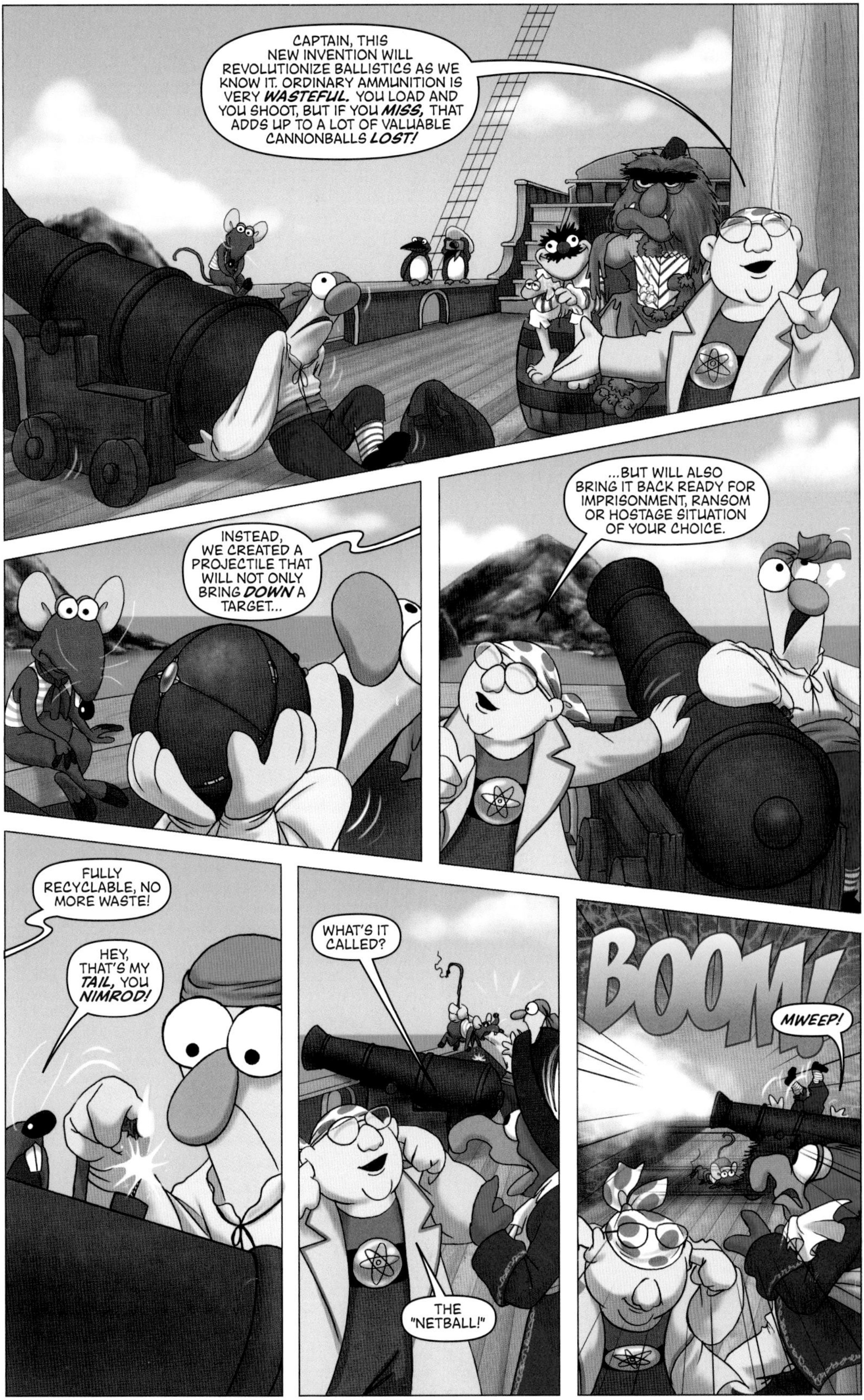
CAPTAIN, THIS NEW INVENTION WILL REVOLUTIONIZE BALLISTICS AS WE KNOW IT. ORDINARY AMMUNITION IS VERY WASTEFUL. YOU LOAD AND YOU SHOOT, BUT IF YOU MISS, THAT ADDS UP TO A LOT OF VALUABLE CANNONBALLS LOST!
INSTEAD, WE CREATED A PROJECTILE THAT WILL NOT ONLY BRING DOWN A TARGET...
...BUT WILL ALSO BRING IT BACK READY FOR IMPRISONMENT, RANSOM OR HOSTAGE SITUATION OF YOUR CHOICE.
FULLY RECYCLABLE, NO MORE WASTE!
HEY, THAT'S MY TAIL, YOU NIMROD!
WHAT'S IT CALLED?
THE "NETBALL!"
BOOM!
MWEEP!

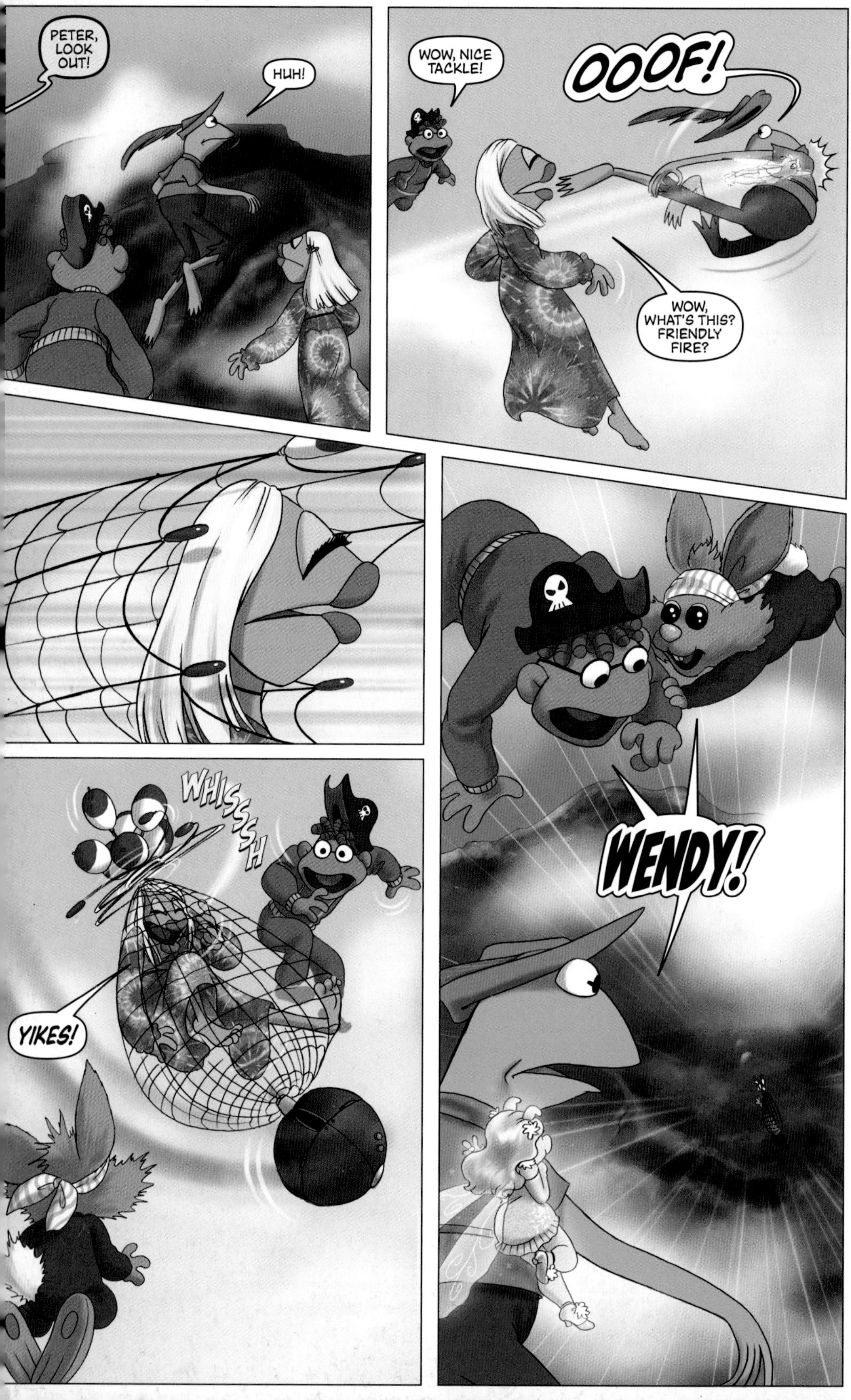

PETER, LOOK OUT!
HUH!
WOW, NICE TACKLE!
OOOF!
WOW, WHAT'S THIS? FRIENDLY FIRE?
WHISSSH
YIKES!
WENDY!

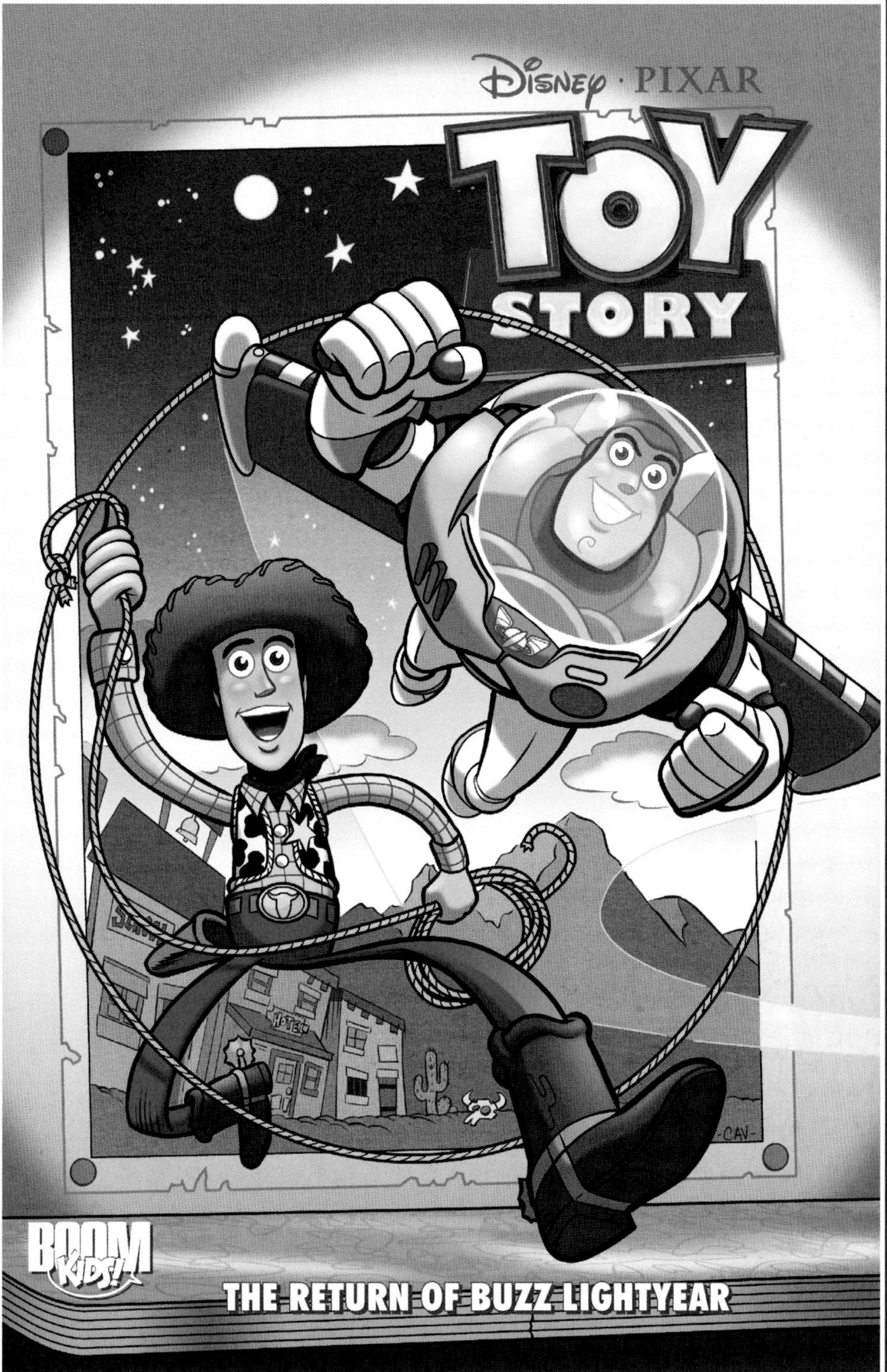
DISNEY · PIXAR
TOY STORY
THE RETURN OF BUZZ LIGHTYEAR

ANDY, HOW MANY TIMES HAVE I TOLD YOU NOT TO RUN DOWN THE STAIRS?!

SORRY, MOM.

WHAT'S A *"GIFT RECEIPT"*? AND WHAT DOES SHE MEAN *"RETURN IT AND GET SOMETHING NEW?"* YOU CAN DO THAT?!

YEAH, BUZZ...YOU CAN.

THAT JUST SEEMS... *WRONG*.

IT'S LIKE THE POOR TOY NEVER EVEN HAD A CHANCE...

TRUST ME BUZZ. IT'S FOR THE BEST.

*"FOR THE BEST?"* I THOUGHT YOU'D BE ON MY SIDE.

I *AM* ON YOUR SIDE.

OBVIOUSLY *NOT*, WOODY.

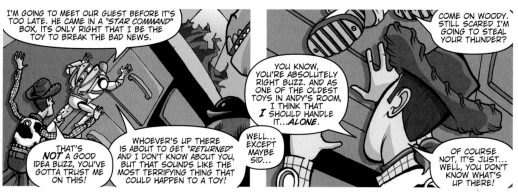

I'M GOING TO MEET OUR GUEST BEFORE IT'S TOO LATE. HE CAME IN A *"STAR COMMAND"* BOX, IT'S ONLY RIGHT THAT I BE THE TOY TO BREAK THE BAD NEWS.

THAT'S *NOT* A GOOD IDEA BUZZ, YOU'VE GOTTA TRUST ME ON THIS!

WHOEVER'S UP THERE IS ABOUT TO GET *"RETURNED"* AND I DON'T KNOW ABOUT YOU, BUT THAT SOUNDS LIKE THE MOST TERRIFYING THING THAT COULD HAPPEN TO A TOY!

YOU KNOW, YOU'RE ABSOLUTELY RIGHT BUZZ. AND AS ONE OF THE OLDEST TOYS IN ANDY'S ROOM, I THINK THAT *I* SHOULD HANDLE IT...*ALONE.*

WELL... EXCEPT MAYBE SID...

COME ON WOODY. STILL SCARED I'M GOING TO STEAL YOUR THUNDER?

OF COURSE NOT, IT'S JUST... WELL, YOU DON'T KNOW WHAT'S UP THERE!

YOU'RE RIGHT. THAT'S WHY I'M GOING UP THERE TO FIND OUT!

OH...

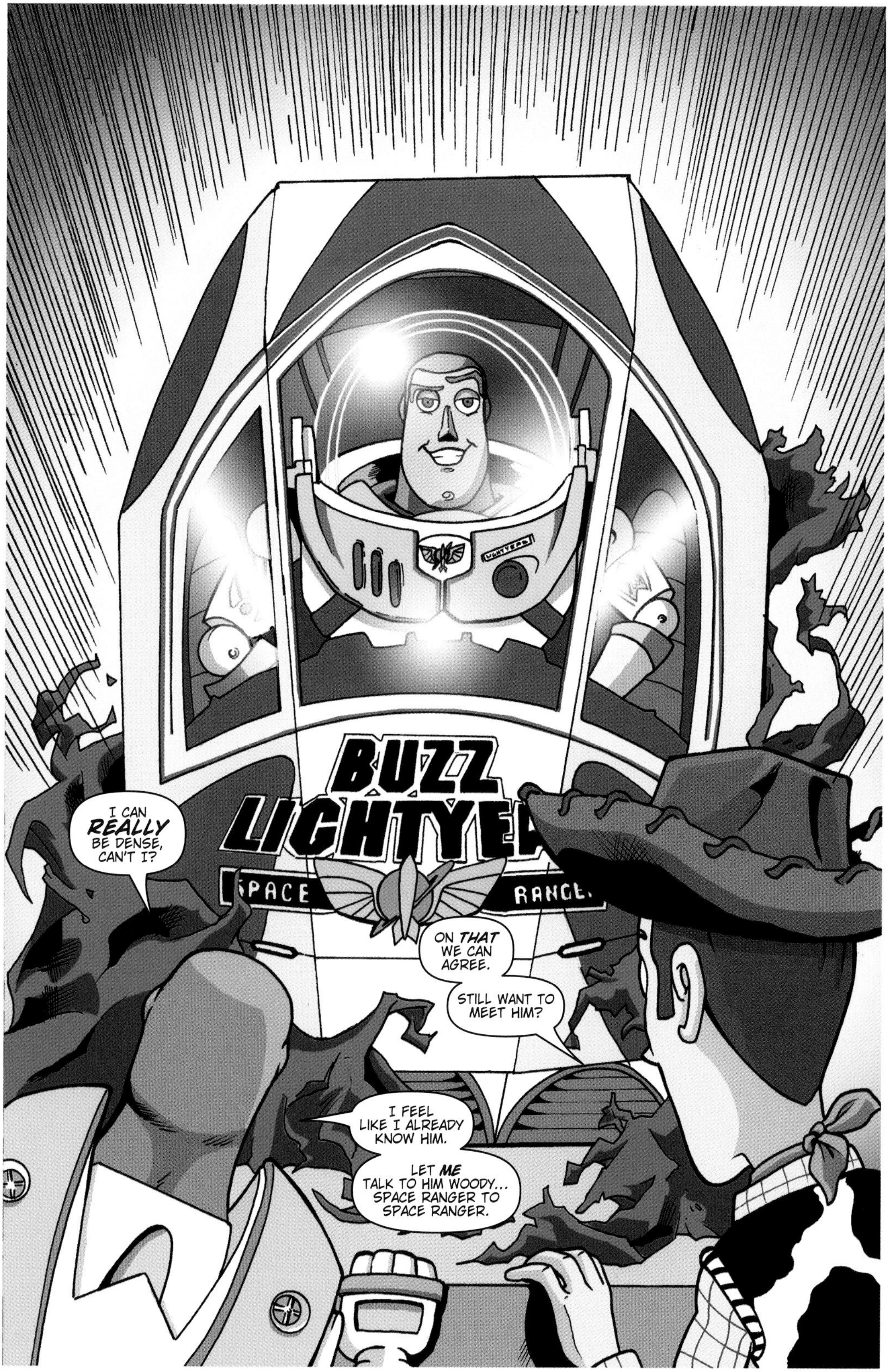
BUZZ LIGHTYEAR
SPACE RANGER
I CAN *REALLY* BE DENSE, CAN'T I?
ON *THAT* WE CAN AGREE.
STILL WANT TO MEET HIM?
I FEEL LIKE I ALREADY KNOW HIM.
LET *ME* TALK TO HIM WOODY... SPACE RANGER TO SPACE RANGER.

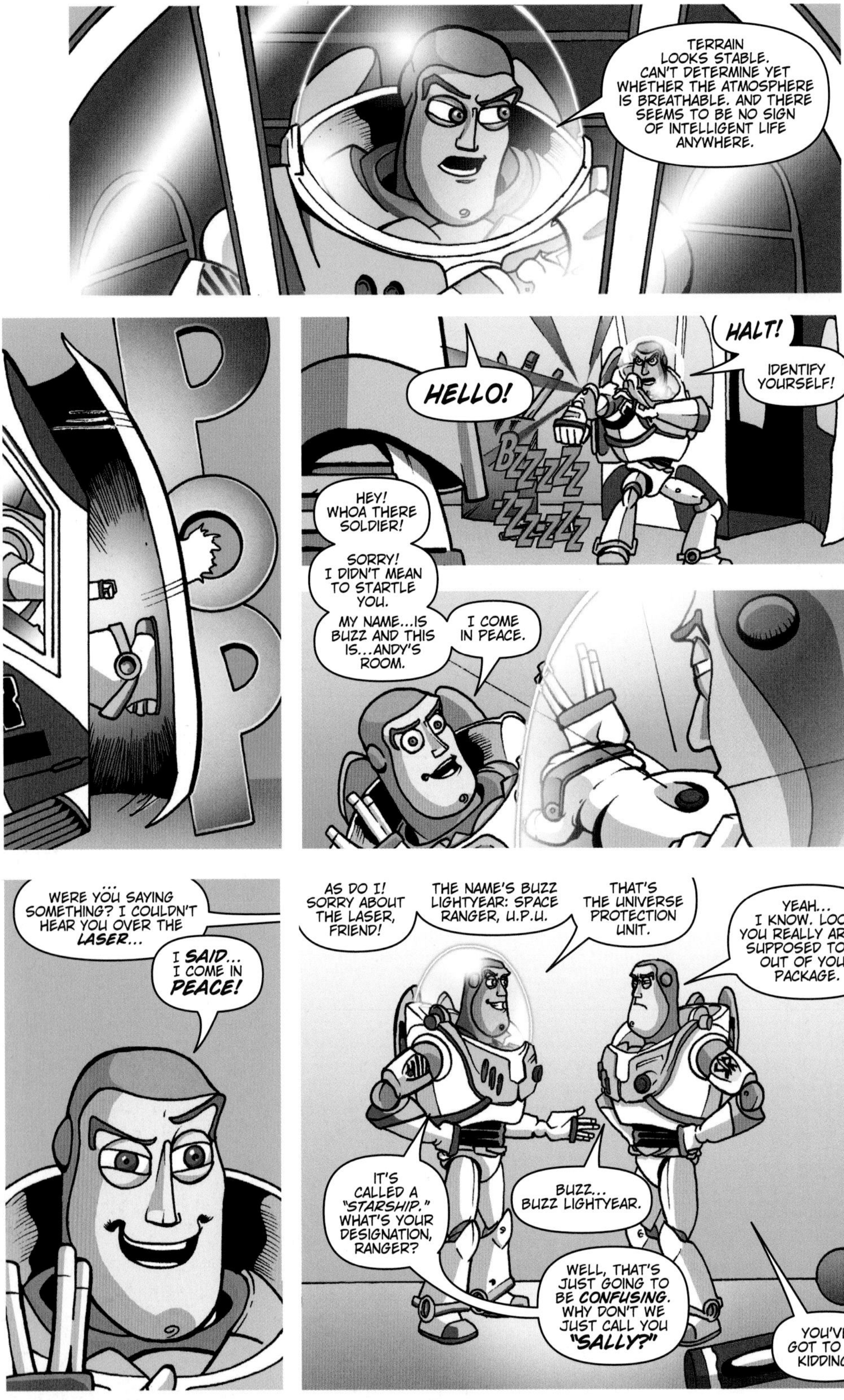
TERRAIN LOOKS STABLE. CAN'T DETERMINE YET WHETHER THE ATMOSPHERE IS BREATHABLE. AND THERE SEEMS TO BE NO SIGN OF INTELLIGENT LIFE ANYWHERE.
POP
HELLO!
HALT!
IDENTIFY YOURSELF!
HEY! WHOA THERE SOLDIER!
SORRY! I DIDN'T MEAN TO STARTLE YOU.
MY NAME...IS BUZZ AND THIS IS...ANDY'S ROOM.
I COME IN PEACE.
...WERE YOU SAYING SOMETHING? I COULDN'T HEAR YOU OVER THE *LASER*...
I *SAID*... I COME IN *PEACE!*
AS DO I! SORRY ABOUT THE LASER, FRIEND!
THE NAME'S BUZZ LIGHTYEAR: SPACE RANGER, U.P.U.
THAT'S THE UNIVERSE PROTECTION UNIT.
YEAH... I KNOW. LOOK, YOU REALLY AREN'T SUPPOSED TO BE OUT OF YOUR PACKAGE.
IT'S CALLED A *"STARSHIP."* WHAT'S YOUR DESIGNATION, RANGER?
BUZZ... BUZZ LIGHTYEAR.
WELL, THAT'S JUST GOING TO BE *CONFUSING*. WHY DON'T WE JUST CALL YOU *"SALLY?"*
YOU'VE GOT TO BE KIDDING.

# GRAPHIC NOVELS AVAILABLE NOW!

BOOM KIDS!

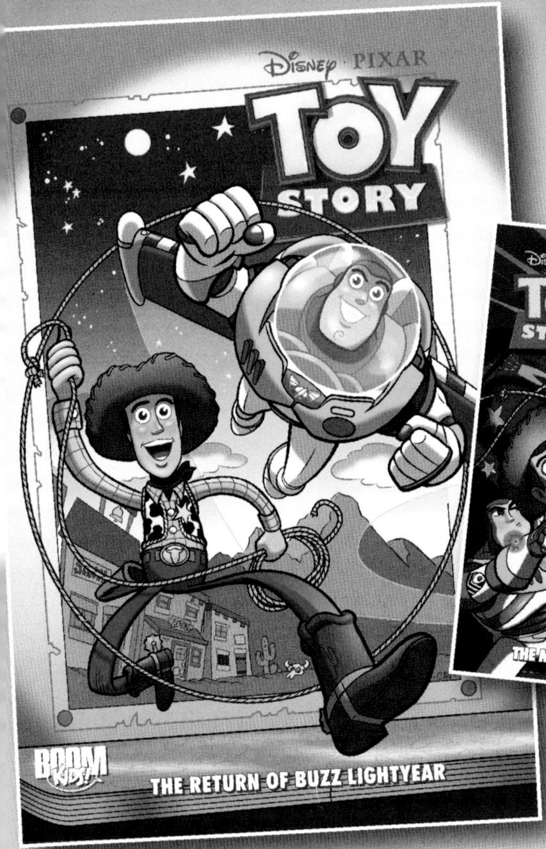

Disney · PIXAR
TOY STORY
BOOM KIDS!
THE RETURN OF BUZZ LIGHTYEAR


## TOY STORY: THE RETURN OF BUZZ LIGHTYEAR

When Andy is given a surprise gift, no one is more surprised than the toys in his room...it's a second Buzz Lightyear! The stage is set for a Star Command showdown when only one Buzz can stay!


SC $9.99 ISBN 9781608865574
HC $24.99 ISBN 9781608865581


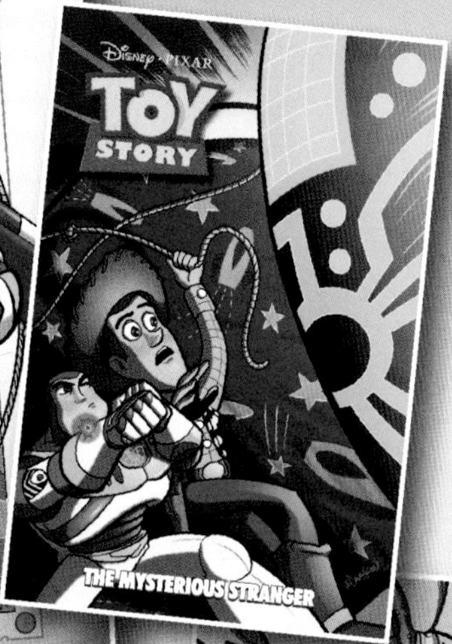

Disney · PIXAR
TOY STORY
THE MYSTERIOUS STRANGER


## TOY STORY: THE MYSTERIOUS STRANGER

Andy has a new addition to his room—a circuit-laden egg. Is this new gizmo a friend or foe? This adventure kicks off the first of four self-contained stories featuring all your favorite characters from the TOY STORY movies – Woody, Buzz and the gang!


SC $9.99 ISBN 9781934506912
HC $24.99 ISBN 9781608865239


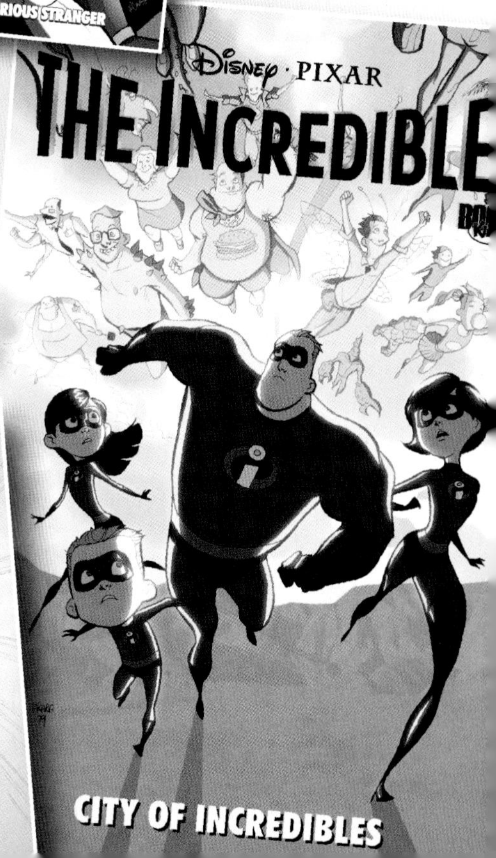

Disney · PIXAR
THE INCREDIBLE
CITY OF INCREDIBLES


## THE INCREDIBLES: CITY OF INCREDIBLES

Baby Jack-Jack, everyone's favorite super-powered toddler, battles...a nasty cold! Hopefully the rest of the Parr family can stay healthy, because the henchmen of super villains are rapidly starting to exhibit superpowers!


SC $9.99 ISBN 9781608865031
HC $24.99 ISBN 9781608865291


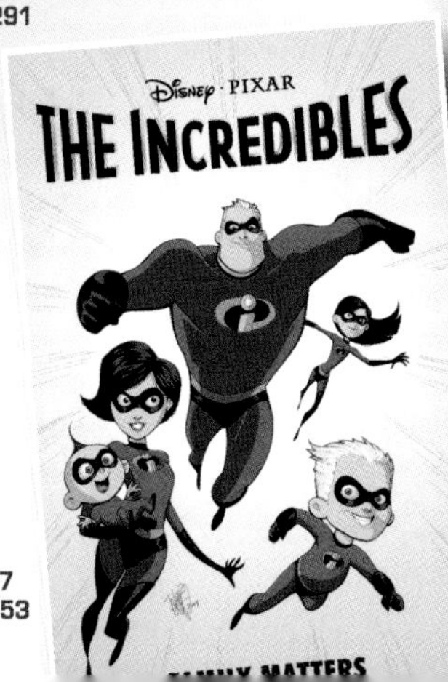

Disney · PIXAR
THE INCREDIBLES


## THE INCREDIBLES: FAMILY MATTERS

Acclaimed scribe Mark Waid has written the perfect INCREDIBLES story! What happens when Mr. Incredible's super-abilities start to wane...and how long can he keep his powerlessness a secret from his wife and kids?


SC $9.99 ISBN 9781934506837
HC $24.99 ISBN 9781608865253

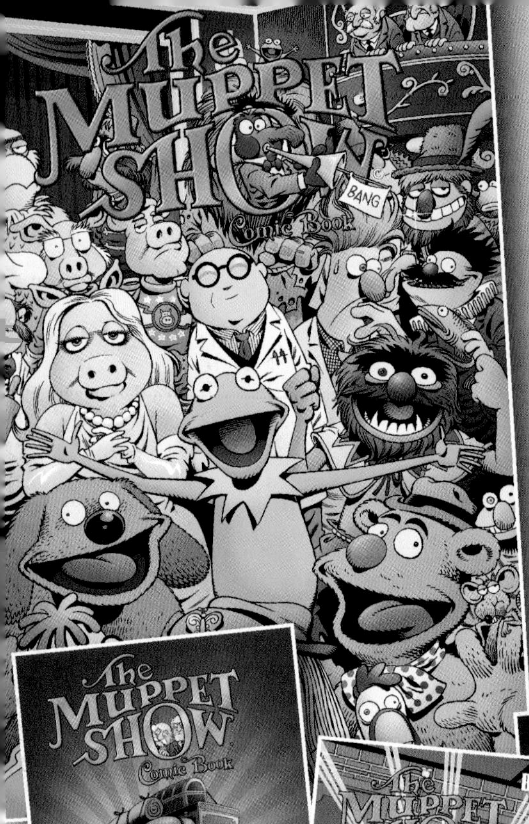
The
MUPPET
SHOW
Comic Book
BANG

## THE MUPPET SHOW COMIC BOOK: MEET THE MUPPETS

Collecting the first four issues of the Eisner Award-nominated THE MUPPET SHOW COMIC BOOK, written and drawn by the incomparable Roger Langridge! Packed full of madcap skits and gags, this trade is certain to please old and new fans alike!

SC $9.99 ISBN 9781934506851
HC $24.99 ISBN 9781608865277

## THE MUPPET SHOW COMIC BOOK: THE TREASURE OF PEG-LEG WILSON

Scooter discovers old documents which reveal that a cache of treasure is hidden somewhere within the Muppet Theater...and when Rizzo the Rat overhears this, the news spreads like wildfire! Can Kermit keep everyone from tearing the theater apart?

SC $9.99 ISBN 9781608865048
HC $24.99 ISBN 9781608865307

## THE MUPPET SHOW COMIC BOOK: ON THE ROAD

With the Muppet Theater destroyed, the Muppets take their act on the road...but with two very familiar hecklers in every town, will the show be a hit, or will our Muppet minstrels be run out of town in tar and feathers? Also: PIGS IN SPACE!

SC $9.99 ISBN 9781608865161

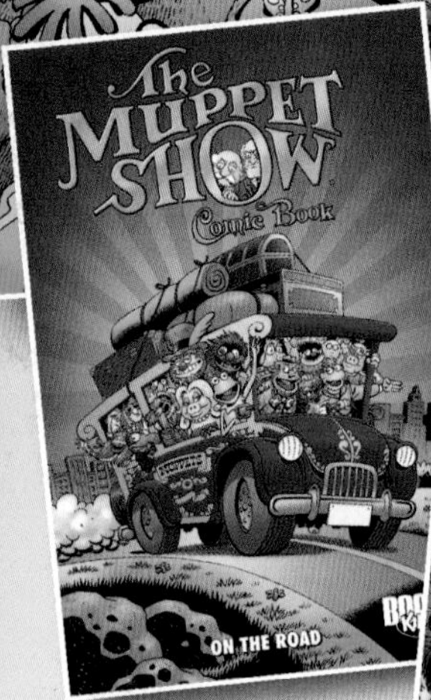
The
MUPPET
SHOW
Comic Book
ON THE ROAD

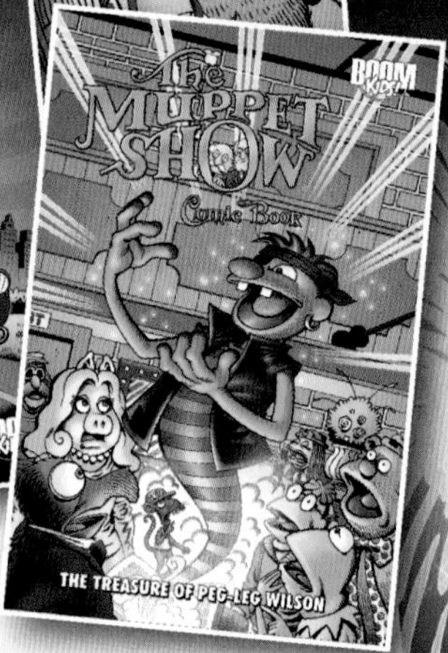
The
MUPPET
SHOW
Comic Book
BOOM KIDS!
THE TREASURE OF PEG-LEG WILSON

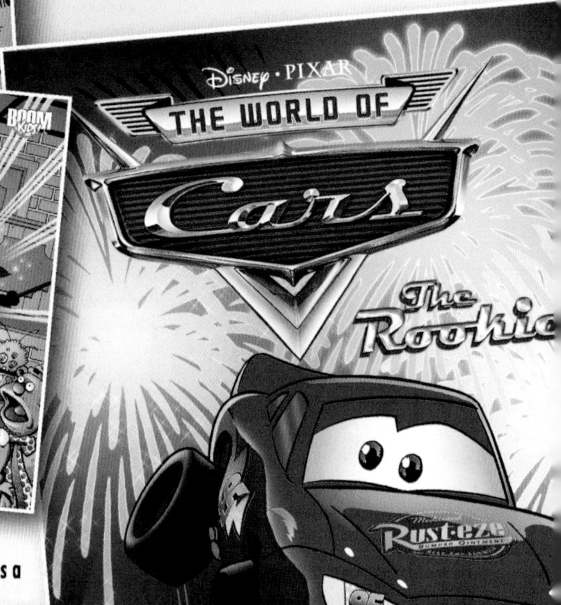
DISNEY · PIXAR
THE WORLD OF
Cars
The Rookie
Rust-eze
95

## CARS: THE ROOKIE

See how Lightning McQueen became a Piston Cup sensation! CARS: THE ROOKIE reveals Lightning McQueen's scrappy origins as a local short track racer who dreams of the big time... and recklessly plows his way through the competition to get there!

SC $9.99 ISBN 9781934506844
HC $24.99 ISBN 9781608865222

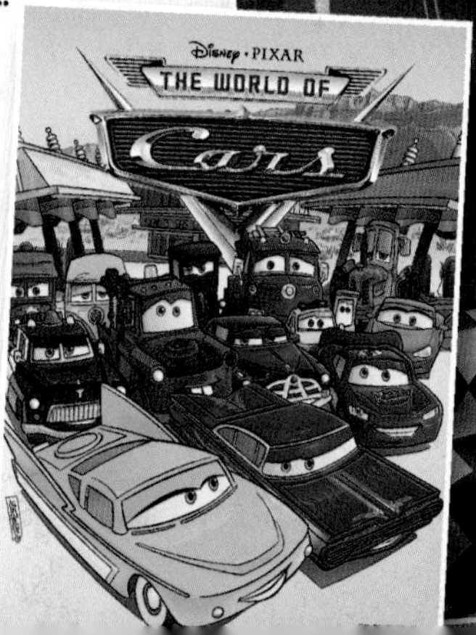
DISNEY · PIXAR
THE WORLD OF
Cars

## CARS: RADIATOR SPRINGS

Lightning McQueen is hanging out with his friends at Flo's V8 Café when he realizes that everyone knows his story...but he doesn't know anyone else's! Lightning wants to know how his friends ended up in Radiator Springs...and more importantly, why they decided to stay!

SC $9.99 ISBN 9781608865024
HC $24.99 ISBN 9781608865284

## WALL•E: RECHARGE

Before WALL•E becomes the hardworking robot we know and love, he lets the few remaining robots take care of the trash compacting while he collects interesting junk. But when these robots start breaking down, WALL•E must adjust his priorities...or else Earth is doomed!

SC $9.99 ISBN 9781608865123
HC $24.99 ISBN 9781608865543

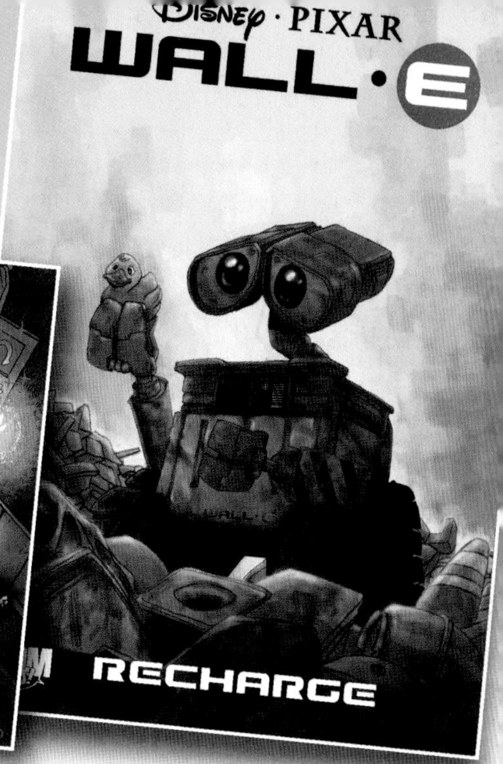
DISNEY · PIXAR
WALL·E
RECHARGE

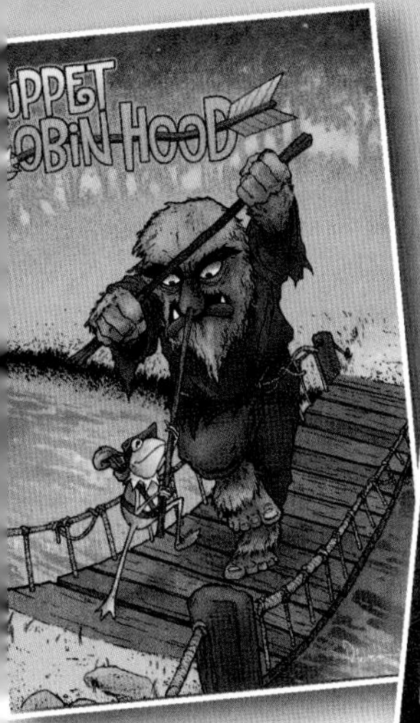

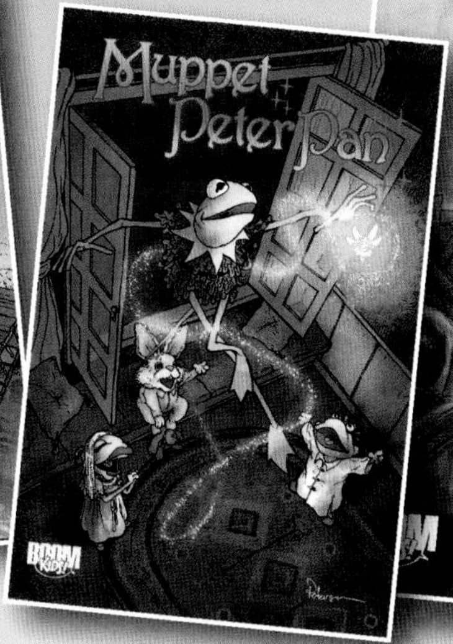
Muppet Peter Pan

## MUPPET ROBIN HOOD

The Muppets tell the Robin Hood legend for laughs, and it's the reader who will be merry! Robin Hood (Kermit the Frog) joins with the Merry Men, Sherwood Forest's infamous gang of misfit outlaws, to take on the Sheriff of Nottingham (Sam the Eagle)!

SC $9.99 ISBN 9781934506790
HC $24.99 ISBN 9781608865260

## MUPPET PETER PAN

When Peter Pan (Kermit) whisks Wendy (Janice) and her brothers to Neverswamp, the adventure begins! With Captain Hook (Gonzo) out for revenge for the loss of his hand, can even the magic of Piggytink (Miss Piggy) save Wendy and her brothers?

SC $9.99 ISBN 9781608865079
HC $24.99 ISBN 9781608865314

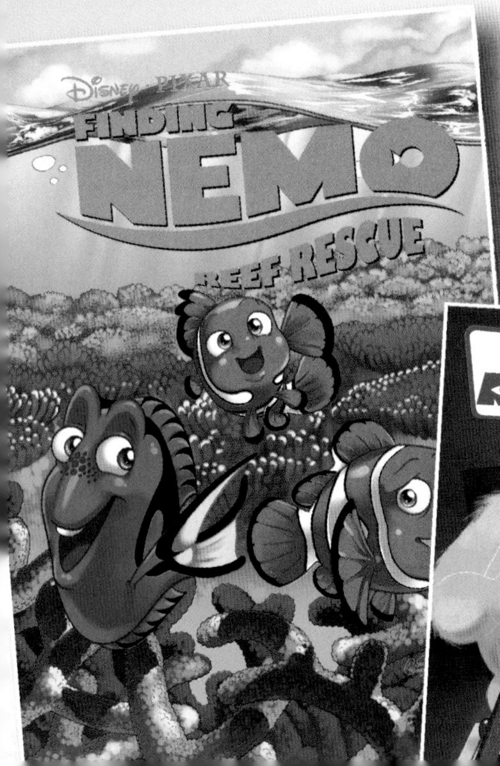
Disney · PIXAR
FINDING NEMO
REEF RESCUE

## FINDING NEMO: REEF RESCUE

Nemo, Dory and Marlin have become local heroes, and are recruited to embark on an all-new adventure in this exciting collection! The reef is mysteriously dying and no one knows why. So Nemo and his friends must travel the great blue sea to save their home!

SC $9.99 ISBN 9781934506882
HC $24.99 ISBN 9781608865246

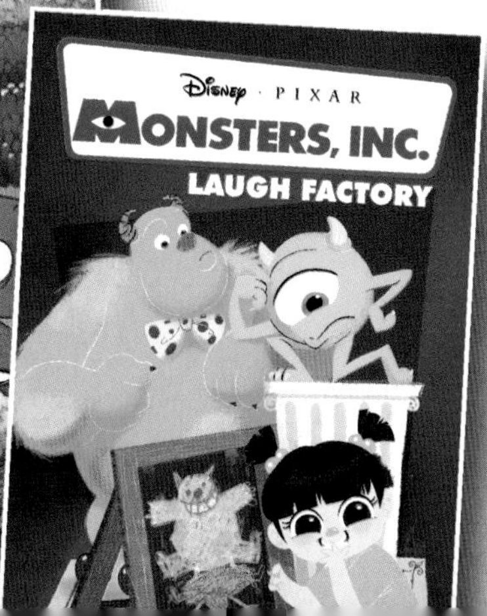
Disney · PIXAR
MONSTERS, INC.
LAUGH FACTORY

## MONSTERS, INC.: LAUGH FACTORY

Someone is stealing comedy props from the other employees, making it difficult for them to harvest the laughter they need to power Monstropolis...and all evidence points to Sulley's best friend Mike Wazowski!

SC $9.99 ISBN 9781608865086
HC $24.99 ISBN 9781608865338

## DISNEY'S HERO SQUAD: ULTRAHEROES VOL. 1: SAVE THE WORLD

It's an all-star cast of your favorite Disney characters, as you have never seen them before. Join Donald Duck, Goofy, Daisy, and even Mickey himself as they defend the fate of the planet as the one and only Ultraheroes!

SC $9.99 ISBN 9781608865437
HC $24.99 ISBN 9781608865529

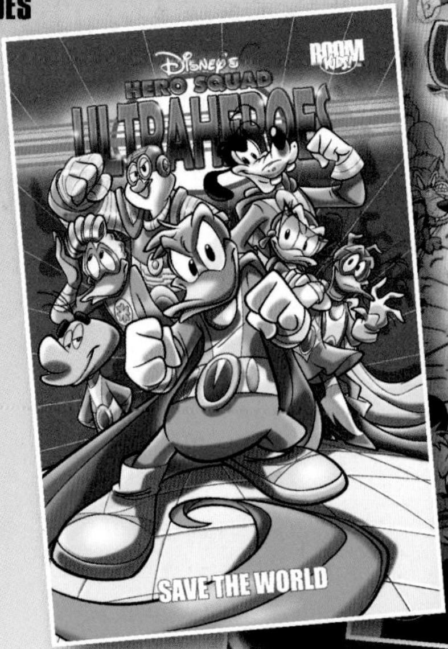
Disney's
HERO SQUAD
ULTRAHEROES
BOOM! KIDS!
SAVE THE WORLD

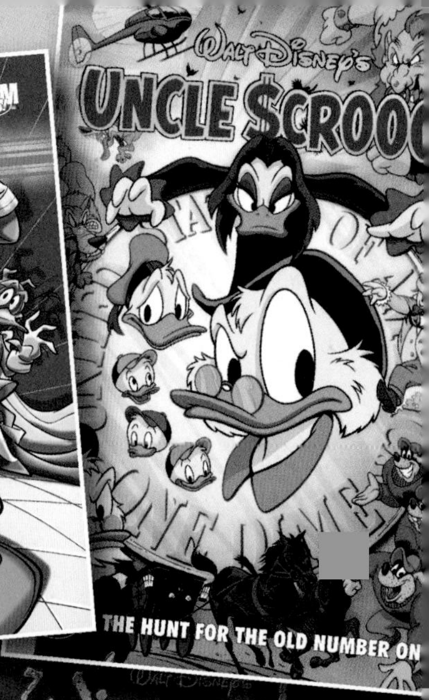
Walt Disney's
UNCLE SCROOGE
THE HUNT FOR THE OLD NUMBER ON

## UNCLE SCROOGE: THE HUNT FOR THE OLD NUMBER ONE

Join Donald Duck's favorite penny-pinching Uncle Scrooge as he, Donald himself and Huey, Dewey, and Louie embark on a globe-spanning trek to recover treasure and save Scrooge's "number one dime" from the treacherous Magica De Spell.

SC $9.99 ISBN 9781608865475
HC $24.99 ISBN 9781608865536

## WIZARDS OF MICKEY VOL. 1: MOUSE MAGIC

Your favorite Disney characters star in this magical fantasy epic! Student of the great wizard Nereus, Mickey allies himself with Donald and team mate Goofy, in a quest to find a magical crown that will give him mastery over all spells!

SC $9.99 ISBN 9781608865413
HC $24.99 ISBN 9781608865505

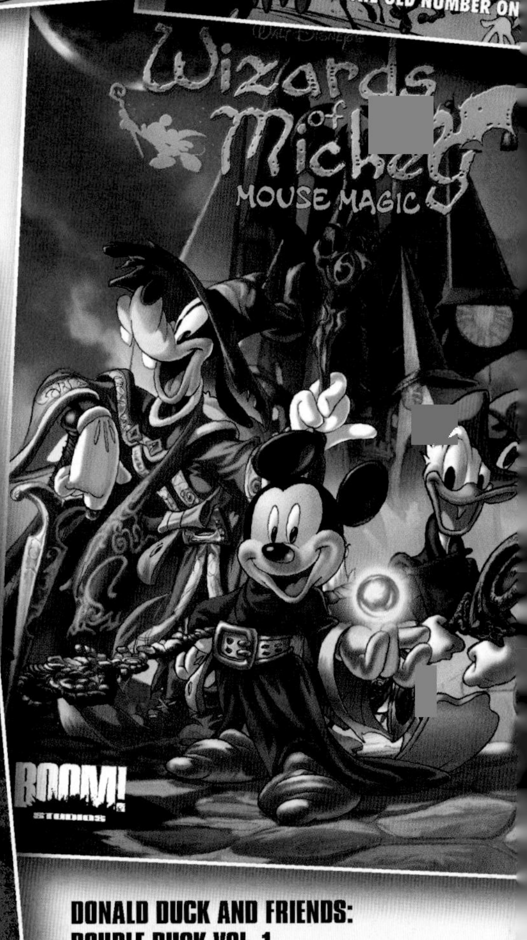
Wizards of Mickey
MOUSE MAGIC
BOOM! STUDIOS

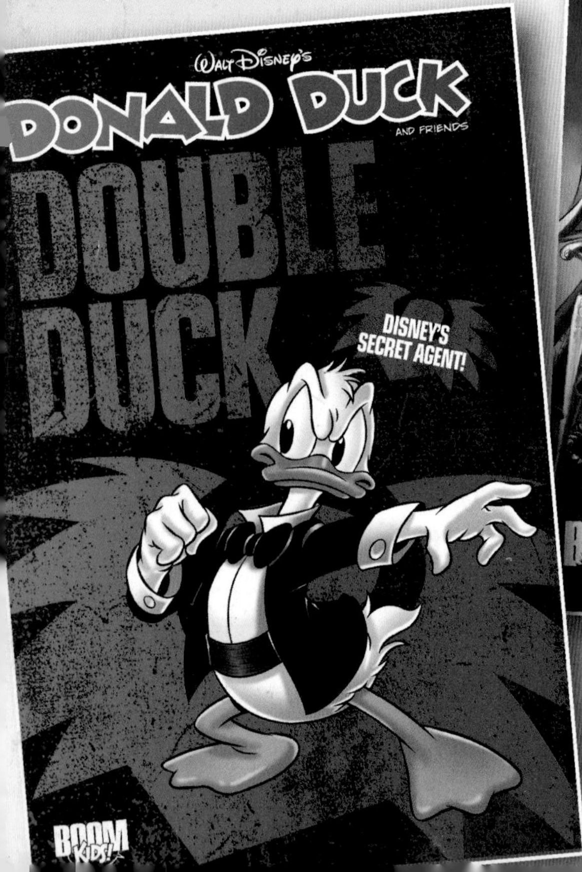
Walt Disney's
DONALD DUCK
AND FRIENDS
DOUBLE DUCK
DISNEY'S SECRET AGENT!
BOOM KIDS!

## DONALD DUCK AND FRIENDS: DOUBLE DUCK VOL. 1

Donald Duck as a secret agent? Villainous fiends beware as the world of super sleuthing and espionage will never be the same! This is Donald Duck like you've never seen him!

SC $9.99 ISBN 9781608865451
HC $24.99 ISBN 9781608865512

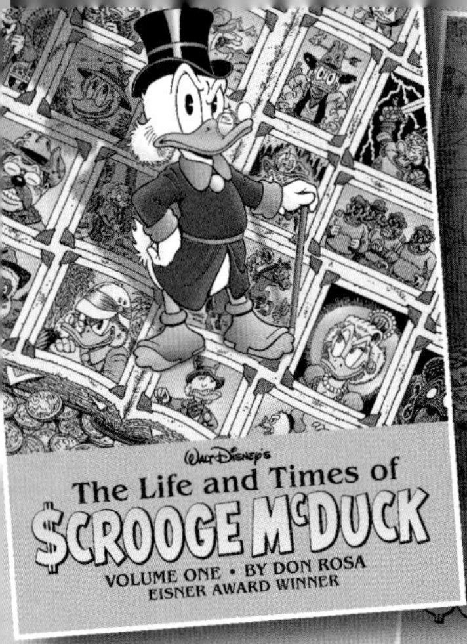
Walt Disney's
The Life and Times of
$CROOGE McDUCK
VOLUME ONE • BY DON ROSA
EISNER AWARD WINNER

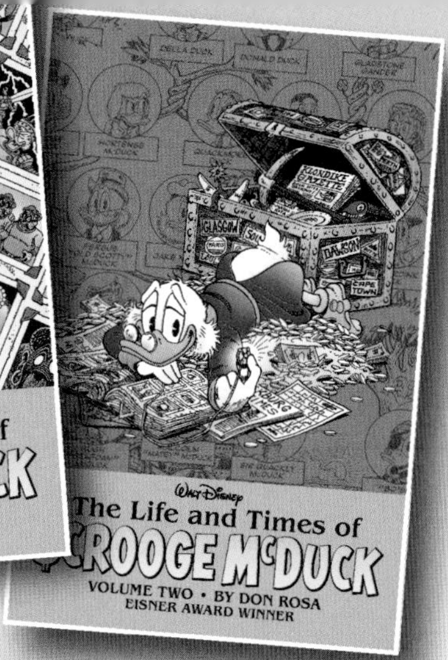
Walt Disney
The Life and Times of
$CROOGE McDUCK
VOLUME TWO • BY DON ROSA
EISNER AWARD WINNER

## THE LIFE AND TIMES OF SCROOGE McDUCK VOL. 1

BOOM Kids! proudly collects the first half of THE LIFE AND TIMES OF SCROOGE MCDUCK in a gorgeous hardcover collection – featuring smyth sewn binding, a gold-on-gold foil-stamped case wrap, and a bookmark ribbon! These stories, written and drawn by legendary cartoonist Don Rosa, chronicle Scrooge McDuck's fascinating life.

HC $24.99 ISBN 9781608865383

## THE LIFE AND TIMES OF SCROOGE McDUCK VOL. 2

BOOM Kids! proudly presents volume two of THE LIFE AND TIMES OF SCROOGE MCDUCK in a gorgeous hardcover collection in a beautiful, deluxe package featuring smyth sewn binding and a foil-stamped case wrap! These stories, written and drawn by legendary cartoonist Don Rosa, chronicle Scrooge McDuck's fascinating life.

HC $24.99 ISBN 9781608865420

## MICKEY MOUSE CLASSICS: MOUSE TAILS

See Mickey Mouse as he was meant to be seen! Solving mysteries, fighting off pirates, and generally saving the day! These classic stories comprise a "Greatest Hits" series for the mouse, including a story produced by seminal Disney creator Carl Barks!

HC $24.99 ISBN 9781608865390

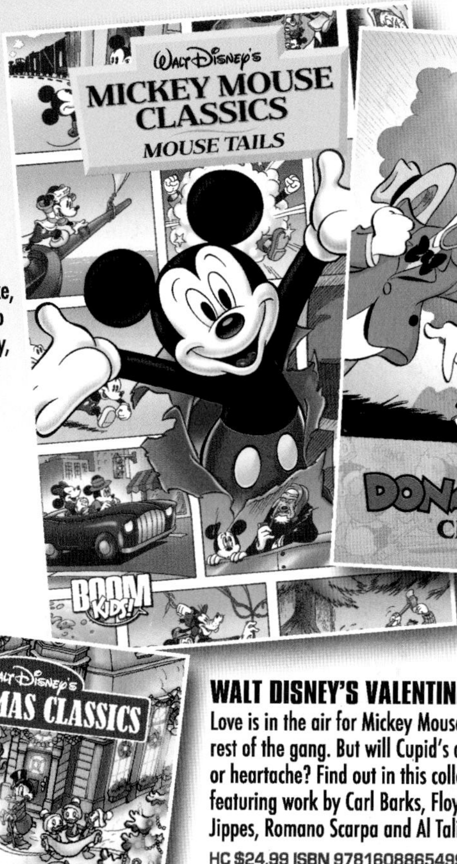
Walt Disney's
MICKEY MOUSE CLASSICS
MOUSE TAILS
BOOM KIDS!

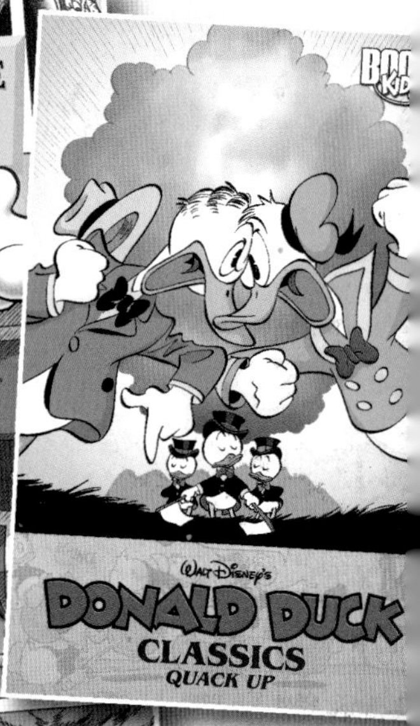
Walt Disney's
DONALD DUCK
CLASSICS
QUACK UP

## DONALD DUCK CLASSICS: QUACK UP

Whether it's finding gold, journeying to the Klondike, or fighting ghosts, Donald will always have the help of his much more prepared nephews – Huey, Dewey, and Louie – by his side. Featuring some of the best Donald Duck stories Carl Barks ever produced!

HC $24.99 ISBN 9781608865406

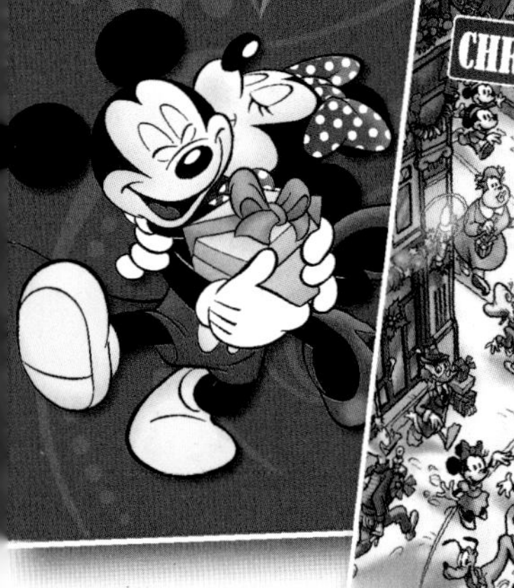
Walt Disney's
Valentine's
Classics

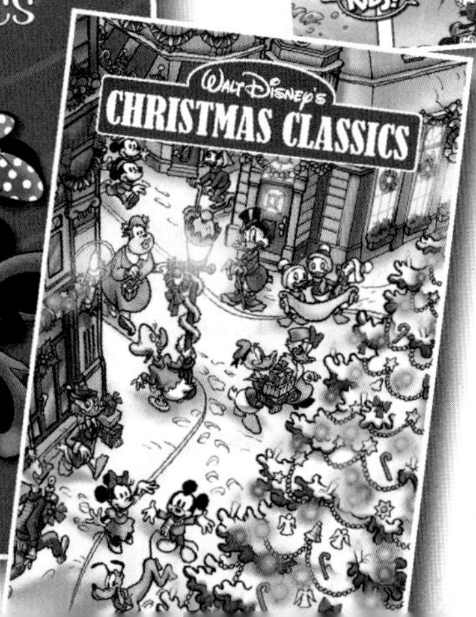
Walt Disney's
CHRISTMAS CLASSICS

## WALT DISNEY'S VALENTINE'S CLASSICS

Love is in the air for Mickey Mouse, Donald Duck and the rest of the gang. But will Cupid's arrows cause happiness or heartache? Find out in this collection of classic stories featuring work by Carl Barks, Floyd Gottfredson, Daan Jippes, Romano Scarpa and Al Taliaferro.

HC $24.99 ISBN 9781608865499

## WALT DISNEY'S CHRISTMAS CLASSICS

BOOM Kids! has raided the Disney publishing archives and searched every nook and cranny to find the best and the greatest Christmas stories from Disney's vast comic book publishing history for this "best of" compilation.

HC $24.99 ISBN 9781608865482

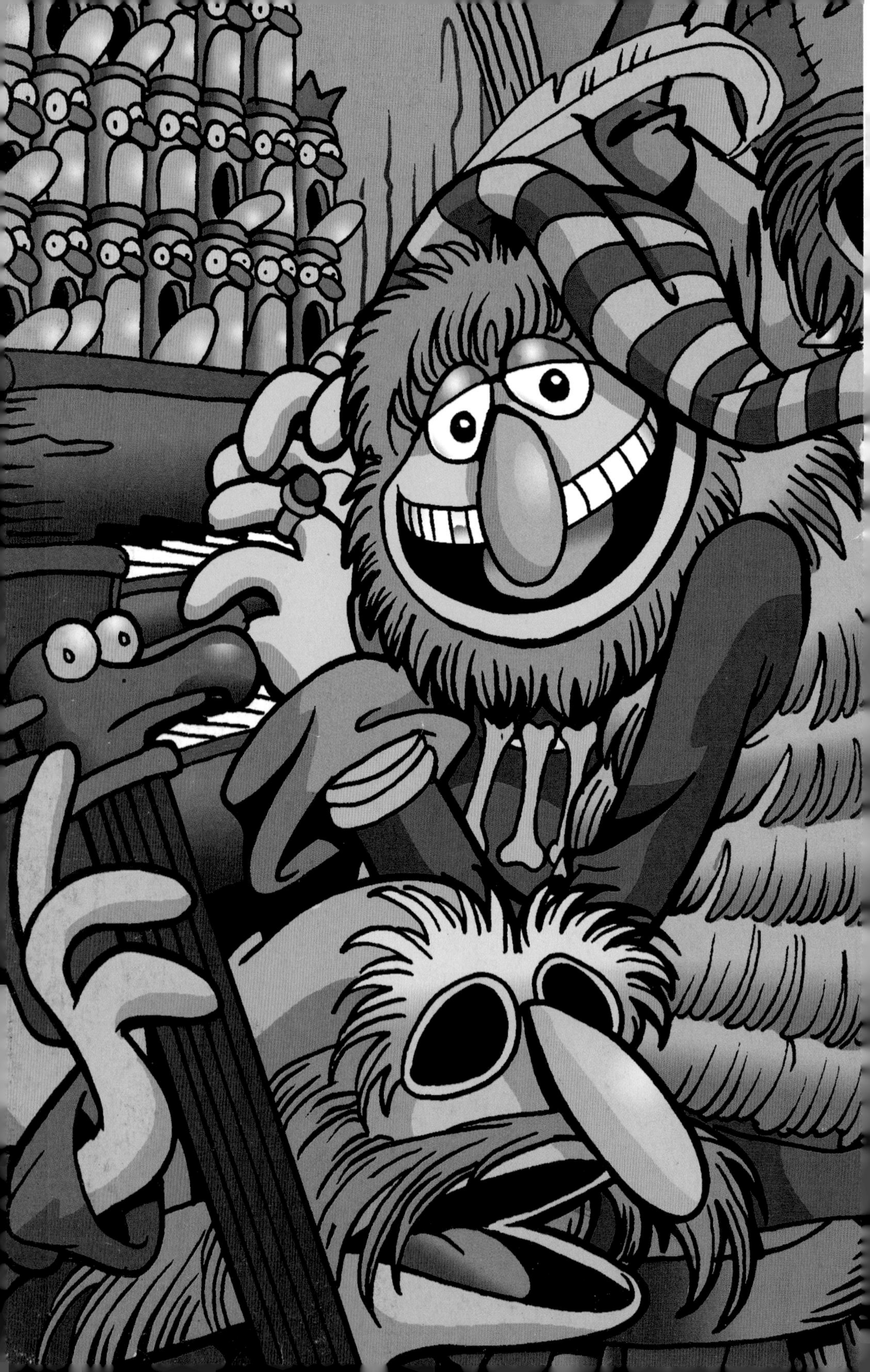